KNOW YOUR RIGHTS—
WHEREVER AND HOWEVER YOU LIVE
TOGETHER!

There are more than 1.3 million unmarried live-in couples in the United States—and the numbers are growing. If you are among them—how should you handle income taxes, credit, inheritance, insurance, breaking up, alimony?

If you're married—is it better to spell out in a formal agreement your understanding as to ownership of material assets?

When a man supports a wife *and* a mistress, can property rights pass to both women?

Is "boomerang" divorce the solution to an equitable division of property?

Can gay couples establish enforceable property contracts?

Whatever your questions, this authoritative state-by-state guide to the laws of love can help you make wise decisions and safeguard your financial future.

THE LEGALITY OF LOVE

BY JERRY SONENBLICK, ATTY.
WITH MARTHA SOWERWINE

A JOVE BOOK

Requests for permission to make copies of any part of the work should be mailed to: Permissions, Jove Publications, Inc., 200 Madison Avenue, New York, NY 10016

First Jove edition published February 1981

10 9 8 7 6 5 4 3 2 1

Printed in the United States of America

Jove books are published by Jove Publications, Inc., 200 Madison Avenue, New York, NY 10016

THIS BOOK CONTAINS GENERAL INFORMATION ABOUT THE LAW AS IT APPLIES TO PERSONAL RELATIONSHIPS BETWEEN LOVERS, MARRIED OR UNMARRIED. IT IS NOT PERSONAL LEGAL ADVICE AND NO ONE SHOULD RELY UPON THE INFORMATION IN THIS BOOK TO MAKE LEGAL DECISIONS. EACH PERSON'S PROBLEMS ARE UNIQUE AND OFTEN COMPLEX; A BOOK CONTAINING GENERAL KNOWLEDGE OF THE LAW CANNOT FURNISH THE NECESSARY ANSWERS TO SUCH INDIVIDUAL SITUATIONS. ALL READERS SHOULD CONTACT THEIR PERSONAL ATTORNEY FOR SPECIFIC LEGAL ADVICE.

THE LEGAL INFORMATION AND CONCLUSIONS FURNISHED IN THIS BOOK, IN-CLUDING THE STATE GUIDES, IS CURRENT THROUGH THE SUMMER OF 1980. AL-THOUGH ALL LEGAL RESEARCH AND ANALYSIS WAS CRITICALLY REVIEWED, NO REPRESENTATION IS MADE AS TO ITS COMPLETE ACCURACY.

ACKNOWLEDGMENTS

The depth and scope of this book would not have been possible without the help of those individuals who dedicated their efforts to its completion.

The seed was germinated with the aid of the very creative Jeffrey Goodman, whose insights, counseling, and patience were extremely valuable.

Legal research fell upon the shoulders of David Morse, who first rolled up his sleeves as a third-year law student, and continued on with this necessary work as a member of the Arizona Bar. When the practice of law eroded away his availability, Eleanor ter Horst, newly admitted to the bar, then stepped in and, with competence and dispatch, completed a great deal of what still had to be done. Jon Yarger, a capable law student, also assisted. My sincere thanks to them for their interest and the thoroughness of their research.

Jean Smith offered helpful insights and did a great deal of the typing of the state guides. The manuscript itself—or rather the multiplicity of drafts that were necessary to arrive at the final version—descended, seemingly like an avalanche at times, upon my secretary, Kathy Lundberg, who shared many of the frustrations and the eventual brighter moments while nearing the end.

And, of course, I shall always have a warm spot for a very lovely lady and homemate, a talented writer, who had so much to do with this contribution—the dear Martha Sowerwine.

A special tribute to my business associates, Cary Marmis and Fred Steiniger, for their encouragement.

Jerry Sonenblick

CONTENTS

PROLOGUE

LEX DE FUTURO, JUDEX DE PRAETERITO. *(The law deals with the future, the judge with the past.)*

We are foggy, but we do not permit our fogginess to be presumed upon.

—Chorus of Ancestors in
RUDDIGORE. *W. S. Gilbert*

Alvin Toffler's book *Future Shock* was concerned with our fast-paced society and our abilities or inabilities to adapt to, and cope with, anticipated future stresses. This book is my contribution to an anticipated course of human events, from the legal standpoint on that totally encompassing and undefinable subject of love.

The law, whose purpose is to establish principles and guidelines for human conduct, is a slow-moving force that gradually changes as society beckons in new directions. Often a change begins with a landmark case that reverberates in the form of a "future shock" among legal communities as a result of a visionary decision handed down by an appeals court.

Such a decision is *Marvin vs. Marvin*, a case decided in 1976 by the Supreme Court of California. In my opinion, it goes far beyond trying to establish the rights of two (and perhaps more) people who live together in a sustained and meaningful way without a marriage contract. All human relationships, married and unmarried, including relationships among homosexuals, lesbians, groups, adulterous affairs with mistresses, and all other kinds and combinations will be affected by this decision.

From this case, and many others like it, will emerge a growing awareness of legal rights and a determination to protect them. Marriage will become a twofold contract, a social commitment for a stated period of time or for life, and an economic contract that spells out realistic dollars-and-cents understandings between individuals. For those who do not marry, a greater number of property-settlement agreements will be drawn so that fuller understandings are established in case the relationship should end.

As Toffler points out: "As human relationships grow more transient and modular, the pursuit of love becomes, if anything, more frenzied. As conventional marriage proves itself less and less capable of delivering on its promise of lifelong love, therefore, we can anticipate open public acceptance of temporary marriages."[1] This new trend, in itself, will fuel the need for more contractual understandings between individuals living as couples and in other relationships.

So, to all my fellow human beings who, at one time or another, crave a relationship with another person, regardless of sexual preference, and who are concerned about their personal rights and the protection of their property rights, I suggest you gaze into the crystal ball with me and see what lies ahead. I have included a glossary beginning on p. 444, and I have summarized the states' laws in the State-by-State Guides beginning on p. 163, so that you can research and generally understand your legal strengths and weaknesses where you reside, or where you plan to reside.

Jerry Sonenblick

PART I

Chapter One

CONTRACTS IN SPITE OF PASSION

No commune, no tribe, no nuclear family even, will ever achieve real human freedom until the barrier between male and female in the self is dissolved, and along with it the sexual and spiritual capitalism that thrive on that division.

—RICHARD ATCHESON, quoted
in *Mindstyles/Lifestyles*
by Nathaniel Lande[1]

Scientists at New York State Psychiatric Institute announce the discovery of phenylethylamine, a chemical that produces the unique feelings of euphoria commonly known as "being in love." Isn't chemistry wonderful? The effects of phenylethylamine are well known, but the ground rules for those under its influence are changing radically. Love remains the same; the legality of love is in a state of flux. The sexual revolution of the last two decades has been the bellwether for legal evolutions that are bringing about big changes for lovers, particularly those who live together out of wedlock.

UNMARRIED COUPLES INCREASE

According to a 1979 issue of *Newsweek*,[2] over three million of the 50 million American couples currently paired in domestic bliss are not married couples. The 1978 census gave a more conservative figure of over a million cohabiting couples, and we believe the actual number may be double or triple the current estimates. Not all are young—census figures show that the number under thirty-five years of age exceeds those over thirty-

five by only a third. About half have been married at least
once, and around one-fourth have children.

Government figures further indicate that in 1977 there were
four times as many "households shared by two persons of the
opposite sex" as there were in 1970. The 1980 census will
confirm even greater increases. The trend was widely expected
to fade with the flower children; instead, it has taken root as
a genuine alternative to marriage.

Sometimes living together is not an alternative, but rather
a preliminary to marriage. *Apartment Living* magazine took a
survey of its primarily young, well-educated audience, and
found that over a third of the couples responding had lived
together before marrying.[3] In a series of interviews with cohabiting couples all over the country, we found evidence that
social pressure against living together has dropped. Parents
still look forward to marching their daughters down the aisle,
but may advise them to try living with their intended husbands
first. We heard about a college professor in Georgia who is
happily paying his daughter's college tuition while she lives
with her young man, but swears to cut off the funds if she
throws away her education by getting married.

THE MARRIAGE BEDROCK

On the other hand, millions of couples choose marriage in spite
of the widely sounded alarm that the new permissiveness will
be the death of legitimate wedlock. In the 1980s, marriage
thrives, with a liberal diet of divorce. However, marriage now
comes in an unprecedented variety of flavors. There's "open
marriage," group, bisexual, and gay marriage, even a resur-
gence of arranged marriages in organizations like Sun Myung
Moon's Unification Church. There is marriage à la Billy Gra-
ham, side by side with serial monogamy à la Liz Taylor.

But why do couples continue to bother? Today the peace
of the double bed may be enjoyed without recourse to marriage;
living together is legal in about thirty-three states and seldom,
if ever, prosecuted in the others. In fact, most young adults
simply assume that their love lives are their own affair, and
not an appropriate subject for government regulation. To quote
Marsha Rawlins of Logan, Utah: "The concept of the state
being the only body capable of giving our commitment re-
spectability and legal validity leaves us both slightly breath-
less." But this liberated form of domestic bliss has legal com-
plexities all its own.

COHABITANTS BEWARE

The warning for those who choose living together—the starry-eyed freedom fighters in the vanguard of the sexual revolution, the battle-scarred refugees from marital holocausts, and those who are just rehearsing for marriage—is: *Beware! Here be tygers!* Unmarried partners today are adrift on a sea of practical difficulties arising from traditional legal sanctions against cohabitation; they are also heading for an iceberg of unforeseen responsibilities created by the new judicial acceptance of their conduct.

No one but a dedicated hermit could have failed to notice the iceberg's tip. Michelle Triola Marvin's lawsuit against Hollywood actor Lee Marvin—who'd lived with her for nearly six years, then married another woman—was enthusiastically tried in the national press and on the airwaves. Lit up in the same publicity spotlight were a number of trendy persons—Peter Frampton, Alice Cooper, Rod Stewart, Nick Nolte, Rod Steiger, and Flip Wilson, to name a few—whose "exes" (*not* ex-wives) were suing for what the press dubbed "palimony."

Recently quoted in *TV Picture Life,* Nolte, who last year married singer Sharon Haddad, sounded an aggrieved note: "The marriage business is in chaos in California. If a man and woman live together for just a week, she can sue, claiming there is an unwritten marriage contract."[4] Peter Frampton told an interviewer that he was getting more cautious after his palimony bout with Penny McCall: "Girls have to sign little pieces of paper when they walk through the door now, and they're checked for the silverware when they go out, ha, ha, ha."[5]

The *Marvin vs. Marvin* trial was the closest thing to the delicious Hollywood scandals of yesteryear that the shockproof seventies could offer. Alternating old sweet songs—"She gave him the best years of her life"—with revolting revelations of filmland decadence, the press milked the "Marvin Doctrine" for all the celebrity juice it was worth, and then some.

Everyone had a ringside seat, and everyone had an opinion. Some found it hard to believe that Ms. Marvin was finally awarded only $104,000—less than 10 percent of her claim for half of Marvin's earnings for the duration of their romance. Others thought she was lucky to get a cent—after all, living together is supposed to be a no-strings affair. Some saw the decision as "a boon to female golddiggers and an affront to the institution of marriage";[6] others hailed it as a milestone in the liberation of women. But few saw the massive iceberg resting in the shadows beneath the glittering tip. For what the California Supreme Court actually issued in its influential *Marvin* decision was less glamorous and far more important than the license it gave Michelle to sue Lee.

What it comes down to today—not only in Hollywood, not only in California, but in a growing number of moderate and firmly conservative states—is that somebody you love and trust—maybe somebody to whom *you* gave the best years of your life—can sue you and collect, not necessarily on the basis of any clear-cut proof of financial responsibility, but by virtue of looser, more "loverly" circumstances. The justices mentioned "reasonable expectations" and "other tacit understandings" as possible bases for enforceable implied contracts.

A NEW RESPONSIBILITY

The Marvin Doctrine—(punsters have wondered whether it was named after Lee and Michelle—who adopted the actor's last name by legal petition, not by marriage—or after Marvin Mitchelson, the enterprising attorney whose untiring efforts on Ms. Marvin's behalf herded a flock of outcasts to legal recognition) represents a total turnabout in the legal approach to free love, creating a heavy burden of responsibility. Living together, declared the California Supreme Court, is no longer to be sneered at on "alleged moral considerations" by the courts, but now it can lead to anything from property settlements to palimony. The *Marvin* decision announced that it was time that people living together were treated as responsible adults, time for the seriousness and depth of these commitments to be recognized as something different from the casual affairs conjured up by the phrase "shacking up." On the other hand, it may be the death of what was once known as free love. Actually, many of the principles of marriage have been expanded to cover this emerging lifestyle. The feelings of commitment are often the same as in marriage, notwithstanding the lack of the traditional marriage license. The new legal recognition of rights and obligations between lovers owes much to the whole gamut of changing consciousness that has swept the nation's love life in the past twenty years.

A PALLOR ON LOVE?

Let's face it, though—living together under the Marvin Doctrine has lost an element of Byronic panache. To set the kiss of death on untrammeled passion, the court suggested it would be happy to uphold businesslike contracts between lovers.

Lawrence Grillett and Hilary Pollak, stationed together at Davis Monthan Air Force Base in Tucson, Arizona, expressed misgivings about these developments. "I don't exactly want to call it childish," mused Lawrence, "but if people start basing things on contracts, it detracts from the whole purpose of why you're living together—because you love each other." Hilary, a truckdriver with a delightful English-schoolgirl voice, gives short shrift to the whole business of contracts and palimony: "I think it's a bit ridiculous; no, I don't think there could be much love in it if they were willing to do that!"

Marsha Rawlins reassured us that tender sentiments can survive the chill California legal winds. "The *Marvin* case sent Joe into a temporary state of shock," she wrote, "but we reiterated our commitment to each other. . . . We have a verbal agreement to invest as much time, caring, and attempted understanding as the relationship needs. We fully expect it to last as long as we do." They had lived together for one year, and though their situation at the moment resembles the Marvin-Triola setup (Marsha is currently unemployed and Joe is bringing in the money for both), they saw no need for a written contract. But, Marsha allowed, "If other couples would be more comfortable with putting it in writing, then that's what they should do."

ADVANTAGES OF A CONTRACT

What sort of couple, then, does feel comfortable with defining their understandings in a legal contract? Janet Traylor of Tempe, Arizona, has no qualms on the subject. "Contracts between lovers are a good idea, especially important for the couple in which one partner is economically dependent on the other," she argues. "Trust and love should not be insulted by logical, practical arrangements; these emotions should be great enough to surround and contain the practical considerations that allow for the protection of both partners."

She and James Abell started living together in 1972, when they were both fresh out of college. "It started out very simply," says James. "We both had professional aspirations, for graduate school and traveling; we weren't sure of what our commitments were, and it didn't seem like the time to get married." In the next six years, James, now an architect, and Janet, art director for a Phoenix advertising agency, found themselves more and more determined to continue the romance and companionship without merging their identities in marriage. Janet describes the satisfaction of living together: "Being able to tailor our relationship to our needs, having agreements based on individual respect and desires, amounts to having your cake and eating it too—everything that marriage offers, without the drawbacks.

"Marriage," she points out, "brings with it a lot of excess legal baggage, implicit contracts that we do not subscribe to. Perhaps they are too outlandish for many people to believe! The general public is not even aware of these rules and contracts until a specific instance arises."

Says James: "When two people establish a business partnership, they don't buy a standard contract off the shelf; they tailor their contract to suit their needs. It's odd how the law provides a standard contract for marriage, and people don't necessarily know what it holds for them. Unfortunately, when they find out, it's too late."

For their first six years, Janet and James got by with an uncluttered oral understanding that covered everything from housework to the mortgage payments on their townhouse; they agreed to be equal partners. They didn't split hairs to keep their finances exactly fifty-fifty. "I may pay a bill for James's student loan one month," says Janet. "He may drop off a check at my mechanic's the next."

"Saying we're equal partners is enough," James believes, to cover most issues. "It's not much of a relationship unless you can be flexible. You have to believe in the other person; it might be a sixty-forty relationship for a while and then reverse itself." Still, now that their investments are increasing, they feel it's time to formulate a written contract.

Buying a townhouse, James explains, was essentially a business agreement they entered together "on a handshake. Currently we are building a new house, our financial future is even more entwined, and we're still continuing to do business on a handshake. That just doesn't make sense; with your most trusted business associate, you'd want to have a written agreement."

Janet feels strongly, however, that the courts should not attempt to enforce unwritten contracts between lovers. "I think that if society grants any implicit agreements in a living-together arrangement, we will be back where we started with marriage. Any agreement that is not set out in a legal document does not deserve to stand. Of course, this puts the burden squarely upon the participants, requiring that they be aware enough to protect themselves with a mutually acceptable arrangement."

Ellen Holt, an attorney, points out the practical weaknesses of verbal contracts: "They are virtually impossible to prove or disprove, especially under circumstances where no witnesses are likely to be present." She had mixed feelings when Harding Maxwell, the man she lives with, suggested a written contract stipulating strictly separate properties with no implied or intended merging of finances. She thought he didn't trust her, but—"grudgingly"—wrote up a contract.

Harding, who has reached a top executive position, said he had reason to be careful. "I've been married since I was nineteen, but to three different gals, so I've been paying for marriage mistakes since 1945 and am saving a few bucks at sixty-two for the first time in my life. I have no rainy-day protection, so anything that is the slightest suggestion of a threat money-wise scares the living hell out of me." That, and tax costs, keep him leery of marriage: "When two professional people earn close to the same amount over $20,000, you really get into full-time support of a thankless government. If we were married, Ellen and I would have each paid $2,000 more in taxes last year." But the contract, he says, was "to protect us from the distorted law, not from one another. I don't believe either of us feels any threat from the other, should we break up, but the vultures could pounce—her relatives, my ex-wives and eight children—should something serious happen to us."

"I'm glad we have it now," says Ellen. "The monkey's off our backs."

Are they happy? we asked.

"Extremely happy, and it gets better all the time," says Ellen. "As far as I'm concerned, I've made a permanent commitment. I couldn't get enough of him, conversationally, mentally, emotionally, or physically—and I still can't."

"Ecstatic is a simple answer," Harding says. "Why didn't she come along thirty or forty years ago? We've been at it for two and a half years, and I hope it can be at least another twenty-five."

THE HARD LINE

Before *Marvin*, most courts probably would have refused to consider undocumented claims based on cohabitation; in fact, even written contracts between lovers were likely to be struck down as illegal, immoral, or unwholesome. California trends are notoriously contagious in legal as well as social matters, and the effects of the *Marvin* decision are already visible in many states, but resistance runs high in some. Illinois, for example: whether courts there will honor even written contracts covering the financial aspects of cohabitation is doubtful; it is clear, though, that there is no protection for unwritten covenants.

Under this hard-line policy, free love remains a dangerous adventure; perhaps it's fine for the young and hardy, but it leaves room for exploitation of the weak and the trusting. Look what happened to Delia Brooks of Cairo, Illinois:

"I lived with Charlie for three years. I thought I was his common-law wife and his business partner. We worked real hard and built up a trucking business from nothing. I mostly worked in the office, but we made all the decisions together. In three years we went from nothing to owning six delivery vans and some heavy equipment. Then Charlie sold everything to buy an eighteen-wheeler Kenmore truck. He said we needed it to get our business into the big time and we'd just keep on expanding! Well, Charlie just drove off in that rig and I haven't seen him since. Everything was in his name; I never thought I had to have anything in writing between us. It turns out there's no common-law marriage in Illinois, and anything goes if you're just shacking up.

"Having been married before, I still think there's a lot to be said for just living together—but I was really ripped off, and legally there's no way I can do anything about it."

Under the old ground rules, living together without marriage made women fair game for this kind of exploitation, and Illinois is still playing by those rules. The Illinois State Supreme Court recently ruled in the *Hewitt* case that until state law recognizes the legitimacy of unmarried liaisons, the courts must turn a blind eye to individual hardships or even injustices suffered by unmarried partners like Delia.

Illinois' *Hewitt* posture is at the opposite extreme of California's *Marvin* decision; of the other forty-eight states, some lean one way, some the other, and most are caught off balance by the social change. Nationwide pressure for a more uniform body of law is increasing, but the dilemma will probably worsen before any real solution is reached.

THE OUTLOOK

We feel sure that, in time, the influence of the *Marvin* decision will prevail in most jurisdictions. When the dust settles, a new concept of the legality of love will emerge, more responsive to the dignity of women, more sensitive to the demands of individuals, and incorporating a greater range of freedom and responsibility for both married and unmarried couples.

Along the road to this lofty peak of judicial vision, the courts will have to face a thousand questions implicit in the acceptance of the Marvin Doctrine. Avalanches of case law will come down to cover the crucial questions that *Marvin* didn't explore.

Many questions remain unanswered, including the following:

1. Can contract rights, implied or written, exist in the seventeen states now holding cohabitation illegal?

2. What are the social implications of the anticipated increase in marriage and cohabitation contracts?

3. What about homosexual and lesbian couples? Can contract or property rights be established between individuals in such relationships?

4. Will hard bargaining over cohabitation agreements destroy the relationships they are supposed to protect?

5. Are contracts enforceable that deal with personal conduct between the parties—kitchen duties, budgets, number of children, child rearing, private hours versus family time, etc.?

6. In states that hold illegal any agreement (outside of marriage) that mixes sex with money, will a cohabitation contract be deemed an act of prostitution?

7. Will contracts validly prepared in one state be recognized in another state that usually considers such agreements invalid?

8. How long, and on what terms, must a couple live together before implied contractual rights vest?

9. If implied contract rights do vest, does a couple living together receive the same income-tax treatment as a married couple?

10. Is each party obligated to disclose all of his or her assets in order to validate a cohabitation agreement?

11. Will the creditors of one cohabitant be able to seize the assets of the other if property rights have vested?

12. Will the bankruptcy of one cohabitant drag down the other, and if so, can one cohabitant sue the other for fiscal irresponsibility or for withholding of information that threw them into bankruptcy?

13. If a cohabitant dies, will recent new legal conditions allow the surviving cohabitant to collect social security, dower, probate allowances, or other benefits usually due a surviving spouse?

14. Since remarriage ordinarily terminates alimony payments, might living together lead to the same conclusion?

15. Might cohabitants in states where property rights cannot vest get married, then divorced, in order to regulate the division of property when they split up?

16. What about "ménages à trois," or more? Will groups who share a community relationship have a joint venture with vested property rights?

17. How does one conduct a live-in relationship so as to negate the vesting of property rights?

18. What about conflicts of interest based on gender? Is it to a man's advantage not to marry in order to avoid alimony, or to a woman's advantage to marry to receive a larger settlement?

19. Will traditional sexual bias affect vested rights between cohabitants? Will the unemployed male cohabitant of a successful woman be treated in the same way as the female who is dependent on a man?

20. What about a married man who supports a mistress? Could property rights pass to both his wife and mistress? If he breaks up with both women, is it possible that one or both will own all his property?

21. Will a person involved in more than one vested-rights relationship be in effect violating the laws of polygamy?

22. Will the chances of the Equal Rights Amendment being passed be increased as the rights of female cohabitants are enhanced?

Many of these questions will be open to speculation for some time to come, but we will explore anticipated trends in search of possible answers.

PROTECTION IS POSSIBLE

Meanwhile, back at the lovenest, where do you stand while the law tips its mighty balances now one way, now the other? If you live together, are you courting an old-fashioned pillory or newfangled palimony? If you marry, do you sign away your rights as a separate individual in exchange for a shrinking security blanket, or do you negotiate a better deal? Are you getting a lifetime guarantee or only a limited warranty? Will divorce be a financial massacre or a relatively painless operation?

Does this make you feel at sea, riding a small raft toward a big iceberg? In spite of all the uncertainties, there are some lifelines within reach, and this book will show you how to use them. We'll chart the shoals and safe channels of cohabitation and matrimony, show you the ropes of contract law, and generally help you keep the legal winds at your back.

Remember that in these days of changeable legal weather, courts are increasingly willing to recognize an unmarried couple's own definition of their relationship, within certain limits. In most states today, the couple that can face the emotional struggle of clarifying their own understanding of their expectations, and can agree on their mutual rights and obligations, can expect some support from the law in enforcing that agreement, especially if they draw up a contract with the help of an attorney.

If you want a "no-strings, no-expectations" relationship, this too—this *especially*, in light of the Marvin Doctrine's open door for lovers' lawsuits—should be put in writing. But if you plan to share financial burdens, expecting a long haul together, you must be careful that your share is protected in case of a breakup. The period *during* a breakup is the absolute worst time to look for a fair distribution of property. It may seem uncool to think of such contingencies while the romance is still hot—but perhaps that's better than getting burned when the embers of love are cold.

What's seldom understood is that the law, which chugs along slower than the proverbial snail, enacting laws long after the evolution of the concept for which it was designed, is and can be flexible. A contract, carefully drafted, can suit the needs of the most unusual couple's expectations. Married couples, too, can enjoy these benefits—and should.

The following chapters and the State-by-State Guide at the end of this book will examine the whole gamut of legal problems facing married and unmarried couples. A wide range of solutions is available to help each couple. You'll learn the difference between cohabitation contracts and contract cohabitation, how to change the rules of marriage, how to achieve tax and estate benefits through trusts and business partnerships, and how divorce might actually save you some money. You'll also learn to recognize legal no-win situations, where you have to choose between your home state and your home life. Most couples, though, will find ways to reinforce their preferred status without moving to Tahiti.

Chapter Two

TO MARRY OR LIVE TOGETHER?

One should always be in love: that is the reason one should never marry.

—OSCAR WILDE. *A Woman of No Importance*

Cooking, like love, comes after marriage.

—*old French proverb*

WHAT DO YOU CALL YOUR LIVE-IN LOVER?

Before plunging into the maze of legalities, let's have a look at love. Why, when society offers a time-honored institution for lovers to live in, are so many choosing to live outside of it—and what are they doing out there? We'll hear some answers to that question after a vital digression. The problem is, what do you call the person with whom you're sharing bed and board without benefit of a marriage license?

How would you like to be a *significant other*? Well, it's better than "marvinizer." There are the variations on the verb *to cohabit: cohabitor, cohabitant, cohabitator;* at least one may be correct, but none is lovely. *Lover?* A trifle ripe for everyday use, and it means something precious in its own right. *Roommate* undershoots the mark—and, like *lover*, is already spoken for by an entirely different arrangement.

Fiancé(e)? Don't be absurd. Plain *mate*? It lacks couth.

In writing the *Marvin* decision, the court referred to *nonmarital partners*; one of the justices complained that *quasimarital* would be more accurate. Imagine it in real life: "Aunt Edith, I'd like you to meet my nonmarital partner, Henry."

In 1974, *Newsweek*'s Jane Otten worried over a similar list

and came up with a novel suggestion: *s'pose*, as in "Do you
s'pose they'll ever get married?"[1] In a recent *Atlantic*, Ben-
jamin DeMott complained that his usually articulate friends
become tonguetied when confronted with the need to mention
their children's intimate companions. "My son's . . . um," reported DeMott, was the standard solution, and he could find
none better. His own daughter's homemate earned a deadpan
compliment: "Jeffrey," he wrote, "is a good um."[2]

There is some serious competition too. Barbara Hirsh, in
her book *Living Together*,[3] suggests and uses the term *consort*. Clearly, if you're going to write a book about people who
live together out of wedlock, you have to call them something—but we're not comfortable with *consort*; the word is
hopelessly entwined with Princes Albert and Philip. What the
dictionary supports ("*concubine:* a woman living with a man
outside of legal wedlock; a man living with a woman") flunks
the Aunt Edith test. *Leman*, a fine word from Chaucer's day,
means "loved one" or "darling," without regard to gender—
but Chaucer's out of fashion. Acronyms are proposed from
time to time: *LIR* (lover-in-residence), or *WITH* (woman-in-
the-house) and its obvious corollary, *MITH*.

Finally, there is the authentic terminology of the ghetto and
the counterculture, where the woman a man lives with is his
old lady, and he is her *old man*. It's legit—but alas, it forms
no feasible plural. Therefore we suggest *homemate* and *casual
mate*; the distinction depends on the depth and duration of the
relationship.

HOMEMATES AND CASUAL MATES

We have drawn a distinction between homemates and casual
mates in order to do justice to certain legal trends. The courts
are starting to recognize that some mates make substantial
commitments to each other, while others view living together
as a light exchange of companionship and intimacy with few
strings attached. So, throughout this book, we will refer to the
former as homemates, to the latter as casual mates.

There is no clear dividing line. The distinction may vanish
in a few years as the law raises these embryonic concepts to
maturity. But at present it does seem that some state courts are
willing to look for and enforce commitments beyond sex in an
unlicensed relationship. Jointly owned property or bank accounts, or substantial investments of joint labor over an extended period of time, indicate a homemate relationship, while

separate finances and actions of the parties giving little hint of a shared future generally point to a casual-mate relationship. These distinctions are particularly important if one of the mates is trying to enforce an oral contract. Of course, when a couple has defined their mutual commitments in a written contract, there is no question. Had the courts found Michelle Marvin more a homemate and less a casual mate, she might have wrested a larger settlement from Lee.

A lady we'll call Cheryl described to us her involvement with Nicholas, a relationship illustrating how college casual mates become homemates and what the progression implies.

"Moving in together was an easy decision for us to make. We weren't all that serious about each other, but neither of us felt it was morally wrong to save the expenses of another apartment when we were going to spend most of our time together anyway."

Is this really love? we asked.

"Yeah, we went through that. We were madly in love with each other for months . . . it did terrible things to my grade-point average."

At that point Cheryl and Nicholas were casual mates; had they split up then, no court would have given her any money to enable her to restore herself to academic grace, nor ordered him to give up the Indian bedspread.

Four years later, though the euphoric feeling may have faded, Cheryl and Nicholas are committed to a future together. They may or may not find time to get married, but they plan to try for "happily ever after."

Cheryl's still in school, but they no longer qualify as impoverished students; Nicholas has made a pile of money, and the assets—two boats, vacation property in Florida, business investments—have accumulated, mostly in Nick's name. Of course it's not all smooth sailing; Nicholas is in serious trouble with the IRS. In fact he's in jail for tax evasion, though he hopes to be sprung on appeal before long.

Should they split up now, Nicholas' property might be liable not only to the IRS, but to some claims by Cheryl as his homemate. Did it cross Cheryl's mind, we asked, that she and Nicholas were candidates for a Marvin-style lawsuit?

"No! Well, yeah, it did occur to me. I just feel that he would be honest with me. He wouldn't try to keep everything, and I'm honest enough to acknowledge that most of the things would be his. I think he realizes that I've contributed a lot, not just money; right now, I've been handling all of his finances. If we split up, I wouldn't expect to get half the value of everything, but I would expect to get whatever I put into it, whether it was money or some other contribution."

Under the reasoning of the *Marvin* decision, Cheryl, as a homemate, may have enforceable rights to a share of the property, based on her substantial efforts—housekeeping and business assistance—and on their oral understanding that the fruits of their separate labors would be shared. The terms *homemate* and *casual mate* are not used in court, but the concept of legalizing the distinction between no-strings-attached relationships and ones that, tacitly or overtly, raise reasonable expectations of shared property and/or alimony is gaining acceptance.

WHY THIS NEW LIFESTYLE?

Now back to our original question: Why are so many people choosing to live together without getting married? We asked dozens of people all over the country this question, and a large percentage expressed their opposition to the traditional roles and relative status assigned to husband and wife. Many feared the possessive aspect that can creep into any relationship, licensed or licentious. The dislike of possessiveness, a desire to renounce "ownership" of one's partner, or a not entirely unreasonable reluctance to be possessed, may be acting to preserve cohabitation's nameless state and to prevent mass acceptance of any of the more or less ridiculous misnomers proposed recently. Perhaps homemates object not only to the connotations of the words *husband* and *wife,* but also to the possessive pronoun that usually precedes them. If Mary does not want to be John's wife, she probably does not want to be labeled as "his" anything else. If this is at the bottom of the difficulty, then *homemate* will prove as fruitless a solution as *significant other*.

If any social researcher wishes to test this hypothesis, we suggest a survey to find out how many homemates would send a valentine inscribed, "Be Mine."

We asked James Abell and Janet Traylor why they weren't married after six years together. James said that the years had brought "all kinds of positive feelings about continuing the romantic relationship that we had. The really important idea is companionship, society, sharing with other people. But we were both very independent as children, and value our individuality. Janet feels so strongly about her name and her identity that something she shares with all the people she has met would be lost if she were to take on another person's name and be married in the traditional way."

Do they ever consider getting married, now that their plans and commitments as "equal partners" are solid enough to have them thinking about a contract?

"No, as a matter of fact," mused James.

Janet replied with a challenge: "We wanted to be together, and marriage seemed unnecessary. Unfortunately, this question takes marriage as the norm and assumes that any other choice is the alternative. The burden of proof should be on the side of those who choose to get married. After all, marriage requires some real effort; doesn't it make more sense to ask for justification of *that* choice, rather than the choice of remaining an individual simply involved with another individual?"

So we asked a married woman to tell us why she had taken not only the plunge but even her husband's surname. Marilyn Momper, an individual if we ever met one, said, "I felt that while I was Marilyn Coleman and he was George Momper, I was still primarily my daddy's little girl and he was his daddy's little boy. When we got married, that created another family. I took his name to say that my first commitment is to *this* family." She draws the line, though, at taking her husband's first name as well: "My name is Marilyn," she protests, "*not* Mrs. George!"

Of course, many wives take pride in adopting their husbands' entire names. Not all of them are domestic pussycats! A distinctly formidable lady who uses her maiden name, Margaret Mendos, in her New York City dance studio, growls at the hapless visitor who calls her "Miss Mendos" at home in Westchester: "In private life I am Mrs. Dan Sandburg, and don't you forget it!"

We also know a couple, Kent Solberg, a social worker, and Salle Hunter, an artist, who got married "for purely romantic reasons" and adopted each other's last names, but put them in the middle: Kent Allen Hunter Solberg and Salle Elizabeth Solberg Hunter. Then there are married women who keep their maiden names intact, and homemates who ditch theirs, and couples who head for the hyphens. Men do not seem to give up their names under any circumstances short of interstate flight to avoid prosecution. They are supposed to keep them and hand them on to their sons. Why this should hold true even among couples who take drastic steps to insure their permanent freedom from parenthood, we do not know. The only case we know of where a man took his wife's last name for ideological reasons was that of Olive and Samuel (*né* Cronwright) Schreiner, two fervent idealists who married each other in 1894.

Probably no sensible inference can be drawn from any of this, but these phenomena reflect a variety of beliefs about the give-and-take between mutual commitment and personal status. Many homemates feel that marriage tends to give to the husband and take from the wife; there is a widespread emotional allergy to a now largely outdated but not yet forgotten element of American marriage law, the doctrine of the "unity of spouses." As defined by that immortal legal scholar, Blackstone, it conjures up visions of *The Stepford Wives*: "By marriage, the husband and wife are one person in law; that is, the very being or legal existence of the woman is suspended during marriage, or at least is incorporated or consolidated into that of the husband."[4]

Though the law has generally—not universally—outgrown this Gothic idea, feminists feel that it lingers in our behavior and expectations.

"Beyond the legal considerations," Janet Traylor points out, "there are implied contracts of a social nature. Society, for the most part, expects a wife to be subservient—for her career, commitments, and interests to be secondary to the man's. Even among professional people, a woman faces more prejudice if she is married."

Richard Miller, who lives on a sailboat off Portland, Oregon, with his homemate of seven years, Barbara George, thinks of her as his "partner, lover, friend, and financial advisor," but never as his wife. "To him," Barbara reports, "a wife is someone who is dependent, demanding, and a fun-dampener."

Salle Hunter recounted how her first experience with wifedom poisoned her mind against marriage: "My first marriage was a very unhappy situation, and we had really only gotten married so that Alex, who was from Argentina, could stay in the States. When we were living together, Alex and I were friends; after we were married, he treated me like a wife, and I never want to go through that again. I don't like being the appendage 'Mrs.'

"Kent wanted to get married, and I just hated the whole idea of marrying again, but I changed my mind because Kent and I don't play by those rules. After a certain time, I felt it was . . . forever.

"Marriage can be very sweet," Salle concedes, trying not to look smug. "There's the romantic reasons, and it's fun to have a big party and celebrate two people getting together—plus, the anniversaries are a scream. We have three anniversaries every year. We celebrate the first time we made love and the two times we got married—once in Arizona and once in Texas."

Kent, who experienced a brief and enlightening stint as a "househusband" while living with another woman, agrees that rigid roles of husband and wife leave a lot to be desired. Still, he feels, "roles are changing very quickly in this country now, and people have to be willing to allow for growth and change whether they get married or not. The real issue is that people do benefit from long-term relationships, and in order to make that possible, there are certain things you have to work out: sharing, roles, commitments. I think that might be a little easier with marriage, because getting married in itself defines some sort of commitment, whereas if you decide just to move in together, you each have to work a little harder to find out what each other's expectations or commitments are."

Writer Matt Seiden cautioned his readers in the *Baltimore Morning Sun:* ". . . I have a feeling I would think twice before agreeing to share a lease on an apartment before I was ready to share a lease on life. It's too easy to back into marriage. It's too easy to let inertia take over, to make the biggest decision of your life by default—as if marriage were nothing more than a vacant apartment to be filled by the first applicant who can pay the rent."[5]

Another equally compelling reason for not getting married is the fixed idea in many male minds that marriage is an infernal device for wringing money out of men, and that divorce is its most sadistic refinement. For many, divorce leads to living together the next time around. Of course, that line of reasoning didn't do much for Lee Marvin. The grim truth is that now you may need a contract to avoid getting a "divorce," even if you aren't married.

Another set of reasons that keeps people from getting married is purely financial. The tax system, which rewards some couples for marrying but penalizes others, and policies that drive respectable old gentlemen to shack up with widowed ladies because remarriage would cut their pension benefits, both account for a substantial number of couples "living in sin."

Ruth and Jim Stevenson, who have been sharing a house in Palo Alto, California, since 1976, told us that marriage would increase the cost of a college education for Ruth's children from a previous marriage. Although they keep their finances strictly separate, Jim's income would be added to Ruth's if they married, and the kids would lose their scholarships.

Ruth, a German-born marketing analyst who adopted Jim's surname along with her citizenship papers, sees little difference between marriage and living together: "Basically these two relationships are equal; a marriage certificate does not make a relationship. You know in the end it just comes down to living with each other. Our basic attitude toward each other is love and respect, and no piece of paper would ever change that. But marriage does carry a lot of assumptions with it, so since we are able to live together the way we do, I wouldn't take the risk."

Jim, a biostatistician, adds some details: "We were going to get married because we were going to stay together and it would be fun to have a wedding. Then we realized that California is a community-property state, and we really don't have similar ideas on what to do with money at all, so we decided to think it over.

"Ruth lets money slip through her fingers, and I'm very careful. She doesn't even bother to balance her checkbook, and I realized that *her* bad checks would affect *my* credit rating if we were married. I'm an investor; I like to own property. Ruth will never save enough to buy anything because she's always spending it on social causes.

"In my first marriage, my wife and I had different attitudes about money. It caused endless fights. I wish I could tell everyone in high school, as part of their sex-education or marriage courses, not to get into a community-property relationship unless their spending habits are compatible! Once Ruth and I decided we shouldn't have community property, we spent very little time arguing about money."

At this juncture it is important to note that you ordinarily don't *have* to get into a community-property relationship even if you get married in a community-property state! You can make a contract to create separate-property status, within minor limitations that vary from state to state; the opposite is also true. Most couples, unaware that the law is flexible enough to encompass such arrangements, automatically submit to the standard local marriage contract, perhaps missing out on some advantages that will be explored in later chapters. Also, there are advantages to the community-property system that bear looking into.

Some homemates do not want to get married because they take a dim view of the effect of marriage on human character, and even on society as a whole. Marsha Rawlins takes just such a broad view:

"Marriage is an attempt to remove control of my life from me and give it to the state. I see it as an instrument to perpetuate the ideology of women and children as property of men. The current romanticizing of 'two becoming one' that surrounds marriage results in expectations that are seldom met.

"In the process of trying to merge two individuals into one conglomerate, what was once flexible becomes rigid; we find the end-product something less than healthy, less than equitable."

Maria Gonzales, who has lived with Jeff Frye for seven years, feels that even the word *commitment* is best reserved for mental institutions: "Our relationship is based on an agreement to make each other's lives better," she says, "not on a commitment to stay together no matter what. We don't make room for any bad influences." Maria is taking a sabbatical, but thinks she will probably return to Carmel Valley, California, a small town where she works at the general store and Jeff is a fireman.

Some people don't see marriage as a front for Big Brother or as an invitation to abuses ranging from curlers at the breakfast table to wife-beating, but see it merely as a very dull substitute for a love affair. "I think a lot of kids—well, not kids—my age think that way," says a worldly-wise thirty-year-old. "I guess we all grew up on a heavy diet of 'Ozzie and Harriet.' Y'know, that sort of stuff leaves an impression on a young kid: Mommy is a total nitwit and Daddy is just dullsville. Anyway, then we discovered *Mad* magazine and nothing was the same ever again." "And then," chimes in another superannuated kid, "came *Playboy*!"

IT'S AN OLD LIFESTYLE REBORN
As vilely contemporary as this may sound, the attitude has much in common with one that characterized the Golden Age of Greece. Respectable Athenian females were kept uneducated and cloistered, literally confined to their own sections of their homes, while, outside the walls, unfettered minds pushed back

the boundaries of knowledge with joyous explorations of philosophy, science, literature, art, politics, and—lest we forget—sex. The contrast was painful. Young men avoided matrimony in droves, preferring the company of other men and of the livelier, often cultured women of the *hetaira* class. Many formed steady living arrangements with *hetairai* (literally "companions"), and could not be dissuaded even by laws against continued bachelorhood. To do their civic duty by the daughters of Athens, the elder citizens, fathers of marriageable girls growing into disgraceful spinsterhood, passed law after law; the young men laughed over wine, women, and boys, and stayed with their courtesans. Some married their exotic companions.

Pericles, a leading and excessively respectable citizen of Athens, thought up a law forbidding Athenian citizens to marry outside their own class and railroaded it through the governing council. Within a year he was sorry he'd done it; he met Aspasia, a foreign courtesan, and was permanently lovestruck. By his own law he could not marry her, so he gave up on trying to lick the recalcitrant youth and joined them. He divorced his wife (who was, luckily, fond of another man) and installed Aspasia, and they lived together at the center of Athenian life for thirty years, until his death.

Other glorious figures of the Golden Age followed their example. The sculptor Praxiteles lived for a while with the spectacularly beautiful Phryne, who was the model for his famous Aphrodites; Sophocles lived with Theoris, Plato with Archeanassa, Epicurus with Leontion and later Danae, Menander with Glycera; even Aristotle lived with a *hetaira* named Herpyllis after the death of his first wife.

Times were hard for the forces of public morality, which lay low during the years of Periclean dominance over Athenian politics, and then, when his power was waning, hauled him and Aspasia into court on charges of embezzlement and impiety, respectively. Pericles died a broken old man, and Aspasia prudently left town with an apolitical—but not penniless—shepherd. But for nearly a century thereafter, writes Will Durant, "free unions . . . gained ground on legal marriage."[6]

The sentiment that unmarried life can be more exciting than marriage is evidently hoary with age, but is it justified? Does romance have a better chance outside of marriage? One viewpoint, expressed beautifully, is that of Barbara George:

"Richard and I celebrated our seventh anniversary this October 1. This was the day Richard moved me and my then eight-year-old daughter from Spokane to Portland, Oregon, where we lived in a house Richard and I chose together, but bought in his name. From the beginning we have adored each other, held common values, and shared common goals—a life-long love affair being one of them. Another goal is to live and work around the world in our sailboat. The first four years we worked, saved money feverishly, took sailing and navigation classes, and shopped for a boat. Now, for three years, we have lived aboard her in the Puget Sound area and up and down the Columbia River. We plan to sail to Alaska this spring, possibly staying several months, possibly several years. Richard is a talented welder and can work anywhere around the world. I do various things to stoke the family finances. I've had my own housecleaning service for other working women, been a secretary, and run my own temporary secretarial service, but basically Richard is the breadwinner and I am the homemaker. However, all the roles and chores are flexible. We've divided them according to interest, ability, and mutual agreement.

"Why did we choose living together? I have been married and divorced twice. My experience influenced me greatly. I wasn't afraid of marriage, but my divorces were so wrenching that I didn't want to marry again simply to never have to divorce again. Over the years it has become a formula that has worked. There has never been a reason to marry.

"Do we think marriage would change our relationship? Richard says yes, that not being married has kept it fresh, and to marry now would be capitulating to social pressure after the pressure is off. I say yes and no. Now, the only difference would be that the public records would say we are married. In the beginning it would have made a difference. While our relationship was forming, I think it was important we weren't married. It gave us the freedom, somehow, to develop a life-style where each flourished, without the expectations of what a 'wife' or 'husband' should be. I didn't expect Richard to support me; he didn't expect me to cook him three meals a day. I didn't expect him to protect me from life's uncertainties; he didn't expect me to patch all the holes in his jeans. Not having preconceived ideas of how the other should behave gave us the flexibility to decide how the work load was divided, how the money would be spent, or what we wanted to accomplish in life."

As homemates, some people can find that love, that recurring delight in recognizing each other as separate-but-equal partners, and that confidence in a fruitful future together; other people find it as husbands and wives. Many people place emphasis on differences that may become outdated as the concept of marriage broadens and living together gains increasing acceptance under the law.

But should we presume to tell you which path to follow? Not for all the laws in Washington! The following chapters present a map with many possible routes, showing legal minefields here and there, but the route you choose must be true to your emotional destination.

Chapter Three

THE EFFECT OF THE LAW UPON COUPLES LIVING TOGETHER

Whereas the eminent services of Emma Hamilton, widow of the Right Honourable Sir William Hamilton, have been of the very greatest service to our King and Country, to my knowledge, without her receiving any reward from either our King or Country . . . Could I have rewarded these services, I would not now call upon my Country; but as that has not been in my power, I leave Emma Lady Hamilton, therefore, a Legacy to my King and Country, that they will give her an ample provision to maintain her rank in life.[1]

—CODICIL WRITTEN BY LORD NELSON
*on the morning of October 21, 1805,
the day of his death in the battle of Trafalgar.*

Lionized for years as England's preeminent military hero for his dramatic and far-flung naval victories in the Napoleonic wars, Horatio Nelson died an even greater hero, with little but glory to his name. A grateful country heaped titles and wealth on his thoroughly undistinguished siblings, and endowed the abandoned Lady Nelson with a generous annuity. As for Lady Hamilton, Nelson's shoreside companion and constant obsession for the last six years of his life, she plummeted into drink and destitution, embittered by her country's cold shoulder to her lover's legacy.

Ludwig of Bavaria lost his throne over his mistress, Lola Montez. Ludwig went mad, and Lola went to America, where,

STATES WHICH STILL OUTLAW COHABITATION OR CERTAIN SEX ACTS

STATE	OUTLAWS ADULTERY	OUTLAWS FORNICATION	OUTLAWS COHABITATION	OUTLAWS SODOMY AND/OR ORAL COPULATION BETWEEN CONSENTING ADULTS
Alabama	X[1]	X	X	X
Arizona	X		X	X
Arkansas			X[2]	X
Washington, D.C.	X	X		X
Florida	X[3]	X	X	X
Georgia	X	X		X
Idaho	X	X	X	X
Illinois	X[4]	X[4]	X[4]	
Kansas	X			X
Kentucky				X
Louisiana				X
Maine		X[5]	X[5]	
Maryland	X			X
Massachusetts	X	X	X	X
Michigan	X[6]	X	X[7]	X
Minnesota	X	X[8]		X
Mississippi	X	X	X	X
Montana	X[4]	X[4]	X[4]	X

1. Illegal only if combined with cohabitation.
2. Illegal only if seen as "public sexual indecency."
3. Illegal if living openly in adultery.
4. Illegal only if open and notorious.
5. Not a crime if conducted in private.
6. A felony.
7. Illegal only if lewd and lascivious.
8. Not illegal if part of ongoing relationship.
9. Court gives only a warning on first offense.
10. Ruled unconstitutional in a state court between consenting adults.
11. Legal unless openly and notoriously lewd.

STATE	OUTLAWS ADULTERY	OUTLAWS FORNICATION	OUTLAWS COHABITATION	OUTLAWS SODOMY AND/OR ORAL COPULATION BETWEEN CONSENTING ADULTS
Nebraska	x		x	x
Nevada				x
N. Hampshire	x			
N. Mexico			x[9]	
N. York	x			x
N. Carolina	x	x	x	x
N. Dakota	x	x[4]	x[4]	x
Oklahoma	x			x
Pennsylvania				x[10]
Rhode Island	x	x		x
South Carolina	x	x	x	x
Tennessee		x[11]	x[11]	x
Texas				x
Utah	x	x		x
Vermont	x			
Virginia	x	x	x[7]	x
West Virginia	x	x	x[7]	
Wisconsin	x[6]	x	x	x

after a series of affairs with wealthy men, she devoted the last years of her life to the cause of helping fallen women.

Most homemates and casual mates are unlikely to find themselves in danger of losing a crown. A large proportion are young, unencumbered by cares of state or children, and perfectly capable of making their own way in the world. As long as both parties are able to earn their own keep and work out their own terms for living together, most couples are unlikely to suffer any drastic consequences from the dubious legal status of their relationship. Of course, there are always exceptions.

LEGAL PROHIBITIONS

In the states listed on pages 26–7, mates are subject to prosecution for fornication, or "open and notorious" or "lewd and lascivious" cohabitation; as a practical matter, however, unless a mate is living the life of Rod Stewart in Mrs. Grundy's backyard, freedom from direct interference can be expected so long as such "immorality" is not rubbed in the neighbor's noses.

And yet, even with this seeming acceptance of adult behavior, there is a host of laws on the books that Cat Ballou would find hard to believe. Alabama has held that a city ordinance forbidding unmarried occupants to make love in a tourist court is not unconstitutional. Alaska has a law that taking a female under the age of sixteen for prostitution *or marriage* is a crime "against morality and decency." Not to be outdone, Mississippi holds it a misdemeanor to become a natural parent of a *second* illegitimate child. Nevada can charge a person with a crime if he has sexual intercourse with someone afflicted with venereal disease. And from Tennessee comes a Faulknerian whiff of something darker than moonshine: the felony of "begetting an illegitimate child on the body of his wife's sister."

PROBLEM AREAS OF LIVING TOGETHER

While it appears today that no one is in serious danger of going to jail for cohabitation, the effect of anti-cohabitation laws works in a series of indirect ways. In the eyes of the courts, even where cohabitation is legal, mates may still inhabit the realm of the immoral. While distinct from the outright criminal, this designation may leave homemates and casual mates ineligible for many benefits automatically enjoyed by married people, and subject to various sorts of harassment with little recourse to court protection. It reaches out in the following ways:

1. In those states where cohabitation is illegal, a non-earning mate cannot be claimed as a dependent for income-tax purposes.
2. Innkeepers may be subject to criminal penalty for registering mates in the same room. In most states it is also illegal to register falsely, i.e., as Mr. and Mrs. This usually will not be a problem unless you insist on total honesty and your host is either very straitlaced or anxious to collect the rent on two rooms.
3. It can affect employment, especially in elementary education, as justification for not hiring a mate or, more importantly, to justify later discharge.
4. It could affect the chances for citizenship of an alien living as a mate prior to naturalization.
5. It can affect one's ability to obtain credit.
6. It can affect one's ability to obtain insurance; even if it is obtainable, the rates may be higher.
7. If a couple is living together, and one of the pair is below the legal age limit, it can lead to charges of statutory rape or kidnapping. The Mann Act, known as the "white slave traffic act," makes it a crime to knowingly transport in interstate commerce any female for the purpose of prostitution or debauchery or for any other immoral purpose, and may have some bearing. Cohabitation might also be a "status offense" for the minor.
8. An interracial couple living together is more likely to be harassed.
9. It can endanger child-custody rights.
10. Some benefits automatically extended to spouses and widowed persons under retirement plans or Social Security are not available to homemates or casual mates, or can be obtained only through chancy litigation.

FUTURE LEGAL TRENDS

Challenges to the dubious constitutionality of the statutes may in time clear most of these hazards from the path of true love. New Jersey's *Saunders vs. Saunders* case is a landmark: in 1979, the state supreme court overruled two previous cases in which a fornication statute had been upheld. The court extended the "right of privacy" protection to mates, essentially legalizing cohabitation.

The idea that "you can't legislate morality" is spreading, and state legislatures are responding. Total decriminalization of all private sexual acts between consenting adults is on the increase. As of this writing, seventeen states have decided that such bedroom behavior is no longer their business:

STATES THAT HAVE DECRIMINALIZED PRIVATE SEXUAL ACTS BETWEEN CONSENTING ADULTS

Alaska	Illinois[1]	Ohio
California	Indiana	Oregon
Colorado	Iowa	Pennsylvania[4]
Connecticut	Maine[2]	South Dakota
Delaware	New Jersey	Washington
Hawaii	New Mexico[3]	Wyoming

[1]Adultery, fornication, and cohabitation are illegal, but only if open and notorious.

[2]Fornication and cohabitation are crimes, but not if conducted in private.

[3]Although cohabitation is outlawed, a warning only is given on the first offense.

[4]Pennsylvania has an anti-sodomy statute, but a recent state court decision held it unconstitutional.

Will the rest of the country eventually follow suit? Probably so. Legalization of all nonviolent, private, and consensual sexual conduct between adults was recommended by the American Law Institute in its Model Penal Code of 1962, which will ultimately be widely adopted as the law of the land.

But vestiges of the law will clutter the path of unwed love for years to come; we have fifty different legislative bodies and the federal government constantly creating a shifting hierarchy of laws, and at the top a Supreme Court faced with the dilemma of calling a halt to this dizzying, conflict-ridden process. For example, while the Arizona legislature recently demoted the crime of cohabitation from a felony to a misdemeanor, it only narrowly defeated a proposal to define living together as an act of prostitution under the law!

LITTLE CHANCE OF ENFORCEABILITY

Still, as noted above, the anti-cohabitation laws that remain on the books are largely paper tigers. No one, least of all the law-enforcement community, is seriously interested in enforcing them, in part because the police know that the citizenry is in greater danger from muggers, murderers, and traffic violators than from homemates, and partly because prosecutors are aware of the shaky constitutional foundations of such laws and the difficulty of getting convictions without treading on the now-protected privacy rights of individuals. Virginia's

State Attorney General, J. Marshall Coleman, told the *Richmond Afro-American* that the fact that an unmarried couple lives together is not by itself proof that the couple is breaking the law; they could be prosecuted, he said, only if they could be proven guilty of "lewd and lascivious behavior," or of "habitual acts of illicit intercourse."[2] Generally, today's police and prosecutors, whatever their personal beliefs, content themselves professionally with enforcing turn-of-the-century morality according to Mrs. Patrick Campbell's dictum, "I don't care what people do, as long as they don't do it in the street and frighten the horses."

All very jolly, what? Well, don't laugh if you are: (1) a minor mate or living with one; (2) a resident alien mate; (3) a gay mate.

MINORS

One of the few issues on which all fifty state legislatures speak unanimously is that of sex and the single child. It is illegal to make love with minors, and the penalties are not only severe but enforceable. Just how they are enforced will vary from place to place, depending not only on state law but on community standards; an adult male caught in flagrant cohabitation with a sixteen-year-old girl might undergo a shotgun wedding in rural Arkansas, twenty years in prison in Connecticut, or, in Berkeley, an avuncular lecture from the judge admonishing him to be sure the teenager is getting three glasses of milk and a birth-control pill every day. Seriously, anyone living with a minor female may face severe problems with the law involving prosecution for statutory rape, impairing the morals of a minor, Mann Act violations, or even kidnapping. The degree of risk depends on many factors; the age of consent varies from state to state, and local moral standards vary within state borders. Parental acceptance of the relationship is helpful; irate parents, on the other hand, pose a real threat. The wisest solution is to get out of it.

The teenaged girl herself—or a boy, if he's under age—is vulnerable too. Even if cohabitation is legal in her state, she may be turned over to the juvenile authorities as a "status offender." A status offense involves behavior that is illegal only for minors: running away from home, buying cigarettes, drinking, and curfew violations, as well as sexual activity.

In brief, if you want to cohabit with a minor, make sure you have that piece of paper that says you're married.

ALIENS

As for our second high-risk group, the long arm of the Law has strong leverage over the lives of visiting or resident aliens, particularly those who wish to become American citizens. They too are subject to a variation on the status-offender theme, which may make them think twice before taking a mate. The law of the land—in this country as well as in most others— holds that an alien resident may be deported if "convicted" of behavior contrary to moral standards, even if he has not actually broken any law; a finding that he came to this country for the purpose of engaging in immoral sexual acts may lead to deportation. If actually convicted of a crime of moral turpitude, the unfortunate traveler may be allowed to stay long enough to serve a prison sentence first.

Further, the United States Supreme Court gave notice in 1977 that it will not intervene in immigration policies, holding in *Fields vs. Bell* that the rights of aliens and all conditions pertaining to their rights are for Congress to decide, and are outside the courts' control. Technically speaking, then, noncitizens may stand to lose their visas and chances for naturalization if they cohabit openly.

These days, though, living together is becoming so widely accepted that in many courts it no longer reeks of scandal. Courts tend to find that while an alien homemate is not precisely of good moral character, neither is he so terribly immoral as to warrant the Feds' paying his way back to the land whence he came. The conclusion would probably be different in cases involving adultery or any radical departure from the sexual norm. There are more reliable avenues to a valid visa, among which marriage is perhaps too obvious to mention.

GAYS

Our third high-risk group, gay mates, probably represents the largest number of individuals currently courting active legal danger. Their predicament, then, is clearly not the least of our priorities; we treat it last because we cannot discuss it without dragging in some legal mumbo-jumbo.

When gay couples cast in their lot as casual mates or homemates, they will run into many of the same obstacles faced by "straights," but for different reasons. Laws against cohabitation are the least of their problems. It is not illegal for two people of the same sex to live together; society willingly makes room for roommates, and thereby provides deep cover for those who can live within the limitations of this camouflage. This state of quasi-legal grace is called "the closet." It is hardly conducive to long-term domestic harmony; still, for our legal purposes, it is available in every state.

The rules of the "closet game" are more restrictive for male homosexuals than for lesbians. Open lesbianism raises fewer hackles than does male homosexuality, and the law mirrors this attitude with harsher penalties for sexual acts between males. Adoption of the Equal Rights Amendment might balance the criminal sanctions between male and female. In any event, for the foreseeable future, gay couples will not be permitted to marry under the law; no matter how they behave in public, no matter how mature, meaningful, and monogamous their relationship may be, they can't make it legal. The United States Supreme Court refused to hear the case of *Baker vs. Nelson,* in effect supporting a Minnesota Supreme Court ruling that a homosexual marriage cannot exist. The Minnesota ruling said that the statute governing marriage does not authorize matrimony between two persons of the same sex, that accordingly such marriages are prohibited, and that this distinction does not violate Constitutional rights under the First, Eighth, Ninth, or Fourteenth Amendment.

A Kentucky court, in the case of *Jones vs. Hallahan*, refused to sanction marriage between lesbians for a more specific reason: they could not contract a legal marriage because of their physical inability to fulfill the requirement of sexual consummation of the marriage.

According to a generally discredited psychiatric theory, homosexuality was viewed as a form of sexual immaturity; it has been claimed that gay people are emotionally unable to form deep and lasting marriage-like attachments. And yet the law does not demand proof of emotional maturity from heterosexuals before issuing a marriage license. The law does not discriminate against heterosexual marriages of convenience, but gay couples have no such path to security. Marriage is the last line of retreat for legally beleaguered heterosexual homemates, but not for gay homemates. Even the halfway measure of enforceable cohabitation contracts may lie beyond their reach in most states, even the states that no longer hold homosexual activity illegal.

In a broader sense, many states and cities are still actively campaigning to stamp out gay sex. Some of these states penalize sodomy more heavily than cunnilingus; whether this tacit discrimination between male and female homosexual activity would survive under ERA remains to be seen. While about seventeen states have generally recognized the absurdity of holding adults criminally responsible for making love, and have eliminated legal sanctions against all private and consensual sexual activities, the others have not. This will not prevent gay couples from living together, but it will ensure that their legal struggles to live together with dignity, justice, and security will be more risky and protracted than those of heterosexual couples.

PUBLIC POLICY AS APPLIED TO GAYS

In fact, even where no criminal statutes are violated, gay relationships are in jeopardy due to a basic legal principle called *public policy*. A standard legal dictionary defines public policy as: "That principle of the law which holds that no subject can lawfully do that which has a tendency to be injurious to the public or against the public good. . . . Thus, certain classes of acts are said to be 'against public policy,' when the law refuses to enforce or recognize them, on the ground that they have a mischievous tendency, so as to be injurious to the interests of the state. . . ."[3]

Public policy, a term popular with judges, corresponds to the layman's idea of the spirit as opposed to the letter of the law. Things that are neither strictly illegal nor immoral may still be found "contrary to public policy" when the public conscience does not find them good for the community. Although public policy is growing less unfriendly toward cohabitation, in most states it is not ready to embrace homosexual relationships; for, "apart from illegality or immorality," the perpetuation of gay love affairs is not often considered to be in the best interests of the state or the community.

Public policy, then, is what the court believes is good for the plural you; it may be very bad indeed for you, singular, if you are short-sighted enough to pursue individual desires at odds with the compelling interests of society. Public policy, as we will explain in later chapters, makes specific demands on marriages and other contracts, and has often been invoked as a reason for denying judicial protection to mates.

As a result, even though more and more states will decriminalize homosexual activites, many courts will probably still refuse to extend any positive legal comfort such as enforceable contracts or the right to marriage or "palimony" to gay lovers, on the grounds that public policy precludes any overt encouragement of homosexual relationships.

To avoid public-policy hangups, many gay couples, especially in and around San Francisco, are using a new system to prepare agreements among themselves with confidence. Since the courts might still not be quite ready to handle contracts between gays, they provide for arbitration if disputes arise. Gay panels are formed to hear their differences and make judgments. This sidestepping maneuver may carve a legal path. More and more states are adopting arbitration legislation that adds legal muscle to settlements arrived at by panels of arbiters selected by the parties.

MATES IN MILITARY SERVICE

Heterosexual couples enjoy fairly wide latitude in the military today; living with a lover of the opposite sex is often tolerated at the discretion of one's CO. The civilian mate of a serviceman or servicewoman does not qualify for the fringe benefits (housing, medical care, and pensions) available to spouses, but as long as it does not have to foot the bill, the military is largely willing to overlook irregular army liaisons. According to an Air Force couple we interviewed, the military does not expressly provide for unmarried couples to be stationed together, but the peacetime, all-volunteer services currently offer enough latitude in assignments to make such togetherness relatively easy to arrange.

In 1973, military regulations were revised to prohibit discrimination among military personnel on the basis of race, color, age, creed, national origin, political affiliation, sex, or marital status. Whether sexual conduct or nonmarital status falls within these revised regulations remains unclear.

Generally, married men and married men with children benefit the most under the military provisions and regulations. Widows do all right as long as they do not remarry; they usually receive free medical and dental care and pension payments. These benefits and payments end when a widow remarries, but probably would remain if she lives as a casual mate or homemate.

DISCRIMINATION AT THE BUSINESS LEVEL

When outright discrimination against mates does appear, it is generally in the realm of private enterprise. Within limits, landlords, merchants, and bankers have the right to refuse to do business with anyone, and businesses with fewer than fifteen employees are not subject to the Civil Rights Act of 1964, which outlaws discrimination in employment. In effect, this means that a landlord may refuse to rent to an unmarried couple, that a small business may refuse to hire mates or homosexuals—or, for that matter, that a small nightclub operator could choose to hire as waiters only gays. Some of these problems may be combatted if your state or community has passed legislation forbidding discrimination based on marital status, as will be explained later.

INSURANCE FOR MATES

Insurance companies may charge higher rates to homemates or casual mates, claiming that they are "poor risks." There is no legal recourse available, but with a few phone calls you can find out which insurance companies offer family-style packages to homemates as well as spouses, or are willing to cover all "members of the household" without prejudice. Call local agents or write to major insurance firms in nearby cities until you find the coverage you need. Do not, if you value your benefits, misrepresent your relationship; you could end up paying for benefits you will never receive, since the insurance company can refuse to honor contracts obtained by fraud. True, many unmarried couples do slip by as "husband and wife," and some agents are willing to cooperate with the pretense, but the higher the amount involved, the greater the risks. If you can't obtain needed coverage openly as homemates, it is wiser to purchase separate policies than to buy a "family" policy that may not deliver the goods.

A special problem arises with the purchase of life insurance. One homemate may purchase a policy insuring his/her own life and naming the other as beneficiary with no complications (unless it is a case of adulterous cohabitation—when the insured homemate is married to someone else, the spouse might get the benefits), but if one homemate wants to purchase insurance on the *other's* life, it is not so simple. The question of "insurable interest" may be raised—does one have a sufficient interest in the ongoing survival of one's homemate? Husbands and wives are deemed to have such an interest. In the legal sense, it is acknowledged that the death of a spouse is a sufficient pecuniary and personal loss to deserve recompense, and in the business sense, insurance companies believe that spouses will generally not do away with each other in order to collect the life insurance. They are not so sure about homemates; though more and more companies are accepting that homemates have an insurable interest, less certainty exists for casual mates.

MATES AS EMPLOYEES

Another questionable area is the rights of mates as employees. State labor laws, union protection, and community standards vary widely, and cities often have local statutes of their own to complicate the affair.

Employees have certain rights to privacy and due process under the Civil Rights Act of 1964, but the limits of these rights have not yet been clearly defined. It appears that an employer cannot discriminate in hiring or firing solely out of disapproval of an employee's off-hours sexual conduct. At the federal level, the Justice Department, in a consent agreement approved by Chief U.S. District Judge William B. Bryant, conceded:

> A person who resides with, or engages in sexual intercourse with an unrelated member of the opposite sex may not be found unsuitable for employment solely based on unsubstantiated conclusions concerning possible embarrassment to the Department of Justice.

The consent order, however, allows the department to refuse to hire an applicant if it finds that living arrangements would affect job fitness. Bryant also criticized an earlier statement by the Justice Department that cohabitation between unmarried persons is a sign of low moral character.

In theory, then, it is none of your boss's business whom you live with, unless your personal conduct can be shown to adversely affect your job performance, employee discipline and efficiency, or the company's public image. In fact, this protection has been somewhat inconsistently applied: in New Mexico it has been held that pregnancy out of wedlock is not a sufficient reason to fire a schoolteacher, while a Minnesota case upheld a university's refusal to hire a self-declared homosexual on the grounds that hiring him would appear to connote approval of his sexual conduct. In a 1977 Pennsylvania case, the court held that due process was not violated by firing employees who indulged in open adultery in a small community.

Anti-nepotism policies have been upheld as constitutional

because employers have demonstrated that job performance is impaired when both halves of a married couple work for the same company. In 1978, a Nebraska court ruled in the *Espinoza* case that a no-spouse company policy could be extended to unmarried couples as well, but not all employers are so consistent. We recently read of a couple who lived and worked together for two years, then decided to get married. The boss contributed to the wedding-present collection, then fired the bride the day after the wedding, citing the no-spouse rule.

New Mexico's *Stoudt* case to the contrary, schoolteachers in small communities remain particularly vulnerable, and may even face increasing restrictions on their private conduct, because their job performance is held to include a professional duty to influence young minds. In the trades and professions, though, there is increasing pressure on state licensing boards to drop arbitrary moral requirements that seem out of step with modern views, such as the refusal to issue barbers' licenses to gays while allowing them to work as hairdressers.

Would-be lawyers who live with their lovers present a delicate problem for states that hold cohabitation illegal; to be admitted to the bar and thus licensed to practice law, one is required to swear solemnly to uphold the law. In Virginia, where cohabitation is illegal, the state supreme court ruled that cohabitation is no disqualifier of would-be counsellors: "While a homemate's living arrangement may be unorthodox and unacceptable to some segments of society, this conduct bears no rational connection to her fitness to practice law."[4]

MARITAL STATUS AND DISCRIMINATION

A number of communities and states have passed gay-rights legislation, and quite a few more statutes prohibiting discrimination on the basis of marital status. These laws offer some hope of court protection, but do not necessarily guarantee freedom from prosecution under state fornication laws.

A politically progressive town or city may be located within the borders of a more reactionary county. A good example is the ordinance that guaranteed equal rights to homosexuals in Dade County, Florida. This was the issue that so enraged Anita Bryant that she mounted a nationwide campaign variously described as pro-morality and anti-gay. The ordinance prohibited "discrimination in the areas of housing, public accommodations, and employment against persons because of their affectional or sexual preferences." It survived judicial challenge; in 1977, Judge Sam Silver of the Fifth Judicial Circuit Court of Appeals rendered a decision upholding the constitutionality of the statute. It survived political pressure on its sponsors; a few days after Judge Silver's decision, the county commissioners closely defeated a motion to void the ordinance. But those victories did not ensure its survival. Bryant's campaign led to a county-wide referendum, and the citizenry of Dade County voted 2-to-1 to rescind the ordinance.

MARITAL STATUS: INCLUSIVE OF MATES?

Whether marital-status legislation also protects mates and divorced persons remains unclear. Fourteen states—California, Colorado, Connecticut, Delaware, Hawaii, Iowa, Maryland, Massachusetts, Montana, New Hampshire, New Jersey, New York, Oregon, and Washington—have passed such legislation. Alaska also protects against discrimination based on a *change* of marital status.

Many cities and smaller communities, too many to list here, also have marital-status discrimination laws; if you are subjected to any form of harassment as a mate, it is worthwhile to investigate whether your community has such legislation, and if so, whether the courts will consider applying their protection to your nonmarital status.

Such a question is now before the Massachusetts courts. In Framingham, an elderly landlord is trying to evict one of his tenants because she is sharing her apartment with a man. This, he claims, violates Massachusetts' two-century-old law against "lewd and lascivious cohabitation," and constitutes grounds for worse than eviction.

The tenant, Suzanne Roy, and her homemate, Maxwell Oden, do not feel that their conduct violates the law. "The law is against 'lewd and lascivious' cohabitation," insists Roy, asking, "How in the world is my landlord going to prove that? It would take pretty extreme behavior to be lewd and lascivious." Oden says it was not their behavior that started the trouble: "I don't think there would be any issue if I was white."[5] They are fighting the eviction proceedings, invoking Massachusetts' new law prohibiting discrimination based on marital status in housing against the cohabitation statute that dates back to Revolutionary times. The contest is expected to go all the way to the state supreme court, perhaps even to the United

States Supreme Court. This will probably take years, but may eventually result in clarification of the legal status of mates everywhere.

ZONING LAWS AND MATES

In Wayland, Massachusetts, the town's forty-four-year-old zoning by-laws may soon be revised, after more than two years of debate, to make cohabitation locally legal. A proposal allowing unrelated persons to live together and own property is under consideration by the town's planning board. William Sawyer, a board member who wrote the proposals, said, "People who don't conform to the traditional norm have no place to live in Wayland. It [unmarried persons living together] does go on, but I don't see why they should not be able to do so openly."[6]

It does appear constitutional for local communities to enact zoning legislation preventing a specified number of unrelated persons from living together. In 1974, in the *Belle Terre* case, the U.S. Supreme Court approved a zoning ordinance that prohibited more than two unrelated people from living together. This does not mean that a community can ban unmarried couples, but rather that it can limit the number of unmarried people living together, so as to protect "family neighborhoods" from degenerating into seedy rows of transient boardinghouses. Communes, too, would fall under such bans.

Still, many cities are reexamining their zoning laws, and most, like Wayland, no longer see the need to ban unmarried couples from family neighborhoods. Detroit rescinded such a law in 1978.

REPUDIATION OF MATES' RIGHTS

As mentioned earlier, the Illinois Supreme Court repudiates relations between mates. In 1979, it took a firm stand against extending any contractual privileges to homemates, and has recently gone even further, ruling that cohabitation, though not illegal unless open and notorious, constitutes grounds for loss of child custody. The *Jarrett* case was decided on the basis of morality and public policy, with barely a nod to the accepted doctrine that the best interests of the children shall determine the choice of custodial parent. Jacqueline Jarrett lost custody of her three daughters solely because she was living with another man and offending the moral scruples of her ex-husband. Mr. Jarrett admitted she was a good mother, and the girls strongly preferred to remain in the home where they were raised, but the court ruled that Mrs. Jarrett's relationship with her homemate "contravened statutorily declared standards of conduct and endangered the children's moral development."

Obviously, Illinois is not safe territory for homemates who have intentions of sharing property, and it is a very unsafe place for divorced parents who risk losing their kids. Casual mates, or couples with no children or shared property at stake, may find Illinois hospitable—but those who want any court protection for their family or finances must either marry or move. The Illinois Supreme Court's *Hewitt* decision made it clear that all financial agreements, including written ones, between mates would be subjected to the most severe and unfriendly scrutiny. No other state has as yet spoken so harshly *against* the rights of unmarried couples. It is possible that some may follow Illinois, but most states seem likelier to move away from legal interference and toward legal recognition of the rights of mates, especially homemates.

If you have read this far without encountering the story of your life, you may be thinking, "Well, maybe I don't have anything to worry about." Maybe not. If you don't live in Mississippi, Georgia, Illinois, or any of the states that have handed down unfavorable decisions, it's probably true that the law isn't going to do anything *to* you simply for living together; it is also not going to do much *for* you—a fact that might become very important at some point in your life.

Legal advantages accorded spouses outweigh those available to mates. Some of these are: alimony, Social Security and pension benefits, survivor's benefits, and the right to initiate a lawsuit for wrongful death of a spouse.

One of the worst times to discover these omissions is at the death of one's mate. A "widowed" homemate can be left penniless after twenty years of apparent financial security, and even the children of unmarried partners may have to go through lengthy litigation to secure any portion of their parents' estates. All else being equal, a marriage license may be the cheapest form of financial insurance!

The rights of married couples have been developed over thousands of years of legal and social change; they are officially favored in ambiguous cases not only by public policy on the broad levels, but by nearly every judge, magistrate, and Supreme Court justice. The rights of mates are just beginning to emerge, and they will continue to face challenges and prejudice

RIGHTS OF SPOUSES AND MATES COMPARED

	SPOUSES	MATES
Waiting period for marriage	Seventeen states have no waiting period; 22 (including the District of Columbia) have a three-day waiting period, and the other 12 vary from 24 hours to 30 days.	Not applicable; you can move in whenever you want.
Residency for divorce	The most common requirement is six months' residency for either spouse at the time of filing (16 states, including D.C.). There is, however, wide variation among states. Time required varies from six weeks to two years, and in some cases no time is specified, but only residency or domicile of one spouse or both at the time of filing.	Not applicable.
Retaining of maiden name	Most states allow a wife to retain her maiden name after marriage. Although there are some holdouts, the trend is toward freedom to choose.	Mates do not generally adopt one another's names and are never required to do so, but may do so in most instances by petition to the court.
Use of maiden name for voting	Though some states require a wife to register to vote in her husband's name, most states now allow her to register in her own name if she chooses.	Not applicable.
Jury duty	Marital status does not affect the right or duty to serve as juror.	Same as for spouses.
Type of property	Eight states are community-property states; the rest are separate-property states. All but five of the separate-property states allow some sort of equitable division of marital property on divorce.	Mates may hold property separately or jointly (but not as community property). A few states allow for an equitable division of property on termination of cohabitation of homemates, but not for casual mates.

	SPOUSES	MATES
Protection of privacy	The Constitution, through Supreme Court decisions, assures the right of privacy to all citizens.	Same as for spouses.
Welfare benefits	Needy individuals are entitled to welfare benefits for themselves and their dependents, regardless of marital status. However, since a married couple is considered a unit, one spouse would not qualify if the other did not.	Individuals are entitled to welfare benefits for themselves and their dependents, regardless of marital status. In some states, however, a mate would not be considered a dependent.
Federal income tax	Married couples are subject to the "marriage penalty tax" and as a result, most two-earner couples pay more tax than two mates earning the same money.	Mates pay taxes as individuals and are not subject to the "marriage penalty tax."
Choice of domicile	Generally, each spouse may establish his/her own domicile. In some states, the wife must take the husband's domicile.	Each mate may establish his/her own domicile.
Testimonial privilege	All states recognize the concept of the marital testimonial privilege, but the exceptions vary greatly from state to state.	The marital testimonial privilege does not apply to mates.
Property management	Each spouse may generally manage his/her own property and all the community property. A common exception is that both spouses must agree on the sale or mortgage of the family home, whether owned separately or jointly.	Each mate manages his/her own property unless they agree otherwise.

	SPOUSES	MATES
Head of family liable for support	Most states require the husband to support the wife during marriage. About 6 states require each spouse to support the other.	There is no requirement that either mate support the other.
Responsibility for necessaries	About half the states make the husband responsible for the wife's necessaries. In the other states, each spouse is equally responsible.	There is no responsibility of either mate for necessaries of the other.
Litigation between mates or spouses	Most states allow litigation between spouses, but a few ban it entirely and a few others limit it to certain kinds of litigation (contract actions, but not personal wrongs).	There is no restriction on litigation between mates.
Suit for wrongful death of spouse or mate	Either spouse may possibly recover for wrongful death of the other from third parties.	A mate probably may not recover for the wrongful death of the other from third parties.
Suit for loss of consortium	Generally, either spouse may recover from a third party responsible for loss of consortium. In a few states, only the husband may sue.	Mates probably may not recover for loss of consortium.
Death tax marital deduction	Spouses are entitled to the deduction.	Mates are not eligible for the deduction.
Family allowance on death of spouse or mate	Generally, either spouse may receive the allowance, but in a few states it is granted only to the wife.	A mate probably would not receive the family allowance upon the death of the other mate.

	SPOUSES	MATES
Availability of homestead rights	Generally, either spouse is entitled to the homestead exemption. A few states have no homestead law.	In those states in which the exemption applies only to husband or wife, a mate would not be eligible. Where the exemption applies to the head of the family, a mate who could show that he/she is head of family would qualify. A few states allow the exemption to any resident, and in those states a mate would qualify.
Pension and other retirement plans	Although there are a number of different types of plans, generally a surviving spouse continues to receive some or all of the benefits earned by the deceased spouse.	A surviving mate would probably not be eligible to receive benefits previously received by his/her deceased mate.
Workmen's Compensation benefits	A dependent surviving spouse of a worker would be eligible for benefits.	In most states, a surviving mate would not be eligible, but some states grant benefits to any dependent of a deceased worker, whether widow(er) or mate.
Recognition of common-law marriage	Thirteen states and the District of Columbia allow common-law marriage. Most other states will grant recognition if the marriage was validly entered into in one of the 14 jurisdictions where common-law marriage is allowed.	Not applicable.

	SPOUSES	MATES
Recognition of putative marriage	Most states recognize property rights of a putative spouse who believed in good faith that a valid marriage existed. A few states recognize it by statute.	Not applicable.
Recognition of presumptive marriage	Only 6 states recognize presumptive marriage, 1 of these by statute.	Not applicable.
Marriage age	Most states set 18 as the legal age for marriage, and usually those under 18 may marry with parental or court approval.	Not applicable.
Alimony	All states except Texas allow courts to impose alimony upon divorce. A few states still restrict alimony to be paid to the wife, but this restriction has been declared unconstitutional by the U.S. Supreme Court. The trend is to grant alimony only when it is necessary, and often it is now limited to the time needed by the recipient to train him- or herself for employment.	Four states have granted "palimony" to a homemate upon termination of cohabitation. Other states that have followed some or all of the theories of the *Marvin* case might grant it in the future.
Alimony adjustments	Many states allow for an adjustment in amount after divorce upon showing of changed circumstances. In some states, changed circumstances would include living with a mate.	May be adjusted later if "palimony" award is part of court decree, but there are no case-law decisions yet.
Alimony termination	In most states, alimony is terminated upon remarriage of the recipient or upon the death of either spouse. In some states it is also terminated if the recipient lives with a mate.	May later terminate, but there are no case-law decisions yet.

at every level for some time to come. The implications of these emerging rights may of course lead to responsibilities as well; under current legal trends, some of the most disliked liabilities of marriage are being extended to living together! Sacramento attorney Barbara McCallum, as reported in the *Los Angeles Daily Journal*, said, "...the *Marvin* decision has done more to promote marriage in California than any other single event in recent years."[7]

Chapter Four

THE REALITIES OF THE *MARVIN* CASE

Sue me, sue me, what can ya do me—I love you!
—FRANK LOESSER, *Guys and Dolls*

Question: What's black and white and read about all over?
Answer: Thirteen pages of fine print containing the California
Supreme Court's landmark ruling in the case of *Marvin vs.
Marvin*. Handed down on December 27, 1976, the *Marvin*
decision was a long-awaited Christmas present for homemates,
representing legal recognition of their lifestyle from one of the
most influential courts in the nation.

THE DOCTRINE
Under its glamorous wrappings, though, the gift may turn out
to be one of the most powerful booby traps ever set for free
love. Along with the kind words, the justices declared that
property rights could be established between homemates (and
perhaps casual mates) living together without benefit of any
written contract, and that the courts could impose an equitable
division of property in the event of a breakup. They would
enforce cohabitation contracts, whether written, oral, or merely
"implied." And by supporting "additional equitable remedies"
to protect the expectations of parties to nonmarital relationships, the court essentially revoked their unwritten license to
practice economic irresponsibility. The message is that warm
pledges may someday have to be redeemed in cold cash.

The court's revolutionary Marvin Doctrine hit like a large
stone thrown into a quiet pond. The big splash involved Hollywood celebrities, but the ripples, only now beginning to be

felt, are spreading in all directions. As the ripples widen, all sorts of relationships will be affected. No couple, married or unmarried, will remain untouched by the judge's pen. Eventually the impact may reach even the most unorthodox relationships—ménages à trois, homosexual couples, communes, and group marriages.

Yes, this means *you*. California often sprouts the trends the nation follows, and the *Marvin* decision is no exception; already seventeen states have handed down rulings recognizing certain rights and obligations of homemates.

Homemates who think their relationship comes with a no-strings guarantee could be following a primrose path to alimony—or, as the magazines have dubbed it, "palimony." People getting ready to share bed and board may have second thoughts as they learn more about the implications of taking the plunge. No one—not even lawyers or Supreme Court justices—wants to throw cold water on the spontaneous combustion of love, but perhaps it's best that lovers be confronted with some of the realities of their contemplated merger.

LEE AND MICHELLE FROM THE BEGINNING
The Marvin affair started in the spring of 1964 on a Hollywood movie set—which sounds more romantic than it was. Both parties were on the rebound from mangled marriages. Michelle Triola had a bit part in the movie, a hopeful career as a blues chanteuse, a tiny bungalow in Hollywood Hills, and a brand-new divorce whose scars were not quite healed. Before long she also had a roommate: Lee Marvin of the evil image, who had been domiciled in his dressing room as his twelve-year marriage to Betty Marvin was breaking up. He said he still loved his wife and four children, but was bitterly disillusioned with marriage itself.

But Lee's interest in females remained steadfast. As UPI quoted him: "What makes women so attractive to me personally is the element of danger when you fool around with them. They are a constant sexual threat. Why did Samson fall asleep? For the first time in his life he relaxed, and after that, he couldn't push down temples."[1]

The story of their next six years comes in several versions. The most common one comes from Michelle (who, toward the end of her relationship with Lee, legally changed her name to Michelle Triola Marvin) and her attorney, Marvin Mitchelson.

MICHELLE'S VIEWPOINT

Michelle's script went something like this: though Lee never seriously entertained the notion of marrying her, he did agree that they would hold themselves out to the public as man and wife. He promised her everything, or half of everything he earned while they were living together, and said he would support her for life in return for her devoted services. Such devotion, she emphasized, was no sinecure: she cooked, kept house, soothed his unruly spirit, nursed him through his open and notorious drinking bouts.

Lee, whose earnings were skyrocketing in those years, bought a roomier Malibu beach house that was the couple's home for the next six years. They traveled everywhere together, their few separations marked by tender letters.

She had to choose between her career and Lee's demands for full-time companionship. Trusting to love, and Lee's promise to take care of her always, she chose Lee, and thought it was forever...

Until the night Lee called her from Las Vegas with a wedding announcement—he had tied the knot with a *new* Mrs. Marvin!

Shocked, she hoped at first it was nothing but a drunken prank, but when Lee's lawyers gave her notice to clear out of the Malibu house, she had to face a sterner reality. She didn't sue him right away; she didn't even think of it, not until eighteen months later when he stopped sending support payments. (He had promised her $1,050 a month for five years.) Then she went to see Marvin Mitchelson.

The results are history, but they didn't come easily. In the end, they were not entirely satisfactory for Ms. Marvin. If she "gave the best years of her life,"[2] as Mitchelson says, to the care of Mr. Marvin, she gave her second-best years to suing him.

Several lower courts heard her claim that she had had a verbal agreement with Marvin to share everything he earned during their romance on a fifty-fifty basis—or $1.5 million apiece, as she reckoned it. Most of the judges were unimpressed.

The next-to-last judge, however, chose a notably flimsy basis for his dismissal of her lawsuit against Lee, and the case went to the California Supreme Court.

THE SUPREME COURT DECISION

Ruling unanimously that she was indeed entitled to a trial for breach of contract on her claims, all six justices agreed that the lower court was off-base in denying Michelle's petition on the grounds that it would conflict with the community property rights of Betty Marvin, the wife Lee had divorced in 1965.

One, Mr. Justice Clark, wanted to leave it at that. "Here," he wrote, "the opinion should stop."[3] But it didn't. The other five justices decided the time had come for them to wade into the legal mire surrounding the rights and obligations of nonmarital partners.

The majority opinion, written with possibly unprecedented clarity by Mr. Justice Tobriner, started off boldly:

> During the past fifteen years, there has been a substantial increase in the number of couples living together without marrying. Such nonmarital relationships lead to legal controversy when one partner dies or the couple separates. . . . We take this opportunity to resolve that controversy and to declare the principles which should govern distribution of property acquired in a nonmarital relationship.[4]

The opinion firmly dispatched the hoary argument that economic rights between cohabitants could not be recognized in court because they were considered "meretricious," i.e., bartering sexual services for money. The term is derived from the Latin word *meretrix*, meaning "prostitute," and has long been used to impugn the standing of any relationship that involves both sex and money. Any relationship except marriage.

> . . . We believe that the prevalence of nonmarital relationships in modern society, and the social acceptance of them, marks this as a time when our courts should, by no means apply the doctrine of the unlawfulness of the so-called meretricious relationship . . . the nonenforceability of agreements expressly providing for meretricious conduct rested upon the fact that such conduct, as the word suggests, pertained to and encompassed prostitution. To equate the nonmarital relationship of today to such a subject matter is to do violence to an accepted and wholly different practice.[5]

Further, the court noted, past precedent already supported the enforcement of contracts, oral as well as written, between nonmarital partners as long as they did not *explicitly* state that illicit sex was the basis of the bargains. Thus an agreement between homemates that the man would support the woman or share property, in exchange for housekeeping services, would be upheld, but an explicit agreement based on the same essential relationship to exchange support for her services as a mistress would be invalid.

The court added that it could not support the theory, as stated in an earlier California case, that moral considerations prevent an abandoned mate from claiming any part of the "gains of her paramour accumulated during the years of her debasement" (*Vallera vs. Vallera*, 1942).

"Indeed," protests the *Marvin* decision, "to the extent that denial of relief 'punishes' one partner, it necessarily rewards the other by permitting him to retain a disproportionate amount of the property. Concepts of 'guilt' thus cannot justify an unequal division of property between two equally 'guilty' persons."[6]

Having knocked down the broadest legal objections to the establishment of financial rights between mates, the court went on to radically redefine the ground rules for determining whether any enforceable rights exist in a particular case.

Not only an express contract, the court declared, but also "an implied contract, agreement of partnership or other joint venture, or some other tacit understanding between the parties,"[7] as might be demonstrated by the conduct of their relationship, might be sufficient to entitle one homemate to a share in the other's property. In suggesting that trial courts "should inquire into the conduct of the parties" to see if it implies "some other tacit understanding," the ruling opened a real can of worms for the legal system, and a trap for unwary lovers. Tacit understandings, indeed! Tacit understandings are the very fabric of love affairs, but seldom do two lovers tacitly understand quite the same idea. They have rarely been considered the stuff that enforceable property rights are made on.

The facts of the *Marvin* case provide a classic example of a tacit misunderstanding: Lee is said to have murmured to Michelle at the very beginning of their romance, "What I have is yours, and what you have is mine."[8] At the time, he had an estranged but not yet divorced wife and four children, the prospect of steep alimony, and little more than the shirt on his back in separate property. "I never said that," says Lee—but even if he did, it is probable that he was not referring to the millions he was to earn as his status rose in Hollywood over the next six years. Michelle, as we have seen, understood something quite different. Largely on that sweet nothing, she based her claim that Lee had agreed to fork over half of what he made while they lived together.

BACK TO THE TRIAL COURT
At the new trial, some two and a half years later, Superior Court Judge Arthur Marshall thought about this and mused: "The meaning of the phrase is hard to understand. Does it mean a sharing of future as well as presently owned property? Does it mean a sharing of the *use* of property, or is title to be extended to both parties? Does it mean that property is shared even though the relationship may be terminated in a week or weekend?" He concluded that in light of Lee's oft-expressed "antagonism against a person acquiring any [property] rights by means of a certificate of marriage, it is not reasonable to believe that plaintiff [Michelle] understood that defendant [Lee] intended to give her such rights even without a certificate."[9]

The phrase had meant, he decided, anything *but* an express contract to split earnings down the middle after the breakup of the relationship. Nor did the conduct of the parties, duly inquired into, seem to Judge Marshall to imply the existence of any such contract. While they lived together, they had kept their earnings separate and owned nothing as joint tenants or tenants in common. Lee had repeatedly refused Michelle's requests that he put their house and other property in her name. Thus there was no implied contract to be found.

Nor did Judge Marshall find that Lee had contracted to support Michelle for life in return for her giving up her lucrative singing career to be his full-time companion, as she had claimed. On the contrary, he decided, her career—"never very brisk-paced"[10]—was dying of its own inertia in spite of Lee's active attempts to promote it.

Michelle feels that the judge's attitude toward "my so-called career, that I got a 'D' in at the trial," reflected sexist denigration of a woman's work. "If you had relationships that took a man away from the job market for seven years," she told Tom Snyder during a television interview, "there'd be a *law*."[11]

Did the fact that Michelle had, on March 26, 1970, legally changed her last name to Marvin indicate any lifelong commitment on her or Lee's part? No, said Judge Marshall. "Coming at a time so close to the date of separation, and after some indication of difficulties between the parties, the change of name does raise a question whether she wished to acquire the right to use defendant's name after separation."[12]

At the trial, Lee maintained that Michelle had adopted his name against his will and over his objections. Michelle says that he could and would have prevented her, had he wanted to.

Nor, in sum, did the judge discover evidence of any sort of contract, expressed in words or arising out of conduct, between the parties. As Michelle had remarked in a published magazine interview: "We were always very proud of the fact that nothing really held us. We both agreed, and we were really pleased with the fact that you work harder at a relationship when you know that there is nothing really holding you."[13] This, said the judge, "bars the finding of any contract."[14]

So Michelle was not to benefit from the Marvin Doctrine; Judge Marshall, paying diligent attention to the theoretical guidelines of the California Supreme Court's ruling, found it abundantly clear that no such financial agreement, in the whole spectrum extending from "express contract" to "tacit understanding," had ever existed between Lee and Michelle Marvin.

REHABILITATIVE ALIMONY

But the state supreme court decision had also stipulated that in the absence of such an agreement, the trial court should consider whether the facts of the case warranted an award of money on the basis of any other equitable considerations, such as mutual effort or the doctrine of *quantum meruit*—loosely translated, "for what it's worth." Employing this standard, Judge Marshall weighed the monetary value of Ms. Marvin's domestic services to Lee against that of his expenditures on her behalf—some $72,000, plus the fringe benefits of glamorous surroundings and travels to exotic film locations—and noted that "such services as she has rendered would appear to have been compensated."[15] In strictly mercenary terms, this works out to less than $12,000 per year, and much of the value represents gifts, not cash. These are not sweat-shop wages, yet the court could arguably have decided that her services to Lee merited a more generous share of the more than $3 million he made while they lived together.

Still, Judge Marshall is not a heartless man. The last two

paragraphs of his plaintiff-devastating decision softened the blow with a relatively modest award for "rehabilitation purposes."

> [The state supreme court decision directed] the trial court to employ whatever equitable remedy may be proper under the circumstances. The court is also aware of the recent resort of plaintiff to unemployment insurance benefits to support herself, and of the fact that a return of plaintiff to a career as a singer is doubtful. Additionally, the court knows that the market value of defendant's property at time of separation exceeded $1,000,000.
>
> "In view of these circumstances, the court in equity awards the plaintiff $104,000 for rehabilitation purposes so that she may have the economic means to rehabilitate herself and to learn new employable skills . . . and so that she may return from her status as companion of a motion picture star to a separate, independent, but perhaps more prosaic existence.[16]

The fact that Michelle Marvin essentially lost the case in trial does not alter in the slightest the far-reaching implications of the California Supreme Court's decision. Judge Marshall did not openly challenge the theory of the Marvin Doctrine; he found that the facts were weak. Had the judge found Michelle to be a homemate, in effect, the monetary award to her would doubtless have been much greater.

A variety of claims have arisen as to who won the *Marvin* case. Marvin Mitchelson says that Michelle won in principle by establishing a new status of legal equality for homemates. Judge Marshall, quoted after the trial in *The New York Times*, disagreed. The principle, he stated, "did not come at the expense of the defendant. . . . She (Michelle) lost on all points."[17]

Even the questions raised by Lee Marvin's post-trial remark that both he and Michelle had lied extensively in their courtroom testimony failed to disturb the judge. His decision to award Michelle $104,000 instead of the $1.6 million she'd sued for had been based, he said, "virtually not at all"[18] on the often sordid allegations Lee had hurled at Michelle.

Though he avoided using the term, the remedy that Judge Marshall invoked for Ms. Marvin is more commonly known as *rehabilitative alimony*. It is a relatively new leaf in the book of marriage law, and will be more fully discussed in the next two chapters; the significant fact here is that under the new guidelines, a judge not wildly sympathetic to Ms. Marvin's plight saw fit to impose a form of alimony on a relationship in which he himself had declared that no contractual rights existed.

OTHER POSSIBLE THEORIES

Other possible remedies available under the Marvin Doctrine include *constructive* and *resulting trusts*. If a judge were to find that the property held in Lee's name *had* been covered by an oral or implied contract to share equally with Michelle, he might declare the property to be held in constructive trust, with Lee as trustee for Michelle's interest.

In another situation, if the Malibu beach house had been purchased partly with Michelle's money and still put in Lee's name, its ownership might be considered a *resulting trust*. In either case, Michelle would then have become a part-owner of the property. Courts generally find that resulting trusts result only from contributions to the purchase price of an asset, not from contributions in labor or services to its maintenance or development; still, it has been argued that this interpretation arbitrarily discounts the monetary value of labor—not to mention the position of women. Possibly courts will turn to a more liberal interpretation and make wider use of the resulting-trust concept in future cases involving homemates.

This is a clear sign of changing times. Even couples who consider themselves casual mates rather than homemates may find some new strings attached when they try to break up the relationship; the wealthier mate may well be liable for alimony if not actually obligated to cough up a property settlement.

OTHER CASES

Recent cases from New York State better illustrate the implications of the Marvin Doctrine. A judge has ruled outright that alimony is no longer the exclusive domain of the legally married, setting off shock waves by awarding such payments to an unmarried Buffalo woman.

Susan McCullon's lawsuit against Leonard McCullon, a flour-mill supervisor who earned $25,000 a year, arose from a grievance similar to Michelle Marvin's. Though the case lacked star appeal, there was stronger evidence—and stronger measures were taken to protect her rights.

For twenty-eight years the McCullons had shared bed and

board, name and bank account; they had raised three little McCullons but never got around to marriage. According to Susan, they filed joint tax returns, kept a joint bank account, held joint ownership of their home, and held themselves out to the community as married. (This was *not* a common-law marriage, a subject we will clarify in the next chapter.)

When Leonard left to marry another woman, Susan sued. Justice Joseph Mattina backed her claim that a verbal contract had been entered into in 1948 and sealed with a ring; he found her eligible for both a property settlement and alimony.

She was awarded the couple's home, $100 per week in temporary alimony, and additional monies for child support, until a jury can settle the matter permanently. The case is coming up for trial, and while the jurors or a higher court may alter Justice Mattina's decision to take the Marvin Doctrine as far as it can go, it is considered a ground-breaker that will have major impact.

Then, in a case of perhaps even greater legal significance, New York's highest tribunal, the Court of Appeals, ruled in a suit by Frances Morone against her former lover: "We decline to recognize an action based upon an implied contract for personal services between unmarried persons living together."[19] However, the court went on to say that if an "express" contract can be proved, even an oral one, it will be recognized and the sharing of assets between mates will be allowed.

Minnesota's highest court has also handed down an un-equivocal affirmation of the Marvin Doctrine in a less equivocal case, that of *Carlson vs. Olson*. It awarded a fifty-fifty property settlement to Laura Carlson, who had lived with Oral Olson and raised his family for over 21 years. Though the court referred to Laura's "wifely" services and modeled the settle-ment on divorce-law principles, it also specifically asserted its approval of the various other theories suggested in the *Marvin* case for division of property between homemates. However, recent legislation passed in Minnesota may bar similar suits in the future unless a written contract exists between the parties.

New Jersey's Supreme Court, in June 1979, ruled that an unmarried man could be compelled to pay lifetime alimony. The *Kozlowski* case, a lawsuit between Irma and Thaddeus Kozlowski, who shared a surname by coincidence, involved one of Michelle Marvin's contentions. Thaddeus had promised to support Irma for life if she would move in with him, and she called him on the promise when he decided to marry a younger woman. The court, echoing *Marvin*, deemed it an enforceable oral agreement. Subsequently, Thaddeus cheerfully coughed up over $80,000 in an out-of-court settlement based, he declared, "on human association of two persons with good will."[20]

Still, he told the *Paterson* (New Jersey) *Morning News*, he believed there was no legal basis for the ruling in Irma's favor. "It was clear anything could happen in this situation, so we decided to avoid the lengthy legal procedures and come to a reasonable agreement. I'll let the smart people think about it,"[21] he said.

Although Kozlowski isn't bitter about the outcome, he does advise other men to wait until more definite legislation is passed before encouraging their lovers to move in.

PENDING LEGISLATION

Such legislation is on the way. A proposal now before the New Jersey state legislature would set clear standards for court enforcement of homemates' claims. If the proposal becomes law, properly written agreements will be upheld, but claims for settlements, support, or palimony will be unenforceable without written documents to back them up. Until it passes, though, the *Kozlowski* decision sets New Jersey's guidelines, leaving the door open for lawsuits based on verbal agreements and alleged promises.

Predictably enough, the New York, Minnesota, and California legislatures have examined similar measures; we daresay the idea will follow *Marvin*-type decisions from state courts to state legislators everywhere. State Assemblyman Walter Ingalls, sponsor of the California bill, proposes to limit the contractual rights granted homemates under the *Marvin* decision to valid written agreements. The measure would relieve state courts of their new responsibilities to "inquire into the conduct of the parties" in search of verbal, implied, or tacit agreements, and would bar homemates from suing on such claims. The courts would still have the power to use noncontractual remedies such as *quantum meruit,* according to the *San Francisco Post.*

Lee Marvin's attorney, David Kagon, testified that the proposal was "a step in the right direction," and Marvin Mitchelson called it just the reverse. He points out that oral and implied contracts have been enforced for the past two hundred years, and sees no legal justification for denying equal rights to contracts between lovers.

Opponents of the bill argue that it would be full of loopholes, encouraging abuse by cunning lovers who can afford to pay for legal maneuverings. It would work against women, particularly the unsophisticated and economically weak, who actually need the benefits of the *Marvin* decision more than do the Hollywood beauties who brought the issue into the limelight. As mentioned, Minnesota's legislature has just passed a bill requiring that contracts between mates be in writing for court enforcement, and denying recognition to oral agreements. So far, New York and California have warded off pressure for similar bills.

PALIMONY FOR PLAIN FOLKS

Throughout the country, it appears that the "common people" have fared better than the stars when it comes to collecting the new dues. At this writing, the top documented palimony settlement comes from Scotch Plains, New Jersey, where a lady named June Schwartz acquired cash and assets worth over $245,000 from her reneging homemate, Robert Schwartz. She had no written contract to show for their nine years together, but she'd saved all his love letters. With these to back up her claim that Robert had promised she would always be taken care of, Ms. Schwartz collected handsomely; Mr. Schwartz settled out of court.

While Michelle Triola Marvin won a major point of principle, her material award of $104,000 was less than triumphant—and since Lee Marvin is appealing even that, she has not yet seen a penny of it. In the interview with Tom Snyder, she told the world that while she takes pride in having fought for and won important rights for women, she does not plan a second entry into the legal battlefield of unlicensed love. "No, I wouldn't live with a man again, but I might leave a toothbrush at his house."[22] What she *would* like to do, she said, is get married.

A New York judge, using the *McCullon* ruling as a yardstick in another celebrated case, found that Penny McCall's lawsuit against rock star Peter Frampton didn't measure up. She wanted half the money he'd earned during their five years together, plus half the value of the Westchester estate where they'd done their cohabiting, but so far she's gotten nothing.

The judge held their relationship up to the *McCullon* light and found it wanting; Frampton and McCall had never intended to contract, nor held themselves out to the public as husband and wife, as had the McCullons. To make matters worse, both parties had run off from legitimate spouses, making their cohabitation not only open and notorious but also adulterous, and this the law could not condone. Nothing daunted, McCall is appealing the decision, confident that a higher court will agree that she deserves compensation for having been, in her words, "a damn good old lady."

Other celebrities' ex-mates share her hopes. Among them are Cynthia Lang, who is suing Alice Cooper for half of his worldly goods, and Karen Ecklund, who wants not only half of the $5 million Nick Nolte made while living with her, but also an extra $2 million in damages for "oppression, fraud, and malice."

For some people, misfortune never comes singly. Flip Wilson is in double trouble from two successive ex-mates, Katayana Harrison and Rosylin Taylor, who are asking for retroactive salaries of $7,500 and $12,500 per month respectively, plus the usual halves—which could add up to a whole lot of money.

Even a mistress wants her cut, as reported in the *Phoenix Gazette*. Genevieve Gilles, who claims she was Darryl Zanuck's "constant companion" for seven years, has filed a $15 million suit against the movie mogul's estate. The busy Mr. Mitchelson is also representing her, maintaining that palimony claims can reach beyond the grave.

The prominent palimony cases that have come to court at this writing have cost their leading men small change compared to one that was settled out of court. Singer Rod Stewart used to describe himself and Britt Ekland as "*the* beautiful couple"; their affair lasted only two years, but her demand for $15 million, neatly placed between the California Supreme Court's *Marvin* decision and the anticlimactic trial, reportedly netted her a beautiful settlement.

Sherry Steiger, divorcing actor Rod Steiger, wanted the divorce settlement to include reparations for their three years' cohabitation prior to the 1973 wedding. The odds were against her; Steiger had entered the marriage forearmed with a three-page prenuptial agreement prepared by his lawyer. Sherry signed the agreement in the presence of Rod's attorney, but later claimed she had not understood that the agreement waived her rights to any property Rod owned before the marriage, as well as all income he would earn once they tied the knot.

Her claim gave Steiger a good run for his money, collapsing down the stretch when the California Superior Court upheld the contract, though she did receive some compensation in temporary-support payments.

For all the attention they've received, the million-dollar "star wars" currently raging in Hollywood are possibly the least significant result of the *Marvin* decision. With much less publicity, yet with increasing steadiness, courts are applying Marvin Doctrine reasoning to the rest of us and developing local standards by which to measure the rights and responsibilities of homemates.

STRETCHING THE DOCTRINE

Just how far are the courts going to take the doctrine of financial responsibility for homemates? Clearly it is becoming socially and legally acceptable to live together without marriage, and courts all over the country are throwing out the moralistic obstacles that used to bar the enforcement of nonmarital contracts. Documented express contracts, even oral ones, will be honored in most states. The crystal ball is not so clear when it comes to the "implied contracts" or "tacit understandings" of the Marvin Doctrine. California's courts may be willing to sift the ashes of burnt-out love affairs for evidence of broken commitments, but such eager inquiry cannot be expected of judiciaries elsewhere in the near future.

Even in California, what the Marvin Doctrine left unsaid has legal scholars scratching their heads. For in directing the courts to "inquire into the conduct of the parties" in search of implied commitments to enforce, the state supreme court neglected to provide any hints as to what sorts of conduct would meet the test. There are no clear guidelines to help lovers establish a homemate relationship with vested property rights, or avoid liability for palimony demands from out of the blue. Judge Marshall's no-nonsense approach to the *Marvin* trial brought an admirably unequivocal decision out of a maze of conflicting "reasonable expectations"—but he could possibly have chosen to emphasize quite another set of arguments and thus decided in favor of Michelle's claim.

ALIMONY TERMINATION

As the Marvin Doctrine solidifies, the law will have to adapt in many directions to the presence of the so-called quasi-marital status, that of homemates with vested property rights. The subject of alimony will have to be reexamined. As it now stands in most states, alimony ceases when the divorced spouse receiving payments marries again, but not, as a rule, when he or she merely lives with another lover as a casual mate. But already in a few states, when the question of vested rights between homemates has arisen, an ex-husband paying alimony to his former wife has successfully argued that her new relationship gives her financial security, so his duty of alimony should end. The ex-wife's homemate, on the other hand, might claim that *he* has a vested interest in *her* alimony.

In effect, this variation on the *Marvin* theme is that a new homemate relationship is tantamount to remarriage for purposes of terminating alimony.

DEBTS AND JOINT LIABILITY

Another area of upheaval will be the subject of debts, already an important factor in some couples' decisions about marriage and living together, chiefly in the eight community-property states: Arizona, California, Idaho, Louisiana, New Mexico, Nevada, Texas, and Washington. Under the community-property system, spouses share equally in the community-property estate, which consists of all property acquired from the earnings of either spouse during the marriage (property acquired by gift or inheritance is ordinarily excluded unless comingled). They also share liability for any debts incurred by either or both parties during the marriage, but only to the amount of the community-property estate. Contrariwise, the community-property estate is either *not* liable or not fully liable for debts incurred by either spouse prior to the marriage. (If the marriage doesn't last, though, the creditor can resume his suit against the debtor's property as soon as the divorce becomes final—as long as the statute of limitations hasn't run out.) Thus, in a community-property state, a $10 marriage license may serve partially or fully as a cheap and pleasant alternative to bankruptcy proceedings—or, if you marry a spendthrift, it can land *you* in as much trouble as your spouse knows how to create.

At present, unmarried cohabitants are not held liable for their homemates' debts, even in community-property states. But although the Marvin case didn't touch upon debts, it seems to follow that if implied contracts and property rights can arise from a couple's conduct, why not obligations to creditors as well? We believe that if *de facto* community property can be established, eventually homemates with vested rights will probably find themselves liable for debts incurred by their mates during their relationship in the eight states mentioned above. This will not be a problem for casual mates as long as they can establish the independent nature of their relationship. Nor will it arise in separate-property states, unless both mates sign a contract with a creditor, or their conduct somehow imposes a joint obligation.

However, we do not wish to present only problems with the concept of community property. We have many positive things to say about it, and we generally endorse the concept because it is inherently fair to both parties. Actually, as will be pointed out later, basic equitable principles, similar to the rationale of the community-property system, prevail in many separate-property states.

ERA: WHAT EFFECT?
A substantial majority of states work under the separate-property system, but some lawyers are speculating that a drastic change may be on the way. The Equal Rights Amendment, they feel, may provoke a nationwide shift to the community-property system or similar methodology on the grounds that it provides economic equality between the sexes within marriage. But other legal scholars argue that the opposite outcome, a unanimous adoption of separate property, is more likely.

LAWSUITS BETWEEN LOVERS
Taking the debt-related ramifications a step further, another nasty question arises: if one becomes liable for the debts of his or her homemate, can the innocent homemate who coughs up the dough sue the wayward partner for the losses sustained? Married couples cannot obtain such relief unless it is done "through the back door"; that is, when they terminate their relationship by means of separation or divorce, the financial reparations between them become a matter of private negotiation. But the "front door" is closed; one spouse usually cannot testify against the other, or sue the other for debts incurred. On the other hand, if two spouses form a business partnership, they may incur liability each to the other, and it may be recognizable by the courts. How this would affect an otherwise harmonious marriage remains to be seen. Perhaps the liability would continue to exist, and neither spouse would sue the other unless their marriage terminated.

NECESSARIES

Discrimination between men and women prevails on many levels. A continuing problem for husbands in most states (not wives, generally) is liability for the family's "necessaries." As the legal status of a male homemate creeps toward that of a husband, he may become responsible for necessary expenses incurred by his female counterpart from third-party creditors for housing, food, and clothing, whether in a separate- or community-property state.

It is sometimes suggested, in more or less appalled tones, that the Equal Rights Amendment would relieve husbands of their sex-linked legal duty to keep wives and children supplied with the basic necessities of life. A more likely outcome, we believe, is that this responsibility would become mutual, so that neither wife nor husband could be left on skid row by a partner able but unwilling to provide necessaries. If all this comes to pass, liability for a homemate's basic needs may be imposed on females too.

Until case law comes down, the present rule is that a homemate or casual mate owes no duty of support, even for necessaries, to another mate; a creditor will have a tough time collecting except from the mate who ran up the bill. As a result, homemates could find it harder to get credit from merchants than would a legally married couple. This should change as homemates acquire vested rights.

CLAIMS AGAINST THIRD PARTIES

A more welcome effect that should emerge from legal implementation of the Marvin Doctrine is that cohabitants will eventually gain the right to sue or be compensated for the loss of a homemate's companionship, support, etc., due to death or serious injury. As mentioned in Chapter Two, homemates may not be permitted to purchase an insurance policy on their mates, or to sue for loss of "consortium" or for the wrongful death of a partner. Even if the death or loss was caused by negligence, a homemate has no standing to sue the negligent person.

Probably a casual mate will always be denied such relief, not only on the dubious grounds that a short-term or uncommitted relationship is more illicit than long-term cohabitation, but also because a casual mate cannot claim to have been exclusively dependent on the departed or incapacitated mate for emotional or financial support when neither had made a serious, long-term commitment to the relationship. Until recently, most courts considered marriage the only proof of such commitment. Under the new approach, a homemate who has acquired vested property rights, whether by contract or by long years of sharing the ups and downs of domestic life, should be entitled to reparations when his or her legitimate expectations are shattered by personal disaster.

This beachhead in the battle for advancing nonmarital rights might be gained in the near future through a two-part lawsuit in a state whose courts recognize the commitments involved in living together.

First, the bereaved party would petition the court to examine his/her status for a determination that he/she was not merely a casual mate but a homemate, possessing valid contractual or vested interests in the affairs of the deceased. Only after that standing was established would the homemate be permitted to pursue a consortium action or wrongful-death claim against the third party responsible for the loss. And yet, the prospects are poor. Even in jurisdictions where the Marvin Doctrine reigns unchallenged, homemates' rights in this area will probably never be as clear-cut as those of lawfully wedded spouses.

NO THREAT TO MARRIAGE

Coupling these legal currents with the divorce wave, legal weather-watchers frequently observe that the dividing line between marriage and cohabitation is disappearing. Soon, they predict, the two will be indistinguishable; living together will be virtually the same as common-law marriage.

The ultimate folly: A man who supports both a wife and a mistress, suggests *Playboy*, may be found guilty of bigamy.

The California Supreme Court's *Marvin* decision clearly contradicted all of these notions:

> We do not seek to resurrect the doctrine of common-law marriage, which was abolished in California by statute in 1895. Thus we do not hold that plaintiff and defendant were 'married,' nor do we extend to plaintiff the rights of valid or putative spouses; we hold only that she has the same rights to enforce contracts and to assert her equitable interest in property acquired through her effort as does any other unmarried person.[23]

> And:

> Although we recognize the well-established public policy to foster and promote the institution of marriage, perpetuation of judicial rules which result in an inequitable distribution of property accumulated during a

nonmarital relationship is neither a just nor an effective way of carrying out that policy.[24]

NEW BOUNDARIES

Similar disclaimers appear in virtually every court ruling emulating *Marvin*. The law is not abandoning the institution of marriage; rather, the courts are extending their demands for fair play beyond the confines of marriage to reach the new boundaries of adult relationships. In the long run, the new ground rules may actually serve to enhance the stability of marriage. People will become more conscious of the seriousness of their commitments, taking more time for careful communication and planning before exchanging vows.

Further benefits for married couples may eventually develop as an indirect result of the revolution in homemates' rights. In the long process of hammering out the new laws and interpretations that must follow in *Marvin*'s wake, the nation's Solons and Solomons may be impelled to "foster and promote the institution of marriage" by seeking to establish new incentives in its favor. They could get off to an auspicious start merely by eliminating some outworn policies that actively discourage many couples from marrying, and then—though this might be expecting too much—they might establish and adopt a uniform body of laws.

The *Marvin* decision is a bold step toward guaranteeing dignity and fair dealing in all sexual relationships; similar advances are visible in a growing number of states. But it still pays to be sure of your legal status in your state.

THE HEWITT CASE: A SETBACK FOR MATES

An interesting case showing a reversal in the *Marvin* direction is *Hewitt vs. Hewitt*. In 1978, the state appellate court in Illinois ruled favorably on a suit brought by Victoria Hewitt against her homemate of fifteen years, Robert Hewitt, pointing out that the legislature had not intended to proscribe any sexual conduct between consenting adults that was not openly damaging to the institution of marriage. The Hewitts and their three children, said the court, maintained "a most conventional, respectable, and ordinary family life," flawed only by their failure to get married, and Victoria Hewitt deserved a fair share of the property accumulated on Robert's substantial earnings as a dentist.

She had helped put him through dental college and worked

in his office, as well as taking care of their home and children. They had held some joint property, but the bulk of their assets was in Robert's name. Victoria claimed that Robert had promised to share everything with her, and had thus talked her into doing without a marriage license. The facts in the case not only tended to support her assertion that Robert had made definite promises of support, but also showed that she had contributed substantially to the prosperity they enjoyed.

When the appellate court ruled that Victoria Hewitt was entitled to relief, Illinois began to be cited among the states favoring property rights for homemates. But wait! Unpack those bags! On appeal, the Illinois State Supreme Court's 1979 opinion on the *Hewitt* case moved as far away from the Marvin Doctrine as it could get; Victoria ended up out in the cold with no compensation, feeling "like a charter member of Stupid Anonymous."[25]

The court maintained that its duty was to uphold the intentions of the Illinois legislature as expressed in the Marriage and Dissolution of Marriage Act passed in 1977. Though that act did not outlaw cohabitation, the supreme court acted on its mandate "to strengthen and preserve the integrity of marriage and safeguard family relationships" by slamming the door in the face of a hard-working mother of three. They found: "Of substantially greater importance than the rights of the immediate parties is the impact of such recognition upon the society and the institution of marriage."[26] To adopt the reasoning in *Marvin*, this court said, would be to establish a form of common-law marriage by judicial decree. The possibility that mates living together do not want common-law marriage, but *do* want enforceable property rights was quickly dismissed. "Potentially enhancing the attractiveness of a private arrangement over marriage . . . by allowing the parties to engage in such relationships with greater security . . . contravenes the Act's policy of strengthening and preserving the integrity of marriage."[27]

Some Illinois lawyers believe that written cohabitation contracts will fare better as long as they meet the standard conditions of contractual relationships. But in view of the court's brusque declaration that "public policy disfavors private contractual alternatives to marriage,"[28] it seems rash to advise unmarried couples that even written contracts offer any protection in Illinois, unless a substantial and truly independent business interest is involved. The Illinois Supreme Court announced it would not be caught ". . . displaying the naivete we

believe involved in finding in these relationships contracts separate and independent from the sexual activity, and the assumption that those contracts would have been entered into or
would continue without that activity."[29]

Of course, an agreement calling for separate property with
no vested rights, *no* palimony, and *no* compensation for services rendered might come in handy just in case the Illinois
court or legislators should suddenly decide to set a new tack.
The way things stand now, what Victoria Hewitt got is what
you get—and that's nothing, unless you take out a marriage
license.

SOME OTHER REMEDIES

We do have ideas for homemates who want to establish their
mutual obligations in states like Colorado and Ohio, where
Marvin-time has not yet come. Business partnerships, as you
will discover, and "boomerang divorce," referred to in a later
chapter, may work to fix less-than-lawful rights between homemates in most places. But the Illinois position is so uncompromising that we wouldn't advise reliance on anything cute.
Illinois homemates who sincerely desire to establish their intentions to deal fairly with each other have a clear mandate to
marry or to move.

GAY NEEDS

Homosexual and lesbian couples, who cannot legally marry
in any state today, clearly need *Marvin* protection more than
any other group; whether they will get it is another question
with no definite answer. Once again, California may be ahead
of the pack, having recently changed its laws to decriminalize
all sexual activities between consenting adults in private. Absence of criminal sanctions alone may not be enough to establish the possibility of enforceable property rights between gay
couples, since the *Marvin* decision did not take up the question.
The arguments dealing with the questions of meretriciousness
and legality of the homemate relationship seem equally applicable to homosexual mates; the reasoning that involves "alleged
moral considerations" and "social acceptance" does not.

Marvin-modeled lawsuits between male lovers have been
initiated in California and in Washington, D.C., but there is
no score to report as yet.

As more gays openly declare their sexual preference and
demand the right to live together with some measure of dignity,

the courts will have to respond. In time new theories will develop, perhaps out of partnership law, to provide a basis for contractual and property rights for gay homemates that more closely parallel those of the majority. At this point, gays should not rely on the possibility of implied rights arising from conduct, nor even on the enforceability of express contracts, but they may find it useful to define their understandings in a contract between themselves. They should definitely seek competent legal advice if they have any desire to enter into a binding commitment.

FUTURE SHIFTS

What with ERA and *Marvin*, the future is hard to predict. All we can say for sure is that we are entering a period of greater change. The old landmarks—the security of marriage, the freedom of living together—are tottering, and a careless wanderer on the paths of love can get seriously lost. This won't last forever, but it may be twenty to fifty years before society and the legislatures straighten out their shifting priorities and enact a unified code of sensible law governing the status of spouses and homemates across the nation. We must expect years—perhaps decades—of uncertainty, occasional inequity, and just plain confusion.

Meanwhile, couples living together will have to examine their own conduct, look over their own "tacit understandings" for financial or emotional discrepancies, and compare their own "reasonable expectations" with what the law in their state seems to be saying.

They should try to decide for themselves whether they intend to be homemates or casual mates, whether they welcome or loathe the prospect of future financial obligations. If they can reach an agreement, they should try to get it in writing, particularly if their intentions are out of sync with local views on the Marvin Doctrine.

Homemates who fail to take advantage of the *Marvin* mandate to express their intentions and protect their rights may end up being taken for a ride. As Mr. Mitchelson put it: "I would have to say, at this stage of the game, that if this troubles you—if you worry about breaking up and are property conscious—you should, to make sure, draw up an agreement. . . . Of course, if you do all that, you may end up not living together at all. . . . Personally, I think it's a terrible way to start a relationship."[30]

Paradoxically, it is those adventurous lovers who want nothing to do with "pieces of paper"—those who want a carefree, no-strings relationship—who stand in line for real trouble in the wake of the *Marvin* decision. Ask Lee Marvin. If you want an ironclad guarantee of your freedom, you'll have to get it in writing, or move to Illinois!

AN INTERLUDE

...I may take comfort a little.
—JOB 10. 20

Mary Wollstonecraft, the founding mother of feminism, and William Godwin, political philosopher, married on March 29, 1797, in Old St. Pancras Church in London. Thoroughly abashed by the incongruity of the deed, the pair of notorious radicals offered separate but equally self-conscious, stiff, and awkward explanations to their friends, while gossips and political wits spread reports of the spectacle with greater relish The marriage did not entirely succeed in conciliating those who were shocked not so much by Mary's pregnancy as by the not-so-very-unexpected revelation, through this marriage, that Mary had not in fact been previously married to Gilbert Imlay, the father of her daughter Fanny.

Mary Wollstonecraft believed in marriage as an ideal, but objected strongly to its abuses in the practice of her times. As she catalogued them, these abuses included the near-impossibility of divorce, a husband's legal and actual tyranny over his wife and children, the mercenary nature of the alliance given the fact that women were denied any other avenue to respectable survival, and the spiritual emptiness of a union in which neither the husband nor the untrained and uneducated wife could expect any intellectual companionship. Today these seem like reasonable, even obvious, objections to the eighteenth century's version of respectable marriage. It only astonishes us that Mary Wollstonecraft was the first writer to express them systematically.

In Godwin, though, she found a lover who believed as passionately as did she in the ideal of an intellectual partnership and an equal one, who abjured as doggedly as did she the bondage of contemporary marital customs. Godwin had written that "Marriage is a law, and the worst of laws.... Marriage is an affair of properties, and the worst of properties."

Though they could do nothing to protect themselves legally, they pioneered the notion of working out a private agreement of marital responsibilities and rights, in an oral contract taken very seriously by both parties.

Their agreements are recorded in Godwin's *Memoir of the Author of a Vindication of the Rights of Woman*, and witnessed, in bits and pieces, by notes exchanged between the parties.

Chapter Five

MARRIAGE: THE REAL ISSUES

The two pillars upon which God has founded the edifice of civilized society are, after all, property and marriage.

—CHARLES MINIVALE

Marriage: a community consisting of a master, a mistress, and two slaves, making in all, two

—AMBROSE BIERCE, *The Devil's Dictionary*

Lest we be misunderstood, however, we take this opportunity to point out that the structure of society itself largely depends upon the institution of marriage, and nothing we have said in this opinion should be taken to derogate from that institution. The joining of the man and woman in marriage is at once the most socially productive and individually fulfilling relationship that one can enjoy in the course of a lifetime.

—JUSTICE MATTHEW O. TOBRINER *in the* Marvin *decision*

THE INSTITUTION OF MARRIAGE

What *do* you get when you get married besides your spouse? Among the indisputable joys of marriage are income-tax breaks for one-breadwinner couples, death-tax breaks for larger estates, inheritance rights, lower insurance rates, and a host of other legal benefits, like the right *not* to testify against one's spouse (sometimes). Marriage can also confer citizenship on a previously illegal alien and allow a Pennsylvania woman to misbehave without going to jail.

Social Security and military benefits fork over extra bucks for the spouse of a breadwinner; these and pension income continue to flow to the surviving spouse after the earner's death. Certain statutory allowances and property rights are also automatically extended to widows. Further, as a matter of public policy, judges are under orders to "look with favor" upon claims of marriage when conflict arises with other demands. The marriage contract is never thrown out as meretricious; it will be upheld as valid whenever possible. Society, recognizing that there can be too much of a good thing, penalizes bigamy, but aside from that, no one has ever been threatened with imprisonment for open and notorious marriage.

COMMON-LAW MARRIAGE

In sharp contrast to cohabitation contracts, the contract of marriage is considered valid in virtually every state as long as it was valid in the home state, even if it did not fulfill the requirements of the forum state. The popular fallacy that common-law marriages are valid everywhere is true to this extent: almost all the states recognize the validity of valid common-law marriages. The catch is that valid common-law marriages can be created only in thirteen states and the District of Columbia; the other states recognize as marriages only those relationships that begin with a ceremony performed by a clergyman, magistrate, or other authorized person.

The distinction between unwed cohabitation and common-law marriage can be hazy. This is especially true in states like Alabama, Montana, and South Carolina, where cohabitation is unlawful. When—and where—do illegal sinners become lawful spouses?

COMMON-LAW STATES

State	Recognizes common-law marriage*
Alabama	Yes
Colorado	Yes
District of Columbia	Yes
Florida	No[1]
Georgia	Yes
Idaho	Yes
Indiana	No[2]
Iowa	Yes
Kansas	Yes
Kentucky	No[3]

Louisiana	No[2, 6]
Maryland	No[2]
Missouri	No[2]
Montana	Yes
New Hampshire	No[4]
Ohio	Yes
Oklahoma	Yes
Oregon	No[2]
Pennsylvania	Yes
Rhode Island	Yes
South Carolina	Yes
Tennessee	No[5]
Texas	Yes

[1]Florida was the last state to abolish common-law marriage, doing so in 1968. Thus common-law marriages consummated in Florida before January 1, 1968, *are* valid. Long-term homemates in other states should look up the date of abolition in their state, since they may qualify as common-law spouses; a few states recognize common-law marriages dating back to the 1950s.

[2]Courts in these states have recognized "marriage by presumption"; see glossary.

[3]Kentucky holds common-law marriages invalid *except* for purposes of recovery under the Workmen's Compensation Act, where they may be recognized.

[4]New Hampshire law expressly provides for presumption of a legal marriage for "widowed" homemates, when the couple had cohabited for three years or more, acknowledged each other as husband and wife, and generally were known as such.

[5]Tennessee courts have recognized marriage "by estoppel" in cases of lengthy cohabitation.

[6]Louisiana does not recognize common-law marriages entered into outside the state by Louisiana residents.

*Most other states recognize a valid common-law marriage entered into in a state that recognizes them, unless the would-be spouses are residents of a non-recognizing state and go to a state that recognizes them primarily to enter into a common-law marriage. Kentucky, a lone exception, recognizes all common-law marriages entered into in any of the fourteen common-law jurisdictions.

Another myth is that common-law marriage consists of living together for seven years; seven years' cohabitation is neither necessary nor sufficient to create a common-law marriage. Under Pennsylvania common law, says Mark J. Goldberg, head of the Allegheny Bar Association's Family Law Section, "people can be married in a matter of minutes."[1] The requirement is simply that the two people actually agree to be married "in the present sense" (that is, now, not someday) and from then on so conduct their affairs that they hold themselves out as spouses. Idaho, for example, finds that a common-law marriage exists when the parties consent to be married and mutually assume marital rights, duties, or obligations. Most states hold that eligibility for a ceremonial marriage is a prerequisite to a valid common-law marriage; that is, no one can be married at common law who was not legally free to enter a regular marriage. One frequent exception to this requirement is the matter of age; the traditional common-law age of consent to marriage (14 for males and 12 for females) is applied in some states even when one must be considerably older to obtain a regular marriage license. Kansas, for example, requires written parental or judicial consent for issuance of a marriage license to anyone under eighteen, but may find a thirteen-year-old girl married at common law.

The *Hewitt* case, which came to a bad end in Illinois, would most likely have been treated as a common-law marriage in Pennsylvania or Idaho. The couple, according to "Mrs." Hewitt, had simply declared themselves married when they started out, and had lived together as Mr. and Mrs. Hewitt for fifteen years.

Yet another delusion is that common-law marriage is less binding than the regular kind. In fact, when it does exist, it is precisely the same as ceremonial marriage; it can be legally terminated only upon death or by divorce. In practice, a couple could enter a common-law marriage, live together as man and wife for, say, three years, then split up *sans* divorce with no one the wiser, assuming they were able to agree on the terms of the separation. Somewhere down the road, though, the ghost of that marriage might rise up and haunt them. They might discover, when marrying or divorcing again, that the subsequent marriage was invalid because the first had never been legally dissolved. This can lead to another type, known as the *putative marriage*.

PUTATIVE MARRIAGE

More widely recognized than common-law marriage, putative marriage is a relationship that is mistakenly regarded by one or both parties as a legal marriage. Unlike a common-law marriage, it is *not* a valid union, but putative spouses are given some marital rights in most states, despite the technical lapse. The flaw may arise from outright deceit. Consider the man who keeps a wife in Boston and another in Philadelphia—the man is a bigamist and knows it, but the ladies are unaware of each other's existence. The one he married first is his legal wife; the other is a "putative spouse" and will in most states be entitled to some marital rights, since she entered into the bogus marriage in good faith.

Often enough, though, the putative marriage arises innocently all around. The ceremony is performed, but it doesn't take because of a technical lapse or because one of the parties was not, in fact, free to marry. The status of putative spouse lasts only as long as the person believes he or she is legally married. Once the error is brought out, and the parties are no longer ignorant of the unhallowed state of their affairs, their quasi-marital rights cease to accrue. However, if they part, most states will allow the innocent putative spouse or spouses (both if they are both innocent) some or all of the rights and privileges normally accorded spouses, including property adjustments for the time prior to the discovery that the relationship is legally flawed.

THE EFFECTS OF COMMON-LAW MARRIAGE

Under the common-law marriage doctrine, it *is* possible to become married retroactively. Is it, then, possible that a cohabiting couple can be married without knowing it, or even against their wishes? The answer is a qualified yes. The states do not go around slapping unwanted marriages like parking tickets on domestic operations; the status of common-law spouse is generally available to anyone who fills the local bill, but is *imposed* only when one or both parties go to court and successfully claim that status. For example:

Zeke Twombly, a blues guitarist, and his lady, Pinkie, who used to work the graveyard shift at the Top Note Cafe, live together on the outskirts of Mobile, Alabama, for two years. It's love in a cottage surrounded by prim neighbors, and while Zeke and Pinkie haven't really discussed the exact nature of their commitment, they find that the course of true love runs more smoothly when they use his last name and let everyone think that they're married.

Out of the blue, Zeke learns that an elderly fan has left him $4 million, with the stipulation that he enroll in classical music courses and stay off drugs. Zeke, who has always been a closet square, leaps at the terms, taking to his new life like a fish to water; Pinkie is bored stiff and wants out, but she wants to take a piece of the $4 million with her. She files a divorce action.

The court does not know whether Pinkie is telling the truth when she declares that she and Zeke privately agreed to be married. Zeke's denial is taken into consideration, but so are the testimony of their landlord, who swears he would not have rented them the cottage if Pinkie had not been introduced as Zeke's wife, and the records of a New Mexico motel where Zeke and Pinkie spent several blissful days, registered in Zeke's handwriting as Mr. and Mrs. Twombly. Finding no independent evidence to support Zeke's story, the court finds a common-law marriage, entitling Pinkie to some settlement upon the "divorce."

In this unedifying tale, Zeke does indeed find himself married unwillingly and unawares. What this best illustrates is why a majority of states has decided against recognizing common-law marriage; while it certainly offers protection to honest but unsophisticated partners, it also invites abuse, since it is not always easy to tell the fraudulent claims from genuine ones.

However, the courts are extending more recognition to serious relationships that endure without a matrimonial license. As the principles of the *Marvin* case gradually seep throughout the land, the fundamental commitments between homemates may receive much the same protection and acceptance as a common-law marriage.

VARIOUS LIMITATIONS

Other limitations are imposed on marriage in various states, which may leave certain couples bereft of its benefits.

Several Southern states still bar interracial marriages—defined as a marriage between a white or Caucasian person and one who has one-eighth or more Negro or Oriental blood! True, the Supreme Court recently struck down Virginia's antimiscegenation statute, and the ones remaining on the books in Georgia, Mississippi, and Tennessee are lame ducks, no less blatantly unconstitutional—but there they are, until voided or repealed.

In Pennsylvania and you cannot marry the person with whom you committed adultery if that adultery was the grounds for divorce from your ex-spouse, as long as the spouse is still living. Puerto Rico's legislature, perhaps sensing a potentially calamitous loophole in such laws, provides that you cannot marry a person who has been convicted of responsibility for the death of your previous spouse.

Many states won't issue marriage licenses to "insane or imbecile persons"; Ohio goes a step further, declaring the state of matrimony off-limits to habitual drunkards. Some states, carrying on eugenic notions long after their medical obsolescence, include epileptics among the classes of people who may not marry. Consanguinity is generally a bar to marriage, even when the relationship is actually created by marriage or adoption and not by blood kinship. Legal horror of violating the incest taboo comes in varying degrees; some states allow marriages between first cousins, while others forbid them as incestuous.

Since one state may permit what another forbids, disqualified couples often think that they can get around an obstacle to their marriage at home by getting married in a more lenient state. First cousins, epileptics, and habitual drunkards can usually find another state willing to unite them. The problem is that the marriage may not be valid back home. If you marry in another state *solely* to avoid restrictions at home, the marriage will not be recognized; the home state will consider it a sham.

North Dakota must be singled out as a poor prospect for marital asylum for all nonresident couples. Its statutes forbid issuing a marriage license to nonresidents, unless one party has parents residing in North Dakota, or unless the parties can prove, by producing a recent and valid marriage license from another state, that they were going to commit matrimony regardless. Perhaps for similar reasons, Tennessee and Indiana officials may not issue a marriage license when either applicant is under the influence of liquor or narcotics, as was noted in *McAdam vs. Walker:*

> If people are drunk or delirious,
> The marriage of course would be bad,
> Or if they're not sober or serious
> But acting a play or charade.

THE RIGHTS OF THOSE WHO MARRY

Broadly speaking, three major rights immediately accrue to those who take the plunge: the right to enjoy conjugal relations in privacy; the right to a share in marital property; and the right to various benefits, compensations, or reparations in the event of death or disability of a spouse.

Only the first of these applies equally nationwide. The states' right to regulate marriage as they see fit is so sacred in American law that the Supreme Court has seldom ruled in the area, but in the 1965 case of *Griswold vs. State of Connecticut,* it delivered an important ruling striking down a Connecticut law forbidding the use of contraceptives as an intrusion on the right of marital privacy.

The second area, involving spouses' rights in each other's property, falls entirely to the states' discretion; happily for us, marital-property policies can be divided into three parts, rather than fifty, without doing serious violence to local color. These three basic policies are community property, separate property, and a minority view of separate property which we will call "ultra-separate property."

COMMUNITY PROPERTY

Community property is an idea derived from the Napoleonic Code; most states that use the system were strongly influenced by Spanish law (California, Arizona, Nevada, and Texas) or French law (Louisiana) in their formative years. Washington and Idaho are also community-property states.

The basic tenet of community-property law is that all property accruing from the labor of either spouse during the marriage belongs equally to both; this includes all wages, salaries, and income from property or investments acquired with such monies. The same yardstick makes all debts and obligations incurred during the marriage "community property" as well. As the sages declare, there ain't no such thing as a free lunch.

Even in community-property states, each spouse may own separate property; all property acquired before the marriage remains the separate property of the acquiring spouse, along with income derived from such property. Property acquired by gift or inheritance during the marriage is also the separate property of the recipient. Debts incurred before the marriage by either party remain the sole and separate responsibility of the debtor, and only his/her *separate* property may be attached to satisfy such debts. His/her share of the couple's community property is *not* liable for debts incurred before marriage, except if the property is divided upon divorce or death, thus reverting to separate ownership. Of course, the community is liable for debts run up during the marriage that generally benefit both spouses.

Marriage in community-property states thus provides immunity, to the extent of the community property, from premarital creditors—not exactly a free lunch, but payment may be deferred until the marriage ends, by which time the statute of limitations may have run out. On the other hand, we can't recommend marrying a chronic debtor if you're going to live in a community-property state. If the bills continue to mount up after marriage, you stand to lose not only your share of the community property, but your credit rating as well. Another nasty jolt hit an Arizona woman whose husband lost his driver's license because he was unable to pay off damages arising from his negligent driving. He alone was responsible for the bad driving, but she was held equally responsible for its financial consequences, since both the automobile and the bad debt were community property. She lost her license too!

The real strength of community property lies in the financial guarantees it affords to dependent spouses. Upon the death of a spouse, half of the community property automatically remains with the survivor, who may also receive family and homestead allowances from the estate of the deceased spouse. The surviving spouse can, of course, receive the entire estate by will, but cannot be totally disinherited, although the decedent can bequeath his/her separate property and his/her half of the community property elsewhere.

If the marriage ends in divorce, the courts attempt to divide the community property equally, or virtually down the middle. In some states the property can be divided equitably rather than equally; if the court sees fit, the needier spouse may be awarded *more* than half of the community property. Usually separate property in a community-property state cannot be redistributed, but alimony and child-support payments may be awarded in addition to the property division.

The community-property jurisdictions have shaken off the strain of sexism that historically vitiated the admirable fairness of the system. In the bad old days (that is, as recently as last year, in Louisiana), wives enjoyed equal ownership but not equal control of community property; the right of management and disposition belonged more or less exclusively to the husband. Only in 1980 did Louisiana cease to regard the husband as "head and master" of the household and raise the wife to the status of an equal manager. Arizona took the plunge in

1973, with new provisions for equal management, control, and disposition. Nevada still regards the husband as head of the family, and subordinates certain aspects of the wife's legal status to his; but even so, the two spouses are now on equal footing as financial partners.

If you are now beginning to suspect that these states have actually managed to agree on a uniform interpretation of domestic law, disabuse yourself of this rank un-American heresy! There are actually nine different community-property systems (including the Commonwealth of Puerto Rico), with differences ranging from major doctrine to minor administrative detail. About half, for example, will reduce a spouse's share of the community-property settlement in a divorce if he or she is considered the "guilty" party; the others either use the no-fault divorce system (e.g., Arizona and California), or consider the community-property law virtually inviolable (e.g., New Mexico). California and Arizona now apply the community-property system in part to couples who move in from separate-property jurisdictions; Idaho does so when a spouse dies but not when a couple divorces; and the other states do not do so at all.

Among the community-property jurisdictions, the discriminating couple in search of a marital utopia might well choose Puerto Rico. There, husbands and wives are obliged ". . . to live together and mutually help each other, and satisfy each other's needs in proportion to their fortune." Due to the Spanish heritage, perhaps, a wife's last name is treated with due respect, and neither spouse may dictate the couple's residence. As to separate property, each partner has an equal right to disposition and control. A curious detail of Puerto Rican law works against mercenary marriages by holding gifts between spouses legally void—except "moderate gifts on festive days."

While Puerto Rico may deprive a guilty spouse of some property rights in divorce as a penalty for marital misconduct, it also provides the option of non-punitive divorce—a marriage may be terminated after two years' separation.

SEPARATE PROPERTY

The separate-property system adopted by forty-two states and the District of Columbia is derived from English common law and does not confer property-sharing rights upon spouses until death or divorce, if ever. The underlying tenet of the system is "to each his own." However, in the event of divorce, many separate-property states hold that marital property acquired during the marriage, and sometimes separate property acquired by one spouse *before* marriage, can be equitably divided. The same equitable divisions are often made as to property held jointly, such as joint tenancy with the right of survivorship or tenancy in common (see p.120 for the distinctions between these two different methods of jointly holding title to property). For a more specific analysis of the law in each state, please refer to the State-by-State Guides.

The five ultra-separate-property states (Florida, Mississippi, South Carolina, Virginia, and West Virginia) hold to a strict separate-property theory, and do not allow for marital property, which is separate property acquired by one spouse during the marriage, except by gift or inheritance generally, to be equitably divided by the court between the spouses in a divorce action. New York and Pennsylvania have just revamped their laws, and a liberalized separate-property law now exists; they used to be ultra-separate-property states.

SEPARATE-PROPERTY LAWS— GENERAL EXPLANATIONS

1. All income acquired before or during the marriage belongs to the acquiring spouse.
2. All property acquired before or during the marriage belongs to the acquiring spouse.
3. In the event of a divorce, a spouse may make claim upon the separate property of the other spouse, and the courts may, as deemed fair in different states:
   a. award to the non-owning spouse some or all of the separate property (marital property) acquired during marriage, or
   b. award to the non-owning spouse some or all of the separate property acquired before or during marriage, or
   c. refuse to make any award of separate property to the non-owning spouse, and/or
   d. divide jointly held property equally or disproportionately, or assign it according to financial contributions.
4. If he or she is disinherited, the surviving spouse in most states can still make claim upon a portion of the deceased spouse's estate by way of dower, curtesy, family allowance, or other statutory relief.

COMMUNITY-PROPERTY LAWS— GENERAL EXPLANATIONS

1. All earnings acquired during the marriage are owned one-half by each spouse.

2. All property bought with money earned from labor during the marriage is owned equally by each spouse.

3. Property acquired by either spouse through inheritance or gift before or during the marriage is separate property unless it is commingled or expressly or impliedly declared to be in common ownership.

4. Income acquired before or during the marriage from a separate-property investment is usually separate property unless it is commingled or expressly or impliedly declared to be in common ownership.

5. Upon divorce, the court in most states can only divide up the community property and, in some states, property held in joint tenancy or tenancy in common. In some, community property can be divided up disproportionately so that, for example, the less wealthy spouse acquires a greater amount of the community property. In other states, it must be divided substantially equally. The separate property of either spouse in most states cannot be divided up.

6. Upon the death of a spouse, one-half of the community property automatically remains with the surviving spouse. The deceased spouse can disinherit the surviving spouse as to the deceased spouse's share of the community property, and as to the deceased spouse's separate property. The surviving spouse usually has certain family and homestead allowances in the estate of the deceased spouse.

7. In California and Arizona, unlike the other community-property states, if a couple moves from a separate-property state to either of these two states, any separate property that would have been community property had the couple been living in California or Arizona all along is treated as community property. Idaho employs this doctrine if a spouse dies, but not if the couple divorces.

SEPARATE-PROPERTY VARIATIONS

All income and property belong to the acquiring spouse in the separate-property jurisdictions. You can be married to a millionaire and not have a penny to your name.

As mentioned, most of the separate-property states have revised the common law by authorizing court imposition of an equitable division in the event of divorce, so all is not quite so "separate." Almost all have legislated family-allowance and homestead privileges for the surviving spouse to protect against total disinheritance. Some of these survivor's benefits are quite substantial, others are meager; check out your state law, if you are not protected by a will or written agreement.

The five states described as ultra-separate-property states do not permit the courts to reassign the separate property of either spouse in a divorce, even if the separate property is acquired during the marriage. By modern standards, this absolute rule works some unconscionable hardships on the non-owning half of a broken marriage. She—it is usually she—can be utterly deprived of the family home, possessions, or savings, unless the breadwinner has been gracious enough to take title to these acquisitions in both names, or otherwise provide for the dependent spouse. However, as compared to mates, assuming there is no written contract between them, spouses fare better in the legal sense. Upon divorce, he/she has a better opportunity to receive alimony. Upon death, even if disinherited, the surviving spouse is usually entitled to certain vested property rights and allowances in the deceased's estate. Other benefits that are accorded a spouse, which are generally denied to a mate, are pointed out throughout this chapter.

HISTORICAL EXAMINATION OF SEPARATE PROPERTY

The system did not offend traditional English notions of equity, largely because these notions were not generally considered applicable to married women. Under the English doctrine of "unity of spouses," a wife's legal civil existence was submerged into her husband's. A traditional quip summarizes the unity doctrine as follows: In marriage, the husband and wife become one, and that one is the husband.

As early as 1600, complaints against the legal status of English wives drove one learned justice into such a passion that he forgot his grammar:

> "God," quoth he, "hath given the man greater wit, better strength, better courage to compel the woman to obey, by reason or force; and to the woman, beauty, fair countenance, and sweet words to make the man obey her again for love. . . ." I wish, with all my heart, that the women of this age would learn thus to obey, and thus to command their husbands: so will they want for nothing that is fit, and these kind [sic] of flesh-flies shall not suck up or devour their husbands' estates by illegal tricks.[2]

The learned and more dispassionate Dr. Samuel Johnson also thus acquitted English jurisprudence of the charge of injustice to women: "Nature has given Woman so much power that the law has wisely given her very little."

In all fairness, it is a more relevant defense of the common-law rule of the inviolability of separate property to point out that the hardships it may now impose on women were seldom seen in old England, where by custom and by law, divorce was next to impossible.

Today, when it is frequently argued that divorce is nearly inevitable, American states need to take a second look at this policy; the palliative of alimony does not cure all the injustices endemic to the system. In fact, New York and Pennsylvania recently seceded from the ultra-separate-property camp and adopted to a system requiring judges to distribute property in divorce cases on the basis of the needs and contributions of each party. The new laws provide that an "equitable" settlement would be determined by considering such factors as the length of the marriage, the present and future earning potential of both parties, their probable needs (with emphasis on the special needs of custodial parents), and the contributions of each party's services as well as assets. In New York, the term "alimony" would disappear from divorces, but either spouse could receive something like it by way of a monetary award for maintenance, either in periodic installments or in a lump-sum payment, along with tangible assets, and Pennsylvania now expressly provides for alimony. The new laws apply to divorce actions initiated after they took effect.

The ultra-separate-property system theoretically permits another unlovely, unfriendly, and generally abhorred practice: the complete disinheritance of a surviving spouse. Some states (e.g., West Virginia and Mississippi) therefore qualify the rule with provisions that disinherited widows or widowers may "elect against the will," inheriting instead whatever share of the estate would have come to them under the state's laws of intestate succession.

New York is notably overdue for a change in another respect; its current provisions for surviving spouses are sparse to the point of impracticability. A surviving spouse and children may be disinherited of all but $5,000 in money; $150 worth of books; farm animals and machinery to $5,000; and other personal property to $1,000. They do get to keep their clothing, but might be hard-pressed to know where to keep it—the surviving spouse is entitled to only $10,000 worth of the family home, and whoever inherits the rest of it can start charging rent after forty days!

CONTRACTS AND LOCAL LAW
One's property rights as a spouse, then, depend on local law.

In most states, couples may choose to adopt a different system or modify known rights by contract, but some states (e.g., Nevada, Iowa, and Ohio) forbid any individual alterations to marital-property rights, and a few others recognize only those contracts drawn up before the marriage vows are taken. Some also require that any contract modifying property rights between spouses be filed at the courthouse along with the marriage records, or be officially recorded in accordance with statutory procedure.

When an individual contract between spouses faces the acid test of a divorce action, it will generally be followed and incorporated into a divorce decree.

While the judge usually has the authority to impose modifications, or even to throw out the private contract, this power is seldom used. Unless the marital contract is patently unfair to one spouse, or blatantly violates public policy (e.g., by sanctioning adultery or negotiating the division of profits from the family dope-dealing enterprise), you can expect support and cooperation from the courts.

Contracts between homemates are less likely to be treated quite so generously; a cohabitation contract may not receive the same recognition in the courtroom, though the trend is toward enforcement.

Ironically, as the forces of change seemingly march to different drummers, it is possible that in a few states, homemate couples without an express written contract may actually enjoy a greater latitude than spouses without a contract. Possibly an ultra-separate-property state, which does not provide for the division of any separate property between divorcing spouses, might be more liberal in its enforcement of implied contracts between homemates and possible divisions of separate property.

OTHER MARRIAGE BENEFITS

A third category of marital rights, which we have conveniently labeled "miscellaneous but exclusively marital financial benefits," deserves attention. Pension plans, some insurance policies, Social Security, Workmen's Compensation, and other federal and state programs automatically include benefits for the spouses of eligible recipients; generally these are not extended to mates, although occasionally an individual mate has won some benefits by "finding a small hole in the middle of the line," or through litigation.

In addition to these systematic security programs, spouses generally enjoy the right to sue for compensation when the actions of another individual or organization result in death or disability to the other spouse. A widow or widower who wins a wrongful death suit may collect not only an amount proportionate to the direct financial loss caused by the spouse's death, but also something extra for the emotional trauma. Husbands— and in most states, wives—may also file *consortium* (as defined in the glossary) actions seeking compensation for loss of the spouse's companionship and conjugal services—everything from housework to sex—against the third party responsible for the spouse's death or disability.

Widows and widowers fare considerably better than surviving homemates and casual mates under estate-tax (death-tax) laws, since marital deductions are provided in each state and at the federal level. The federal marital deduction exempts as much as $250,000 that is inherited by a surviving spouse from estate-tax levies.

When a spouse dies without making a will, the survivor generally and automatically inherits a substantial portion—at least a third, often a half, and if there are no children, perhaps all of the estate under the laws of intestate succession. A surviving homemate is not covered under these laws; even if the homemate takes the matter to court, the blood relatives of the deceased usually come out with the lion's share of the estate.

TESTIMONIAL PRIVILEGE

Last but not least of the standard benefits for legally married couples is the marital testimonial privilege, recognized in different degrees by all the states and the federal government, yet so fraught with exceptions in some states that the rule seems to operate to the detriment of marriage. Under this doctrine, one spouse cannot be forced to testify against the other in any court of law, whether in civil or criminal proceedings. The privilege arises from two quite different legal theories. The sillier of the two, extrapolated from the doctrine of unity, holds that if a husband and wife are legally one person, to require one to testify against the other is tantamount to requiring him to testify against himself, and thus would violate the Fifth Amendment to the Constitution. A weightier argument for the privilege holds that requiring spouses to reveal marital confidences or to incriminate each other would damage the marital relationship. Since public policy generally forbids the courts to do any such injury to the institution of marriage, the privilege has survived long after the effective demise of the unity doctrine.

A most striking example of the lengths to which the courts will go was recently acted out in Virginia. There the state supreme court ruled on appeal that spousal immunity barred suits even *after* divorce, preventing Janet Young Goldstein from further collection of $65,000 awarded her against her ex, Leonard Goldstein, for assaulting her.

In some courts, however, the privilege of refusing to be a witness against one's spouse is held also to imply that one spouse may not be a witness *for* the other; taken to this length, the privilege is a mixed blessing. While the tenet that "the law does not sanction absurdities" is sufficiently sacrosanct to be usually quoted in Latin, surely some absurdity lurks about the finding of a Southern court that refused to allow a widow to testify about her husband's oral gift to her of certain assets, on the grounds that her testimony would violate a "marital confidence"; another claimant, free to testify, walked away with the property. Surely this ruling did nothing to foster a marital relationship already terminated by the husband's death!

The conflict may be lessened by the recent ruling of the United States Supreme Court that the marital-testimonial privilege should *not* be used to prevent one spouse from testifying voluntarily against the other in federal courts, nor should the consent of the accused spouse be required. This reasoning, which preserves the privilege and removes the handicap, establishes some clarification of the rule.

LITIGATION BETWEEN SPOUSES

Some states have removed a related historic taboo that forbids civil lawsuits between husband and wife. From the Massachusetts Supreme Court comes an example of how far the law has been stretched in this regard. The *Arizona Daily Star*[3] reported a precedent-setting decision by Massachusetts' highest court that a wife can sue her husband for failing to shovel the walk. The court said that Mrs. Brown can sue her husband, William, because he failed to shovel their snowy walk; she later slipped on it and broke her pelvis. Apparently William must cough up for being careless and negligent. Massachusetts lawyers have something to say about all this: "I think this has got to be the most profound change in matters involving husband-and-wife relationships that the court has ever adopted," said Anile Madan, the husband's attorney. He even envisions that if a wife puts too much salt in her husband's meals, and he eventually gets high blood pressure, he can sue her, and maybe recover damages. Charles E. Blumsack, who represents the injured Mrs. Brown, sees the case as simply allowing a neglected class, injured spouses, to pursue their legal rights.

Unknown from all of this is whether Mrs. Brown will be able to collect under the family homeowner insurance policy.

But criminal prosecution for criminal assault by one spouse against the other remains a legal hot potato. For a number of reasons, not *all* of which are bad, traditional legal doctrine postulates that there can be no prosecution for rape between husband and wife.

Oregon broke with this doctrine in 1977, providing that marriage was not a defense to rape. The first case to be tried under the new law vividly illustrated the complexity of the problem. Greta Rideout charged her husband, John (they had been separated but temporarily reconciled), with rape. The couple reconciled after John's acquittal on the rape rap—then she left him again; she has since charged him with trespassing. The rape charge was serious, but the Rideouts' chaotic marriage made it virtually impossible to determine what had actually happened. In Massachusetts, though, James J. Chretien *was* convicted of raping his wife. According to the *Family Law Reporter*,[4] Chretien's nine-year-old son testified that his father, who had been living apart from his mother, had dragged his mother into the bedroom of her home, and then he did not hear them "arguing." Chretien was convicted and later sentenced to three to five years in prison for raping his wife. At the time the couple had been granted a divorce but the decree was not yet final.

This new trend in the law is not without critics. They have mounted a strong campaign against it—*not* on the theory that marriage entitles a husband to use his wife's body whenever and however he likes, but because of the difficulty of proof, and the consequent invitation to vindictive, unfounded, and damaging charges. Courts feel that such charges represent a powerful threat to marital peace.

Whether the difficulty justifies the extension of a virtual license to commit rape, along with other more easily proven acts of physical violence, as a perquisite of marriage is a question that pits traditional policy and judicial convenience against very basic individual rights. The question will probably be reexamined in every state within the next decade; more equitable solutions may emerge when the legal minds of the nation cease to settle for dogma. California has swung toward individual protection; a new law making it a crime for a husband to rape his wife equally penalizes women who rape males.

THE WOMAN'S FREER MARITAL ROLE

American domestic law, true to its largely English roots, used to embody some very Gothic ideas about the rights and status of married women. Centuries of real legal oppression have given wifedom a bad name that still rouses horror in some independent minds; for the most part, though, the law has discarded the notorious disabilities it once imposed on married women. Married women are now as free to contract, dispose of, and manage community property and their own separate property as are their male counterparts. Most of the fifty states have repudiated the unity doctrine entirely, and the few that still keep it on the books (e.g., Nevada and Georgia) have expressly abolished its traditional effects.

Some states (e.g., Ohio and Georgia) still hold that the husband is "head of the family"; Georgia adds that the wife is "subject" to him. This language, loaded with patriarchal connotations, is translated to hold the husband primarily responsible for the support of the family, and to confer on him the right to set its standard of living. Georgia also holds the husband sole owner of the family home, regardless of who paid for it.

DOMICILE

A great number of states still hold to the common-law rule that a wife's legal domicile follows her husband's. New York, West Virginia, Iowa, Kentucky, Minnesota, Montana, Vermont, and Wisconsin traditionally grant the husband the exclusive right to choose the couple's domicile. While the states may view domicile (one's official legal residence) as a matter where administrative convenience takes priority over individual freedom, it does affect many substantive personal concerns, notably in regard to where one may vote, run for public office, or be tapped for jury duty. It can also carry financial consequences: a Pennsylvania woman was required to pay higher out-of-state tuition at the University of Pittsburgh when she married a man whose domicile was out of state. She won in the end, but hangovers of the policy may appear in several states for some time to come. Eligibility for welfare benefits often depends on domicile, and local income tax structures vary widely, so that one domicile may be considerably more expensive than another. Estate and inheritance taxes also vary from state to state, as do grounds for divorce, so domicile, while not precisely a household word, is much more than a technicality.

RETENTION OF MAIDEN NAME

The last and most celebrated area of discrimination against married women concerns their right to maintain or reassume their maiden names during marriage. Although not one state statute or federal law requires a married woman to assume her husband's surname, wives in several states have been and continue to be harassed by policies requiring exclusive use of the husband's surname for such legal documents as drivers' licenses, citizenship papers, and voter registration. Other decisions holding that a woman's only legal name is her husband's have actually worked *for* the material interests, if not the legal dignity, of the individuals involved, for example by allowing them to claim that they had not been legally notified of impending litigation or court-imposed judgments against them.

Some startlingly obnoxious cases have invoked the surname question to the detriment of women's rights. A 1926 case deserves comment. In *Bacon vs. Boston Elevated Railway Co.*, both spouses were denied compensation for damages caused when the company's equipment negligently collided with their automobile, which was registered in the wife's maiden name. The court held that the car was "illegally registered in a false name," thus a "nuisance." Mrs. Bacon was denied recovery because she was "operating a nuisance." Mr. Bacon's claim was also denied, because he was an occupant of a vehicle that he had reason to know was improperly registered.

Another case: In 1974, a hapless Mrs. Hauptly was subjected to remarks ranging from demeaning to slanderous in the arguments with which the state of Indiana opposed her petition to resume her maiden name. The appellate court that finally granted her the change quoted these notably prejudicial excerpts from the state's brief:

> It can be reasonably inferred that she believes the fact that she is the breadwinner of the family should be publicized so that all will know her husband has been emas-

culated and that she is the head of the family. . . . indicating
that perhaps Mrs. Hauptly's need was not for a change
of name but for a competent psychiatrist. . . . namely a
sick and confused woman, unhappy and unsatisfied with
her marriage, unable to determine what she wants to do
with her life.

Several states insist that married women register to vote in
their husband's names; these policies and similar questions
have been upheld by high courts in some states (Illinois, New
York, and, believe it or not, California). In California and
Arizona, some judges have refused to hear divorce petitions
simply because they were filed by wives using their maiden
names. Both were overruled, which brings us to the good news:
a substantial majority of appellate and state supreme court
decisions in recent years have supported a woman's right to
keep or reassume her maiden name. Most, in fact, have found
that there was *never* any solid legal requirement in common
law for a change of name upon marriage, rendering moot the
theoretical question of whether such a requirement would violate the equal-protection clause of the Constitution. Courts
in Maryland, Tennessee, Wisconsin, Ohio, Virginia, Florida,
and Connecticut have so ruled; Hawaii, the only state that ever
expressly required a woman to adopt her husband's last name,
has repealed the offending statute and replaced it with one
specifically authorizing both spouses to keep their individual
surnames, or to adopt the husband's or wife's, or to hyphenate
the two. Massachusetts, home of the Boston Elevated Railway
Company, now specifically allows a woman to retain her
maiden name, and we feel sure this is the wave of the future.

One very important court has not yet felt the approaching
tide; we are sorry to report that the only current United States
Supreme Court ruling on wifely surnames actually upheld an
Alabama policy requiring a woman to use her husband's surname to get a driver's license, and this in 1972. In defense of
the Brethren, we point out that they neither heard arguments
in the case nor read full briefs nor wrote out their reasons for
sustaining the case; they merely affirmed without comment.

Informed sources, and we include ourselves, believe that
if the question were to be argued fully before the High Court,
a different opinion would result, particularly if the case under
review concerned a "fundamental" right, such as the right to
vote, instead of the less important issue of driving identifica-

tion. In any event, the lower courts are industriously clearing away this cobweb of discriminatory state policies, so the question may never arise.

THE MARRIAGE PENALTY TAX

Occasionally the right hand giveth and the left hand taketh away. In 1969, Congress amended the federal tax laws to upgrade the status of single taxpayers, who had been paying considerably more income tax than spouses under the old system. The legislators intended to equalize the tax burden rather than to shift a disproportionate weight onto the shoulders of spouses, but they apparently overlooked two important phenomena in their deliberations: the increase in two-income marriages as a result of social and economic changes, and the availability and wide acceptance of unlicensed alternatives to marriage.

As it turns out, the new tax structure actively discriminates against two-earner families, giving a break to married couples only when one spouse earns from 80 to 90 percent of the income. If each spouse in a given couple earns $35,000, they now pay about $4,234 more per year to Uncle Sam than they would as single taxpayers.

Under this system, two working taxpayers are assessed hundreds or thousands of dollars each year for the privilege of being married. It is estimated that approximately 19 million couples are affected.

Congress is currently considering several proposals aimed at removing this paper parasite from the house of matrimony. A bill sponsored by Representative Millicent Fenwick and Senator Charles Mathias would leave the present tax tables in effect but cancel the marriage penalty tax by giving married taxpayers the option to use the same rates as single people. Another bill would allow a married couple to deduct 10 percent of the first $20,000 of the second income; this would lower but not erase the marriage penalty. If the marriage tax were abolished, the federal budget would lose from $5 to $9 billion in revenue per year. In these days of budget balancing, it may be difficult for the government to correct this situation. As recently reported in the *Baltimore News American,* a Ways and Means Committee source said that there is a "chasm between equity and the price of equity."[5]

While Congress deliberates, some married couples are finding another solution to the dilemma—they get divorced, thereby saving enough on their taxes to make it worthwhile. Angela and David Boyter recently incurred the displeasure of the IRS when it discovered that for three straight years they had been divorcing and remarrying each other annually—Haiti and the Dominican Republic were the sites for two of the severances—and paying for a lovely winter vacation with the tax monies they saved. Of course, the IRS has attacked the Boyters' sidestepping, and has won round one. Federal Judge Richard C. Wilbur of the United States Tax Court ruled that according to Maryland law, where the Boyters live, two of the foreign divorces before the court were not valid, so they will have to pay higher taxes as a married couple. No decision was made by the judge on whether the "marriage penalty" was legal. The Boyters may appeal the ruling to the United States Court of Appeals.

Nevertheless, divorce followed by cohabitation may hold off the revenuers long enough for Congress to remedy this hardship imposed on many marriages. This maneuver, about which we have some qualms, is discussed further in the following chapter.

PART II: A STEP-BY-STEP GUIDE

Chapter Six

LOVERS NEED
CONTRACTS

Lex vigilantibus, non dormientibus, subvenit. *(The law comes to the aid of the vigilant, not the sleeping.)*

A verbal contract isn't worth the paper it's written on.

—SAMUEL GOLDWYN

THE COMMITMENT

To love is to be committed. To express this commitment in writing for a couple's mutual protection, or to provide safeguards in the event the relationship sours, is an expression of care—a way to help each other savor the joys and endure the pangs of life.

An old French proverb goes *"plus ça change, plus c'est la même chose"*; the more things change, the more they're the same old thing. The last word in up-to-date domesticity is the oldest trick in the book: contracts tailored to fit each couple's expectations and purses.

HISTORICAL PRECEDENT FOR
MARRIAGE CONTRACTS

From the days of Babylon until recent times, marriages between people of any wealth were regulated not only by the state but also by the terms of individual marriage contracts. In fact, in the Code of Hammurabi, the oldest legal system known, the privilege of contractual—i.e. legal—marriage was reserved for the propertied classes.

Progress and Judeo-Christian philosophy extended the benefits of marriage to all, but the upper crust preserved the spirit of Hammurabi's law in a tradition of entirely businesslike

99

marriage contracts. Hammered out well in advance of the wedding, these agreements concerned questions of marriage settlements, dowries, inheritance, and rank; they controlled the financial future of the parties, often with an iron hand.

Marriage contracts were also used to protect the inheritance rights of those children not lucky enough to be firstborn males, and children of previous marriages. There were forms of marriage designed to preclude inheritance: a *morganatic marriage* was an alliance between two persons of unequal rank, providing that neither the lower-born spouse nor the children would enjoy the titles or inherit the estate of the higher-born.

Thus, for centuries, whenever the prospective spouses brought anything more than their hands and hearts to the marriage, they got it in writing. If this seems cold-blooded, it was. People did expect a certain degree of affection to develop in a good marriage, but the primary ambitions to be realized in matrimony were those of social status, financial comfort, and orderly inheritance. These matters were settled beforehand, and love had to take care of itself. The idea was that lasting domestic happiness arose from well-regulated domestic security.

Another French proverb is apposite: "Cooking, like love, comes *after* marriage."

CONTRACTS ARE SELDOM USED NOW

This is nearly the reverse of modern expectations. In recent generations, Americans have married for love and expected financial security to take care of itself. Although housewives expected to be dependent on their husbands' financial providing, they were willing to start at the bottom and climb together without knowing how far they'd get. Love and marriage went together like horse and carriage, proclaimed a popular song of the fifties, and most young people would no sooner have married without love than they would have bought a carriage without owning a horse. A lady who frankly confessed to marrying for money would get as little open sympathy in this era as did an eighteenth-century lady who eloped for love. More and more starry-eyed near-strangers rushed into—and out of—wedlock with less and less thought for the morrow; sentiment rebelled at the very idea of superimposing lawyerlike clauses on the promise to "love, honor, and cherish."

In the sixties and seventies, even this light bond seemed oppressive to many. For married and unmarried couples alike, speaking of love and contracts in the same breath might seem a hideous breach of good taste, and the hapless homemate, spouse, or fiancé who proposes a codified relationship runs the risk of censure for unlovely conduct.

Never before in the history of civilization has love without contracts been so widely accepted, but the pendulum may be swinging back again. Contracts are coming back into style, not only in a sudden stroke of reaction to palimony suits, but as an evolutionary response to contemporary mores. Men who are aware of the financial consequences of divorce (or breaking up) are considering contracts limiting their future liability. Women in this ERA era are becoming painfully aware that the housewife in a broken marital partnership may find herself, especially in those states with stricter laws, up the creek without an asset, with limited support payments, and with the unlovely status characterized by social workers as "displaced homemaker."

However, we must all be aware that this trend is not a matter of men's interests versus women's. Men and women in love, both becoming sensitive to the injustices they unwittingly inflict on each other, are as anxious not to exploit each other as they are to protect themselves from exploitation. Susie Coelho, living with Sonny Bono after his expensive divorce from America's favorite vamp, deplores *Marvin*-madness. "I wouldn't dream of taking a man to court for half of what he made when I didn't contribute," she told an interviewer from *People*. "Sonny and I are not building a unit. He was already established."[1]

Many men share feminist concerns. James Abell, a Phoenix architect, feels strongly about the tendency of marriage to obscure people's view of the woman as an individual, and adds that, for an unmarried couple "where one partner is economically dependent on the other, a clear written agreement is important."

Couples may be very much in love and yet contemplate the potential pain of a future divorce. Mere statistical probabilities prompt many people to decide how they'll divvy up their earthly goods while they're still speaking to each other, or even better, to identify and work out some of the conflicting expectations that might lead to tension in the marriage. Unmarried couples are discovering that they may need a written contract not only to share their property, but also to keep their separate ways intact.

Love, or rather the ideal of love, has governed our choices, and the law is gradually coming to terms with this new state of affairs. The formerly starry-eyed are now plotting detailed charts for their course of true love. This is chiefly because the reigning laws won't take them where they want to go.

STATE LAWS: A SOCIAL CONTRACT

It should now be apparent that social contracts already govern the behavior of couples; each state imposes a unique set of rules on domestic relationships conducted within its borders. Furthermore, until domestic law catches up to our differing and changing lifestyles, each state will continue to maintain two, or possibly three or more, different codes for casual mates, homemates, and married couples.

Although the law provides a variety of roles, and rules to choose among, it demands that you stay within the confines of the rights and obligations of the social contract you have chosen. This contract is found in state statutes and court decisions, and governs all personal relationships. You might not *like* the legal interpretation of your current status, but that is irrelevant to the court. You must recognize that such a contract *does exist;* it's as legally and morally binding as any personal contract drawn up between two individuals.

PUBLIC POLICY: A FURTHER RESTRAINT

However, even though society these days is stretching its rules to accommodate the demand for many emerging domestic patterns, "public policy" still sets substantial limits to the elasticity of the social contract, beyond which individual agreements cannot legally trespass, even with the existence of a written contract.

But within these limits there is abundant room for individual solutions. For instance, if a person wants to marry but does not agree with the pattern of marriage cut out by the law in his state, he may be able to cut his own pattern, so long as he doesn't stretch it beyond the limits of the socially imposed contract or the other outer limit defined by public policy. If he wants to live with his true love, but needs more monetary protection than his state offers to homemates, he can write a contract to protect himself, if his true love agrees. Or, if she wants to share her luscious Malibu beach cottage with a luscious Malibu beachboy, but doesn't want to risk her life savings in California's palimony-prone courts, she may also turn to a personal contract tailored to her needs.

STRINGS ARE ATTACHED

After the *Marvin* decision, it is no longer safe to assume that living together is liability-free. To put it bluntly, though paradoxically, if you believe in a no-strings free union, get it in writing. The *Marvin* decision essentially licensed judges to treat their interpretation of an unmarried couple's conduct as an enforceable contract. This "contract" may not be at all what you had in mind.

As Toni Ihara and Ralph Warner—attorneys, homemates, and authors of *The Living Together Kit*—told a *People Weekly* interviewer, the *Marvin* case "has made having a contract more important than ever." In its well-intentioned search for a couple's tacit understandings, they said, ". . . the court could drag in every aspect of their relationship. It might be worse than a contested divorce."[2]

Public mudslinging, invasion of privacy, court-imposed reparations—doesn't this sound like everything you didn't like about marriage and divorce?

Arthur L. Messinger, an Annapolis attorney, feels that Maryland's lack of guidelines and definite rulings on nonmarital rights puts unmarried couples in an insecure position. Thus, he suggested in an article written for the Annapolis *Capital*, ". . . it is important for cohabiters to draw up an agreement to avoid potential disputes and to establish the respective rights of the individuals involved. Such an agreement is necessary, even if both parties 'trust' each other . . . as the laws may not otherwise carry out individual intentions or expectations."[3]

Does this mean that homemates can't, or shouldn't, *trust* each other? Not at all. No contract is potent enough to enable two people who don't trust each other to cohabit in any degree of happiness. Trust is just one prerequisite for living together, as well as for making it through the writing of a really helpful contract. True, the permanently starry-eyed may suffer hurt feelings when the subject of contracts comes up at the breakfast table; the very cool or hard-bitten, at the other extreme, might accuse, "You're trying to take advantage of me." Ihara and Warner respond: "Contracts have gotten a bad reputation because they have been used by the legal system to take things away from people. But you have to remember that you're not making a contract with GM or IBM."[4]

If handled wisely, developing a contract can be constructive. It can add foresight and insight to romantic visions, and can solidify the practical foundations of the lovenest.

So go ahead and trust each other—but look ahead and create a contract that provides for the contingencies and hazards you hope you never have to face. Love and contracts both work best when both parties offer self-respect, mutual respect, and flexibility.

CAREFUL PREPARATION IS NECESSARY

Practical contracts between mates will usually be upheld (except, possibly, in Illinois), even in most of the states where cohabitation or fornication is illegal, but remember to watch the wording. It is most unwise to rely on any legal protection from a document that explicitly promotes an illegal relationship such as the establishment of a sham marriage, or one that explicitly provides for a meretricious exchange of sexual favors for economic ones. In recent years, many courts have agreed to uphold the "legitimate" portions of contracts between homemates, finding that a couple's financial agreements are "separable" in a cohabitation contract, but some states are not so permissive. Even married couples run a similar risk if parts of their agreement violate public policy. So long as such attitudes run loose in the courts, careful drafting is necessary so as not to endanger a workable contract by tainting it with legally suspect provisions.

THE CONTRACT-PREPARATION PROCESS

1. Read about contracts and their legal significance.
2. Obtain sample copies of cohabitation and/or nuptial agreements and study them.
3. Prepare notes of salient points.
4. Prepare a complete list of all known assets and liabilities, including anticipated rights to inheritance or lifetime gifts from parents and others.
5. Preferably retain your own separate lawyer.
6. Exchange your list of assets and liabilities with your mate, spouse, or fiancé(e).
7. Make an appointment to see your lawyer and discuss all legal, social, and personal aspects with him or her.
8. Decide on what is important to you, and separate the sensitive issues that could lead to disharmony in your personal relationship with your mate or spouse.
9. Arrange for your lawyer to lead all negotiations and to set up a meeting with your mate or spouse and his/her lawyer.
10. Establish a friendly atmosphere at the meeting, and put off the sensitive or difficult issues for the last.

11. Allow enough time for the meeting, and plan on more than one meeting so that no one feels pressured to make quick decisions.
12. If the meeting gets heated, adjourn it and schedule another. Make a list of the unresolved points so that everyone knows what still has to be decided.
13. It may be wise to avoid further private discussions of the unresolved issues with your mate or spouse; feelings can become exacerbated.
14. Set up another private meeting with your lawyer to discuss the unresolved issues.
15. Allow time to think about the unresolved issues before the next meeting.
16. Set up the next meeting and make sure that both lawyers attend. (Sometimes it may be advisable for the lawyers only to meet. Sometimes it may be advisable to bring in other third parties to further counsel one or both of the mates or spouses, and to add objectivity to the discussions.)
17. Once substantial agreement is arrived at, prepare a first draft of the contract with the understanding that it is subject to modification and that it does not constitute a firm commitment.
18. Freely ask questions and/or offer changes to the contract; make sure that it is clear and unambiguous.
19. Make sure that the contract allows for future contingencies, since it is a long-term commitment.

PERSONAL CONDUCT AS DISTINGUISHED FROM LEGAL RIGHTS

National magazines carry advertisements for mail-order cohabitation contracts or contract workbooks. Many of the issues covered by them concern personal conduct, and while these may be of great interest to the contracting couple, one should bear in mind that clauses and considerations relating to private personal behavior are largely unenforceable. It would be foolhardy to expect the courts to find a homemate liable for failure to walk the dog each evening! Still, ideas like these help you decide what to include in your contract.

THE NEED FOR LEGAL ASSISTANCE

The issue of whether professional advice is necessary is not so simple. Marvin Mitchelson, who does not even like the idea of premarital or pre-living-together contracts, still suggests in his book *Made in Heaven, Settled in Court* that couples likely to acquire much property should draw up a formal agreement. To ensure that it will stand up in court, he recommends that each party retain a lawyer—as the best way to protect against problems that may arise later.

An otherwise legal contract prepared by one lawyer representing both parties could be challenged on the grounds of undue influence exerted by the more powerful party or his/her attorney, or perhaps conflict of interest on the attorney's part. If, in spite of a well-thought-out agreement, the couple has reached the point of litigation, fatal flaws in the contract may defeat the whole purpose, leading to nastier wrangles and more court involvement. A couple's best bet is to study the potential benefits of contracts, decide in general what they want theirs to provide or proscribe, and then each should retain competent assistance from a lawyer familiar with local laws.

Who needs legal help the most? It depends on circumstances. If two people start out as casual mates, if they're young and strong and haven't much property, there is considerably less need for an attorney. Among homemates, however, even if their holdings are modest, there is greater need for an attorney's advice. Property rights may be implied or expressed between them or, contrariwise, they may be expecting more protection than their state is ready to extend to unmarrieds. And finally, if a couple is planning to marry, they should seriously consider a written agreement *before* exchanging vows; they should take the time to inform themselves as to their state's marriage laws and try to identify any policies that might cause future friction.

No matter what your circumstances, something in writing is better than nothing when it comes to protecting your relationship and your rights as a mate or a spouse. Realtor Herb Goldman put it succinctly: "The faintest of ink is better than the keenest of memories."

REQUISITES FOR A WRITTEN CONTRACT

In order to ensure that a contract will later be enforceable, it is necessary that certain requirements be met:

1. Offer and acceptance (evidenced by signatures of both parties).
2. Adequate consideration (something promised in return for the promise of the other).
3. Legal consideration (a promise of sexual favors in exchange for property or support is illegal).
4. Clear and reasonably exact terms with little ambiguity or vagueness.
5. Absence of unconscionability (must not be grossly unfair to one party).
6. Absence of duress, coercion, or undue influence.
7. Full and fair disclosure of all relevant facts, assets, and liabilities.

AN AID TO COMMUNICATION

If nothing else, an agreement helps a couple to plan before they start living together. It's worse to leave matters hanging and let possible conflicts build up; the resulting tensions can be explosive, particularly when one is earning more than the other. A contract also opens lines of communication, preventing later misunderstandings. A couple may think that their expectations are the same, only to find out that when he said, "We will share expenses," he meant equally, while she thought he would pay three-fourths because he earned three times as much as she.

Let's consider the following case:

Rick Parker, an adventurous and prosperous geologist employed by a mining corporation headquartered in Nebraska, meets Emily Gordon, a dental hygienist, on a business trip to Culver City, Nevada. Sparks fly and letters follow, and soon Emily is thinking of the bright lights of Lincoln. She finds a comparable job—at a slightly lower salary, but it appears that Rick may be part of the fringe benefits. Their affair kindles, and they decide to live together in a glossy new apartment that Emily couldn't afford on her salary alone. She's nervous about signing a lease without a guarantee that Rick will hold up his end of the expenses, but they haven't any desire to commit themselves to any further obligations. They are, at this stage, budding casual mates. Rick, who is making $30,000 a year against Emily's $10,000, offers to pay a similar proportion of their living expenses, asking her to take responsibility for the housework in exchange (but he agrees to pitch in on weekends).

THE SIMPLE CONTRACT

Feeling that neither is risking very much, they might draw up the following written understanding without an attorney:

Rick Parker and Emily Gordon agree to a full disclosure of their present assets and that:

1. They will share living expenses, including rent, food, utilities, and maintenance, according to any one of three alternatives:
   a. equally; or
   b. 3-to-1, the ratio of Rick's income to Emily's; or
   c. 2-to-1. [Perhaps the most practical arrangement, since Rick's tax bite is larger than Emily's, and he is likely to have higher fixed expenses as well. Obviously this sword cuts both ways;

Emily could be struggling to pay off student loans, or Rick could be supporting three ex-wives and nine children. It makes sense to compare discretionary rather than gross income when dividing expenses].

2. In consideration for lower costs, Emily will be chiefly responsible for doing the laundry, cooking, food shopping, and housecleaning.
3. Rick shall attempt to do all household repairs and once a week shall equally participate in housecleaning.
4. Each party shall maintain a separate bank account and separate property.
5. Neither party will purchase linens, lamps, furniture, or other items for the apartment without the agreement of the other party. Emily shall decide on food purchases.

Dated this_____day of_____, 19_____.

_____   _____
Rick Parker   Emily Gordon

Or they can add provisions to allow for joint purchases according to the following terms:

1. If any joint purchases are made, each party shall own one-half unless otherwise agreed to in writing.
2. Each shall make one-half of the down payment and all monthly payments unless otherwise agreed to in writing.
3. If either party fails to make his or her payment, the other shall have the right to make the payment; the nonpaying party shall be indebted to the paying party, and interest at two percent above the current prime rate shall accrue until paid. [Alternatively, a formula could be worked out for the paying party to acquire more than 50-percent ownership.]
4. Upon the death of either party, the equity of the deceased party shall belong to the survivor, unless the deceased party has provided in his or her will to the contrary, and the surviving party shall be responsible for all future payments still due and owing. [Alternatively, the parties can provide for title to be acquired in joint tenancy with the right of survivorship, so that the survivor will automatically acquire title notwithstanding any contrary terms in the will of the deceased.]
5. If the parties shall stop living together, and they cannot come to an agreement in which one party buys out the other's share, the property shall be sold and the proceeds divided according to each person's ownership, after the payments of debts as provided in paragraph 3 above.

If Emily still worries about incurring expenses she could not meet if her relationship with Rick were to end suddenly, she may doubt the wisdom of joint purchases. A variation could kill two birds with one stone: they could agree that all major purchases involving credit would be made in Rick's name. Rick could then lower his taxes by deducting all the interest expenses, and Emily would be liable only to Rick for her share of the payments.

POSSIBLE ADDITIONS TO THE CONTRACT
The foregoing agreements, with or without provisions for joint purchases, may be simple enough to draw up without a lawyer. If Rick and Emily wish, they may also include:

1. a more detailed budget;
2. career priorities (Emily might agree to move if Rick is offered a better job elsewhere; Rick might agree to take on all their expenses while Emily goes back to school to become a dentist);
3. inventory of smaller items of property (they might agree to keep records of who owns which antiques, furnishings, even books and records, and to initial each other's lists);
4. custody of the cat (probably not legally enforceable; *de minimis non curat lex*[5]);
5. insurance, illness, or death.

PALIMONY
Perhaps Rick suffers from fear of palimony. He doesn't really believe that Emily has designs on his assets, but the mere thought puts a damper on his fires. Emily agrees that theirs is a no-strings relationship. Fast—though possibly temporary—relief comes from a simple proviso: *Neither party shall owe alimony, support, nor any form of reparations to the other.*

Perhaps changes in their relationship may later justify a provision for alimony. If Emily does give up her job at Rick's request, she might want him to promise rehabilitative alimony for as long as it takes her to brush up her technical skills, catch up on the state of her art, and find a new job. Or suppose Rick promises, in the alleged words of Lee Marvin, to "take care of her always." He might want to qualify that promise in a clause providing that alimony will cease if Emily marries, or even if she lives with another man for, say, longer than six months.

NO-NO'S
Subjects that should be avoided in a written contract are clauses

concerning birth control, exchanges of sexual favors, or promiscuity with others; to include such provisions may give the nasty impression that the contract is based upon (legal horrors!) sexual considerations. This could invalidate the whole agreement, especially in any state that holds fornication illegal, and it may raise the question of meretricious considerations or violation of public policy. Furthermore, little or nothing is gained through such provisions. The court has not yet sat that would enforce a woman's promise to undergo an abortion or to be mellow about her lover's other lovers.

Although if they are poorly worded there is less chance of enforceability, homemade contracts do, at the minimum, provide a step toward clarification, and carry some moral weight. If Rick and Emily clearly understand their mutual commitments, chances are they will do their best to honor them even if their romance comes unstuck. Much of the bitterness that turns sweethearts to swine actually arises from simple misunderstanding of what they agreed to expect of each other. Given reasonable wisdom in your choice of a mate and concern for fairness in your agreements, the contract will most likely work well enough to keep the courts out of the picture.

POSSIBLE UNFORESEEN RISKS

Although Rick and Emily, by virtue of their homemade contract described above, are now clearly defined as casual mates, they ought to bear in mind certain uncomfortable possibilities. Changes, travels, or legal snafus could throw them for a loop! Consider:

1. Void contract: If their home state calls cohabitation or fornication a crime, their agreement could be completely void; it is perfectly possible, though not likely, that a whimsical court might assess restorative alimony after throwing out their original waiver.
2. Common-law marriage: Emily and Rick buy a farm, settle down, and have a child in a state that recognizes common-law marriage. Relying on their contract to keep their single status inviolate, they proceed to rent a house as "Mr. and Mrs. Parker," keeping up the same facade to protect Rick's new job and Emily's reputation. Emily hates the whole setup, splits for Alaska with their six-month-old daughter, and takes up with David, who is married to Jenny. This adulterous relationship leads to Rick's claiming a common-law marriage with Emily and eventually getting child custody, which probably would not have occurred had they not moved to a common-law state.
3. Common debts: Emily finds herself liable for Rick's debts; their

contract to maintain separate property is found to be waived by their conduct, because they have mingled their funds in joint accounts and joint investments. (Or the court holds after they split up that they agreed to share the assets since they commingled their assets.)

4. Contract cohabitation: Emily quits her job and becomes a full-time homemaker; the government tells Rick that he must pay Social Security taxes and other benefits on Emily's account because their relationship is construed as "contract cohabitation."

5. Palimony: After years as casual mates, Rick strikes oil. So will Emily; she could be entitled to regular alimony or rehabilitative alimony just like Michelle Marvin (assuming alimony was not waived in their contract).

6. Injury or illness: Having signed the foregoing no-strings contract with Rick, Emily is crippled in a mountain-climbing accident. Rick, the geologist, says it's her own damn fault for driving her pitons into a cliff of crumbling rhyolite, and refuses to support her. Emily's been had. The contract didn't say anything about letting Emily stay with Rick if she couldn't earn her share of the rent.

7. Gap in contract: The same, except the court construes that since Rick and Emily's contract is silent on the subject of illness or injury, Rick must still pay the contracted amount of Emily's living expenses, which are now $2,500 per month and climbing.

8. No will protection: Emily and Rick buy a house together; when the house is paid for, Rick has made three-quarters of the payments and Emily one-quarter. The house, beautiful but termite-ridden, is assessed at $30,000. Emily quits her job to concentrate on carpentry, and the next day Rick is struck by lightning. Alas, Rick allowed his life-insurance policy to lapse a few months previously. He has not made a will, and his dissolute nephew Murgatroyd inherits as next-of-kin. Murgatroyd would normally be delighted to give Emily time to buy out his share in food stamps, but alas (again!) he owes his bookie $15,000. The house is sold to the fastest bidder for $24,000, Murgatroyd pays his debts—and Emily, whose blood has boiled, pays a thug $6,000 to have Murgatroyd murdered.

Most, if not all, of these unpleasant surprises could have been warded off with the aid of a competent attorney.

HOMEMATES RATHER THAN CASUAL MATES
What if Rick and Emily considered themselves homemates? If their lifestyle came closer to that of a married couple, would that offer them a comparable degree of shelter from the shifting winds of the law? It all depends.

Homemates enjoy more secure relationships than do casual mates; legally the advantages are greater and the disadvantages more plentiful. A homemate is more likely to face a palimony suit, liability for debts incurred by the mate, or responsibility for the mate's children; in addition, a deserted or "widowed" homemate may be less prepared to stand on his/her own two feet than would the casual mate who has not come to depend on the relationship for economic as well as emotional support. While homemates may be able to take advantage of a wide range of legal stratagems largely unavailable to less committed twosomes, their legal snarls, tighter-wound, are sometimes more baffling to untangle. For example, homemates tend to overlook the details of daily spending, they tend to hold more property jointly, and they may wrongly assume that property rights are held in common simply because the property is used by both together.

Homemates, then, tend to need the well-tempered contract more than any other class of couples. Let's give a few new twists to Rick and Emily, seven years later, now living in California:

Emily, having completed dental school with Rick's financial help, has now had her own practice for three years and builds up a large following. She's now bringing in $25,000 a year. After buying a piano she can't find time to learn to play, she accumulates $15,000 in the bank.

Rick is thrilled with Emily's success. Thinking that he, too, would like more money and more independence, he quits his position with the Megalithic Mining Company and invests all his savings in an unprepossessing square mile of darkest Nevada in which his trained but excitable eye has discerned mineral promise. But, oh—promises, promises! Not only is his mile less than miraculous, but he has borrowed $200,000 to develop its nonexistent potential, and when all is said and foreclosed on, he still owes $50,000.

Emily feels that they should apply her $15,000 and their future earnings toward settling the debt. Rick reasons that he can declare bankruptcy, thus protecting Emily's funds and credit rating. Of course their separate-property agreement, drawn up seven years ago in Nebraska, may protect her from Rick's creditors, but there is uncertainty.

Had they remained in Nebraska, a separate-property state, Emily's assets and credit rating would probably be quite safe from Rick's creditors as long as she hadn't co-signed for any of the loans. But California, as a community-property state with advanced ideas about cohabitation, may hold a different view of the matter.

It is quite likely, after seven years in which each has shared freely in the fortunes of the other, that Emily and Rick are now homemates, and that a community-property state may look upon all the assets acquired during those seven years as something similar to community property (it can't be community property because they're unmarried). This conclusion could only be strengthened by the fact that, unlike the celebrity couples that have come to court for palimony settlements, Rick and Emily intend to continue living together, perhaps happily ever after. The court may hold that they now have a common interest not only in each other's assets but also in each other's debts!

What would happen, then, if a sharp-eyed creditor were to lay claim to Emily's $15,000 bank account?

Rick and Emily will maintain that their contract protected the separate status of their assets. California's policy of upholding cohabitation contracts as stated in the Marvin decision will certainly be in their favor, and California would probably abide by Nebraska law.

But the creditors, ready to grasp at legal straws to get their hands on some compensation for their loss, might argue that:

1. Since cohabitation is a crime in Nebraska, Rick and Emily could not legally contract to live together there. The California court, therefore, should not honor the contract, since it would be held invalid in Nebraska where it was executed. (This may not be true. Nebraska might have held the contract valid, but no such cases have been decided there, so it is uncertain).
2. The benefits bargained for in Rick and Emily's agreement were primarily sexual. Thus, the consideration upon which the contract rests is not only illegal but also meretricious, and therefore not valid.
3. Rick and Emily themselves had waived the provisions of their agreement. The provision calling for separate property had been altered by their joint checking account, jointly owned '68 Rambler, and "his and hers" towel set.
4. Even if it were valid, Emily's contract with Rick is not binding upon anyone else, particularly not upon Rick's creditors.

These arguments may sound specious, particularly if we're rooting for Emily and Rick, but each one has some legal merit.

RULES FOR WOULD-BE CONTRACTORS

Rule 1. Consideration: To be valid, a contract must provide some "valuable consideration" to each party. If X contracts to give Y five dozen red roses or $5,000, the contract is not valid (enforceable) unless Y contracts to give X something in exchange. This may be almost anything—a piece of real estate, five years' laundry service, or lessons in organic gardening—as long as it is neither frivolous nor illegal, but it must represent at least an arguably sufficient value. It must also be something that Y has in his power to give—*not* the Brooklyn Bridge—and further, something that X does not already own or have an independent right to expect—*not* what the Mafia calls "protection." And it must *never* be sexual. A contract that promises material rewards for sexual favors is considered meretricious unless, of course, the exchange starts with a wedding band.

For a dreadful example of how a contract may fail for lack of consideration, consider this real-life boorishness. A husband, having agreed to pay his wife wages for her work around the house, reneged and got away with it; the contract was void for lack of consideration. True, wages were a valid consideration; ditto housework. The catch? Under most current family law, the husband *already owns,* free and clear, the right to his wife's services as a housekeeper.

Rule 2. Sister-State Recognition: States generally try to uphold each other's laws, and will enforce contracts and court orders across state lines. This policy is called *sister-state recognition*. If a contract is invalid or illegal in the state where it is prepared, most likely it will be held invalid everywhere. The converse is usually, but not always, true: a cohabitation contract drawn up in California might be considered binding in Arizona, but probably not in Illinois, where it would be against public policy.

Whether the benefits of sister-state recognition will be extended to cohabitation contracts remains to be seen. We expect that most states will decide in the affirmative, since more and more courts are now upholding such contracts at home, even where cohabitation itself is illegal.

The question of the creditors' claim is not as cut-and-dried. In Rick and Emily's case, the California court will probably base its decision on the broader question of whether a Nebraska court would uphold the contract, not merely on whether their relationship offends Nebraska statutes. Had their contract originated in Illinois, where the state supreme court has recently declined to do any favors for homemates, California might strike it down, unless to do so would violate the public policy of California; still, the California courts might choose to abide by their own laws rather than those of the original state.

In contrast, the fifty states *have* reached a clear agreement to honor each others' marital laws, granting sister-state recognition to any marriage that was valid under the original jurisdiction *(home state)*. If the couple moves to a new jurisdiction (the *forum state*), and the validity of their marital contract becomes an issue, the forum state will usually go by the home state's rules. Thus, two people married only by common law in Texas remain legally wed once they move to New York, even though New York law does not provide for common-law marriage, and Nevada's quickie divorces are valid even in states whose local requirements are much more stringent.

Practices that fall on the wrong side of public policy unfortunately arouse no such universal spirit of tolerance in the breasts of judges and legislators. But we do predict that most states will honor contracts that they believe would have been honored in the home state, *unless* the contract is flagrantly contrary to public policy in the forum state.

In any event, once a couple moves, they should have their contract reviewed and updated in the new state. They should also discuss their present contract to determine whether they want to make any changes to it.

Rule 3. Clearer in Writing: Your agreements *are* safer in writing. Remember, if Rick and Emily had no contract at all, only their conduct and oral statements would be considered in determining their financial understandings.

After Emily and Rick had prepared their contract, they all but forgot it as their relationship grew. They stopped worrying about how they would split their expenses when it became clear that neither was trying to take advantage of the other. They stopped worrying about the housework when they were able to hire a cleaning lady, and they laughed indulgently over that childish notion of keeping records of which toys were whose.

But when the creditors were at the door, they unearthed their contract and pointed to the clause about their separate-property status. Did the chastened creditors slink off into the night? No. They brandished the following technicality:

Rule 4. Waiver by Conduct: Even if a contract is perfectly valid, it can atrophy from disuse. To keep a contract strong, keep your conduct consistent with its terms. Failure to operate by its guidelines may be construed as a waiver of its rights. If you flout your own contract, so can your partner and the courts.

Here are some things that may look like good ideas, but aren't if your future security depends on the solidity and legitimacy of your contract:

If your contract calls for equal division of work and joint ownership of all property, do not let your mate take separate title to anything big; you might be waiving your half-interest. If you need to preserve your separate financial status, credit rating, etc., do not buy property together, open joint bank accounts, or co-sign for each other's loans and credit cards. Do *not* go about telling your partner you'll support her for life if you want the anti-palimony clause to stick. In a common-law state, do not hold yourselves out as a married couple unless you want to *be* a married couple. Even in court, actions may speak louder than words. "We are what we pretend to be, so we must be very careful what we pretend to be," wrote Kurt Vonnegut, Jr.; the law may agree when you least expect it.

As for the creditors' claim that the contract is not binding on them as third parties—it depends. If the court found that Rick and Emily had followed the terms of the contract, keeping their assets separate and sharing expenses only as provided in the contract, the creditors probably could not establish waiver. If their recent conduct indicated that they now intended to share each other's fortunes, though, the creditors might win.

What if there had been no written contract? Then the court would look at the conduct between them and the creditors, and any implied or express agreements between them. Certainly if they share property rights, it's likely, although there is no case law on the subject, that obligations follow: if you share the benefits, you assume the burdens. If a valid business purpose existed, creating an implied partnership between Rick and Emily, then, as partners, they would share profits *and* losses and both would be liable to the partnership's creditors.

PROTECTIVE STEPS

Emily and Rick could have taken certain steps at various times that would have protected them:

When they first moved to California, they might have amended their contract to be sure it was valid in California.

Had they desired to maintain their separate status, they could simply have touched up the old contract to reflect any changes in lifestyle, such as the provisions involving expenses, which are now shared equally; thus the contract would match their actions. Had they anticipated any problems arising out of Rick's debts, they could have written a formal abrogation of common debts.

Later, when Rick first contemplated taking out loans to finance his venture, he might have protected Emily by informing his bankers that he was doing so in his sole and separate right. A signed disclaimer from Emily accepted by the bank would have been extremely helpful. None of this need chill the hearts of lovers. Going into debt should always be considered with a cool head.

HOUSEBREAKING INSTEAD

But what if we consider the two of them in different coloring—a shade less capable, a few shades less loving, considerably paler in integrity? A turn of bad luck might pit these two against each other, and the contract would have to bear a heavier load.

Once Rick's business venture turns sour, he feels like a failure and behaves like a wretch. Emily's patience erodes, and her soothing noises slowly turn to self-righteous recriminations. Though she is technically correct, her "I told you so" portends no good.

Rick demands that Emily help him pay his debts, since she owes her present professional income to his previous support. She reminds him that she did all the housework along with her homework while he was putting her through dental school, and that he has since shared her earnings, so she feels they're even. Shocked by his disregard of their written and unwritten understandings, Emily packs her little black bag and leaves.

Shortly, she receives notice that Rick and his creditors are jointly suing her for $50,000. Rick sends along, for good measure, a torn-up copy of their agreement and a letter, intact, casting aspersions on her character, her figure, and her mother. While her mother does not in fact wear combat boots, the lady advises Emily to countersue.

Emily retains the services of Mitchell Marvinson and files for big bucks in palimony, arguing that if their agreement was invalid, the anti-alimony clause is null and void. Further, she claims, she had no legal advice and did not understand what she was signing, so the contract was based on fraud.

ANTICIPATION IS IMPORTANT

This version is an invitation to the confrontations characteristic of the courtroom. To avoid this set of snafus, Emily and Rick should have:

1. had *legal advice,* preferably separate, in drawing up their contract;
2. *amended* their contract to clarify the new status quo when Emily quit her job to finish her education;
3. drawn up a separate agreement to cover the money Rick contributed to Emily's support and tuition, perhaps as a loan or a gift; or
4. tried marriage, followed by *boomerang divorce,* which we will discuss, but not necessarily recommend, later in this chapter.

The importance of all this? If you are creating a contract with your homemate, think about the fact that your relationship *will* change. Two people in good faith can make false assumptions. If changes are anticipated in the agreement, it may be beneficial not only in fending off later litigation but in launching serious discussion that will eventually deepen the relationship.

OTHER CONTRACT IDEAS

Topics that could be covered might include:

1. **Change to alimony:** If a casual-mate relationship matures into a deeper bond and the two become homemates, they should decide whether they would then owe each other some form of support or alimony; if so, a mathematical formula linking the amount to their years together, or to the ratio of their incomes, might be worked out and the agreement amended to reflect this new understanding.
2. **Reject alimony regardless of change:** Conversely, they might abjure the whole idea of alimony and swear to maintain a totally separate status no matter how long or how lovingly they live together.
3. **Estate planning:** At some specified point, each would prepare a will in each other's favor.
4. **Children:** They might agree that if they later have children, financial and child-care responsibility would be shared equally while both continue their careers, or the one who gave up a job to stay home with the kids would earn "wages" from the breadwinning mate; a value or percentage arrangement might be worked out.
5. **Illness or disability:** Illness or disability might be provided for.
6. **Tax benefits:** Changes in their relative financial status might be considered, and provisions made to seek maximum advantage of the tax laws.

Homemates may use a wide variety of legal agreements to implement their understandings. Their contracts may be as simple as an agreement to share everything each mate acquires or earns during the relationship on a fifty-fifty basis, holding most assets as joint tenants with right of survivorship, and depositing salary checks in a joint bank account until one party gives notice in writing that he/she wishes to terminate the arrangement. In our opinion, this is probably the best means of ensuring fairness and long-term domestic serenity, especially when one mate earns most of the money and the other contributes most of the homemaking efforts.

Such an arrangement, however, is less than ideal from a tax standpoint. As noted, when one mate contributes most of the earnings, the couple would pay lower taxes if they were married. The IRS will probably define the division according to who earns the money, even if there is a legal agreement that it belongs equally to both mates, so the breadwinner will be taxed at the highest rate, and may not even be able to claim a deduction for the dependent mate (if cohabitation is illegal where they live). If a couple has reasonably equal earnings, they will fare better as mates than as spouses, but in no case can they compound the advantage by income-splitting (each declaring 50 percent of the total), unless they can set up a valid business partnership, which will be explored later. The only couples who can automatically split income equally for tax purposes are spouses in community-property states.

CERTAINTY OF TERMS AND LANGUAGE

When homemates draw up a contract providing that most or all of their assets shall be shared equally, its provisions should be spelled out in minute detail. This will ensure that both parties clearly understand the extent of the agreement, and will fortify the contract against future challenges. For example, a simple statement that they agree to hold all property as community property, as if they were married, will not suffice, since the term "community property" cannot be applied to mates. It would be better if they gave it another title, such as "joint property" or "common ownership" (and spelled out what it meant). Even then, what about property later acquired by gift or inheritance? And what if the parties own one or two items they do not wish to share?

If they wish to hold property jointly, the contract should state precisely which assets and earnings are included and whether the property is to be held in "joint tenancy with right of survivorship" or "tenancy in common."

DIFFERENT TYPES OF JOINT PROPERTY

Joint tenancy with right of survivorship is often the method used by mates and spouses for holding title to real or personal property. It provides that the surviving co-owner, whether a mate or spouse, shall receive all the joint tenancy upon the death of the other joint owner. Consider the following case:

Edgar establishes a savings account in joint tenancy with the right of survivorship with Rose, his casual mate. All of the funds come from Edgar's salary and are his separate property. Edgar sets up joint tenancy as a matter of convenience so that if he dies, Rose has easy access to the funds. Edgar also prepares a will leaving all of his property to his mother, who is still alive. Edgar's other property consists of stocks and bonds worth $40,000, a car and other valuables worth $7,500, and a checking account of $2,500.

If Edgar dies, his mother will get the stocks and bonds, the car and other valuables, and the checking account funds, totalling $50,000. Although there is a conflict between the provisions of the will and the joint-tenancy account, the terms of the joint tenancy prevail, and Rose will receive the $10,000 in savings.

But joint tenancy can prove disadvantageous for either mates or spouses in larger estates, if estate taxes will be due. In such instances, joint tenancy should not be set up without competent tax advice.

Another method is *tenancy in common*. If two or more people hold title as tenants in common, there is no survivorship provision. If one of the tenants dies, his or her share (usually half) of ownership will not automatically pass to the survivor, but will pass according to the terms of the deceased tenant's will. The surviving mate will share ownership of the once-joint property with the beneficiaries specified in the will. The same is true if that person dies without a will, and title then passes to relatives according to the laws of intestate succession (see glossary). Property held by tenants in common *does not* avoid probate. Joint-tenancy ownership with the right of survivorship *does* avoid probate.

There are other types of joint ownership, some obscure or no longer applicable: tenancy by the entireties, trust bank accounts, POD (pay-on-death) bank accounts, etc. These and others fall, with slight modifications, under one of the two foregoing definitions. Legal counsel will clarify the distinctions.

Keep in mind that neither tenancy in common nor joint tenancy is community property. Community property exists *only* between spouses and *only* in community-property states. It is most analogous to tenancy in common, but not completely; tax laws and divorce laws, for example, are applied differently.

CONTRACT COHABITATION

A different legal tack for mates is called *contract cohabitation*, a term that refers to a contract under which one mate is employed by the other at a specified rate of remuneration. Generally this covers domestic services, but conceivably a secretary and her boss might draw up such an agreement, or a prosperous novelist might "hire" her homemate as a live-in editor or exterminator. This is clearly less egalitarian a framework than the fifty-fifty split, but may exactly satisfy the needs of less idealistic couples. Such a contract may later protect against vague claims for alimony or against estate-poaching by a survivor. The IRS may demand that the employer pay Social Security taxes for the employee. This too is unromantic, but could be very practical if the employer is rich enough to afford the contributions; if the couple breaks up or the employer dies, the employee is likely to need his/her eligibility for government benefits.

Before Social Security was born, W. C. Fields maneuvered an amiable young woman named Carlotta Monti into a state of apparent contract cohabitation. The contract was oral, not written, although Fields' letters to Carlotta during their brief separations often allude to it. Sometimes the letters changed the terms of the contract, and at least once he wrote that it was kaput—but they always picked up exactly as before when she came home again.

As his biographer, Robert Lewis Taylor, explains: "Fields had undergone certain hardships with female companions; he was wary of encroachments."[6] Thus the terms were clear, and not generous. Miss Monti was provided a salary of $25 per week for her services, and though she was, at least at first, his lover, the contract was entirely unmeretricious. Fields, a notoriously miserly millionaire, made it plain that their love earned no dividends; when he paid her $25 per week, plus free room and board, he demanded his money's worth in service.

She served as his companion, kitchen supervisor, practical nurse, and general dogsbody. His style as her lord and master was not markedly different from his celebrated film persona: an outrageous olio of the courtly autocrat and the unscrupulous bamboozler.

Carlotta adored his style and discerned a true heart in the flinty performer. But he made it tough on occasion. Once, she recalls, he inexplicably ordered her to go to his bank and withdraw five thousand dollars. She protested, nervous about carrying such a sum through the city alone, but he brooked no denials and sent her, miserable, on her way in his flashy sedan. Finding his paranoia contagious, she decided the car was being followed, and returned with the cash in a taxi. Fields had just finished telephoning the police to "have that thieving Mexican bitch arrested at the airport," where he was convinced she would run with the money. Finding his suspicions unjustified, Fields promptly began to berate Miss Monti for squandering his hard-earned cash on cab fare!

Miss Monti, says Taylor, was "one of the least mercenary of girls."[7] Surely she was also better-natured than most. She stood by him for fourteen years. For the last few years before his death, she became more his nurse than his mistress, as his phenomenal consumption of alcohol slowly destroyed him. She recently told the *Los Angeles Times:* "There was a big romance for maybe a year, but I was mostly a nursemaid. We got along really well—and he didn't get along with many people."[8] She was with him through his last illness, holding him as he died, and he remembered her as one of the chief beneficiaries of his $800,000 estate.

But she never saw very much of it. The will was broken by Fields' long-estranged wife, who took charge of his estate; Miss Monti eventually won rights to a 16-cylinder 1938 Cadillac and about $50 per week for life, which, according to Miss Monti, stopped in 1954. Social Security benefits would have come in very handy.

Of course, not everyone can identify with the situation of Fields and Monti. Still, for those who feel the need to protect their assets, contract cohabitation may be the answer.

FLEXIBLE CONTRACT ARRANGEMENTS

More complicated contracts may be in order if the couple needs a flexible arrangement or faces possibilities of significant change. Agreements to take turns supporting each other make sense for some couples, assuming they are ready to make such long-term commitments. Eligible persons include penniless artists, premed students, and anyone who feels that regular vacations are the spice of life. The specific provisions could vary from six-month stints at odd jobs for the patron of an artist to a six-year career for someone supporting a prospective MD. Putting a mate or a spouse through years of professional training is a notoriously risky occupation, as thousands of ex-wives can testify; it is surely fair and wise to make sure such a heavy investment of emotional and financial support is protected by legal covenants.

Suppose, on the other hand, two people plan to spend their lives together, and in order to avoid dependency, they insist on separate finances? Homemates and even spouses can set up situations similar to that of casual mates, if that is their agreement.

Or, homemate couples may value their separate identities and independence, but allow their possessions to become entangled as time goes by. Marlene Doherty, a feminist counselor and therapist, relates that she takes pride in supporting herself and her children and prefers to—lovingly—resist her wealthier homemate's desire to take care of her. Still, she moved from New England to New York City to live with him and is just beginning to reestablish herself professionally—and the two of them are jointly buying a condominium apartment and a country house.

Rainbow Goodsky wrote us from the orchards of Washington, where she and Elmo, her homemate of eight years, were toiling, as they have for the past four summers, to earn the money that goes into the forty acres of farmland on which they eventually plan to build their future. They both know the land is "theirs," but the bank thinks it's Elmo's; they took title in his name because a rocky divorce ruined her credit rating. Elmo has made a will in her favor—but her common interest in the farm should also be protected by contract.

LATER DISPOSAL OF JOINT PURCHASE

If for any reason either homemate wishes to dispose of his/her interest in common property, the other should have the *right of first refusal* to match the price and terms of a bona fide third-party offer (or another method of purchase can be set up).

If they desire to terminate their togetherness and the joint ownership, but neither wishes to sell, they could (choose one):

1. flip a coin to determine which party shall buy out the other's interest according to a prescribed payment plan;

2. submit the issue to arbitration; or

3. change their joint tenancy to tenancy in common and agree that each shall enjoy access to the property during certain months. Caveat: this practice can lead to Bad Scenes if the parties are inclined to be uncompromising or vindictive; only couples who are capable of realistic give-and-take should attempt to continue sharing after their relationship breaks up.

CHOOSING STATE LAWS

Within limits, as described in the previous chapter, married or marrying couples in most states have the right to decide for themselves whether their home state's system meets their needs, and if not, to adopt an equitable alternative by written contract. Consider this strategy:

John and Mary are planning to get married in New York, a separate-property state. As devout Baptists, they believe strongly in a traditional family life and agree that John shall be the sole breadwinner while Mary devotes herself exclusively to home and children. They feel that their marriage makes them one, but realize that New York law does not treat them as such, so they opt for a community-property agreement.

They should be aware that the community-property concept is applied differently in different states. It is not sufficient simply to declare that they intend to adopt community property; they should spell out precisely how they intend to own assets. For example:

> John Smith and Mary Jones agree that after their marriage, John shall earn the family's keep, and Mary shall not seek employment outside the home. It is understood between them that all property accumulated during the marriage, whether by John's earnings or investments, or any other means, including [or excluding] gifts and inheritance, shall belong equally to John and Mary, although John shall have the right of management [or they may agree to mutual management of all or part].

Or:

> John and Mary agree to hold all property, however acquired during their marriage, as joint tenants with right of survivorship, and that neither party shall keep any property separate except that which belonged to each before their marriage. [As mentioned previously, joint tenancy is not community property. The parties should

still have an understanding concerning management of their joint tenancy holdings.]

They could also study the laws of eight community-property states and choose the system that comes closest to their intentions, and declare:

> We agree that all property acquired by either party during our marriage shall be considered community property, and intend to adopt the community-property laws of the state of Idaho.

John and Mary's polar opposites are—oh, let's revisit Rick Gordon and Emily Parker. We'll assume that Rick's finances are back in the black, that Emily continues to practice dentistry, and that a child is on the way. For one reason or another they feel it's time to get married. Both, however, have ideological objections to the idea of community property. Since they still live in California, they decide to draw up a new contract reiterating their intention to keep all their finances separate, and to waive any rights to community property or alimony.

Their new agreement might read in part:

> Rick Gordon and Emily Parker, residing at 34 Elm Street, Venice, do hereby agree:
>
> That while they intend to marry, they wish to renounce any community-property rights and to waive any community-property obligations their marriage might create under California law, and:
>
> That all monies or property acquired by either party shall be deemed sole and separate property of the acquirer, except as otherwise agreed upon in writing, and:
>
> That they intend to follow the marital property laws of the state of Iowa [caution: it is extremely unwise to adopt the laws of another state without expert legal counsel], and:
>
> That both parties agree to contribute equally to the support of any children they may have, both financially and emotionally, and:
>
> That each party shall arrange his or her work schedule to facilitate equal sharing of child-rearing time, and neither party shall be expected to give up his or her career, and:
>
> That while the obligation to participate equally and contribute equally toward the support of any children they may have will continue should the marriage terminate, neither party will receive any additional alimony from the other.

WAIVER OF ALIMONY

It should be pointed out that the waiver of alimony has possibly critical implications. Once waived—always waived. One method that is close to being a waiver is to provide for $1.00 a year in alimony to one or both spouses; this keeps the doors open so that the courts have continuing jurisdiction to order increased financial aid, should a spouse be in need later on. In this respect, courts take very different stands regarding agreements between spouses from those prevailing for mates.

If mates break up after having drawn up a valid agreement, the court will enforce its terms and probably cannot order any adjustments later on. If an ex-mate, receiving only $75.00 per month as palimony per agreement, should later suffer a crippling auto accident and lose her independent livelihood, the court cannot step in and order the other party to assume greater financial responsibility for her support; it generally has no after-the-fact jurisdiction over the affairs of mates, unless, perhaps, the palimony award was made pursuant to court order and there was no agreement between the mates.

For spouses, though, different rules prevail. Whatever the terms of their private agreements, the courts retain the right after divorce to revise or readjust their obligations, should a change in circumstances warrant special allowances. An ex-husband might well be ordered to increase his support to his disabled ex-wife, assuming she had not completely waived alimony, when she could no longer support herself. Between mates, only contract law underlies the enforceability of their agreements; between spouses—or even between ex-spouses— the courts in most situations retain the power to supervise relations "till death do them part."

"LATER-LIFE" CONTRACTS

Some couples may wish to enter into very complex prenuptial contracts of a more old-fashioned sort—in fact, ones very similar in style to those commonly employed in earlier centuries. Most commonly, such agreements are prepared for mature couples planning marriage who have had previous marriages, still have children to provide for, or may have fairly substantial property interests to protect. At their stage in life, they are more concerned with security, maintaining their property, providing for the children, and avoiding legal complications. In this situation the couple might do well to consider living together, thus avoiding the marriage-penalty tax and minimizing the chance of mingling their estates. If they are not so liberated, they should proceed to marry. In either case they should retain a lawyer to prepare a pre-cohabitation or prenuptial agreement; better yet, each should retain separate counsel to represent his/her respective legal position. Full disclosure of all assets is vital to the enforceability of such contracts.

"DECLINING-YEARS" CONTRACTS

A set of circumstances familiar to lawyers, which would require an agreement, might be called the Groucho Syndrome:

Illness and incapacity may render an elderly person unable to live alone, and his or her assets often attract conniving, though not necessarily unkindly, attentions. Nurses and other aides may easily influence lonely widows or widowers to reward their services out of all proportion, or even to disinherit children whose visits are infrequent by comparison. An effective legal instrument in such cases is an employment contract setting forth *all* compensation to the aide, which might include the promise of a reasonable bequest; this clarifies and stabilizes the relationship, avoiding the risk of false post-mortem claims of lavish promises. Such a contract is also interpreted by the courts as negating the possibility of marriage or promise of marriage between the parties.

Certainly a prenuptial agreement is in order if marriage is planned with the companion. At such a time, if the aged party has children, the family should be called in and a fair arrangement worked out in writing. Of course, it may be the children who are the connivers, and the elderly parent may be more than justified in wishing to disinherit them in favor of a new wife or devoted housekeeper. In such a case, the elderly party should retain the meanest lawyer in town to ensure that the children do not succeed in breaking the will or contract.

Some, of course, may be perfectly capable of dealing with the brats singlehandedly. The Greek playwright Sophocles left his wife to spend his declining years with the courtesan Theoris. As he approached ninety, his legitimate son, fearing that the old man planned to disinherit him, petitioned the Athenian court to declare the great dramatist senile and make the son his legal guardian. Sophocles proved his competence undiminished by reciting from memory the whole of his latest masterpiece, and won the day.

THE BUSINESS PARTNERSHIP

Another way of averting potential problems is by going into

business and defining your relationship as a partnership:

Susan and Harry Landow of Providence, Rhode Island, have been happily married for three years when she learns that she has inherited the estate of her eccentric Uncle Ebenezer. This twist of fate seems unlikely to alter the course of their lives drastically, as the estate consists of seven Persian cats, one 1937 Pierce-Arrow, and the patent rights to Uncle Ebenezer's magnum opus, the Rotating Turbo-Widget.

They sell the Pierce-Arrow to an antique car buff and ditch the cats by abandoning them at a meeting of the Providence Persian Cat Lovers' Society; Susan, giggling a little at her memories of Uncle Ebenezer's houseful of Rube Goldberg contraptions, tucks the patent papers into the family scrapbook as a memento.

Leafing through the book one evening, Harry is intrigued by the old man's designs. The Rotating Turbo-Widget begins to haunt his dreams; he takes the papers down to the basement, builds a prototype, and tests it in his homemade wind tunnel. "Eureka!" cries Harry. "This will revolutionize the automotive fuel-economy testing process!"

With Susan's encouragement, Harry withdraws $5,000 from their joint savings and hires an engineer to produce ten custom-made RTWs; before long he has orders from General Motors and the EPA, and the RTW goes into mass production. Success beckons, and arrives nearly instantaneously: a rival firm offers to buy the RTW for an enormous sum.

Susan and Harry, dazzled by the brightness of their prospects, spend an evening deliriously proposing various dispositions of this fabulous loot. A castle in Spain, says Susan; solid investment in blue-chip stocks, says Harry. "We'll move out of this burg and spend the rest of our lives roaming the world in a yacht," says Susan. "We'll buy up the old Cheswick farm, and build a shopping mall to revitalize the local economy," says Harry.

They discover, appalled, that their notions of Easy Street are entirely incompatible. Susan discovers that Harry, who seemed so endearingly steady, is really just a New England banker at heart. Harry realizes that Susan's imagination, which brightened their simple life together, is just a first-class ticket to the poorhouse; she's really quite unstable. Soon they're barely speaking to each other.

Susan sulks, and finally announces that she is going to buy

the yacht no matter what Harry thinks, because the patent is *hers*.

Harry goes into shock. If it weren't for him, the Rotating Turbo-Widget would be nothing but a piece of paper moldering away in a scrapbook! The patent may be hers, but all the money it generated should be his! Furthermore, he has decided to devote his life to the production of RTWs and to turn down the dazzling offer anyway. Susan begins to cry.

"Don't cry," says Harry. "We can have the RTW company *and* the yacht, if you'll be a little patient—say, in ten years."

"I want a divorce," sobs Susan. "You'll hear from my lawyer as soon as I get one." Susan's lawyer files her divorce papers and arranges her acceptance of the rival company's offer for the patent; Harry's lawyer gets a court injunction against the sale, and from that day forward, most of the money earned by the RTW goes into lawyers' fees and court costs, not to mention Harry's increasing debt to the liquor store and Susan's bills from the psychiatrist.

In short, they'd have done better to get legal advice at the very beginning of their venture. A lawyer would have helped them set up a business partnership, perhaps with more mutual involvement; they would at least have reached a workable understanding and accepted equitable terms of ownership *before* the property reached a mind-boggling value.

Probably the agreement would have enabled them to deal more sensibly with the yacht question, and even if they still decided to go their separate ways, the partnership agreement would ensure an orderly division of the fruits of the RTW. It would have cost them far less in legal fees than the later hassles.

An additional advantage to a business partnership is that it is the one system under which a couple, married or not, *can* arrange a fifty-fifty income-splitting for tax purposes with the blessing of the IRS. It might be the ideal contract for mates, since partnership agreements are legitimate in every state, although partnership law varies somewhat from state to state. Generally, the right to create a business contract is one of the most sacred privileges of American citizenship; prospective partners have much more leeway to arrange the precise terms they desire than do prospective spouses, and much more assurance that their contract will be enforceable than do mates! A business partnership can provide for everything from cheaper auto insurance to tax-sheltered retirement plans; the fact that the partners sleep with each other should not be written into the contract, but it does not affect its validity!

You do need legal help to be sure of setting up a legitimate business partnership, but don't grudge the cost; it's a sound investment, and may pay off handsomely if the lawyer is clever enough to grasp all the possible advantages and put them to work for you.

There is only one catch to this proposition: there must be a real business effort involved, not a sham or dummy with no purpose other than to legitimize an illegal relationship or whittle down a couple's tax bite. The business does not have to be a roaring success, nor does it have to be a couple's sole means of support; a little imagination and some competent legal advice could set almost any couple on the path to a bona fide business partnership.

Use of a partnership agreement may be especially advantageous for gay couples who are otherwise unable to provide themselves with a reliably legal basis for a durable contract. They cannot marry, and their cohabitation contracts are vulnerable. Even where homosexual activity is not illegal, it may be considered illicit, immoral, or unacceptable. A contract furthering the security of a gay relationship runs a high risk of being disqualified as meretricious. Courts in some places may also decline to enforce a contract for gay cohabitation as being against public policy. The more businesslike their agreement, then, the stronger their chances; the more it mentions their personal relationship, the weaker.

Whether a gay "displaced homemaker" could ever obtain rehabilitative alimony or a settlement like Michelle Triola Marvin's remains unclear. Current legal trends may eventually extend some protection to gay homemates; courts may look to the intentions of the parties rather than their marriage impediments and find enforceable contractual rights, implied or expressed. Of course, expressed obligations beat implied ones by a country mile.

Gay couples' agreements require careful legal planning and drafting, and where a personal contract looks risky, partnerships, joint tenancy, and other legal methods should be examined.

MORE COMPLEX SITUATIONS

Let us now look more deeply into the potential of contracts and a series of complex financial tactics to redistribute the wealth of deeply committed partners. Homemates and spouses who have reached total union and who have accumulated a substantial worth can cement their promises and lower their taxes by the judicious use of gifts and trusts.

While *income* is usually not transferable between homemates or spouses for tax purposes (the one who earns it must pay taxes on it, even if there is an agreement to share on some other basis), income-producing *assets* or property can be divided; the income can then be shifted, equalized both for tax savings and for the protection of the new owner.

Let us introduce Leslie Chadwicke and Bob Mudge, homemates for ten years who plan to live together forever. Leslie is as rich as Croesus, while Bob is as poor as a churchmouse, a status difference that bothers them only around April 15, since they share the fruits of Leslie's assets with perfect equanimity. Leslie earns a salary of $150,000 per year, and receives another $75,000 in dividends from blue-chip stocks. Bob, a composer of entirely incomprehensible music, earns nothing. To save on taxes, then, Leslie wants to make a gift of the dividend income to Bob, who would still enjoy a considerably lower income-tax bracket, particularly if Bob had dependent children by a previous marriage to soak up deductions.

CLIFFORD TRUSTS: INCOME SHIFTING

One way to accomplish this redistribution is for Leslie to set up a nonrevocable trust. The so-called *Clifford trust* is often used, putting property in trust for a period of ten years or more, during which time the income is taxed only to the beneficiary, Bob. At the end of the ten years (or more, if desired, but not less), the principal of the trust can be transferred back to Leslie as the original owner, or the trust can be reestablished for another ten years (or more, but not less).

A practical pitfall of this arrangement is that even if the homemates—Leslie as the trustor and Bob as the beneficiary—split suddenly, the income from the trust will continue to go to Bob, as the beneficiary, until it expires. If Leslie reserves the right to revoke the trust, or even gives such powers to a third party, the tax advantages disappear; a revocable trust does not transfer income for tax purposes.

If Leslie, despite their devoted relationship, does *not* wish to provide Bob with such an unconditional meal ticket, she might prefer to invest in tax-exempt bonds and maybe buy a substantial life-insurance policy benefiting Bob as a consolation.

At any rate, there are other technical limitations to the use of Clifford trusts, which must be carefully drawn up by a lawyer to achieve the desired income-tax savings. Clifford trusts are also useful to transfer income to minor children or aged parents in lower tax brackets. It's one way to satisfy a part of your duty of support with more after-tax dollars.

GIFT-TAX

One hitch is that a gift-tax return must be filed when a Clifford trust is set up. Usually there will be no gift tax to pay even though the return is filed, unless the donor has previously used up the $175,625 lifetime gift-tax exemption allowed to him in 1981 and after that. The gift-tax regulations are an awful bore to read about; they work differently for spouses than for mates, and involve a lot of arithmetic. If you want to know how gift taxes may apply to your own financial situation, ask your lawyer. Agreements between mates to share equally the benefits of unequally earned income may also contain gift-tax considerations. Keep in mind that $3,000 apiece can be given away each year, tax-free, to as many people as you like and it doesn't consume any part of the $175,625 gift-tax exemption. If a spouse or mate has six kids and three grandmothers, he/she can give away $27,000 each year with no gift-tax impact.

LIVING TRUSTS

Another type of trust arrangement that may be useful to home-mates is called a *living trust*, which again should be set up by an attorney, or possibly two. With it, the beneficiary can save estate (death) taxes, and avoid probate. It's a great way to maintain privacy when one passes away; there's no publicity telling who's getting what and how. To top it off, the one with the bucks who sets it up can also be the trustee, so he can maintain control over the property while he's alive and avoid paying trustee fees to a bank. The trust can be revocable or irrevocable, and as complex as you care to make it, but when you're through, you've got the legal equivalent of a fine piece of clothing from a custom tailor.

Provisions of Bob and Leslie's living trust might include:
1. That all the assets of Bob and Leslie would be conveyed into the trust, but would retain their separate-property character. The trust would be divided into two parts so that the separate property of each party could always be readily identified, though they would be managed together by the trustee. (Common property can also be placed in the trust, with disposition provided for as agreed to between the parties).

2. The initial beneficiaries, as well as the trustors (donors), would be Leslie and Bob, and they would receive income from the trust in proportion to their respective property holdings in the trust. If they wish to control the assets, they may also name themselves, or one of them, as trustee.
3. Upon the death of either party, all of the assets in the trust could continue to be held in trust for the benefit of the surviving mate, or all or part of the assets could be distributed to the survivor, or to someone else.
4. If Leslie and Bob should later decide to marry (each other), the trust would be modified to take advantage of the marital deduction for further savings on estate taxes.
5. If they should have children, protection would be provided to ensure that the offspring cannot later be deprived of their share of the assets in the trust.

ESTATE TAXES

For those who have larger property holdings, it costs to die! Estate planning to save on taxes is rather complex. It applies when an individual's net worth exceeds $175,625 during 1981 and thereafter. Spouses may take advantage of an additional $250,000 marital deduction, which is *not* available to mates. Planning an estate to achieve tax savings is complex and requires the services of a competent lawyer who specializes in this intricate field.

DISPOSITION OF PROPERTY AT DEATH

No matter how small the prospective estate, all couples should give some thought to its post-mortem disposition. The precedent-setting *Trimble* case, involving the inheritance rights of "illegitimate" children, went all the way to the Supreme Court, even though the estate in question consisted only of a dilapidated automobile. Spouses and mates should have wills or other dispositive instruments such as living trusts prepared, but the need is greatest for homemates and casual mates.

If there is no will or other valid documentation of the deceased's intentions, property is divided up by the court in accordance with state *laws of intestate succession.* These laws universally favor relations by blood or marriage over any other consideration, and surviving mates are generally not protected at all.

All the property of a deceased mate, then, is likely to pass to blood relatives if there is no will or other dispositive instrument, and no provision has been made for joint ownership with right of survivorship; tenancy in common, as we explained, does *not* give the surviving mate any right to inherit

TAX COMPARISON CHART

For review, the following tax-comparison chart should be useful:

Item of Tax Significance	Spouses	Homemates	Casual Mates
Marriage penalty tax	Applicable. For two-earner marriages, the penalty generally applies, though if one spouse earns 20 percent or less of total income, the penalty has little significance. If one spouse earns all the income, there is no marriage penalty tax. For spouses who each earn about the same, the penalty is at its maximum. The greater the earnings, the higher the penalty.	Not applicable. If each homemate earns income, they generally pay less than would two spouses each earning income. On the other hand, if one mate is the sole support of both mates, they would pay lower income taxes if they were married.	Not applicable. If each casual mate earns income, they generally pay less tax than would two spouses each earning income.
Marital deduction	Available. This is an estate-tax (death-tax) savings device, which allows one spouse to leave up to $250,000 to his/her surviving spouse tax-free.	Not available.	Not available.
Gift tax marital deduction	Available. This allows one spouse to make tax-free lifetime gifts to the other spouse.	Not available.	Not available.
Head-of-household favorable tax treatment	Available to either spouse upon divorce.	Available to mates who support children or others according to IRS rules.	Same as for homemates.

Item of Tax Significance	Spouses	Homemates	Casual Mates
Annual gifts	Available. $3,000 per year per recipient is tax-free. With community property the gift can be $6,000 tax-free. With separate property it also can be $6,000 tax-free if both spouses consent.	Available. $3,000 per year per recipient is tax-free.	Same as for homemates.
Tax deduction for dependents	Available.	Available for children if strict tax rules are followed. Available for dependent homemates in those states where cohabitation is legal.	Same as for homemates.
Alimony/ Palimony	Upon divorce alimony is deductible for the payor spouse and reportable as taxable income to the recipient spouse.	It is doubtful whether the payor homemate can deduct palimony payments and whether the recipient homemate must report them as taxable income. Most likely, palimony will be treated as taxable income.	Same as for homemates.
Sale of house	Gain on sale of house can be deferred if a new home is purchased within 18 months after sale, or a new home is	Same as for spouses, except that the first $200,000 of gain is not taxable if *both* homemates are 55 or older, and share	Same as for homemates.

Item of Tax Significance	Spouses	Homemates	Casual Mates
	constructed within 24 months after the sale that is equal to or greater in value than the sale of the old home. If one of the spouses is 55 years of age or older, the first $100,000 of gain is not reportable even if a new home is not purchased or constructed, provided that spouse resides within the home a required period of time.	co-ownership. If only *one* mate is 55 or older, then only the first $100,000 of gain is not taxable.	

the decedent's share of the property. Children born to casual mates or homemates qualify as blood relatives of the mother, but their status as heirs of the father may have to be established by court action, so it is particularly important for unmarried parents to provide for them by will.

WILL CONTRACTS

Surviving spouses and "legitimate" children are better protected; each state has its own prescribed formula for intestate succession, but all provide for the surviving spouse and children to inherit from the estate. Of course, if the spouses wish to arrange any alternative distribution, or to set up trusts, they must do so in writing. They may even want to draw up a *will contract*, a very practical legal tool, seldom used, which is a document pledging that the surviving spouse will not alter the terms of his/her will, or otherwise enter into any agreement that later disinherits the children or other loved ones. This is a good protection against later marriages, when the surviving parent, now remarried and consumed with love and affection, might become disenchanted with the children.

ESTATE SUMMATION FOR MATES

To sum up the estate status of mates:

1. If a casual mate dies without a will or other dispositive instrument, the surviving mate will receive nothing, unless property was placed

in joint tenancy or other common ownership prior to death.

2. If a homemate dies without a will or other dispositive instrument, the surviving homemate (except in New Hampshire) will probably receive nothing, unless property was placed in joint tenancy or other common ownership prior to death. (However, a homemate has a much stronger chance of claiming implied ownership rights in the estate.)

3. Mates are not entitled to the gift-tax marital deduction (pertaining to tax-saving lifetime transfers between spouses) or the marital deduction pertaining to transfer of property to a spouse at death, which means that mates pay higher death taxes on larger estates.

4. Under most retirement plans a mate is not entitled to receive benefits, with possible exceptions for homemates or mates who are dependents as defined under the Internal Revenue Code.

5. No benefits for a surviving mate are provided under Social Security.

6. No death benefits (with rare exceptions) are granted to a surviving mate under Workmen's Compensation.

A surviving mate might be able to claim that an oral contract had existed between him and his deceased mate, giving him the right to claim all or part of the decedent's property. As mentioned in paragraph 2 above, a homemate is certainly in a stronger position to make such a claim than is a casual mate; substantiating factors that might tip the balance in his favor include:

1. the rendering of homemaking services or other services for a substantial time;

2. a history of previous joint purchases with mutual-survivorship understandings;

3. contributions of money or services into the deceased mate's property;

4. evidence of certain promises that were made by the deceased mate during his lifetime; or

5. children.

Remember, though, that the blood relative who would otherwise inherit the deceased mate's estate has the law on his side, and he is likely to press his claim. Just to be sure, your intentions should be expressed in a valid will or other document, and be sure to search for the right attorney!

FINDING THE RIGHT LAWYER

Be careful of lawyers who prepare contracts between lovers without considering all the legal possibilities, due to a kind of professional tunnel-vision. They may be excellent trial attorneys but lack the necessary expertise to cover all bases in an agreement. Though experienced in one side of domestic law, they may be quite unfamiliar with the terms of practical business negotiations and dealings, tax shelters, income-tax laws, estate law, trusts, wills, corporations, partnerships, etc. They may fail to consider such alternatives as life insurance and its many settlement options, vesting formulas for acquisition of property rights between mates, or the many varieties of retirement plans that may be useful to homemates. They might not effectively provide for the effects of inflation, or understand the auditing procedures used to seek full disclosure of assets. The law profession is becoming more specialized all the time. It is wise to choose a lawyer carefully. Perhaps two should be retained, one to handle courtroom proceedings and the other to deal with negotiations and contract preparation. Such specialization may not be necessary in the case of modest estates, but should be given due consideration where more substantial holdings are involved.

Selecting a lawyer is a difficult task. The best way is for one lawyer to recommend another. Most lawyers know who is qualified and respected among their peers. However, if the selection is based upon friendship rather than objective standards, or because the referring lawyer is receiving a fee, then the selection may be prejudiced; a second opinion may be necessary. Other methods of selection are to seek out a qualified friend or business advisor who has had experience dealing with attorneys and has some general knowledge as to who are the more respected domestic-relations lawyers. A passing remark at a cocktail party, or even a recommendation from a friend who has just gone through a divorce, is not enough. Further probing is necessary. Even if a recommendation is made by a competent party, a preliminary interview with the lawyer is necessary to obtain a basic understanding of what will take place and, just as important, to make sure that the right mixture—the proper blend of personality, communication, and trust between client and lawyer—exists. Even a good meeting doesn't make a lasting relationship, but it's good to get off on the right foot and have the right initial feeling.

Many bar associations, some three hundred throughout the country, provide lawyers' referral services. Your local agency will recommend one or more attorneys who devote their time to domestic-relations matters. Generally there is little or no fee for the initial interview, providing it does not go beyond a predetermined time. Though such referral systems are helpful, they may provide less than adequate legal representation because the lawyers who are referred are simply those who volunteer for the program.

Similarly, more and more lawyers are advertising and often list their areas of devotion in the classified section of the telephone directory. Legal areas of devotion are to be distinguished from specialization in medicine. In order for doctors to become specialists they have to undergo special training in a certain field of medicine. No such requirement is imposed upon domestic-relations lawyers. Devotion is not necessarily synonymous with skill, but devotion ordinarily does lead to more experience within a specialized area of the law.

SEPARATE LEGAL REPRESENTATION

In addition, where substantial interests—assets or risks—are involved, one lawyer should not represent both parties. To expect him or her to represent the best interests of each party while simultaneously maintaining objectivity and fairness toward both is unrealistic. Lawyers in this position may rationalize, "Well, the clients already negotiated everything between themselves; they only want me to reduce those understandings into print."

That's true enough—but what if one party isn't playing quite fair? One of the clients may have superior knowledge, or be withholding key financial information, or may actually expect to take advantage of the other. One of them may misrepresent the provisions because of intentional or honest misunderstanding. If one party does all the talking in the lawyer's office, it may seem as if the couple shares the same assumptions, a mistake that would quickly come to light in the adversary-style maneuvers of separate legal representatives.

If a contract does later come to court in litigation, the court will presume that it was drawn in good faith, and will seek a reasonable interpretation of any ambiguous language. Still, it is difficult to determine which party is telling the truth once the parties have taken opposite interpretations, and Jane claims she told Linus all about her $10,000 debt to her bookie, while Linus swears he wouldn't have touched her with a ten-foot pole if he'd known about it.

For a contract to be valid, a full disclosure of the total financial status, assets, and liabilities of both parties must be made at the beginning.

If one contracting party is wealthier, and the poorer one

gains little or nothing by the agreement, another question may
be raised. If, say, an impoverished lady farmer marries a prosperous gentleman farmer, and he extracts from her a document
relinquishing all her marital rights in his property, including
any rights to alimony, the fact that she receives little or nothing
in return may be considered a factor supporting a later claim
of fraud, or of "undue influence," especially if full disclosures
were not made.

An even stronger case could be made if the bride were also
pregnant and in debt to the groom; in such a case, a contested
prenuptial agreement might well be broken on the grounds that
the groom was in a position to exert undue influence on the
bride. Actually, this last example approaches conditions of
outright duress! A less obvious example:

Clarissa LeMarr, a bright nineteen-year-old sophomore at
the University of Frambesia, who hopes to rise from poverty
to moderate independence through a career in bilingual education, falls head-over-heels in love. The object of her affec-
tions is Dr. Sebastian Morley, her faculty advisor, a distinguished semanticist and accomplished flirt. A childless widower,
he inherited a generous nest egg from his late wife, but chooses
to pretend that he lives on his salary and royalties.

His benevolent concern for Clarissa's academic progress
flowers above and beyond the call of duty; Clarissa, walking
on roses and not looking where she's going, becomes pregnant.
Professor Morley's concern now turns to his own career—this
situation could do his status at the university considerable damage. And, yes, he always *did* want children. His proposal of
marriage puts Clarissa in seventh heaven. She does not demur
when he starts to hedge, pointing out that of course she cannot
expect him to support her impoverished parents and twelve
worthless siblings. Flinching at this not entirely accurate de-
scription, but somewhat awed by her circumstances, Clarissa
signs the prenuptial agreement he proposes, consenting to
waive any rights in his property, and further to expect no aid
except child support from him should their marriage shatter.

Clarissa's fledgling career dissolves in infant formula when
she and Sebastian have two children. Lo! She then discovers
that he has taken a benevolent interest in another pretty sophomore. Clarissa divorces Sebastian, not much caring about his
scholarly reputation, and contests the premarital contract. She
wins; the court cites not only undue influence but also Sebas-

tian's failure to disclose his independent income before the marriage, and awards her a lump-sum settlement sufficient to support the children on its income alone; *and* she receives rehabilitative alimony for five years to enable her to resume her interrupted education and career.

Along these same lines, such disparity of circumstances between the parties to a prenuptial contract places a strong burden of proof on the wealthier spouse to demonstrate that the poorer and possibly less sophisticated partner actually understood the consequences of the agreement.

In the Steiger case discussed in Chapter Four, Sherry Steiger's suit for alimony was based on her claim that she had not understood that she was signing away her marital rights by their agreement. As reported in the *Los Angeles Herald Examiner,* Judge Schafer said he couldn't "buy her position."[8a] The judge said he felt it was "ill-advised" for Steiger to engage his own law firm to advise his bride-to-be on the agreement, but said it did not represent sufficient conflict of interest to invalidate the agreement.

BREAKING THE CONTRACT

True, even if a contract is drawn up in proper style and in good faith, an embittered ex-lover may turn around and try to break it. However, a well-prepared contract probably won't break, and a *wisely* prepared contract greatly reduces grounds for serious bitterness.

Perhaps some insights into divorce and other breakups are in order to reflect upon the breadth and scope of a wisely prepared contract.

DIVORCE AND HOUSEBREAKING

The most obvious caveat to would-be wedded pairs is the painful prospect of divorce. Government statisticians estimate that nearly 40 percent of all first marriages and 45 percent of all second marriages end in divorce, and the *Family Law Reporter* announced in 1979 that the total number of marriages terminated in American courts has hit an all-time high.[9] In spite of these chilling numbers, the *Wall Street Journal* gave front-page billing to the cheerier news that the overall divorce *rate* was at last leveling off,[10] and a recent survey of nearly four thousand husbands and wives claimed that one-third of these spouses simply ruled out the possibility of their ever getting a divorce.[11]

Divorce is no longer a social disgrace, a legal Mount Everest, nor even a statistical improbability. We can't call it unthinkable—but we can cling to the belief that it will happen to someone else. When it comes to marrying, Americans—who must lead the world in numbers of non-arranged marriages between almost complete strangers—still earn their national reputation as idealists and optimists. "Full speed ahead and damn the statistics" might be blazoned over the door of City Hall, particularly in Oregon and California, which boast among the highest divorce rates in the nation.

A common belief among the wary unmarried is that the "marrying kind" prance to their weddings with fingers crossed behind their backs, assuming that they can always get a divorce if it doesn't work out. Not so, say husbands and wives and exes. At the altar, nearly all Americans sincerely embrace a lifetime commitment, and the decision to separate before death do them part is not taken lightly. A marriage that shows signs of strain brings out the Protestant ethic: we "work at" our marriages, and invest enough in them to support a brisk trade in marriage manuals, consciousness-raising groups, and expert counseling. We can be philosophical about the neighbors' divorce, but view our own as a personal failure.

Divorce is emotionally grueling, no matter how mechanical the legal process becomes; every marriage, except the most mercenary, evolves into an intimate tangle of personal hopes, visions, and commitments that cannot be cut away with a single stroke. We do not get divorced casually; we get married carelessly, and pay handsomely in the spectacular divorce rate that follows.

Many husbands and wives decide they simply cannot afford a divorce. The male half of a marriage gone sour may find that the bacon he brings home is shrinking fast in the inflationary frying pan and will not stretch to feed two households. His wife finds that the going pension for ex-wives won't cover her expenses, nor has she much prospect of future earnings. Her skills as a homemaker are not readily marketable, and few employers will invest the time and money to teach her new skills when younger workers are competing for available jobs.

In about thirty states, the question of fault may still enter the divorce process, and the demand for reparations or severance pay may lead to substantial alimony—which, since the United States Supreme Court's 1979 *Orr* decision, is now an option for both sexes. The most equitable division of means may leave both parties poorer even in the best of divorces; the worst, aggravated by overzealous attorneys or by marital vengeance turned venal, can be ruinous. The process alone can cost more than the couple can afford to lose. This is one reason why more and more states have legislated either mandatory or optional no-fault divorce.

In the past decade, thousands of lovers have tried another route to no-fault separation. Living together once provided some freedom from the stigma of "failure" attached to a broken marriage, and it was guaranteed to be free of alimony. Plain, unvarnished blackmail probably raised its ugly head from time to time, but not in court. Since *Marvin*, though, the breaking up of unwed households promises financial risks more unpredictable than mere divorce. Even *sans* acrimony, cohabiting couples are increasingly likely to face financial complications; there are Gordian Knots where once there were no strings.

To designate this type of separation, we'll take a hint from Gilbert and Sullivan. As Learned Counsel in *Trial by Jury* declares that "marrying two wives at once is Burglaree," the end of a domestic liaison that was never legally begun shall be hereinafter known as *housebreaking*.

Housebreaking homemates, and even casual mates, also encounter rude awakenings: they discover that the emotional web they've spun together is stickier than they expected. Breaking away from a homemate can be especially bewildering for young couples—perhaps even harder than divorce.

Divorce does have much in common with the funeral ceremony, apart from universal grimness; both serve a personal and social need to know when something is over, and when it is time to begin something else. Long before people viewed marriage as a matter of success or failure—even before it became a religious rite separating virtue from sin—the law demanded a legal rite to dissolve a legal marriage.

For one reason or another, the law has stepped back from refereeing divorces as moral boxing matches. The current trend toward no-fault divorce prevailing in more and more states makes it easier for splitting couples to achieve "peace with honor" between themselves, while the legal designation of marriage as a civil contract (as opposed to divine law) in most states also leaves it to the divorcing parties to make their own peace with the Almighty. There are still couples who divorce because one spouse has committed a dastardly deed of marital malfeasance. They must still go through a trial by ordeal in any of the fault-divorce states, and are free to do so in some of the "modified" no-fault-divorce states. In the eighteen or so true no-fault-divorce states, the divorce court no longer provides a theater for intimate jousting—although the questions of financial settlements and child custody are still often resolved in trial by combat.

EXPANDED THEORIES

Divorce cases are becoming more civilized, at least legally, while housebreaking is losing its vaunted freedom from judicial interference. In time, perhaps, there will be proposals from scandal-sated Solons to extend no-fault divorce across the lines of marriage to unwed mates as well. Certainly there will soon be at least a bias, if not a statute, favoring couples with written contracts over those who try to work out all the gory details in court. New rulings extending the right to receive alimony to needy ex-husbands, granting smaller alimony awards for ex-wives capable of supporting themselves, and approaching equal rights for fathers in custody cases, all reflect a strong desire to place the sexes on a meticulously equal footing in the divorce court. Nonsexist divorce law, which is the trend, is truly a giant step for mankind, although it is cold comfort for the man who, after winning custody of his children, finds that he cannot get time off from work to care for them when they fall ill. Similarly, the woman who finds that all her skills as a homemaker won't get her a paying job may feel less than grateful to the liberated judge whose respect for female self-sufficiency led to an insufficient alimony award. It appears, though, that a majority of American women are willing to take these risks. According to a 1980 study conducted by the Roper Organization, three out of five women feel that a divorced wife who can support herself should not receive alimony.[12] Still, there remains a gap between the increasingly stringent economic reality of today and the expansive vision of the law. This will inevitably create a pitfall for thousands of individuals—and hard cases for hundreds of judges.

MAJOR PROBLEM AREAS

In divorce cases there is an eternal triangle of troublemakers which causes the bitterest battles of the exes. Three Furies—Infidelity, Property, and Offspring—with their immeasurable permutations and combinations, have pursued marriages with deadly loads of acrimony since the first nuptials were recorded, and time has not sapped their troublemaking powers.

It is here that marital and homemates' contracts come into their own. Lovers with 20/20 hindsight discover that it is far, far better—and cheaper—to work out the legal papers in advance, when hearts are warm and minds are cool. Contracts cannot erase the sting of jealousy nor divide babies into two equal portions, but they can ensure that property divisions upon divorce or housebreaking come in two parts (his and hers) rather than three (his, hers, and a military-sized budget for legal fees).

Nevertheless, if you have come to the parting of the ways with no contractual amulet to protect you, we won't try your equanimity with any more I-told-you-so's. If you must separate, here are some considerations toward a better-late-than-never negotiation:

1. Is the divorce or housebreaking going to take place in a separate-property or community-property state?
2. What assets are involved? What about life insurance and participation in retirement plans?
3. Are the assets community property, joint property, or separate property?
4. Are the parties mates or spouses? If they are mates, are they casual mates or homemates?
5. What are the applicable state laws regarding mates or spouses?
6. What skills and abilities to earn in the future does each party possess?
7. What was the length of the relationship?
8. What provisions must be made for the health, education, and welfare of children born or adopted during the relationship?
9. What is the position of each mate or spouse concerning property, future earnings, age, health, general attitude, and the like?
10. Does the applicable state law provide for no-fault divorce, or does it require grounds for divorce? To what extent does it affect the division of property and/or support or alimony payments?
11. What planning should be made for inflation?
12. Could the parties establish a business partnership or corporation, or possibly continue a business partnership or corporation already in existence, to obtain certain tax-savings benefits, such as business-expense deductions, a Keogh retirement plan, group insurance benefits, and the like? (Caution: legitimate business purposes must be satisfied, otherwise such deductions may be considered unlawful and set aside as a sham.)
13. Is there an estate-tax (death-tax) problem, and if so, what protective methods can be worked out?
14. What contingency planning should be worked out if one of the parties dies without fulfilling all of his/her obligations?

15. What visitation rights should be worked out for the non-custodial parent? (See the checklist beginning on page 153 for a detailed itemization of the steps to consider concerning children and their rights.)
16. Should trusts, will contracts, special bank accounts, and other legal protections be established?
17. What are the tax consequences, if any, of divisions of property between the parties?

KNOWLEDGE

Divorce or housebreaking is a turbulent experience. Ping-Pong balls cross the net at a slower pace than the emotions that gnaw at even the hardiest of cast-iron stomachs. A person's capacity for reasoning understandably diminishes. Bitterness, if it exists, only adds to the hardships.

During these times, knowledge can be a strengthening resource. In addition to close counseling with your lawyer, take time to learn the law; it will build confidence and remove suspicions. With confidence comes a calming effect, so that a more mature perspective can be attained. This can accomplish one of two things: it can perhaps lead to a reconciliation, if that is the eventual desire of both parties; or possibly lead to a fairer understanding of each party's financial position so that extreme demands and prolonged negotiations are minimized if not eliminated.

PROPERTY

One of the first issues that must be dealt with is how the spouses will divide whatever material assets the marriage has been blessed with. Each separate-property and community-property state exercises different powers in the disposition of property in the event of divorce, assuming no agreement was previously worked out between the spouses. There are other tax and practical aspects to be considered:

1. In separate-property states, if one spouse transfers property to the other spouse, and if the property has a fair market value that is greater than cost, then the transferor spouse pays income taxes at ordinary gain rates. If the transfer is made after the divorce decree, or is sold to a third party after the divorce decree, then the tax is at lower capital-gains rates. It may be advisable to pledge assets as collateral and borrow rather than make transfers before the decree. In states such as New York, which provide for an "equitable distribution" of property acquired during the marriage, the law is unclear, once property in the name of one spouse is transferred to the other spouse as part of an equitable distribution, whether it

constitutes a taxable sale or exchange, or a nontaxable division of property similar to a nontaxable division of community property.

2. In community-property states, the equal division of community property between divorcing spouses is not taxable. If, however, one spouse receives more than one-half of the community property, there is a tax on the excess valuation over cost.

3. If the family home is sold, the taxable gain can be deferred if a new house is purchased within eighteen months of the sale and the new one costs as much as, or more than, the old one; or the eighteen-month period can be extended to twenty-four months if the new residence is constructed rather than purchased. If either spouse is fifty-five or older, then the first $100,000 of gain upon the sale of the family home is not taxed, even if a new home is not purchased or constructed. Mates are also entitled to this benefit if *both* are fifty-five or older and the home is jointly owned; otherwise, if only one owning mate is old enough to qualify for the exemption, only the first $50,000 of gain is tax-free.

The first servings having been made, we now refer you to the State-by-State Guides for more specific information on property law in your state, which, in the broad sense, should round out the menu of understanding.

PROPERTY MANAGEMENT AND CONTROL

A further warning: "Separate" doesn't quite mean what it implies, and "community" is not necessarily "togetherness."

While a couple is living in harmony, or at least not yet divorced, in almost all separate-property states the spouse who owns separate property, even marital separate property acquired during the marriage, is the manager of that property. He or she can sell it, mortgage it, hock it, even give it away. But whoa! As pointed out earlier, once the couple divorces, unless they live in one of the ultra-separate-property states, some of this separate property may be awarded by the court to the other spouse. Or, if they stay married until death do them part, and the wealthier spouse disinherits the other spouse by will, the survivor spouse usually can carve out a small niche in the estate with a family allowance, a homestead right, a dower or curtesy right, or a combination of these rights. So all is not completely owned when a parting occurs.

Community-property states generally give each spouse full and equal power to manage the community property, but there are usually special requirements that both sign to sell or put a mortgage on the family home. In some states, this joint-signature requirement applies to all real estate. Once again, when the marriage is ended by divorce or death, different rules apply; the courts then have the power to divide the property according to the state's community-property laws or provide for the surviving spouse according to its succession laws at death. And rules play tricks!

If Charlie Braun wishes to disinherit Hilda, his wife of twenty-six years, and bequeath his half of the community-property estate to the residents of a dog-and-cat hospital, he may do so. Fits, tantrums, and F. Lee Bailey will do her no good as long as Charlie was of sound mind and wasn't unduly influenced by a scheming pussycat. Granted, Hilda will still own her half of the community property, but she will no longer have a free hand in its disposal. The community is no longer in existence; Hilda now co-owns the family home and bank account as tenant-in-common with the dogs and cats. As a result, she cannot sell the entire home or use the money without their approval.

On the other hand, if Charlie had divorced Hilda in a community-property state, the court could impose a more sensible settlement, assuming they couldn't work it out between themselves. In most community-property states, divorce courts have jurisdiction over the entire community property, with the power to divide it "equitably" rather than equally. Conceivably, Hilda could receive the lion's share of the community property and poor old Charlie would find himself in the doghouse. More than likely, however, the court would divide the assets in such a way that each had exclusive ownership over some of the assets, thus avoiding further co-ownership and possible future hassles.

PROPERTY SETTLEMENTS FOR HOMEMATES

Keep in mind that the states' views of property rights between homemates vary widely, to say the least (see Chapter Four and the State-by-State Guides). California's Supreme Court has directed judges to sift through the ashes of burnt-out lovenests in search of implied contracts or other enforceable agreements between unmarried couples; the Illinois Supreme Court, at the other extreme, has declared open warfare against "private contractual alternatives to marriage."[13] Several courts in between have awarded property settlements to homemates at the end of a long relationship; casual mates should not expect such treatment.

JOINT AND SEPARATE PROPERTY
OF HOMEMATES

One aspect that may be examined by the courts to determine whether any contractual rights exist between housebreaking mates is the manner in which their assets are owned. Home-mates may own property separately or jointly (never as community property), and the manner of ownership usually is taken literally by the courts:

If John and Laurie, after living together for six years, have acquired a $40,000 house in Laurie's name and three cars, worth about $12,000, in John's name, chances are the courts will allow Laurie to kick John out of the house and let John take all the wheels. In most states, no judge would interfere *unless* John proved an oral or written contract calling for an agreed-upon division of some or all of their earthly goods, or unless Laurie were able and willing to prove that the cars had been bought and maintained with her money and registered to John to avoid unpleasantness due to his extensive police record for car theft.

If property is owned jointly between mates, the courts will probably not step in to divide it (as they might for married couples), unless there is a valid contract authorizing division, or unless one mate can prove he or she put up most of the bucks and did not intend to make a gift to the other. If the assets in question can be amicably shared after the housebreaking, the ex-homemates may continue as joint owners, perhaps changing their status from joint tenants with right of survivorship to tenants-in-common. Still amicably, they may work out an arrangement for one party to buy out the other's interest within a certain period of time. If they can't agree on anything, one co-owner may file a partition lawsuit; the courts may then either divide the property into separately owned parts, or order the property sold and the proceeds divided, either according to each party's contribution or equally.

ALIMONY

As is commonly understood, divorce settlements may go beyond dividing the couple's current assets. Alimony may be agreed upon in private negotiations, or it may be imposed by a judge; it may be paid in one or many installments as a lump sum, or as fixed periodic income. Texas is the only state that does not permit courts to award alimony. (Pennsylvania was also a holdout but changed its law, allowing for alimony as of July 1, 1980.) In Texas, a community-property state, the dependent spouse's one-half share of the community property would cushion the financial impact.

No one needs to be told that alimony has been a nightmare to ex-husbands; there is, however, a strong tendency nowadays toward lower alimony awards, particularly in no-fault-divorce states. A contributing factor in the slimming of alimony payments is the increasing expectation that women can and should support themselves.

A new concept gaining influence in the courts—and we cast a sideways salute to Michelle Marvin for her contribution to this contemporary idea—goes by the names of *restorative* or *rehabilitative* alimony. It refers to money awarded, usually to ex-wives, for a limited period of time—time that is supposed to be spent developing or improving job skills with a view toward future independence. Since many wives gave up a career to raise children, or for other reasons, they may reenter the job market after a divorce either totally or partially disadvantaged as potential breadwinners. Growing awareness of this practical weakness in the theory of equality has led to a new notion of postmarital obligations. An ex-husband may be ordered to pay rehabilitative alimony for a few years to support his ex-wife while she learns a trade or seeks training to update and sharpen her skills. Theoretically, of course, men are equally eligible for awards of rehabilitative alimony.

TAX TREATMENT OF ALIMONY, PALIMONY, AND CHILD SUPPORT

Generally, alimony must be reported as taxable income to the recipient spouse and is deductible by the payor spouse. Child-support payments have no tax consequences; they do not constitute taxable income to the recipient, nor are they deductible by the payor.

Whether palimony is taxable income to a recipient mate is not clear. Probably the IRS will regard it as a gain and try to tax it. Whether a mate who pays palimony is entitled to an income-tax deduction also remains unclear. Conceivably, then, it could work to the tax disadvantage of mates at both ends.

Individual legal counsel is needed on these subjects, but here are some fairly universal legal and tax pointers:

1. If alimony is waived by a spouse, it is waived forever. If the divorce decree provides for a payment of $1.00 per year to either or both spouses, it can later be increased for the recipient spouse in the event of an emergency. (In some states token alimony is no longer allowed as a means of reserving later jurisdiction.)

2. Alimony awarded in a divorce decree can later be adjusted if either spouse suffers a serious change of circumstances, such as an unforeseen medical catastrophe or career setback. Whether such adjustments will be made for recipients or payors of palimony remains to be seen. Probably the courts will not step in to modify private contractual agreements, unless the palimony award was incorporated into a court decree.

3. Alimony usually ceases when the recipient spouse remarries. There are exceptions to this rule in a few states. Recently, some courts have terminated alimony payments to recipients who have entered homemate relationships, but what constitutes "living together" to form a basis for alimony termination is as yet unsettled. Alimony paid in a lump sum, rather than in periodic installments, is of course not subject to termination. In one case, a judge ordered the termination of alimony payments to a divorced woman whose homemate was another woman; the judge let her ex-husband off the hook because the lesbian relationship precluded the possibility of her remarriage. Usually, though, sharing living quarters with a person of the same sex does not endanger one's alimony payments.

4. Lump-sum alimony awards will most likely not have tax consequences; it may be advisable to switch to periodic payments to get tax deductions as defined within the Internal Revenue Code (and, of course, the recipient would then pay income taxes).

5. In order to get tax deductions *before* the divorce decree is final, there must be a court order for temporary alimony, or the parties must sign a written agreement so providing. What constitutes a satisfactory written agreement is unsettled as of this writing. If the order or agreement does not set out how much is alimony and how much is child support, most likely all of the payments will be treated as alimony.

CHILD-CUSTODY DISPUTES

The second Fury of divorce discord, the couple's offspring, rouses the deepest difficulties of all. There is simply no way to create an equitable division of kids. It's a good thing that most divorcing spouses are able to agree on which parent shall have custody of the children; those who can't agree go through child-custody battles that range from merely heartrending to downright vicious. The courts try to confine the battlefield to areas directly related to the children's welfare, making their decision on the basis of "the best interests of the child." Most judges sincerely do not want to hear about the private skeletons in each parent's cupboard as long as these issues do not affect the parent's capacity to care and provide for the child.

Still, problems may arise if one parent openly violates laws or local standards in his/her private life. Gay parents are particularly vulnerable, though in recent years a dramatic broadening of legal thought in this area has taken place. More and more courts are finding that gay parents do qualify as fit; strategic information for individuals facing such custody battles can be found in the "Gay Parents' Support Packet" put out by the National Gay Task Force in New York City.

Occasionally a parent may lose custody rights because he/she "lives in sin" with a new partner. Usually the courts will accept a homemate relationship as long as it does not harm the children's home life. The higher-ranking courts in most states have supported custodial rights for homemates, but here again Illinois is bucking the trend. The Illinois Supreme Court upheld a decision to deprive Jacqueline Jarrett of custody of her two daughters solely because the justices and her ex-husband objected to her cohabiting with another man. No one questioned Jarrett's excellence as a mother, nor suggested that her homemate was in any way personally objectionable, yet the court held that the best interests of her teenaged daughters required a more moral environment.

What do the children have to say about it? Generally they are not consulted about custody matters unless they are fourteen or older. Seldom do the children have separate legal counsel; this omission may deprive them of some of their rights.

CHILD CUSTODY AND
SUPPORT ARRANGEMENTS

An old proverb advises, "Take revenge—live long enough to be a trial to your children." Nonetheless, it's our duty to support them until they become adults. The age of majority varies from state to state; it used to be twenty-one virtually everywhere, but is now as low as eighteen in some states.

Most child-custody and -support agreements are fairly simple, spelling out payment schedules and reasonable visitation rights. It might be wise at least to discuss and possibly to incorporate more detailed questions into the agreement. Lawyers disagree on the amount of detail that should be covered in a binding agreement, but the following issues should be considered as rationally as possible.

CHILDREN'S BASIC NEEDS

1. Does your state or community provide a legal representative for children of divorcing parents? If not, what about hiring an independent attorney for the children to ensure that their interests are carefully represented and protected in the divorce arrangements?

2. Is the proposed child-support agreement realistic? Is the paying parent likely to keep faith? It's important to provide adequately for the children's needs, but if one parent is expected to provide impossible levels of support, the risks of skipping out altogether are increased.

3. Should the noncustodial parent be denied visiting rights if he/she fails to keep up the support payments? (The law generally does not impose this penalty.)

4. What about future increases or decreases in child support because of emergencies, illness, or loss of income?

5. Has the weakening effect of long-term inflation been considered and provided for?

6. Will the children have adequate medical insurance? Who pays for it?

7. Should each parent contribute to a fund providing for orthodontic, dental, or other care that might not be covered by medical insurance?

8. If the children end up in expensive universities, will both parents contribute to their educational costs beyond the age of majority when the legal duty of support terminates?

9. What about fixed long-term protection in the form of a trust, will contract, or other legal instrument?

10. Does life insurance covering the life of the parent who furnishes the major support name the children as beneficiaries?

11. Has any thought been given to joint custody? How would it work?

12. Which parent should have custody on holidays and vacations? For how long? Should they alternate?

13. Should the children have anything to say about the frequency of visitation, the hours, and whether all of the children or one at a time should visit with the noncustodial parent?

14. Should the custodial parent be restrained from moving out of the state or becoming a member of a cult without permission from the noncustodial parent?

15. If one parent seems to be poisoning the children's minds against the other, should either parent have the right to insist on counseling to rectify the problem? If disputes arise, should they be resolved by arbitration rather than through the courts?

16. If the custodial parent dies or is incapacitated, should the noncustodial parent automatically get custody, or should the courts or an able counselor decide who should assume care of the children?

17. Would it be wise to set up a separate conservatorship to manage

the children's assets? (It is possible to make one person the children's guardian and leave the finances in the hands of another individual or a bank.)

18. What if the custodial parent remarries or begins a homemate relationship? Should the children be adopted by the new partner? Should child support be decreased or terminated?

19. Have the tax laws been carefully investigated? Which parent should be entitled to claim the children as dependents? (Some parents split the deductions.) Have the different tax consequences of alimony and child-support payments been considered?

20. Should payments be lowered if a "child" marries, or be reinstated if the "child" gets divorced and is still below the age of majority?

CHILDREN AND CONTRACTS

Can these and other child-related conflicts be averted by prior precautions, such as contractual agreements at the beginning of the marriage or cohabitation? Can a couple prepare a sensible agreement anticipating separation before emotional attachments cloud their parental judgment? For the most part, yes. The courts do, however, reserve the right to alter or reject any agreement that is not in the best interests of the child. Children's rights are clearly affected by their parents' negotiations; if the custodial parent makes too many concessions, the child stands to lose benefits. This is a further argument for separate counsel for children.

One sort of contract that will never stand up in court is an agreement not to bear children; no penalties for breach of this contract will be imposed. Nor can people sign away their duty to support any child they bring into the world, voluntarily or otherwise.

Similarly, a parent's waiver of child-support rights in a divorce or housebreaking is not binding on the child and, in most states, cannot be imposed even upon the parent who originally waived support claims. Arizona, Arkansas, California, Colorado, Florida, Idaho, Illinois, Iowa, Kansas, Missouri, New York, and Ohio hold that an ex-wife may contractually relinquish her right to collect child support from the father, but the child would still have the right to sue for support; the funds could then be dispensed through another agent for the child's upkeep. One of the few clear facts in this whole vast area of law is that a child has the inalienable right to be supported by both natural parents.

Of course there's a catch. In order to exercise that last right fully, a child must be reasonably certain who his/her parents are. Mothers tend to be biologically obvious and reasonably available; fathers, on the other hand, are not so clearly identifiable and sometimes make themselves scarce. Regardless of rights, you cannot collect child support from "father unknown." This brings us to:

LEGITIMACY OF CHILDREN

Under early English common law, a bastard had no rights at all and was doomed to a lifetime of that dismal status unless his parents later married. Most state courts today favor placing children born out of wedlock on an equal footing with the offspring of legalized unions, and several states have abolished the status of illegitimacy, echoing the sentiments of Judge Leon Yankwich, proclaimed in 1928: "There are no illegitimate children—only illegitimate parents."

This is a wonderful idea; unfortunately it does not entirely dispatch the central issue of legitimacy, which is a legal and social convention adopted thousands of years ago to deal with the biological dilemma of paternity. Long ago our forefathers decided that it would be better to allow children to suffer stigma and deprivation than to permit grown men to be humiliated and exploited by taking responsibility for another man's offspring. This is not the only way to look at the issue, but it has been entrenched in our legal system for so long that we can hardly expect to dig our way out overnight with good intentions.

Many important decisions have served to upgrade the status and conditions of "illegitimate" children. Years ago the United States Supreme Court struck down discrimination against illegitimates in state welfare assistance, ruling that all children were equally entitled to such benefits. The High Court has also turned thumbs down on state laws that automatically deny illegitimate children the right to inherit or receive other benefits through the father, saying that such blanket prohibitions violate the equal-protection clause of the Fourteenth Amendment. The Court has, however, upheld certain laws that discriminate between legitimate and illegitimate children, on the grounds that these laws serve a compelling state interest such as promoting family life, establishing a workable method of estate disposition, or guarding against questionable or fraudulent claims.

DISABILITIES OF "ILLEGITIMATE" CHILDREN

The law does hold, with a few highly technical exceptions, that all children are the legitimate heirs of their mothers, and that they are entitled to receive benefits like Social Security through the mother. Complications set in when children born out of wedlock try to exercise similar rights to compensation or inheritance arising from their relationship to the deceased father, unless the father has taken steps to legitimize or clarify his paternity of the child.

A Louisiana statute upheld in 1971 by the United States Supreme Court prohibits illegitimate children from inheriting from the father unless he has no legitimate heirs. (This one, we were told, promotes family life.) In the other states, illegitimate children may inherit if they are named in the father's will, but they remain at a disadvantage if the father dies intestate; they can, of course, be expressly disinherited by will. Generally it is possible, though not easy, for an illegitimate child to qualify as an heir under the laws of intestate succession: once paternity is convincingly demonstrated or proven, the child is entitled to inherit.

To collect government benefits arising out of the death or disability of the father may be more difficult. Under the Social Security Act, legitimate children below the age of majority automatically receive such benefits, while their unlicensed brothers and sisters must prove that they were actually dependent upon the deceased or disabled wage-earning father. Some federal programs further require that the child be living with the father at the time of death, and/or that the child be entitled to inherit from the wage-earning father under the laws of their home state. In addition, it must be shown that the deceased worker was declared by court order to be the child's father, or that the father acknowledged the child to be his, or that he was ordered by a court to provide for the child, or that it was actually proven that the deceased worker was the biological father.

Most of these barriers (except the Louisiana inheritance law) exist not to punish children for the sins of their deceased fathers, but to enable the courts to distinguish between genuine and spurious claimants; nevertheless, the decision-making process seldom gives children the benefit of the doubt.

Whether or not the legal stigma of illegitimacy still exists in local statutes, the child whose paternity is not clearly established before the father's death may be forced to run a gauntlet of prying, trying routines in order to collect any of the benefits to which he/she is theoretically entitled.

YOU DON'T HAVE TO BE MARRIED
TO HAVE LEGITIMATE KIDS!

It will make the state very happy if you choose matrimony as
the means of ensuring your children's legitimacy, and it doesn't
matter if the marriage takes place before or after the babies are
born. A child is automatically legitimated by the marriage of
his/her natural parents, whether the wedding occurs twenty
minutes before or twenty years after the child's birth. If, however, your own happiness depends on remaining legally single,
you can still protect the children.

In most states, children born to homemates can be made
entirely legitimate in one or more simple steps. In some states,
we repeat, all children are held legitimate, and the father may
seal the bargain by placing his name on the child's birth certificate and welcoming it into his home. Even so, the child
may not be quite legitimate enough to satisfy federal standards
and qualify for Social Security or other compensation if the
father dies. Wise parents, therefore, will take whatever extra
precautions may be necessary to make the child's legitimacy
airtight. Some states hold a written declaration of paternity or
an order of filiation sufficient; others may prescribe an uncon-
tested paternity suit in order to obtain a judicial affirmation of
the relationship. Generally the child may also be given the
father's surname if the parents so desire, although at some
courthouses this may require additional wrangling.

An unmarried father can also legitimate his child by going
through the rigmarole of legal adoption, but this is apt to entail
huge and unnecessary complications. Legitimating the child,
incidentally, protects the father's rights as well, ensuring that
the child cannot later be adopted by someone else without his
consent, and giving him status to seek custody should he and
the child's mother split up.

CLARIFICATION OF PATERNITY

If the parents do not choose to go through procedures for
legitimizing the child, the father should at least acknowledge
paternity in a written statement. Even if this doesn't satisfy
local requirements for legitimacy, it will help the child collect
material benefits if the father dies without otherwise providing
for him/her.

The Uniform Parentage Act of 1973 prescribes a presumption of paternity arising out of the marriage of the biological
parents *or* out of their conduct toward the child, especially

when the man has substantially assumed parental responsibilities or acknowledged the child as his. This act, which will make things easier for homemates' and casual mates' offspring, is now law in California, Hawaii, Montana, North Dakota, Washington, and Wyoming, and will probably be spreading south and east in the near future.

SUMMATION ON LEGITIMACY

To condense the many spokes that often do not converge upon the same axle, we submit:

1. The trend is to place all children on an equal legal footing.
2. All natural parents have the legal duty to support their children.
3. At this writing, six states have enacted the Uniform Parentage Act, which sets up certain presumptions establishing paternity; they would apply to homemates who keep up normal parental responsibilities.
4. In the other states there are various ways to establish paternity or legitimacy. Some or all of the following apply in the various states:
    a. A later marriage legitimizes the former illegitimate status of a child born out of wedlock.
    b. A father signs a paternity statement acknowledging that he is the father of the child(ren), or gets an order of filiation in court.
    c. A father welcomes the child into his home and/or assumes responsibility.
    d. A court ruling adjudicates parenthood based upon a voluntary petition or as a result of a contested hearing.

BOOMERANG DIVORCE

Unlike the typical divorce, which occurs as a result of torn heartstrings, there are sometimes merely practical reasons for severing the nuptial knot. Can married couples actually improve their legal position by divorcing and living as homemates? Yes! Increasingly, once-wedlocked couples are enjoying the benefits of "boomerang divorce." *Boomerang* is a term we've adopted for purposely getting divorced, and yet continuing to live together, or to stretch the idea a bit further, getting married after living together and *then* getting divorced, and, naturally, continuing to live together. Why? For good reasons, but we wonder if they are quite good enough.

Before we probe further into this Machiavellian strategy, some legal and ethical questions must be addressed. Even in a no-fault-divorce state, anyone seeking divorce must testify under oath that the marriage is irretrievably broken. In fault states, it must be proved that one spouse is a marital bad guy. Thus, if a party seeks a divorce to avoid the marriage-penalty tax or for some other legal or financial reason, he/she must either state under oath that the marriage is irretrievably broken or prove fault; either case involves possible ethical, not to mention criminal, problems. We have pored over case law in search of justifications in judicial remarks, but it seems clear that the law does not view marriage as a disposable convenience that can be thrown away when no longer advantageous. Even in California, it is perjury to state that your marriage is irremediably broken when in fact the two of you are happy as clams together.

In fault states, one might achieve a boomerang divorce without perjury, but only by descending to the sort of evil behavior that constitutes grounds for divorce. Adultery, extreme cruelty, personal indignities rendering life intolerable—questionable tactics, potentially hazardous to the health of your relationship if not your immortal soul.

Some practitioners of boomerang divorce advocate doing the dirty deed outside the country to circumvent these difficulties, but that leads to other problems. Most foreign divorces are not recognized as valid in American courts. The Bahamas, where nonresidents can get virtually instant divorces, attract boomerang vacationers; the Internal Revenue Service has its eye on such divorces, preparing for battle.

Probably the best route, if not the most convenient, is that old Hollywood standby, the Reno divorce. But we would recommend that you contact your lawyer and request an ethics opinion from the bar association in your state before setting any boomerangs in motion.

Assuming this hurdle is overcome, there are practical reasons for considering a boomerang divorce:

1. **Marriage-penalty tax:** If both spouses are bringing in income, they pay a lot more in taxes than they would if they were single and living together;
2. **Creditor protection:** Do you trust your spouse? If creditors are after your hide, you could give all your assets to your spouse as part of a divorce settlement. This sounds shabby and might be set aside as a sham. But, for example, a doctor who can't obtain enough malpractice insurance or doesn't want to pay the high cost of the premiums, and has no claims pending, might find divorce in this

manner a big protection. Pity the poor doctor if the spouse then runs off with the assets.

3. **Income splitting:** As we already pointed out, income cannot be split between spouses except in a community-property state or unless a business partnership is established. But if the spouses divorce and the higher-earning spouse agrees to pay alimony, he/she gets a tax deduction, which is tantamount to splitting income, and his/her former spouse pays taxes on the "alimony" at a lower tax rate!

4. **Eligibility for financial assistance:** Sometimes the combined incomes of both spouses will make a child ineligible for an educational scholarship or other advantage. If the parents divorce, generally only the separate income of the custodial parent is considered and eligibility may be established.

5. **Social security benefits:** If two spouses are both receiving Supplemental Security Income (increased benefits under the Social Security system to those who are blind, disabled, and/or over sixty-five and possess limited resources), they would receive more as single individuals living together.

6. **Deductions:** A divorce settlement can shift interest payments and other tax-deductible items to the spouse with the higher income, and achieve greater tax savings.

7. **Conflict of interest:** Sometimes being married can result in a conflict of interest according to the law, and trigger a divorce. The *Arizona Daily Star* reported that Buckeye Police Chief Paul Mullenix and his wife, Justice of the Peace Lorraine Vose, are divorcing—partly because their jobs create a conflict of interest. Arizona Attorney General Bob Corbin ruled in a formal opinion, "It is obvious that a police chief's job could well depend in part on the number of arrests made by his department, and of those arrests, the number of convictions that result." Corbin went on to say that the Code of Judicial Conduct requires a judge to disqualify herself in cases where she knows her husband has a financial interest. Query: Will Paul and Lorraine continue to live together after they get divorced, and if so, will that continue to be a conflict of interest?

8. **Hit and run marriage:** Happy homemates may derive substantial benefits from a brief plunge into marriage followed by divorce. Possible advantages:
   a. The move can legitimize their personal contract if they fear it is unenforceable in the state where they reside; divorce agreements are most often enforceable.
   b. They can use the gift tax marital deduction while married.
   c. They can establish alimony to achieve tax savings.
   d. They can acquire life insurance on each other and not worry about the question of insurable interest.
   e. Their children will be legitimated.

The list goes on and on...

Lawyers can be so full of neat solutions that they may seem to overlook the subtle personal qualities of life. The very thought of a boomerang divorce would be traumatic to some people and offensive to others; across the fence, some home-mates despise the idea of getting married for convenience. Each couple should be acquainted with the legal and tax conse-quences of their options, but their choice in the end must be true to their personal vision. Boomerang divorce or hit-and-run marriage may be splendid for couples who don't care whether they're mates or spouses as long as they're together; if marriage is just a piece of paper, why pay good money for it? But when two people's love is deepened by the solemnity of marriage or the integrity of a freely created union, they have a treasure in the house; it should not be sold for a mess of pottage.

FUTURE AFTER DIVORCE OR HOUSEBREAKING

Still, not every love affair is fated to live happily ever after. For the casualties, the wounds can be deep. Learn from the breakup, but don't shy away from lasting relationships. Plan well and plan legally.

During or after divorce or housebreaking, women in par-ticular may have a difficult time getting credit, buying insur-ance, getting a job, buying a home, etc. If a housewife is relying upon alimony and/or child-support payments for in-come, it is difficult for her to establish bank credit. Unless the bank is sure that the former husband will continue to support her, it will be reluctant to rely upon the ex-housewife's ability to repay, since she will probably need time to reestablish her earning powers. A cooperative ex-husband may be able to help reassure the moneylenders. If everyone is being nasty, though, it may help to learn to recite whole paragraphs of the Federal Equal Credit Opportunity Act.

Here are some survival pointers for women about to be divorced:

1. Talk to a banker as soon as possible and find out what should be done to establish bank credit. Perhaps certain protections can be built into a property settlement agreement or a divorce decree.
2. While the divorce is pending, find out what can be done to get credit without the necessity of a husband's signature. It may be wise to open new charge accounts before the divorce is final. If you will have to get a job, learn early about the attitudes of em-ployers. Often, prospective employers have to be convinced that a woman, particularly one who has not worked in a while, is

emotionally capable of taking on employment while maintaining negotiations and suffering the trauma associated with divorce.

3. Read applicable state laws. Find out about the rights of women, where discrimination may occur, and what can be done to fight back.

4. Find out about income-tax laws as they apply to a head-of-household, if you have children, or to a newly divorced individual, so that you can prepare a budget based on after-tax dollars.

5. Find out about the purchase of a home and the requirements of VA, FHA, or conventional mortgage lenders.

6. If you have been covered by a family medical insurance policy, make sure that you and/or the children get a new policy after the divorce. Most insurance companies will stick by you, but if the policy was a small group arrangement at your spouse's workplace, you may have to seek elsewhere.

Housebreaking is not necessarily any easier than divorce. A University of Colorado psychologist's research indicated that breaking up after living together is almost as traumatic as getting a divorce. Thirty-four-year-old Kitty Mika, a CU graduate student who earned her Ph.D in Clinical Psychology, interviewed fifty Boulder County people for a study on cohabitation. All were over twenty-one and had recently broken up with their live-in lovers. She found that the stress they experience is similar to that experienced by married kpeople going through a divorce.[14]

Many people tend to underestimate the complications involved in letting go of a homemate or even a casual mate. Perhaps there is really no such thing as a no-strings relationship. Adjustments must be made to develop a new life after divorce or housebreaking, and most people do not perform well for some time. Eventually, though, you will bounce back and be ready to try again. And when love beckons again, we wish you a long journey down lovers' lane.

PART III: STATE-BY-STATE GUIDES

2

ALABAMA

I. MARRIAGE

A. Legality:
1. Age: 18; under 18, need consent of parents and bond of $200, unless previously married; under 14, not permitted.
2. License: Required; expires 30 days after issuance.
3. Medical examination: Certificate of freedom from venereal disease required.
4. Waiting period: None.

B. Common-law marriages: Recognized

C. Out-of-state marriages: Presumably valid if valid in state where entered into, but there is no statutory provision for their recognition

D. Adultery: Illegal only if combined with cohabitation; fine and/or sentence.

E. Property: Separate.

F. Partnerships: A partnership agreement between spouses is probably enforceable as long as there is a valid business purpose.

II. COHABITATION

A. Legality:
1. Cohabitation: Illegal; fine and/or sentence.
2. Fornication: Illegal; fine and/or sentence.

B. Common-law marriage:
1. Since common-law marriages are recognized, cohabitation can result in marriage.
2. Continued cohabitation after the removal of the reason for an invalid marriage is a common-law marriage.

C. Putative marriage: Courts will adjust the property rights of couples who mistakenly believe in the validity of an invalid marriage.

165

D. Property: Express agreements between mates would probably be enforced.

E. Partnerships: A partnership agreement between mates is probably enforceable as long as there is a valid business purpose and the agreement is not primarily based on sex.

III. DIVORCE (DISSOLUTION) AND LEGAL SEPARATION

A. Divorce or dissolution (grounds):
1. Incapacity at time of marriage.
2. Adultery.
3. Physical violence.
4. Abandonment for one year.
5. Imprisonment for two years under sentence of 7 years or more.
6. Crime against nature before or after marriage.
7. Habitual drunkenness or habitual use of drugs.
8. Five successive years in insane asylum or incurable insanity.
9. Irretrievable breakdown of marriage (no-fault).
10. Final decree of legal separation in effect for more than two years (no-fault).
11. Complete incompatibility of temperament (no fault).
12. For husband: wife's pregnancy by another man at time of marriage without husband's knowledge.
13. For wife: nonsupport for two years.

B. Legal separation (grounds):
1. Cruelty: Any grounds for divorce.

C. Residency requirements:
1. One spouse must be domiciled in state.
2. Spouse filing for divorce must have resided in state for 6 months if other spouse is a nonresident.
3. A wife seeking divorce for nonsupport must have resided in the state for two years and husband and wife must have been separated for two years.

D. Remarriage:
1. Each must wait at least 60 days after divorce.
2. Guilty party may be expressly forbidden by the court to remarry in which case he/she may not marry without the consent of the court.

E. Court orders after filing for divorce and before divorce is final:
1. Court costs and attorneys' fees.
2. Allowance for support during divorce.
3. Temporary child support and custody.

F. Alimony:
    1. Granted to wife when she has no separate estate or if estate is insufficient for her maintenance.
    2. If divorce is granted to wife for misconduct of husband, alimony may be granted to wife.
    3. May be terminated on proof that wife has remarried or is cohabiting with member of opposite sex.
    4. The U.S. Supreme Court has recently ruled that the Alabama scheme imposing alimony only on husbands violates equal-protection laws.

G. Child support and custody:
    1. No specific statute on support; support is probably ordered when custody is decided.
    2. Custody granted at discretion of court and in best interests of child.

H. Property division by court in absence of written or oral agreement:
    1. Separation agreements dividing property will not necessarily be followed by the court.
    2. Division of joint property is within the discretion of the court; it must be fair, but need not be equal.
    3. Separate property retained by owner.
    4. No division of property is required; alimony may be given instead of property division.

IV. TERMINATION OF COHABITATION

A. Court jurisdiction: No judicial control; voluntary parting.

B. Court orders: A court may make orders for child support and custody similar to those made in a divorce, once paternity is established.

C. Property division (decisions in other states suggest the following possibilities):
    1. Courts could infer partnership agreements as a means of dividing property and money.
    2. Courts could order return or division of property and money if there had been an implied or express agreement.
    3. Courts could order return of property to rightful owner or grant an interest in property or an award of money to a mate to the extent of his/her contribution toward its purchase.
    4. Since cohabitation is illegal, courts would probably not honor an agreement if relationship was primarily sexual. However, even when sex is a part of the agreement, it will be honored if the primary purpose of the

agreement is to protect property rights and recovery might be had for performing household duties as well as for direct financial contributions, so long as the implied or express agreement was not primarily based on sex.

D. Putative marriage: Courts will adjust the property rights of a putative spouse.

E. Palimony: There have been no court decisions to indicate that rehabilitative alimony, temporary, or permanent alimony would be awarded to a mate, and such an award seems unlikely.

V. SPECIFIC SUBJECTS (No written agreements, except for A,E,I.)
Reference to "BOTH" means married and unmarried couples.

A. Prenuptial or precohabitation agreements:
MARRIED: Valid.
UNMARRIED: Probably valid if sex is not the basis of the agreement and if meant for protection of property interests.
BOTH: Agreements must be made without duress and with full disclosure of assets and other important information.

B. Property:
BOTH: All property is separate property of acquiring spouse or mate.

C. Liability of separate property for other spouse's or mate's debts:
BOTH: No liability.

D. Management and control of separate property of each:
BOTH: Each controls own property.

E. Contracts made during marriage or cohabitation settling property rights:
MARRIED: Separation agreements are valid, but the court is not bound by them.
UNMARRIED: Probably enforceable if based on earnings, property, etc. rather than on sex.

F. What can be willed?
MARRIED: Each spouse's separate property, subject to dower rights (see subject L). Widow may disregard will and receive her dower and intestate share of personal property instead. Widower may not elect to disregard wife's will.
UNMARRIED: Each mate's separate property.

G. Automatic protection for surviving spouse or mate:
MARRIED: Survivor has dower or curtesy rights, and widow

and/or minor children have $6,000 homestead exemption for life of widow or for minority years of children. (See subjects K, L, M.)

UNMARRIED: No protection for surviving mate. Minor children receive homestead exemption until eighteen and support allowance until estate is distributed if they are entitled to inherit (see subject H).

H.   If no will:

MARRIED: 1) Real estate: Surviving spouse receives dower or curtesy share; surviving children of deceased spouse or their descendants receive remainder. Surviving spouse receives all if there are no surviving children, their descendants, or other relatives. 2) Personal property: All, one-half, or one-third to widow, depending on number of surviving children; one-half to widower, regardless of number of survivors.

UNMARRIED: Surviving mate receives nothing. Illegitimate children inherit from mother; may inherit from father if he recognizes them as his children.

I.   Contracts:

BOTH: Each may contract with anyone, including each other.

J.   Lawsuits:

BOTH: Each may sue or be sued separately unless both involved.

K.   Homestead law:

BOTH: Homestead of a resident exempt up to $2,000 over liens. Homestead owner must file a sworn declaration describing property in office of probate judge of county where property is located.

L.   Dower:

MARRIED: If there are no surviving descendants, widow has one-half interest when estate is solvent; one-third when insolvent; if there are surviving descendants, widow has one-third interest, whether estate is solvent or not.

M.   Curtesy:

MARRIED: If wife dies without a will, widower has lifetime interest in wife's separate real estate.

N.   Civil suits by spouses or mates against each other:

BOTH: Permitted.

O.   Legitimacy:

MARRIED: Children born during marriage are legitimate.

UNMARRIED: Illegitimate are children of mother; father may

legitimize children by written declaration to make them capable of inheritance.

BOTH: Marriage of mother and father makes children legitimate if father also recognizes children as his.

P.   Adoption:

MARRIED: Spouses may adopt jointly.

UNMARRIED: Any proper adult may adopt.

BOTH: Investigation required to determine whether parents are financially able and morally fit.

Q.   Division of property upon termination of relationship:

MARRIED: Division of joint property must be fair but not necessarily equal; each spouse keeps his/her separate property.

UNMARRIED: Implied or express contracts, value of services, or unfair economic gain may create rights to property.

VI. RECENT EVENTS, TRENDS, AND CONCLUSIONS

A.   When real property is sold during the administration of a deceased husband's estate, the dower interest may be sold with the widow's consent, and the fair value of the dower may be fixed by the court (not exceeding ⅓ of purchase price) and paid to her in cash. In other situations, the widow can petition the court to ascertain the present value of her dower interest and receive payment in cash.

B.   A law denying a wife the power to sell her real estate without her husband's consent signature was held unconstitutional.

C.   The U.S. Supreme Court has recently ruled that imposing alimony on husbands but not on wives is unconstitutional.

D.   Common-law marriages are recognized, and courts have been willing to adjust property rights in a putative marriage. Although cohabitation and adultery are illegal, courts have been willing to recognize rights of a mate when there was an agreement, or when a mate paid part of the purchase price. Perhaps some of the theories of the *Marvin* case would be followed.

ALASKA

I. MARRIAGE

A.   Legality:
1. Age: 18; between 16 and 18 need parents' consent; between 14 and 18, may get court approval with parents' consent or if parental nonconsent is unreasonable.
2. License: required.
3. Medical examination: Required, plus blood test not more than 30 days before issuance of license.
4. Waiting period: 3 days between application for license and issuance.

B.   Common-law marriages: Not recognized.

C.   Out-of-state marriages: Probably valid if valid where entered into.

D.   Adultery: Not a crime.

E.   Property: Separate.

F.   Partnerships: A partnership agreement between spouses is probably enforceable as long as there is a valid business purpose.

II. COHABITATION

A.   Legality:
1. Cohabitation: Not a crime.
2. Fornication: Not a crime.
3. All private, nonviolent sexual acts between consenting adults are legal.

B.   Common-law marriage: Not recognized.

C.   Putative marriage: Recognized for the purposes of compensation for services and pro rata adjustments for specific contributions to an asset.

D.   Property: Courts will not adjust property rights of mates who do not believe they are married, but if the precise amount of the contribution of one mate to the purchase of an asset is known, a pro rata division could be made.

E.   Partnerships: A partnership agreement between mates is

probably enforceable as long as there is a valid business purpose and the agreement is not primarily based on sex.

III. DIVORCE (DISSOLUTION) AND LEGAL SEPARATION

A. Divorce or dissolution (grounds):
1. Failure to consummate at time of marriage and continuing at time of suit.
2. Adultery.
3. Conviction of felony.
4. Wilful desertion for one year.
5. Cruelty impairing health or endangering life or personal indignities making life burdensome.
6. Incompatibility of temperament (may be based on fault).
7. Habitual and gross drunkenness contracted after marriage and continuing for one year before commencement of action.
8. Incurable mental illness when spouse confined to institution for 18 months proceeding suit.
9. Addiction after marriage to habitual use of drugs.
10. Incompatibility (no fault) when other spouse's whereabouts unknown and spouse can't be served personally in or out of state.
11. Incompatibility (no fault) if both spouses have mutually agreed on custody, support, property rights, and payment of debts.

B. Legal separation (grounds): Not obtainable.

C. Residency requirements: None. For dissolution when spouses file together (A-11 above) both must consent to jurisdiction of court.

D. Remarriage: Possible immediately after divorce is final.

E. Court orders after filing for divorce and before divorce is final:
1. Court costs and attorneys' fees to either spouse.
2. Care, custody, and maintenance of minor children.
3. Freedom of one spouse from control of the other.

F. Alimony:
1. Granted to either spouse as needed.
2. Marital misconduct is not considered.

G. Child support and custody:
1. Support imposed by court on either spouse or both.
2. Neither parent is given preference for custody; court considers best interests of child.

H.   Property division by court in absence of written or oral agreement:
1. Court divides all separate property, including joint property, as it deems fair.

IV. TERMINATION OF COHABITATION

A.   Court jurisdiction: No judicial control; voluntary parting.

B.   Court orders: A court may make orders for child support and custody similar to those made in a divorce, once paternity is established.

C.   Property division (in spite of the fact that courts in the past have refused to adjust the property rights of mates upon termination of cohabitation, recent decisions in other states suggest the following possibilities):
1. Courts could infer partnership agreements as a means of dividing property and money.
2. Courts could order return or division of property and money if there had been an implied or express agreement.
3. Courts could order return of property to rightful owner or grant an interest in property or an award of money to a mate to the extent of his/her contribution toward purchase of property.
4. Since living together is not illegal, recovery might be had for performing household duties as well as for direct financial contributions, so long as the implied or express agreement was not primarily based on sex.

D.   Putative marriage:
1. A putative wife may receive compensation for services rendered during an invalid marriage.
2. Pro rata adjustments are made for the contribution of putative spouses to the purchase of property.

E.   Palimony: There have been no court decisions to indicate that rehabilitative alimony, temporary, or permanent alimony would be awarded, but such an award is a possibility.

V. SPECIFIC SUBJECTS (No written agreements, except for A,E,I.)
Reference to "BOTH" means married and unmarried couples.

A.   Prenuptial or precohabitation agreements:
MARRIED: Probably valid.
UNMARRIED: May be valid if sex is not the primary basis of the agreement and if meant for protection of property interests.

BOTH: Agreements must be made without duress and with full disclosure of assets and other important information.

B. Property:
BOTH: All property is separate property of acquiring spouse or mate.

C. Liability of separate property for other spouse's or mate's debts:
BOTH: No liability.

D. Management and control of separate property:
BOTH: Each controls own separate property.
MARRIED: Both spouses must sign to sell family home.

E. Contracts made during marriage or cohabitation settling property rights:
MARRIED: Valid.
UNMARRIED: May be enforceable if based on earnings, property, etc., rather than on sex.
BOTH: Agreements must be made without duress and with full disclosure of assets and other important information.

F. What can be willed?
BOTH: Each spouse's or mate's separate property.

G. Automatic protection for surviving spouse or mate:
MARRIED: Homestead allowance is $12,000; exempt personal property of $3,500 over liens; family allowance in a reasonable amount.
UNMARRIED: No protection for surviving mate. Minor children receive allowances and exemptions. Illegitimate minor children would also receive them if entitled to inherit (see Subject H).

H. If no will:
MARRIED: Surviving spouse shares with surviving children or parents of deceased; if no children or parents survive, surviving spouse receives everything.
UNMARRIED: Surviving mate receives nothing. Children inherit from mother; from father if paternity is acknowledged or decreed by court.

I. Contracts:
BOTH: Each may contract with anyone, including each other.

J. Lawsuits:
BOTH: Each may sue or be sued separately unless both are involved.

K. Homestead law:
BOTH: Exemptions up to $19,000 over liens, including mort-

gages for family home. May be claimed by owner or wife of owner. No filing necessary, but notice must be given to officer who levies upon property that it is claimed as homestead.

L.   Civil suits by spouses or mates against each other:
      BOTH: Permitted.

M.   Legitimacy:
      MARRIED: Children born during marriage are presumed legitimate. Subsequent marriage of parents legitimizes.
      UNMARRIED: Children may be legitimized by marriage of parents, by acknowledgment of paternity, or by court decree of paternity.

N.   Adoption:
      BOTH: Both spouses or either may adopt. A single adult mate may adopt. Any person may be adopted. Investigation of home required.

O.   Division of property upon termination of relationship:
      MARRIED: Court may divide separate property, including joint property, as it deems fair. Marital misconduct not considered.
      UNMARRIED: Implied or express contracts, value of services, or unfair economic gain may create rights to property.

VI. RECENT EVENTS, TRENDS, AND CONCLUSIONS

A.   A divorced wife was given a share of her husband's vested federal civil service retirement benefits, although the husband was not yet retired or receiving his pension. Property division to provide for the needs of a dependent spouse rather than alimony is encouraged by the courts.

B.   Military retirement pay, unlike civil service retirement benefits, is not subject to division on divorce.

C.   It appears that the court will not adjust the property rights of mates, but may divide on a pro rata basis when the precise amount of a mate's contribution is known. In a 1976 case, two mates lived together for eight years prior to an invalid marriage. The court, in adjusting the property rights of the couple, noted that it would be wrong to go back to the period of cohabitation to calculate the putative wife's contributions to property acquired, but that her contribution during the invalid marriage should be considered in dividing the property. However, since cohabitation and fornication have recently been decriminalized, a liberalizing trend has occurred in other areas (e.g., alimony, child custody, discrimination), and the court has shown an interest in individual choice and divergent lifestyles, some or all of the theories of the *Marvin* case might be followed.

ARIZONA

I. MARRIAGE

A. Legality:
1. Age: 18; under 18, need parents' or guardian's consent; under 16, approval of court.
2. License: Required.
3. Medical examination: Physician's certificate required showing blood test for syphilis negative not more than 30 days before issuance of license.
4. Waiting period: None.

B. Common-law marriages: Invalid; will recognize if valid in another state where entered into.

C. Out-of-state marriages: Valid if valid in state where entered into.

D. Adultery: Illegal (misdemeanor); fine or sentence.

E. Property: Community.

F. Partnerships: A partnership agreement between spouses is probably enforceable as long as there is a valid business purpose.

II. COHABITATION

A. Legality:
1. Cohabitation: Illegal (misdemeanor); fine or sentence.
2. Fornication: Not a crime.

B. Common-law marriage: Not recognized.

C. Putative marriage: Not recognized, but the courts are willing to recognize property and legal rights acquired in a good-faith relationship.

D. Property:
   1. Mates who agree to pool earnings and to share property acquired during cohabitation are entitled to judicial enforcement of such agreements.
   2. D-1 does not apply if sexual relations are a part of the agreement.

E. Partnerships: A partnership agreement between mates is probably enforceable as long as there is a valid business purpose and the agreement is not primarily based on sex.

III. DIVORCE (DISSOLUTION) AND LEGAL SEPARATION

A. Divorce or dissolution (grounds): Marriage irretrievably broken (no-fault).

B. Legal separation (grounds): Same as for divorce.

C. Residency requirements:
   1. Divorce: 90 days by either spouse before legal action is filed.
   2. Legal separation: Either spouse living in state at time legal action is filed.

D. Remarriage: Possible any time after divorce is final.

E. Court orders after filing for divorce and before divorce is final:
   1. Restraining orders preventing selling of property, removal of children, disturbing peace of a spouse or children, excluding spouse from family home.
   2. Orders granting temporary alimony, temporary child support, court costs, and attorneys' fees.

F. Alimony:
   1. Granted to either spouse.
   2. Considerations:
      a. Health of each spouse.
      b. Length of marriage.
      c. Standard of living.
      d. Education and skills.
      e. Financial capability of each spouse.

G. Child support and custody:
   1. Support can be imposed by court on either parent, based on earning power of supporting parent.

       2. Custody granted according to best interests of children, without preference for either parent.

H.   Property division by court in absence of written or oral agreement:
       1. Court divides in a substantially equal manner all the community property, quasi-community property, and property held in tenancy in common and in joint tenancy with right of survivorship acquired after 1973.
       2. Separate property is not divided, but is retained by the owner.
       3. Marital misconduct is not considered in property division unless the misconduct is economic (dissipation of community funds, for example).

IV. TERMINATION OF COHABITATION

A.   Court jurisdiction: No judicial control; voluntary parting.

B.   Court orders: A court may make orders for child support and custody similar to those made in a divorce, once paternity is established.

C.   Property division (decisions in other states suggest the following possibilities):
       1. Courts could infer partnership agreements as a means of dividing property and money.
       2. Courts could order return or division of property and money if there had been an implied or express agreement. Previously, express agreements between mates had been required.
       3. Courts could order return of property to the rightful owner or grant an interest in property or an award of money to a mate to the extent of his/her contribution toward purchase of property.
       4. Since cohabitation is illegal in Arizona, the court would probably not honor an agreement if the relationship was primarily sexual in nature; thus it would be difficult to collect for performing household duties when no direct financial contribution can be shown.

D.   Putative marriage: Courts are willing to recognize property and legal rights acquired in a good-faith relationship.

E.   Palimony: Court decisions seem to indicate that a mate would not be entitled to receive rehabilitative alimony, or temporary or permanent alimony.

V. SPECIFIC SUBJECTS (No written agreements, except for A,G,K.)
Reference to "BOTH" means married and unmarried couples.

A.   Prenuptial or precohabitation agreements:
     UNMARRIED: Probably valid if sex is not part of the agreement and if meant for the protection of property interests.
     BOTH: Valid if made without duress and with full disclosure of assets and other important information.

B.   Separate Property:
     MARRIED: Property owned by either spouse before marriage or acquired after marriage by gift or inheritance; property acquired after marriage using separate property.
     UNMARRIED: All property is separate property of acquiring mate.

C.   Community property:
     MARRIED: Property acquired during marriage, including earnings, unless classified as separate (see subject B) property. Spouses can agree to give up right in community property either before or during marriage.

D.   Liability of community property for debts contracted by one spouse:
     MARRIED: If it is a community debt (one benefiting the community even if contracted for by only one spouse), community property is liable.

E.   Management and control of separate property of each:
     BOTH: Each controls own property. Both spouses must sign conveyance, lease, or encumbrance of family home.

F.   Management and control of community property:
     MARRIED: Either spouse may buy, sell, or transfer, except for real property, which requires signatures of both spouses.

G.   Contracts made during marriage or cohabitation settling property rights:
     MARRIED: Usually recognized and enforced by courts.
     UNMARRIED: Probably enforceable if based on earnings, property, etc., rather than on sex.
     BOTH: Must be made without duress and with full disclosure of assets and other important information.

H.   What can be willed?
     MARRIED: Each spouse's half of the community property.
     BOTH: Each spouse's or mate's entire separate property.

I.   Automatic protection for surviving spouse or mate:
     MARRIED: Surviving spouse retains his/her half of the community property and receives allowances totaling $15,500 free of creditors' claims.
     UNMARRIED: No protection for surviving mate. Same allowances to minor children.

J. If no will:
MARRIED: Surviving spouse receives everything if there are
no children of deceased from another marriage. If there
are children from another marriage, surviving spouse
receives one-half of separate property. Children of former marriage receive the other half of separate property
and all of deceased spouse's one-half community-property interest.
UNMARRIED: Surviving mate receives nothing. Children inherit from deceased parents whether they are married
or not.

K. Contracts:
BOTH: Each may contract with anyone, including each
other.

L. Lawsuits:
MARRIED: If subject of the suit is a community contract or
a wrong that concerned the community, both spouses
must sue or be sued and are liable.
BOTH: Each can sue and be sued separately unless both
involved.

M. Homestead law:
BOTH: Resident head of family has $20,000 in value in fam-
ily home above liens, including mortgages, exempt from
creditors. Must be claimed by sworn statement filed in
office of county recorder in county where property is
located.

N. Civil suits by spouses or mates against each other:
MARRIED: Not permitted.
UNMARRIED: Permitted.

O. Legitimacy:
BOTH: All children are legitimate children of natural parents.

P. Adoption:
UNMARRIED: Both mates living together cannot adopt.
BOTH: Either spouse or mate may adopt unless mates are
living together.

Q. Division of property upon termination of relationship:
MARRIED: If spouses are unable to agree on division, court
divides all community property, quasi-community property, and property held in joint tenancy or in tenancy
in common in substantially equal shares. Separate property not divided.
UNMARRIED: Implied or express contracts, value of services,
and unfair economic gain may create rights to property.

VI. RECENT EVENTS, TRENDS, AND CONCLUSIONS:

A.   Prospective spouses may contract before marriage that property and rights which would otherwise be community will be separate. Such an agreement is also possible during marriage.

B.   A husband's or wife's earnings during a period of legal separation are community property.

C.   A personal injury recovery by the injured spouse for injuries suffered during marriage is the separate property of the injured spouse.

D.   A partnership interest owned by a husband and wife is a community-property interest.

E.   Retirement pay of one spouse earned during marriage is community property.

F.   The concept of quasi-community property (property acquired in another state which would have been community property if it had been acquired in Arizona) applies to division of property upon divorce but not to distribution of property upon the death of one spouse. This means that upon divorce the separate property of either spouse acquired out of state may be divided as community property if it is the kind of property that would be community property if it had been acquired in Arizona. The Supreme Court recently decided that this applies only to property acquired after 1973. Before 1973 it would be classified according to state law where spouses resided at time of acquisition.

G.   Early cases have not granted property division when there was nothing more than the sexual relationship on which to base an agreement, but relief has been granted when a partnership agreement or joint venture could be found, so long as sex was not a part of the agreement. Although cohabitation is illegal, it is unclear whether some or all of the theories of the *Marvin* case would be followed, but the courts will honor express agreements.

ARKANSAS

I. MARRIAGE

    A.   Legality:
        1. Age: Male, 17; female, 16; under 18, need consent of parent or guardian.
        2. License: Required; issued 3 days after application.
        3. Medical examination: Physician's certificate and blood test required.
        4. Waiting period: 3 days between application for license and issuance.

    B.   Common-law marriages: Invalid; will recognize if valid in state where entered into.

    C.   Out-of-state marriages: Valid if valid where entered into.

    D.   Adultery: Not a crime.

    E.   Property: Separate.

    F.   Partnerships: A partnership agreement between spouses is probably enforceable as long as there is a valid business purpose.

II. COHABITATION

    A.   Legality:
        1. Cohabitation: Not a crime unless it is seen as "public sexual indecency." Then it is a misdemeanor.
        2. Fornication: Not a crime.

    B.   Common-law marriage: Not recognized.

    C.   Putative marriage: Rights of putative spouses have not been generally recognized.

    D.   Property:
        1. Generally the courts refuse to honor an agreement between mates if any part of the agreement is based on sex.
        2. However, Courts have honored a business partnership agreement between mates or a separation agreement providing that the male would retain property accumulated and pay the female mate an allowance during her life.

E.   Partnerships: A partnership agreement between mates is probably enforceable as long as there is a valid business purpose and the agreement is not primarily based on sex.

III. DIVORCE (DISSOLUTION) AND LEGAL SEPARATION

A.   Divorce or dissolution (grounds):
   1. Impotency.
   2. Desertion for one year.
   3. Bigamy.
   4. Felony conviction.
   5. Habitual drunkenness for one year.
   6. Cruel and barbarous treatment.
   7. Indignities to person of innocent party.
   8. Living separate and apart for three years (no fault).
   9. Nonsupport.

B.   Legal separation (grounds): Not obtainable.

C.   Residency requirements: At least one spouse must have resided in state for 60 days before legal action is filed and for three months before decree is obtained.

D.   Remarriage: Possible immediately after divorce is final.

E.   Court orders after filing for divorce and before divorce is final: Temporary alimony, court costs, and attorneys' fees to either spouse.

F.   Alimony:
   1. Court may order alimony as well as attorney's fees for enforcement of alimony.
   2. Court may enforce decree by sequestration of property or securities.
   3. Later cohabitation of the recipient does not necessarily terminate alimony but it may be considered as one reason for termination.
   4. Marital misconduct may be considered.

G.   Child support and custody:
   1. Court may order child support to either parent and may require bond for compliance. Attorneys' fees are allowed for enforcement. Court may enforce decree by sequestration of property or securities.
   2. Mother preferred for custody of young children unless contrary to best interests of children. Otherwise parents have equal rights to custody.

H.   Property division by court in absence of written or oral agreement:

1. Each spouse retains separate property either spouse brought to the marriage.
2. Court has power to distribute separate or joint property acquired during marriage equally or as it deems fair. Estate by entirety is dissolved.
3. Marital misconduct may be considered even under no-fault ground.

IV. TERMINATION OF COHABITATION

A. Court jurisdiction: No judicial control; voluntary parting.

B. Court orders: A court may make orders for child support and custody similar to those made in a divorce, once paternity is established.

C. Property division (decisions in other states suggest the following possibilities):
   1. Courts would probably honor partnership agreements and could infer them as a means of dividing property and money.
   2. Courts could order return or division of property and money if there had been an implied or express agreement.
   3. Courts could order return of property to rightful owner or grant an interest in property or an award of money to a mate to the extent of his/her contribution toward purchase of property.
   4. Courts would probably not honor an agreement if the contractual relationship was primarily sexual; thus it might be difficult to collect for performing household duties when no direct financial contribution can be shown.

D. Putative marriage: The courts have been reluctant to divide the property of mates, even with a good-faith belief in marriage, except as under II.D.2. above.

E. Palimony: There have been no court decisions to indicate that rehabilitative alimony or temporary or permanent alimony would be awarded to a mate, but such an award is a possibility.

V. SPECIFIC SUBJECTS (No written agreements, except for A,E,I.)
Reference to "BOTH" means married and unmarried couples.

A. Prenuptial or precohabitation agreements:
   MARRIED: Valid if acknowledged before a court of record in state where made.
   UNMARRIED: Probably valid if sex is not the basis of the

agreement and if meant for the protection of property interests.

BOTH: Agreement must be made without duress and with full disclosure of assets and other important information.

B. Property:

BOTH: All property is separate property of acquiring spouse or mate.

C. Liability of separate property for other spouse's or mate's debts:

BOTH: No liability.

D. Management and control of separate property of each:

BOTH: Each controls own separate property.

MARRIED: Wife may not claim her separate property if she allows husband to use it as his own. Wife may defeat husband's curtesy interest by conveying her separate property, but husband may not convey wife's dower interest without her consent.

E. Contracts made during marriage or cohabitation settling property rights:

MARRIED: Valid if acknowledged before court of record in state where made.

UNMARRIED: Probably enforceable if based on earnings, property, etc., rather than on sex.

BOTH: Agreement must be made without duress and with full disclosure of assets and other important information.

F. What can be willed?

MARRIED: Each spouse's separate property, subject to dower rights. Wife may defeat husband's curtesy by will.

UNMARRIED: Each mate's separate property.

G. Automatic protection for surviving spouse or mate:

MARRIED: Surviving spouse has dower or curtesy interest, homestead rights, household furnishings, and support up to $500 for two months. Widow receives property worth $2,000 before heirs or $1,000 before creditors.

UNMARRIED: No protection for surviving mate. Minor children have homestead rights and allowances; illegitimate minor children probably would not have them on father's death.

H. If no will:

MARRIED: Surviving spouse receives dower or curtesy, plus homestead rights and allowance, plus entire estate if there are no surviving children or their descendants. If married less than three years, surviving spouse receives only 50 percent of remainder after dower or curtesy and other allowances.

UNMARRIED: Surviving mate receives nothing. Illegitimate children inherit from mother; inherit from father only if father marries mother and acknowledges children.

I. Contracts:
BOTH: Each may contract with anyone, including each other.

J. Lawsuits:
BOTH: Each may sue and be sued separately unless both involved.

K. Homestead law:
MARRIED: Either spouse or head of family receives exemption not exceeding $2,500 in value in family house over liens, including improvements.
UNMARRIED: Available to head of family whether married or not.
BOTH: No filing necessary; may be claimed at any time before forced sale.

L. Dower:
MARRIED: Widow has life interest in one-third of all real and personal property of husband. If husband dies without descendants, dower is one-half of all real and personal property as against his relatives and one-third as against creditors.
UNMARRIED: Not available.

M. Civil suits by spouses or mates against each other:
BOTH: Each may sue other.

N. Legitimacy:
MARRIED: Children born during marriage are presumed legitimate.
BOTH: Children born before marriage may be legitimized only by subsequent marriage of parents and recognition by father.

O. Adoption:
MARRIED: Both spouses must sign for adoption.
UNMARRIED: Unmarried person twenty-one or older may adopt.

P. Division of property upon termination of relationship:
MARRIED: Each retains separate property brought into marriage. All marital property is divided equally or as court deems fair. Estates by the entirety are dissolved and divided. Fault may be considered.
UNMARRIED: Implied or express contracts, value of services, or unfair economic gain may create rights to property.

VI. RECENT EVENTS, TRENDS, AND CONCLUSIONS

A.   A husband, on divorce, was granted one-half of the contributions and improvements he put into the family home which was jointly owned by his wife and her mother, even though generally a husband's improvements to his wife's property are presumed to be a gift. In this case, the home had been purchased with the proceeds from the sale of a home owned jointly by husband and wife.

B.   An adoption statute was held unconstitutional because of the vagueness of the term "a proper home." Under the statute a guardian could be appointed who had authority to consent to a child's adoption if the child's parents were "unable to provide a proper home for the child." "A proper home" does not provide sufficient guidelines when a procedure as important as the termination of parental rights is involved.

C.   The courts have generally not recognized putative marriages and have been reluctant to divide property of putative spouses. However, since cohabitation is not illegal, there is the possibility that courts would honor express oral or written agreements between mates, especially if the agreement concerned business or property. It is doubtful that many of the theories of the *Marvin* case would be followed.

CALIFORNIA

I. MARRIAGE

A.   Legality:
1. Age: Not fixed; need consent of parent or guardian if under 18.
2. License: Required; license expires 90 days after issuance.
3. Medical examination: Physician's certificate of freedom from syphilis required within 30 days prior to issuance of license.
4. Waiting period: None.

B.   Common-law marriages: Invalid; out-of-state common-law marriages recognized if valid in state where entered into.

C.   Out-of-state marriages: Valid if valid where entered into.

D.   Adultery: Not a crime.

E.   Property: Community.

F.   Partnerships: A partnership agreement between spouses is probably enforceable as long as there is a valid business purpose.

II. COHABITATION

A.   Legality:
  1.   Cohabitation: Not a crime.
  2.   Fornication: Not a crime.
  3.   All private, nonviolent sexual acts between consenting adults are legal.

B.   Common-law marriage: Not recognized.

C.   Putative marriage: Recognized by the courts if at least one mate believed the marriage was valid.

D.   Property: Property agreements between mates based on joint economic reasons rather than sex are enforceable.

E.   Partnerships: A partnership agreement between mates is probably enforceable as long as there is a valid business purpose and the agreement is not primarily based on sex.

III. DIVORCE (DISSOLUTION) AND LEGAL SEPARATION

A.   Divorce or dissolution (grounds):
  1.   Irreconcilable differences causing irremediable breakdown of marriage (no fault).
  2.   Incurable insanity.

B.   Legal separation (grounds): Same grounds as for divorce.

C.   Residency requirements: Either spouse a resident of state for 6 months and of county for 3 months before filing for divorce.

D.   Remarriage: Possible immediately after divorce is final.

E.   Court orders after filing for divorce and before divorce is final:
  1.   Either spouse may be ordered to pay temporary support and maintenance of the other spouse or children, reasonable court costs and attorneys' fees.

  2. Orders for or against transfers of property, molestation, exclusion from family dwelling, temporary child custody are permissible.

F. Alimony:
  1. Court may order either spouse to pay.
  2. Considerations:
     a. Duration of marriage.
     b. Best interests of children.
     c. Other relevant circumstances.
  3. Terminates upon death of either or remarriage of recipient.
  4. There is a presumption of decreased need for alimony if the recipient is cohabiting with a mate of the opposite sex.

G. Child support and custody:
  1. Court may order either parent or both to pay.
  2. Court orders custody according to best interests of child.

H. Property division by court in absence of written or oral agreement:
  1. Court divides community property, quasi-community property, and family home equally. ("Equally" has been interpreted to mean "substantially equally," allowing the court to balance one piece of property against another.)
  2. Family residence held in joint tenancy is assumed to be community property. Other joint tenancy property is not divided; each owns a half-share.

IV. TERMINATION OF COHABITATION

A. Court jurisdiction: No judicial control; voluntary parting.

B. Court orders: A court may make orders for child support and custody similar to those made in a divorce, once maternity is established.

C. Property division (decisions in California and in other states indicate the following possibilities):
  1. Courts could infer partnership agreements as a means of dividing property and money.
  2. Courts could order return or division of property and money if there had been an implied or express agreement.
  3. Courts could order return of property to the rightful owner or grant an interest in property or an award of

money to a mate to the extent of his/her contribution toward purchase of property.

4. Since living together is not illegal, recovery could be had for performing household duties as well as financial contributions to the relationship, so long as the implied or express agreement was not primarily based on sex.

D. Putative marriage: If proven, each party accorded same rights as spouses.

E. Palimony: Court decisions indicate that rehabilitative alimony or temporary or permanent alimony would be awarded to a mate if circumstances warranted.

V. SPECIFIC SUBJECTS (No written agreements, except for A,H,L.) Reference to "BOTH" means married and unmarried couples.

A. Prenuptial or precohabitation agreements:
MARRIED: Authorized.
UNMARRIED: Valid if sex is not the basis of the agreement and if meant for protection of property interests.
BOTH: Agreements must be made without duress and with full disclosure of assets and other important information.

B. Separate property:
MARRIED: All property owned before marriage and all acquired after marriage by gift or inheritance; earnings and accumulations from such property while living separately.
UNMARRIED: All property is separate property of acquiring mate.

C. Community property:
MARRIED: All real estate and personal property acquired during marriage except as provided in Subject B. Spouses have equal ownership. All property located or acquired out-of-state which would have been community property if acquired in California is treated as community property upon divorce or upon death of one spouse; this is called quasi-community property. Spouses may agree before or during marriage to change the community or separate status of their property.

D. Liability of separate property for other spouse's or mate's debts:
MARRIED: None except for necessaries purchased by other spouse.
UNMARRIED: None, but it is possible that a homemate could be held liable for necessaries purchased by the other mate.

E.   Liability of community property for debts contracted by one spouse:
     MARRIED: Liability for debts incurred during marriage on behalf of community.

F.   Management and control of separate property of each:
     BOTH: Each controls own property.
     MARRIED: Each spouse must sign to sell or mortgage homestead.

G.   Management and control of community property:
     MARRIED: Each has management and control, but both must give written consent to disposition of community property other than real estate, and both must sign for the lease, conveyance, or encumbrance of real estate.

H.   Contracts made during marriage or cohabitation settling property rights:
     MARRIED: May make written agreements dividing community or separate property.
     UNMARRIED: Enforceable if based on earnings, property, etc., rather than on sex.
     BOTH: Agreements must be made without duress and with full disclosure of assets and other important information.

I.   What can be willed?
     BOTH: Each spouse's or mate's separate property.
     MARRIED: Each spouse's half of community property. If one spouse attempts to dispose of more than one-half of the community property by will, surviving spouse must choose whether to take according to will or to take his/her half of community property.

J.   Automatic protection for surviving spouse or mate:
     MARRIED: Homestead up to $40,000 over liens, including mortgages, some personal property, and reasonable family allowance, exempt from creditors.
     UNMARRIED: No protection for surviving mate. Dependent children receive same exemptions and allowances; dependent illegitimate children receive same if entitled to inherit (see Subject K).

K.   If no will:
     MARRIED: Surviving spouse receives deceased spouse's half of community property and all of deceased's separate property if there are no surviving children of deceased spouse. If children survive, division of separate property is made between them and surviving spouse. In all instances, surviving spouse receives deceased spouse's half of community property.

UNMARRIED: Surviving mate receives nothing. Legitimized children will inherit from father, and will inherit from mother whether legitimized or not (see subject P).

L. Contracts:

BOTH: Each may contract with anyone, including each other.

M. Lawsuits:

BOTH: Each may sue or be sued separately, unless both involved.

N. Homestead law:

BOTH: Head of family with or without children or any person 65 or older has exemption up to $40,000 in family home, over and above liens including mortgages. Declaration of homestead must be signed and acknowledged and recorded in office of county recorder where land is located.

MARRIED: Exemption applies to head of family with or without children.

UNMARRIED: Any person who is not head of family receives $25,000 exemption over and above all liens, including mortgages. Head of family includes unmarried person whose minor children are living with him/her.

O. Civil suits by spouses or mates against each other:

MARRIED: May sue each other only for personal wrongs or to recover separate property appropriated by the other.

UNMARRIED: Each may sue the other.

P. Legitimacy:

MARRIED: Children born during marriage are presumed legitimate.

UNMARRIED: Father is considered father of children if parents later marry and he consents to being named father on birth certificate, or he is obligated by written contract or court order to support children, or if he receives children in home and openly holds children out as his.

Q. Adoption:

BOTH: Any adult may adopt any child or any adult younger than self. Investigation must ascertain that home is suitable for child.

R. Division of property upon termination of relationship:

MARRIED: If no written agreement, court divides community property, quasi-community property, and family home equally (as defined under III, H 2). Each spouse retains his/her separate property. Joint property (except family home) is not divided; each owns a half-share.

UNMARRIED: Implied or express contracts, value of services, and unfair financial gain may create rights to property.

VI. RECENT EVENTS, TRENDS, AND CONCLUSIONS

A. Social Security benefits previously were community property subject to division on divorce. Since then the US Supreme Court has held that federal law preempted state law for railroad retirement benefits. A California Court of Appeals has reconsidered the status of military pensions and declared them to be separate property.

B. Courts can incorporate pension plans in divorce actions and order distributions between an employee and employee's former spouse.

C. A man who fathered a child at the mother's request and upon her oral promise that she would not hold him financially responsible is not relieved of financial support obligations. The mother's contention that, according to the *Marvin* case, the contract was void because the basis of the agreement was sexual services of the father was accepted by the court.

D. Permanent support can be determined based on a husband's ability to earn rather than on his actual earnings. The husband in the case on which the decision was based was a psychiatrist who worked only 20 hours a month because he had found no work that interested him.

E. Court can consider the income of the new wife of a former husband in determining his ability to pay alimony to former spouse. Since the additional burdens of remarriage are considered when alimony is awarded, the additional benefits should also be considered.

F. *Marvin vs. Marvin*, decided in 1976, set out the types of recovery available to a mate. They include: 1) recovery in accordance with an express contract to share property unless the basis of the agreement was primarily sexual; 2) recovery in accordance with the conduct of the couple from which the court could imply a contract, partnership agreement, joint venture, or other understanding; 3) recovery for value of services performed; 4) recovery of property to the extent of the mate's contribution toward its purchase; 5) recovery to prevent unfair economic gain of one mate as against the other; 6) recovery for the reasonable value of household services less the reasonable value of support received. In 1979 the court, finding that none of these bases for recovery existed in the particular case, decided that it had the power to fashion "additional equitable remedies" and provided an alimony-like award for economic rehabilitation of the female mate.

COLORADO

I. MARRIAGE

A.   Legality:
1. Age: 18; 16–18, need consent of parents or guardian; under 16, need consent of parents or guardian and judge of juvenile court.
2. License: Required; valid for 30 days.
3. Medical examination: Physician's certificate required saying applicant is not infected with venereal disease and that female under 45 has been tested for rubella immunity and Rh factor.
4. Waiting period: None.

B.   Common-law marriages: Recognized.

C.   Out-of-state marriages: Valid if valid in state where entered into.

D.   Adultery: Not a crime.

E.   Property: Separate.

F.   Partnerships: A partnership agreement between spouses is probably enforceable as long as there is a valid business purpose.

II. COHABITATION

A.   Legality:
1. Cohabitation: Not a crime.
2. Fornication: Not a crime.

       3.   All private, nonviolent sexual acts between consenting adults are legal.

B.   Common-law marriage: Recognized; cohabitation may result in marriage.

C.   Putative marriage: Recognized. Children of such marriages are legitimate. Putative spouse acquires rights of legal spouse, including alimony following termination.

D.   Property: An early case held that a contract is void if made in contemplation of sexual relations.

E.   Partnerships: A partnership agreement between mates is probably enforceable as long as there is a valid business purpose and the agreement is not primarily based on sex.

III. DIVORCE (DISSOLUTION) AND LEGAL SEPARATION

A.   Divorce or dissolution (grounds): Irretrievable breakdown of marriage relationship (no fault).

B.   Legal separation (grounds): Same as for divorce. Converted to divorce after 6 months, or upon motion of either party and notice to other.

C.   Residency requirements: Either spouse resident of state for 90 days before divorce action filed.

D.   Remarriage: Possible after divorce decree is issued and time for appeal has expired.

E.   Court orders after filing for divorce and before divorce is final:
       1.   Either spouse may be ordered to pay temporary alimony, court costs, and attorneys' fees.
       2.   Orders granting or prohibiting transfers of property, molestation of other spouse, exclusion from family dwelling, temporary custody of children, etc., are permissible.

F.   Alimony:
       1.   To either spouse, but only if he/she lacks sufficient support for self, is unable to secure sufficient employment, or is custodian of child and it is inappropriate to work.
       2.   Later modified or terminated after divorce only upon showing of substantial and continuing changed circumstances.
       3.   Terminates on remarriage of recipient.

G.   Child support and custody:

      1. Court may order either parent or both to pay support.
      2. Court awards custody according to child's best interests; each parent is equally considered.

H.   Property division by court in absence of written or oral agreement:

      1. Court may order division of marital property acquired during marriage, except by gift or inheritance, without regard to marital misconduct. Marital property includes joint property and increases in value of separate property during marriage. Court may not order division of separate property acquired before marriage.

      2. Considerations:
          a. Contribution of each spouse (including contribution as homemaker).
          b. Value of property of each.
          c. Economic circumstances of each.

IV. TERMINATION OF COHABITATION

A.   Court jurisdiction: No judicial control; voluntary parting.

B.   Court orders: Orders may be made for support and custody of children similar to those made in a divorce, once paternity is established.

C.   Property division (decisions in other states suggest the following possibilities):

      1. Courts could infer partnership agreements as a means of dividing property and money.

      2. Though an early case held that contracts in contemplation of sexual relationships are void, courts could order return or division of property and money if there had been an implied or express agreement.

      3. Courts could order return of property to the rightful owner or grant an interest in property or an award of money to a mate to the extent of his/her contribution toward purchase of property.

      4. Since living together is not illegal, it is possible that recovery could be had for performing household duties as well as for direct financial contributions so long as the implied or express agreement was not based primarily upon sex.

D.   Putative marriage: On termination, courts may divide property as if the marriage had been valid.

E.   Palimony: There have been no court decisions to indicate that rehabilitative alimony or temporary or permanent alimony would be awarded to a mate, but such an award is a possibility.

V. SPECIFIC SUBJECTS (No written agreements, except for A,E,I.)
Reference to "BOTH" means married and unmarried couples.

A.   Prenuptial or precohabitation agreements:
MARRIED: Valid, but will not necessarily be followed by the court in dividing property on divorce.
UNMARRIED: Probably valid if sex is not the basis of the agreement and if meant for protection of property interests.
BOTH: Agreements must be made without duress and with full disclosure of assets and other important information.

B.   Property:
BOTH: All property is separate property of acquiring spouse or mate.

C.   Liability of separate property for other spouse's or mate's debts:
MARRIED: None except for family expenses.
UNMARRIED: No liability.

D.   Management and control of separate property of each:
BOTH: Each controls own property.

E.   Contracts made during marriage or cohabitation settling property rights:
MARRIED: Property-settlement agreements are valid.
UNMARRIED: Probably enforceable if based on earnings, property, etc., rather than on sex.
BOTH: Agreements must be made without duress and with full disclosure of assets and other important information.

F.   What can be willed?
BOTH: Each spouse's or mate's separate property.

G.   Automatic protection for surviving spouse or mate:
MARRIED: Exempt property allowance of $7,500 divided among dependent children. Family allowance up to $6,000 lump sum or $500 per month are available to spouse and/or dependent children. $7,500 homestead exemption for surviving spouse and minor children if they are joint tenants of deceased spouse.
UNMARRIED: No protection for surviving mate. Minor children receive same homestead exemption and allowances if they were being supported by decedent or were legally entitled to support.

H.   If no will:
MARRIED: Surviving spouse receives everything if there is no issue of deceased spouse. If issue survives, division is made between surviving spouse and issue.

UNMARRIED: Surviving mate receives nothing. Illegitimate children would inherit from father if paternity had been established by adjudication. Any children inherit from mother.

I. Contracts:
BOTH: Each may contract with anyone, including each other.

J. Lawsuits:
BOTH: Each can sue and be sued separately unless both involved.

K. Homestead law:
BOTH: Home occupied by owner or family receives up to $7,500 exemption in excess of liens, including mortgages. Created automatically if occupied as home by owner, but for exemption to apply to debts created before July 1, 1975, owner or owner's spouse must file claim in clerk's office of county where property is located.

L. Civil suits by spouses or mates against each other:
BOTH: Permitted.

M. Legitimacy:
MARRIED: Children born during marriage are presumed legitimate.
UNMARRIED: Children born outside marriage are illegitimate. Such children are the children of mother; also of father if couple marries after birth, or if paternity is established by adjudication prior to father's death, or established after his death by a preponderance of the evidence, or if father adopts children.

N. Adoption:
MARRIED: Both spouses must consent to adoption.
UNMARRIED: A single adult may adopt.
BOTH: Investigation made to determine good moral character, ability to support, and suitability of home.

O. Division of property upon termination of relationship:
MARRIED: Court orders fair division of marital property (see III, H), including joint property, without regard to marital misconduct, but cannot divide separate property acquired before marriage or by gift or inheritance after marriage.
UNMARRIED: Implied or express contracts, value of services, or unfair economic gain may create rights to property.

VI. RECENT EVENTS, TRENDS, AND CONCLUSIONS

A. Future military retirement pay is not property, but it may be considered as an economic circumstance when property is divided at the time of divorce.

B. Contributions on deposit with a state employees' retirement association are marital property and subject to division at the time of divorce.

C. The value of the goodwill incident to a husband's dental practice is marital property subject to division on divorce.

D. Since cohabitation, fornication, and common-law marriages are legal, it seems likely that some or all of the theories of the *Marvin* case would be followed.

CONNECTICUT

I. MARRIAGE

A. Legality:
   1. Age: 18; under 18, need written, witnessed, and acknowledged consent of parent or guardian; under 16, need written, witnessed, and acknowledged consent of judge of probate.
   2. License: Required; good for 65 days. If applicant is divorced, certified copy of divorce or certification from clerk of court required.
   3. Medical examination: Physician's certificate required showing blood test for syphilis negative not more than 35 days before license issued.
   4. Waiting period: 4 days after filing of application for license.

B. Common-law marriages: Not recognized; unknown whether out-of-state common-law marriages recognized.

    C.   Out-of-state marriages: Probably recognized unless contrary to strong public policy.

    D.   Adultery: Not a crime.

    E.   Property: Separate.

    F.   Partnerships: A partnership agreement between spouses is probably enforceable as long as there is a valid business purpose.

II. COHABITATION

    A.   Legality:
        1. Cohabitation: Not a crime.
        2. Fornication: Not a crime.
        3. All private, nonviolent sexual acts between consenting adults are legal.

    B.   Common-law marriage: Not recognized.

    C.   Putative marriage: A marriage entered into in good faith and thought to be valid by one or both parties will be recognized.

    D.   Property: Agreements between mates will probably be recognized.

    E.   Partnerships: A partnership agreement between mates is probably enforceable as long as there is a valid business purpose and the agreement is not primarily based on sex.

III. DIVORCE (DISSOLUTION) AND LEGAL SEPARATION

    A.   Divorce or dissolution (grounds):
        1. Irretrievable breakdown of marriage (no fault).
        2. Living apart for eighteen months (no fault).
        3. Adultery.
        4. Fraudulent contract.
        5. Wilful desertion for one year.
        6. Seven years' absence.
        7. Habitual intemperance.
        8. Intolerable cruelty.
        9. Sentence to imprisonment for life.
        10. Imprisonment for more than one year for infamous crime.
        11. Hospitalization for five years for mental illness.

    B.   Legal separation (grounds): Same as for divorce. Converted to divorce on petition of either spouse at any time after separation.

C. Residency requirements: Either spouse a resident for one year before filing for divorce; either spouse domiciled in state at time of marriage and intends to remain permanently; or the cause of the divorce occurred after either spouse came to the state.

D. Remarriage: Possible immediately after divorce is final.

E. Court orders after filing for divorce and before divorce is final:
   1. Temporary alimony and support to either spouse.
   2. Exclusive use of family home to either.
   3. Attorneys' fees to either.
   4. Orders protecting property of either.

F. Alimony:
   1. May be granted to either spouse; fault may be considered.
   2. Court may modify or terminate alimony after divorce if the recipient is living with a mate.

G. Child support and custody:
   1. Court may order support as seems fair.
   2. Court assigns child to either parent or to third party. No preference for either parent over the other.

H. Property division by court in absence of written or oral agreement:
   1. Court may assign all or part of either spouse's separate property to other spouse as it deems fair. Court may divide joint property or assign it to either spouse.
   2. Considerations: length of marriage, cause for divorce, age, health, station, occupation, amount and source of income, vocational skills, employability, estate, liability and needs of each, opportunity of each for further acquisition.

IV. TERMINATION OF COHABITATION

A. Court jurisdiction: No judicial control; voluntary parting.

B. Court orders: A court may make orders for child support and custody similar to those made in a divorce, once paternity is established.

C. Property division (decisions in Connecticut and in other states suggest the following possibilities):
   1. Courts could infer partnership agreements as a means of dividing property and money.
   2. Courts could order return or division of property and

money if there had been an implied or express agreement.

3. Courts could order return of property to the rightful owner or grant an interest in property or an award of money to a mate to the extent of his/her contribution toward purchase of property.

4. Since living together is not illegal, recovery could be had for performing household duties as well as for direct financial contributions so long as the implied or express agreement was not primarily based upon sex.

D. Putative marriage: Property adjustments would probably be made to compensate a mate who believed in the validity of an invalid marriage.

E. Palimony: There have been no court decisions granting rehabilitative alimony, temporary or permanent alimony to a mate, but such an award seems a likely possibility.

V. SPECIFIC SUBJECTS (No written agreements, except for A,E,I.)
Reference to "BOTH" means married and unmarried couples.

A. Prenuptial or precohabitation agreements:
MARRIED: Valid.
UNMARRIED: Probably valid if sex is not the basis of the agreement and if meant for the protection of property interests.
BOTH: Agreements must be made without duress and with full disclosure of assets and other important information.

B. Property:
BOTH: All property is separate property of acquiring spouse or mate.

C. Liability of separate property for other spouse's or mate's debts:
BOTH: No liability.

D. Management and control of separate property of each:
BOTH: Each controls own separate property.

E. Contracts made during marriage or cohabitation settling property rights:
MARRIED: Permitted on contemplation of divorce or separation.
UNMARRIED: Probably enforceable if based on earnings, property, etc., rather than on sex.
BOTH: Agreements must be made without duress and with full disclosure of assets and other important information.

F.   What can be willed?

BOTH: Each spouse's or mate's separate property.

MARRIED: Surviving spouse may elect to take one-third of deceased spouse's estate instead of accepting provisions of the will.

G.   Automatic protection for surviving spouse or mate:

MARRIED: Reasonable sum for support of surviving spouse and family if needed during administration of estate.

UNMARRIED: No protection for surviving mate. Children would probably receive support allowance if entitled to inherit (see subject H).

H.   If no will:

MARRIED: If issue or parents of deceased spouse survive, division if made between surviving spouse and issue or parents; otherwise, surviving spouse receives everything.

UNMARRIED: Surviving mate receives nothing. Issue includes children born out of wedlock; such children inherit from mother and from father if parents intermarry, if paternity has been adjudicated, or if father has acknowledged paternity.

I.   Contracts:

BOTH: Each may contract with anyone, including each other.

J.   Lawsuits:

BOTH: Each can sue and be sued separately unless both involved.

K.   Homestead law:

BOTH: No homestead laws.

L.   Civil suits by spouses or mates against each other:

BOTH: Permitted.

M.   Legitimacy:

MARRIED: Children born during marriage are presumed legitimate.

UNMARRIED: Illegitimate children inherit from mother; inherit from father if paternity has been adjudicated, or if father acknowledges parenthood.

BOTH: Children born before marriage are legitimized if parents later marry.

N.   Adoption:

MARRIED: Both spouses must consent to adoption.

UNMARRIED: A single adult may adopt.

BOTH: Adult younger than the person adopting may be adopted.

O. Division of property upon termination of relationship:
MARRIED: Court may divide separate property, including joint property, as it deems fair.
UNMARRIED: Implied or express contracts, value of services, or unfair economic gain may create rights to property.

VI. RECENT EVENTS, TRENDS, AND CONCLUSIONS

A. Statutory interference with private sex has been held to be an unconstitutional invasion of privacy.

B. Agreements between mates dividing property upon termination are honored. Since there are no criminal sanctions against private sexual relationships, there is no reason not to enforce such agreements. The *Marvin* case has been relied on in reaching these conclusions.

DELAWARE

I. MARRIAGE

A. Legality:
1. Age: Male, 18; female, 16; female under 18, need consent of parents or guardian.
2. License: Required; good for 30 days.
3. Medical examination: Physician's certificate and laboratory statement showing freedom from syphilis not more than 30 days before license issued.
4. Waiting period: 24 hours.

B. Common-law marriages: Not valid; recognized if valid in another state where entered into.

C. Out-of-state marriages: Valid unless the particular marriage would be prohibited by Delaware law.

D. Adultery: Not a crime.

E.   Property: Separate.

F.   Partnerships: A partnership agreement between spouses is probably enforceable as long as there is a valid business purpose.

II. COHABITATION

A.   Legality:
1. Cohabitation: Not a crime.
2. Fornication: Not a crime.
3. All private, nonviolent sexual acts between consenting adults are legal.

B.   Common-law marriage: Although common-law marriages are not valid, the courts give limited recognition to a presumption of marriage resulting from cohabitation.

C.   Putative marriage: Courts would probably adjust the property rights of a mate who mistakenly believed in the validity of an invalid marriage.

D.   Property: No decisions, but see IV,C.

E.   Partnerships: A partnership agreement between mates is probably enforceable as long as there is a valid business purpose and the agreement is not primarily based on sex.

III. DIVORCE (DISSOLUTION) AND LEGAL SEPARATION

A.   Divorce or dissolution (grounds): Marriage irretrievably broken, which is deemed to occur when:
1. Voluntary separation (no fault).
2. Separation caused by respondent's misconduct.
3. Separation caused by respondent's mental illness.
4. Separation caused by incompatibility (no fault). Parties must be separated for at least 6 months between the time of filing and the hearing to grant divorce.

B.   Legal separation (grounds): Not available.

C.   Residency requirements: 6 months for either spouse before filing for divorce.

D.   Remarriage: Possible immediately after divorce is final.

E.   Court orders after filing for divorce and before divorce is final:
1. Temporary alimony.
2. Court costs and attorneys' fees.

F.   Alimony:
   1. Court may award to dependent spouse if marriage is irretrievably broken because of incompatibility or mental illness.
   2. May be awarded to plaintiff if ground for divorce is not that marriage is irretrievably broken.

G.   Child support and custody: Court has power to order support and custody. No preference to either parent for custody.

H.   Property division by court in absence of written or oral agreement:
   1. At request of either, court divides marital property, including joint property, as it deems fair, without regard to marital misconduct. Marital property includes all property acquired during the marriage except in exchange for property acquired before the marriage or the increase in value of such property.
   2. Separate property acquired before marriage retained by owner.

IV. TERMINATION OF COHABITATION

A.   Court jurisdiction: No judicial control; voluntary parting.

B.   Court orders: A court may make orders for child support and custody similar to those made in a divorce, once paternity is established.

C.   Property division (decisions in other states suggest the following possibilities):
   1. Courts could infer partnership agreements as a means of dividing property and money.
   2. Courts could order return or division of property and money if there had been an implied or express agreement.
   3. Courts could order return of property to the rightful owner or grant an interest in property or an award of money to a mate to the extent of his/her contribution toward purchase of property.
   4. Since living together is not illegal, recovery could be had for performing household duties as well as for direct financial contributions so long as the implied or express agreement was not based primarily upon sex.

D.   Putative marriage: Courts would probably adjust property rights of a mate who mistakenly believed in the validity of an invalid marriage.

E.   Palimony: There have been no court decisions to indicate
     that rehabilitative alimony or temporary or permanent ali-
     mony would be awarded to a mate, but such an award is
     a possibility.

V. SPECIFIC SUBJECTS (No written agreements, except for A,E,I.)
Reference to "BOTH" means married and unmarried couples.

A.   Prenuptial or precohabitation agreements:
     MARRIED: Valid.
     UNMARRIED: Probably valid if sex is not the basis of the
          agreement and if meant for protection of property in-
          terests.
     BOTH: Agreements must be made without duress and with
          full disclosure of assets and other important information.

B.   Property:
     BOTH: All property is separate property of acquiring spouse
          or mate.

C.   Liability of separate property for other spouse's or mate's
     debts:
     BOTH: No liability.

D.   Management and control of separate property of each:
     BOTH: Each controls own property.

E.   Contracts made during marriage or cohabitation settling
     property rights:
     MARRIED: Valid.
     UNMARRIED: Probably enforceable if based on earnings,
          property, etc., rather than on sex.
     BOTH: Agreements must be made without duress and with
          full disclosure of assets and other important information.

F.   What can be willed?
     BOTH: Each spouse's separate property.

G.   Automatic protection for surviving spouse or mate:
     MARRIED: Surviving spouse receives allowance of cash up
          to $2,000. He/she may elect either $20,000 or one-third
          of decedent's estate, besides share under will or intestate
          share (see subject H).
     UNMARRIED: No protection for surviving mate. No provision
          for minor children.

H.   If no will:
     MARRIED: If issue or parents of deceased spouse survive,
          division is made between them and surviving spouse.
          Otherwise surviving spouse receives everything.
     UNMARRIED: Surviving mate receives nothing. Illegitimate

children may inherit from mother; from father if parents marry before or after child's birth, or if paternity is judicially established.

I. Contracts:
BOTH: Each may contract with anyone, including each other.

J. Lawsuits:
BOTH: Each may sue or be sued separately unless both involved.

K. Homestead law:
BOTH: No legislation.

L. Civil suits by spouses or mates against each other:
MARRIED: Generally cannot sue each other, but allowed in certain cases.
UNMARRIED: Each may sue other.

M. Legitimacy:
MARRIED: Children born during marriage are presumed legitimate.
UNMARRIED: Children may be legitimized if parents marry before birth, or after birth if paternity adjudicated or acknowledged, or upon written acknowledgment of paternity by both parents.

N. Adoption:
MARRIED: Both must consent to adoption of minor child.
BOTH: Spouses or mates must be residents over 21 for adoption of minor child. Adults may be adopted. Adopting parents or parent must be of same religious affiliation as natural mother or child.

O. Division of property upon termination of relationship:
MARRIED: Court divides marital property, including joint property, without regard to marital misconduct, as it deems fair, and at request of either party. Separate property acquired before marriage retained by owner.
UNMARRIED: Implied or express contracts, value of services, or unfair economic gain may create rights to property.

VI. RECENT EVENTS, TRENDS, AND CONCLUSIONS

A. Modification of alimony is considered a continuation of original divorce action; a spouse originally subject to court's jurisdiction is bound by a subsequent order.

B. An increase in retained corporate earnings may be included in the calculation of a couple's marital property.

C.   A vested but not yet matured pension plan is subject to
     division on divorce.

D.   A separation agreement signed by the husband while he was
     in a hospital being treated for paranoid schizophrenia is
     voidable because of his mental incapacity due to medication,
     lack of counsel, undue influence, and unfairness.

E.   Since neither cohabitation, fornication, nor adultery is il-
     legal, and a limited form of common-law marriage is rec-
     ognized, it would seem likely that some or all of the theories
     of the *Marvin* case would be followed.

DISTRICT OF COLUMBIA

I. MARRIAGE

A.   Legality:
     1. Age: 18; under 18, need consent of parents or guard-
        ian, unless previously married; under 16, not per-
        mitted.
     2. License: Required.
     3. Medical examination: Physician's certificate that blood
        test shows freedom from syphilis; not more than 30
        days before license application.
     4. Waiting period: 3 days between application for license
        and issuance.

B.   Common-law marriages: Recognized.

C.   Out-of-state marriages: Void if prohibited in D.C. and en-
     tered into in another state by a D.C. resident; otherwise
     recognized.

D.   Adultery: Illegal; fine and/or imprisonment; between mar-
     ried woman and unmarried man, both are guilty; between
     married man and unmarried woman, man only is guilty.

E.   Property: Separate.

F.   Partnerships: A partnership agreement between spouses is

probably enforceable as long as there is a valid business purpose.

II. COHABITATION

A. Legality:
   1. Cohabitation: Not a crime.
   2. Fornication: Illegal; fine and/or sentence.

B. Common-law marriage: Recognized.

C. Putative marriage: Courts would probably recognize the property rights of a putative spouse.

D. Property: A mere promise to a mate to transfer title to property to another mate does not confer title, although monthly payments and repairs had been made.

E. Partnerships: A partnership agreement between mates is probably enforceable as long as there is a valid business purpose and the agreement is not primarily based on sex.

III. DIVORCE (DISSOLUTION) AND LEGAL SEPARATION

A. Divorce or dissolution (grounds):
   1. Voluntarily living apart for 6 months without cohabitation (no fault).
   2. Living apart for one year without cohabitation (no fault). Couple is deemed to have lived apart if they pursue separate paths and live separately even if housed under the same roof.

B. Legal separation (grounds): Same as for divorce, and in addition:
   1. Adultery.
   2. Cruelty.

C. Residency requirements: 6 months for one spouse before filing for divorce.

D. Remarriage: Possible immediately after divorce is final.

E. Court orders after filing for divorce and before divorce is final:
   1. Temporary alimony for either spouse.
   2. Court may order child support payments and child custody to either parent.

F. Alimony:
   1. Court may require payment of alimony to either spouse.
   2. No provision for termination upon remarriage.
   3. Illicit sex after divorce does not cause termination.

G. Child support and custody:
   1. Court may order either father or mother to make support payments.
   2. Court determines custody according to best interests of child; neither parent given preference.

H. Property division by court in absence of written or oral agreement:
   1. Each spouse retains separate property acquired prior to marriage or acquired by gift or inheritance after marriage.
   2. Marital separate property is divided by court whether held individually or jointly.
   3. Considerations: duration of marriage, ages, health, occupation, employability, assets, debts, provision for custody of minor children, contributions of each.

IV. TERMINATION OF COHABITATION

A. Court jurisdiction: No judicial control; voluntary parting.

B. Court orders: A court may make orders for child support and custody similar to those made in a divorce, once paternity is established.

C. Property division (decisions in other states suggest the following possibilities):
   1. Courts could infer partnership agreements as a means of dividing property and money.
   2. Courts could order return or division of property and money if there had been an implied or express agreement.
   3. Courts could order return of property to the rightful owner or grant an interest in property or an award of money to a mate to the extent of his/her contribution toward purchase of property.
   4. Since living together is not illegal, recovery could be had for performing household duties as well as for direct financial contributions, so long as the implied or express agreement was not primarily based upon sex.

D. Putative marriage: Courts would probably adjust the property rights of a putative spouse.

E. Palimony: There have been no court decisions to indicate that rehabilitative alimony or temporary or permanent alimony would be awarded to a mate, but such an award is a possibility.

V. SPECIFIC SUBJECTS (No written agreements, except for A,E,I.)
Reference to "BOTH" means married and unmarried couples.

A.   Prenuptial or precohabitation agreements:
        MARRIED: Valid.
        UNMARRIED: Valid if sex is not the basis of the agreement
           and if meant for protection of property rights.
        BOTH: Agreements must be made without duress and with
           full disclosure of assets and other important information.

B.   Property:
        BOTH: All property is separate property of acquiring spouse
           or mate.

C.   Liability of separate property for other spouse's or mate's
        debts:
        MARRIED: Each spouse may be liable for necessaries fur-
           nished to the other; otherwise, no liability.
        UNMARRIED: No liability.

D.   Management and control of separate property of each:
        BOTH: Each controls own property.

E.   Contracts made during marriage or cohabitation settling
        property rights:
        MARRIED: Separation agreements (if not made in contem-
           plation of future possible separation) will be enforced
           if provision for wife's support is reasonable and fair.
        UNMARRIED: Probably enforceable if based on earnings,
           property, etc., rather than on sex.
        BOTH: Agreements must be made without duress and with
           full disclosure of assets and other important information.

F.   What can be willed?
        BOTH: Each spouse's or mate's separate property.
        MARRIED: A spouse who receives property through a de-
           ceased spouse's will does not receive dower share in
           addition to will share unless the will specifically so
           provides. Surviving spouse may elect to disregard will
           and take either intestate share or dower share instead
           (see subjects H and L).

G.   Automatic protection for surviving spouse or mate:
        MARRIED: Both spouses have dower interest (see Subject L).
           Surviving spouse or minor children have $2,500 allow-
           ance. Surviving spouse may remain in family home for
           forty days (until dower assigned).
        UNMARRIED: No protection for surviving mate. Minor chil-
           dren receive $2,500 allowance if entitled to inherit (see
           subject H).

H.   If no will:
   MARRIED: Surviving spouse receives one-third if there are
      surviving children of deceased spouse or their descen-
      dants; one-half if no surviving children, but there are
      surviving parents or their descendants. Surviving spouse's
      share is instead of dower unless he/she elects to take
      dower share.
   UNMARRIED: Surviving mate receives nothing. Illegitimate
      children inherit from mother; from father if legitimized
      by later marriage of parents or if paternity is judicially
      established.

I.   Contracts:
   BOTH: Each may contract with anyone, including each
      other.

J.   Lawsuits:
   BOTH: Each may sue and be sued separately unless both
      involved.

K.   Homestead law:
   BOTH: No homestead law.

L.   Dower:
   MARRIED: One-third interest for life in real estate acquired
      by spouse during marriage. Applies only to wife before
      November 29, 1957. Applies to husband and wife since
      March 16, 1962.

M.   Curtesy:
   MARRIED: Abolished with respect to wife dying after No-
      vember 29, 1957. Husband has same dower rights as
      wife after March 16, 1962 (see subject L).

N.   Civil suits by spouses or mates against each other:
   BOTH: Each may sue other.

O.   Legitimacy:
   MARRIED: Children born during marriage are legitimate.
      Children born before marriage are legitimized if parents
      later marry and father acknowledges them.
   UNMARRIED: Children born out of wedlock are legitimate
      children of father and mother when relationship to
      mother established by birth, and relationship to father
      presumed by preponderance of evidence.

P.   Adoption:
   BOTH: Any person may petition for adoption of any minor
      or adult.
   MARRIED: Both spouses must sign petition.

Q.   Division of property upon termination of relationship:
     MARRIED: Each retains separate property acquired before
        marriage or after marriage by gift or inheritance. Marital
        property accumulated during marriage is divided as court
        deems fair.
     UNMARRIED: Implied or express contracts, value of services,
        or unfair economic gain may create rights to property.

VI. RECENT EVENTS, TRENDS, AND CONCLUSIONS

A.   An antenuptial agreement providing that the wife waives
     all rights to financial support on divorce, regardless of the
     couple's respective health or financial positions, is unen-
     forceable and contrary to public policy. The agreement is
     not deemed voluntary, fair, and reasonable under the cir-
     cumstances, and an award of alimony is just and proper,
     considering the financial conditions of both as well as other
     factors.

B.   It is illegal for a lender to refuse to combine the incomes
     of mates living together to determine their creditworthiness
     when they apply jointly for a mortgage loan.

C.   Property acquired as marital property during the marriage
     will remain as such, notwithstanding subsequent dealings
     between the two spouses. Thus a sale of a house from
     husband to wife did not alter its classification as marital
     property divisible by the court as it deems fair.

D.   A 1976 case enforced an oral agreement between mates
     because of the possibility of great injury to the party who
     relied on it, the perpetration of fraud, and unconstitution-
     ality. Although cohabitation is legal, fornication and adul-
     tery are not; there is a possibility that some of the theories
     of the *Marvin* case would be followed.

FLORIDA

I. MARRIAGE

A. Legality:
1. Age: 18; under 18, need written and acknowledged consent of parents.
2. License: Required; valid for 30 days; issued three days after application.
3. Medical examination: Required within 60 days before license application; must include blood test for venereal disease.
4. Waiting period: 3 days.

B. Common-law marriages: Not recognized unless entered into before 1968.

C. Out-of-state marriages: Presumably valid if valid in state where entered into, but there is no statutory provision for their recognition.

D. Adultery: Living openly in adultery is illegal (misdemeanor); fine and/or sentence.

E. Property: Separate.

F. Partnerships: A partnership agreement between spouses is probably enforceable as long as there is a valid business purpose.

II. COHABITATION

A. Legality:
1. Cohabitation: Illegal (misdemeanor); maximum 60-day sentence.
2. Fornication: Illegal (misdemeanor); maximum 60-day sentence.

B. Common-law marriage: Not recognized unless entered into before 1968. A marriage which is invalid because of a previously undissolved marriage unknown to one party becomes a common-law marriage if the previous marriage was ended prior to 1968 and cohabitation continued afterward.

C. Putative marriage: If property is transferred upon the mis-

- taken belief of a valid marriage, the court may order its return.

D. Property: A contract based on sex is void.

E. Partnerships: A partnership agreement between mates is probably enforceable as long as there is a valid business purpose and the agreement is not primarily based on sex.

III. DIVORCE (DISSOLUTION) AND LEGAL SEPARATION

A. Divorce or dissolution (grounds):
   1. Marriage is irretrievably broken (no fault).
   2. Mental incompetence for at least 3 years.

B. Legal separation (grounds): Legal separation not recognized.

C. Residency requirements: 6 months for plaintiff before filing for divorce.

D. Remarriage: Possible immediately after divorce is final.

E. Court orders after filing for divorce and before divorce is final: Court may make appropriate orders for temporary support, alimony, preservation of property, and attorneys' fees.

F. Alimony:
   1. May be granted to either spouse in the form of either rehabilitative or permanent alimony.
   2. Adultery and economic factors may be considered.
   3. May be modified upon changed circumstances after divorce.
   4. May be periodic, lump sum, or both.

G. Child support and custody:
   1. Court makes orders for care, custody, and maintenance of children.
   2. Each parent has equal consideration for custody.

H. Property division by court in absence of written or oral agreement:
   1. Court has no power to distribute separate property; title alone controls.
   2. Jointly owned real estate may be ordered sold and the proceeds divided at the request of both spouses. Jointly owned real estate or personal property becomes tenancy in common if sale and division are not requested.

IV. TERMINATION OF COHABITATION

A. Court jurisdiction: No judicial control; voluntary parting.

B.   Court orders: A court may make orders for child support and custody similar to those made in a divorce, once paternity is established.

C.   Property division (decisions in other states suggest the following possibilities):
  1. Although courts disapprove of cohabitation, courts would probably honor partnership agreements between mates and might infer them as a means of dividing property and money.
  2. Though contracts based on sex are void, courts might order return or division of property and money if there had been an implied or express agreement based on something other than sex.
  3. Courts could order return of property to rightful owner or grant an interest in property or an award of money to a mate to the extent of his/her contribution toward purchase of property.
  4. Since cohabitation is illegal and a contract based on sex is void, courts would probably not honor an agreement between mates if the relationship was primarily based on sex; thus it might be difficult to collect for performing household duties when no economic contribution can be shown.

D.   Putative marriage: Courts would probably adjust the property rights of a couple who mistakenly believed in the validity of an invalid marriage.

E.   Palimony: There have been no court decisions to indicate that rehabilitative alimony or temporary or permanent alimony would be awarded to a mate, and such an award seems unlikely.

V. SPECIFIC SUBJECTS (No written agreements, except for A,E,I.)
Reference to "BOTH" means married and unmarried couples.

A.   Prenuptial or precohabitation agreements:
  MARRIED: Valid.
  UNMARRIED: Probably valid if sex is not the basis of the agreement and if meant for protection of property interests.
  BOTH: Agreements must be made without duress and with full disclosure of assets and other important information.

B.   Property:
  BOTH: All property is separate property of acquiring spouse or mate.

C. Liability of separate property for other spouse's or mate's debts:
    BOTH: No liability.

D. Management and control of separate property of each:
    BOTH: Each controls own property.
    MARRIED: Both spouses must sign to sell family home.

E. Contracts made during marriage or cohabitation settling property rights:
    MARRIED: Valid.
    UNMARRIED: Probably enforceable if based on earnings, property, etc., rather than on sex.
    BOTH: Agreements must be made without duress and with full disclosure of assets and other important information.

F. What can be willed?
    MARRIED: Separate property except family home.
    UNMARRIED: Each mate's separate property.

G. Automatic protection for surviving spouse or mate:
    MARRIED: Surviving spouse receives elective share (30 percent of fair market value of all net assets after valid claims deducted); homestead exemption passes to surviving spouse and heirs; family home may not be denied by will to a surviving spouse or heirs. Surviving spouse also receives household furnishings, appliances, and automobile up to $5,000 in value, personal effects up to $1,000, and reasonable family allowance up to $6,000.
    UNMARRIED: No protection for surviving mate. Children would receive homestead exemption and allowance if entitled to inherit (see subject H).

H. If no will:
    MARRIED: Surviving spouse receives everything if there are no descendants of deceased spouse; if there are descendants, they share with surviving spouse.
    UNMARRIED: Surviving mate receives nothing. Illegitimate children inherit from mother and from father if parents marry, or if paternity established by adjudication or acknowledgment.

I. Contracts:
    BOTH: Each may contract with anyone, including each other.

J. Lawsuits:
    BOTH: Each may sue or be sued separately unless both involved.

K. Homestead law:

BOTH: $1,000 in personal property plus net value over liens in family home accrues to head of family for most purposes. Homestead designation must be filed before a forced sale levy by recording in office of clerk of circuit court.

L.   Dower and/or curtesy:
MARRIED: Abolished and replaced by elective share (see subject G).

M.   Civil suits by spouses or mates against each other:
MARRIED: Uncertain; no provision.
UNMARRIED: Each may sue other.

N.   Legitimacy:
MARRIED: Children born during marriage presumed legitimate. Children born before marriage are legitimized if parents later marry.
UNMARRIED: Illegitimate children are descendants of mother; of father if parents later marry, or if paternity established judicially, or if acknowledged in writing by father.

O.   Adoption:
BOTH: Any adult may adopt child or adult. Adopter must be more than ten years older than adoptee.

P.   Division of property upon termination of relationship:
MARRIED: Court has no power to divide separate property; title alone controls. Joint property may be sold upon request of both spouses and proceeds divided evenly; otherwise hold title as tenants in common.
UNMARRIED: Actions based on implied or express contracts, on value of services, or on unfair economic gain are uncertain because of courts' attitude toward cohabitation. Action for return of property toward which one contributed might be possible.

VI. RECENT EVENTS, TRENDS, AND CONCLUSIONS

A.   Although rehabilitative alimony, rather than permanent alimony, is commonly recognized, an appeals court rejected an award of rehabilitative alimony to a wife after a 32-year marriage when the husband had a $516 weekly military pension and the wife had only a high-school education, no work experience, and no employable skills. Instead she was awarded permanent alimony.

B.   Another appeals court upheld rehabilitative alimony rather than permanent alimony for a college-educated wife of a dentist, despite the fact that she had been married 25 years, had worked only one year at the beginning of the marriage, and had little chance at age 45 of beginning a new career. The same court held that an award of 20 years of rehabilitative alimony to a wife was excessive because, although she was 43, she had good possibilities of employment.

C. A separation agreement providing for the husband to pay $100 a week for the wife's life or until she remarried was held to be terminable because her income had increased to a level that she had while married.

D. Although an adulterous relationship may reduce alimony, the prime considerations are need and ability to pay.

E. A wife's alimony was increased by 60% when it was learned that the former husband's financial condition had substantially improved.

F. A wife's alimony cannot be lowered for not allowing the husband child visitation rights, but the payments can be suspended when other legal efforts to enforce visitation rights have failed.

G. Overnight visitation of a 5-year-old daughter with her divorced father who lives with a mate may not be canceled unless the arrangement is shown to have an adverse effect on the child.

H. Since cohabitation is illegal and common-law marriages are no longer recognized, it seems likely that few, if any, of the theories of the *Marvin* case would be followed.

GEORGIA

I. MARRIAGE: "The husband is head of the family and the wife is subject to him; her legal existence is merged in the husband except so far as the law recognizes her separately, either for her own protection, or for her benefit, or for the preservation of public order."

    A.   Legality:
1. Age: 16; under 16, need consent of parents or guardians.
2. License: Required.
3. Medical examination: Required examination for veneral disease.
4. Waiting period: 3 days, unless both over 18.

    B.   Common-law marriage: Recognized.

    C.   Out-of-state marriages: Valid if valid in state where entered into.

    D.   Adultery: Illegal (misdemeanor).

    E.   Property: Separate.

    F.   Partnerships: A partnership agreement between spouses is probably enforceable as long as there is a valid business purpose.

II. COHABITATION

    A.   Legality:
1. Cohabitation: Not a crime.
2. Fornication: Illegal (misdemeanor).

    B.   Common-law marriage:
1. Cohabitation could result in a common-law marriage.
2. If the parties divorce but continue to cohabit, a common-law marriage can result.

    C.   Putative marriage: A ceremonial marriage invalid because of a previously existing marriage unknown to one partner becomes a common-law marriage when the previous marriage is dissolved.

    D.   Property: Courts would probably not recognize rights of a mate to the property of the other, since cohabitation is viewed as immoral.

    E.   Partnerships: A partnership agreement between mates is probably enforceable as long as there is a valid business purpose and the agreement is not primarily based on sex.

III. DIVORCE (DISSOLUTION) AND LEGAL SEPARATION

    A.   Divorce or dissolution (grounds):
1. Incest.
2. Mental incapacity.
3. Impotency.
4. Force, duress, or fraud in obtaining marriage.

       5. Pregnancy, unknown to husband, at time of marriage, by another man.
       6. Adultery.
       7. Desertion for one year.
       8. Conviction of offense involving turpitude and imprisonment for 2 years or more.
       9. Habitual intoxication.
     10. Cruel treatment.
     11. Incurable mental illness.
     12. Habitual drug addiction.
     13. Marriage irretrievably broken (no fault).

B.   Legal separation (grounds): No grounds.

C.   Residency requirements: 6 months for either spouse before legal action for divorce is filed.

D.   Remarriage: Possible immediately after divorce is final.

E.   Court orders after filing for divorce and before divorce is final:
       1. Temporary alimony.
       2. Husband may not transfer property after separation and before divorce is final.
       3. Temporary support and custody of children.
       4. Attorneys' fees.

F.   Alimony:
       1. Awarded to either party according to needs of recipient and ability of other to pay.
       2. Adultery and desertion are absolute bars to alimony.
       3. Conduct of parties is irrelevant to amount of alimony when ground is irretrievable breakdown.
       4. Cohabitation of recipient spouse after divorce is ground for modification or termination.

G.   Child support and custody:
       1. Support imposed on either parent.
       2. Parents have equal rights to custody, based on best interests of child.

H.   Property division by court in absence of written or oral agreement:
       1. Court has the power to divide all jointly owned property as it deems fair.
       2. Each spouse's separate property is retained by owner.

IV. TERMINATION OF COHABITATION

A.   Court jurisdiction: No judicial control; voluntary parting.

B.   Court orders: A court may make orders for child support and custody similar to those made in a divorce, once paternity is established.

C. Property division (decisions in Georgia and in other states suggest the following possibilities):

1. Courts could enforce express partnership agreements but would probably not infer them.

2. Georgia courts presume immorality when there is cohabitation, and would probably find contracts between cohabitants to be based at least partly on illicit sex. The possibility that a court would enforce implied or express contracts between mates is unlikely.

3. Courts might order the return of property to the rightful owner, but it is unlikely that they would award property to a mate who had simply contributed to its purchase.

4. Even though living together is not illegal, fornication is, and courts look upon cohabitation as immoral if not illegal. Thus it would be unlikely that a mate could collect for performing household duties.

D. Putative marriage: Might be recognized to the extent of adjusting property rights.

E. Palimony: Court decisions seem to indicate that a mate would not be entitled to receive rehabilitative alimony or temporary or permanent alimony.

V. SPECIFIC SUBJECTS (No written agreements, except for A,E,I.) Reference to "BOTH" means married and unmarried couples.

A. Prenuptial or precohabitation agreements:
   MARRIED: Valid.
   UNMARRIED: Doubtful, but may be valid if sex is not the basis of the agreement and if meant for protection of property interests.
   BOTH: Agreements must be made without duress and with full disclosure of assets and other important information.

B. Property:
   BOTH: All property is separate property of acquiring spouse or mate.

C. Liability of separate property for other spouse's or mate's debts:
   BOTH: No liability.

D. Management and control of separate property of each:
   BOTH: Each controls own property.

E. Contracts made during marriage or cohabitation settling property rights:

MARRIED: Valid.

UNMARRIED: Doubtful, but may be valid if based on property, and clearly not on sex.

BOTH: Agreements must be made without duress and with full disclosure of assets and other important information.

F.   What can be willed?

BOTH: Each spouse's separate property.

G.   Automatic protection for surviving spouse or mate:

MARRIED: Widow and minor children entitled to support from estate for one year, minimum of $1,600, and homestead exemption (see subject K).

UNMARRIED: no protection for surviving mate. Minor children may receive one year's support and homestead exemption if entitled to inherit (see subject H).

H.   If no will:

MARRIED: If children of deceased spouse or their descendants survive, division made between them and surviving spouse; otherwise, surviving spouse receives everything.

UNMARRIED: Surviving mate receives nothing. Illegitimate children inherit from mother, and from father if legitimized.

I.   Contracts:

BOTH: Each may contract with anyone, including each other.

UNMARRIED: Contracts based on sex would not be enforced.

J.   Lawsuits:

BOTH: Each may sue and be sued separately unless both involved.

K.   Homestead law:

BOTH: Head of family may choose between (1) $5,000 over liens, including mortgages, in real property, in personal property, or both; or (2) homestead exemption, which includes real estate up to $500 and other subjects such as horse, cow, beds, cooking utensils. Wife may apply for exemption on husband's property, but reverse is not true. Application is made by petition to probate judge in county of residence.

L.   Civil suits by spouse or mates against each other:

UNMARRIED: May sue on contract or for wrongs related to property rights, but not for personal wrongs.

BOTH: Each may sue other.

M.   Legitimacy:

MARRIED: Children born during marriage are legitimate.

UNMARRIED: Children legitimized if father establishes paternity judicially. An illegitimate inherits from mother only.

BOTH: Children born before marriage are legitimized if parents later marry.

N. Adoption:

BOTH: Any adult may adopt if not below the age of 25, or if married and living with spouse. There must be not less than a ten-year age difference, and adopter must be financially, physically, morally, and mentally fit and able.

O. Division of property upon termination of relationship:

MARRIED: Court has power to divide jointly owned property as it deems fair, and no power to divide separate property.

UNMARRIED: Property division is not favored unless the presumption of immorality can be rebutted.

VI. RECENT EVENTS, TRENDS, AND CONCLUSIONS

A. Visitation privileges and support duties are not conditioned one on the other; if the mother denies visitation to the father, he is not relieved of support payments.

B. Statutes allowing alimony only to wives are unconstitutional.

C. A change of custody from a wife living apart from her husband was ordered because she was cohabiting with another man in violation of a statute, the "live-in-lover law." Her alimony was not lowered.

D. In May 1979, new divorce laws were enacted, removing sex-based classification and establishing equal rights and obligations for both spouses.

E. Although a female mate contributed to the price of land and improvements to which the male mate took title, in 1958 a court offered no relief, finding that illicit sex formed part of the contract.

F. In 1977, a female mate sued for monthly compensation based upon 18 years of cohabitation, and for her property rights in a house that had been jointly purchased. Her claim was denied because she could not present sufficient evidence to overcome the presumption of immorality.

G. These court decisions, and the fact that fornication and adultery are illegal, seem to indicate that the theories of the *Marvin* case would not be followed.

HAWAII

I. MARRIAGE

A. Legality:
1. Age: 16; under 18, need consent of parents or guardian; 15, need written approval of family court; not permitted under 15.
2. License: Required.
3. Medical examination: Required.
4. Waiting period: 30 days between application for license and issuance.

B. Common-law marriages: Not recognized.

C. Out-of-state marriages: Valid if valid where entered into.

D. Adultery: Not a crime.

E. Property: Separate; however, modified form of the community-property system is in effect.

F. Partnerships: Partnership agreements between a husband and wife are valid if there is a valid business purpose.

II. COHABITATION

A. Legality:
1. Cohabitation: Not a crime.
2. Fornication: Not a crime.
3. All private, nonviolent sexual acts between consenting adults are legal.

B. Common-law marriage: Not recognized.

C. Putative marriage: Not recognized, but property rights of a putative spouse would probably be recognized.

D. Property: No recent court decisions, but see IV-C. for possibilities as to division of property.

E. Partnerships: A partnership agreement between mates is probably enforceable as long as there is a valid business purpose and the agreement is not primarily based on sex.

III. DIVORCE (DISSOLUTION) AND LEGAL SEPARATION

A. Divorce or dissolution (grounds): All grounds are no-fault, including:
1. Irretrievable breakdown of marriage.
2. Voluntarily living apart for two years.
3. Expiration of term of legal separation (2 years maximum) without reconciliation.
4. Living apart under court decree of separate maintenance for 2 years.

B. Legal separation (grounds): Court decree of legal separation lasts up to two years. If no reconciliation is effected during this period, divorce may be declared under A, 3 above. A spouse may also petition for separate maintenance, which can result in divorce under A, 4 above.

C. Residency requirements: 6 months by either party before legal action is filed.

D. Remarriage: Possible immediately after divorce is final.

E. Court orders after filing for divorce and before divorce is final:
1. Orders preventing disposal or encumbrance of property.
2. Temporary alimony to either spouse.
3. Court costs and attorneys' fees.

F. Alimony:
1. May be granted to either spouse at discretion of court.
2. Alimony may be modified or terminated if recipient remarries.

G. Child support and custody:
1. Court may order either parent to furnish support.
2. Neither parent has preferred status for custody.

H. Property division by court in absence of written or oral agreement:
1. Community property is divided by the court as it deems just.
2. Court may divide joint or separate property acquired before or during marriage as it deems just.
3. Court allocates responsibility for payment of all debts.
4. Considerations: respective merits of spouses, relative abilities, condition of each, burdens imposed because of children, financial resources, ability to support self, duration of marriage, standard of living, age, physical and emotional condition, occupations, needs, custodial and child-support responsibilities.

IV. TERMINATION OF COHABITATION

A. Court jurisdiction: No judicial control; voluntary parting.

B. Court orders: A court may make orders for child support and custody similar to those made in a divorce, once paternity is established.

C. Property division (decisions in other states suggest the following possibilities):
 1. Courts could infer partnership agreements as a means of dividing property and money.
 2. Courts could order return or division of property and money if there had been an implied or express agreement.
 3. Courts could order return of property to the rightful owner or grant an interest in property or an award of money to a mate to the extent of his/her contribution toward purchase of property.
 4. Since living together is not illegal, recovery might be had for performing household duties as well as for direct financial contributions, so long as the implied or express agreement was not primarily based on sex.

D. Putative marriage: Although early cases are to the contrary, courts would probably adjust property rights of a mate who mistakenly believed there was a valid marriage.

E. Palimony: There have been no court decisions to indicate that rehabilitative alimony or temporary or permanent alimony would be awarded to a mate, but such an award is a possibility.

V. SPECIFIC SUBJECTS (No written agreements, except for A,G,K.)
Reference to "BOTH" means married and unmarried couples.

A. Prenuptial or precohabitation agreements:
 MARRIED: Probably valid.
 UNMARRIED: Probably valid if sex is not the basis for the agreement and if meant for protection of property interests.
 BOTH: Agreement must be made without duress and with full disclosure of assets and other important information.

B. Separate property:
 MARRIED: Presumption is that all property acquired before or during marriage is property of spouse in whose name it was acquired.
 UNMARRIED: All property is separate property of acquiring mate.

C.   Community property:
     MARRIED: Community-property system was in effect from July 1, 1945, to June 30, 1949, and still applies for property acquired during those years.

D.   Liability of separate property for other spouse's or mate's debts:
     BOTH: No liability unless both involved.

E.   Management and control of separate property of each:
     BOTH: Each controls own property.

F.   Management and control of community property:
     MARRIED: Each has individual control over community property acquired during time period referred to in subject C.

G.   Contracts made during marriage or cohabitation settling property rights:
     MARRIED: Agreements in contemplation of divorce or separation are valid.
     UNMARRIED: Probably enforceable if based on earnings, property, etc., rather than on sex.
     BOTH: Agreements must be made without duress and with full disclosure of all assets and other important information.

H.   What can be willed?
     MARRIED: Each spouse's own half of any community property.
     BOTH: Each mate's or spouse's separate property.

I.   Automatic protection for surviving spouse or mate:
     MARRIED: Surviving spouse receives homestead allowance of $5,000, exempt personal property allowance up to $5,000, reasonable maintenance allowance, and possession of family home until ended by estate administrator.
     UNMARRIED: No protection for surviving mate. Minor or dependent children receive equal shares of $5,000 homestead allowance, reasonable-maintenance allowance, and same rights to possession of family home if they are entitled to inherit (see subject J).

J.   If no will:
     MARRIED: Surviving spouse receives everything if there are no surviving children or parents. Otherwise surviving spouse receives one-half and the children or parents divide the other one-half.
     UNMARRIED: Surviving mate receives nothing. Illegitimate

children inherit from mother, and from father if acknowledged.

K.   Contracts:
BOTH: Each may contract with anyone, including each other.

L.   Lawsuits:
BOTH: Each may sue and be sued separately unless both
involved.

M.   Homestead law:
BOTH: $20,000 exemption in family home for head of family
or person over 65. Exemption applies over and above
liens including mortgages; value determined on basis of
tax assessment.
UNMARRIED: $10,000 exemption for any owner other than
family head.

N.   Dower and/or curtesy:
MARRIED: None for marriage entered into after July 1, 1977.

O.   Civil suits by spouses or mates against each other:
BOTH: Permitted.

P.   Legitimacy:
MARRIED: Children born in wedlock are legitimate.
UNMARRIED: Legitimized by voluntary acknowledgment
supported by affidavits of both parents, by adjudication
of paternity, or by adoption.
BOTH: Children are legitimized if parents later marry each
other.

Q.   Adoption:
BOTH: Any proper adult may adopt a child.

R.   Division of property upon termination of relationship:
MARRIED: Property-settlement agreements are valid. If no
agreement, court divides joint, separate, and community
property as it deems just; situations of parties may be
considered.
UNMARRIED: Implied or express contracts, value of services,
or unfair economic gain may create rights to property.

VI. RECENT EVENTS, TRENDS, AND CONCLUSIONS

Since neither cohabitation, fornication, nor adultery is illegal, it
would seem likely that the court would apply some or all of the
theories of the *Marvin* case upon the termination of cohabitation
between mates.

IDAHO

I. MARRIAGE

A. Legality:
    1. Age: 18; between 16 and 18, need consent of parent or guardian; under 16, need consent of parent and order of probate court after hearing.
    2. License: Required.
    3. Medical examination: Physician's certificate that applicant is free from venereal disease and has had blood test not more than 30 days prior to issuance of license.
    4. Waiting period: None.

B. Common-law marriages: Recognized.

C. Out-of-state marriages: Valid if valid where entered into.

D. Adultery: Illegal (misdemeanor); fine or sentence.

E. Property: Community.

F. Partnerships: A partnership agreement between spouses is probably enforceable as long as there is a valid business purpose.

II. COHABITATION

A. Legality:
    1. Cohabitation: Illegal (misdemeanor); fine and/or sentence.
    2. Fornication: Illegal (misdemeanor); fine and/or sentence.

B. Common-law marriage: Recognized. A common-law marriage results after the removal of the reason for an illegal marriage.

C. Property:
    1. Neither mate in an illicit sexual relationship acquires, by reason of the cohabitation alone, any rights in property accumulated by the other during the relationship.
    2. However, courts have, in the past, allotted to a female mate a share of property accumulated during an illicit relationship, either according to an agreement or according to other theories.

D.   Partnerships: A partnership agreement between mates is probably enforceable as long as there is a valid business purpose and the agreement is not primarily based on sex.

III. DIVORCE (DISSOLUTION) AND LEGAL SEPARATION

A.   Divorce or dissolution (grounds):
1. Adultery.
2. Extreme cruelty.
3. Willful desertion.
4. Habitual intemperance.
5. Conviction of felony.
6. Willful neglect.
7. Permanent insanity with 3 years' confinement.
8. Living separate and apart for 5 years (no fault).
9. Irreconcilable differences (no fault).

B.   Legal separation (grounds): Not obtainable.

C.   Residency requirements: 6 weeks before legal action is filed.

D.   Remarriage: Possible immediately after divorce is final.

E.   Court orders after filing for divorce and before divorce is final: Temporary alimony, child support and custody, court costs and attorneys' fees.

F.   Alimony:
1. Allowed only to wife for fault of husband. (The U.S. Supreme Court has recently ruled that such a provision is unconstitutional as a violation of equal protection.)
2. Subsequent cohabitation of recipient does not necessarily terminate alimony.

G.   Child support and custody:
1. Husband may be required to pay support. Wife's duty unknown, but in view of recent equal-protection decisions, she would probably have same duty.
2. Both support and custody are subject to control of court.
3. Although a statute equalizes parental rights to custody, a fit mother is still given preference for younger children.

H.   Property division by court in absence of written or oral agreement:
1. Each spouse retains separate property whether acquired before or after marriage.
2. Community and joint property is divided as court deems fair.
3. Family home is assignable to innocent spouse.

         4. Retirement or pension benefits are part of the community and are therefore divisible upon divorce.

IV. TERMINATION OF COHABITATION

A.   Court jurisdiction: No judicial control; voluntary parting.

B.   Court orders: A court may make orders for child support and custody similar to those made in a divorce, once paternity is established.

C.   Property division (decisions in other states suggest the following possibilities):
      1. Courts could infer partnership agreements as a means of dividing property and money.
      2. Courts could order return or division of property and money if there had been an implied or express agreement.
      3. Courts could order return of property to rightful owner or grant an interest in property or an award of money to a mate to the extent of his/her contribution toward purchase of property.
      4. Courts would probably not honor an agreement if the relationship was primarily sexual; thus it might be difficult for a mate to collect for performing household duties when no direct financial contribution can be shown.

D.   Common-law marriage: Courts have applied principles of fairness to adjust property rights of partners whose union was originally illicit and later became a common-law marriage; courts have also enforced agreements of such parties.

E.   Palimony: Court decisions seem to indicate that a mate would not be entitled to receive rehabilitative alimony or temporary or permanent alimony.

V. SPECIFIC SUBJECTS (No written agreements, except for A,H,L.)
Reference to "BOTH" means married and unmarried couples.

A.   Prenuptial or precohabitation agreements:
MARRIED: Valid. May modify or abrogate community property by contract.
UNMARRIED: Doubtful. May be valid if sex is not the primary basis of the agreement and if meant for protection of property interests.
BOTH: Agreement must be made without duress and with full disclosure of assets and other important information.

B.   Separate property:
MARRIED: All property owned by either spouse before mar-

riage, acquired after marriage by gift or inheritance, or acquired with the proceeds of separate property.

UNMARRIED: All property is separate property of acquiring mate.

C. Community property:

MARRIED: All property acquired during marriage, including income from separate property, is community property. All personal property, wherever situated, and all real property in Idaho acquired while domiciled elsewhere, but which would have been community property if acquired while domiciled in Idaho, is treated as community property on death of one spouse. This property is called quasi-community property.

D. Liability of separate property for other spouse's or mate's debts:

MARRIED: A community obligation incurred by one spouse without consent of the other does not bind separate property of the other.

UNMARRIED: No liability.

E. Liability of community property for debts contracted by one spouse:

MARRIED: Liable for community debts made by one spouse only if consent if other spouse is in writing. Community property is not liable for separate debts.

F. Management and control of separate property of each:

BOTH: Each controls own property.

MARRIED: Both spouses must sign conveyance or encumbrance of family home.

G. Management and control of community property:

MARRIED: Either husband or wife may manage and control community property. Either may bind the community, except that neither may sell, convey, or encumber community real estate unless the other spouse also signs.

H. Contracts made during marriage or cohabitation settling property rights:

MARRIED: Valid. Marriage settlements may change the property rights provided for by statute.

UNMARRIED: Doubtful. May be enforceable if based on earnings, property, etc., rather than on sex.

BOTH: Agreements must be made without duress and with full disclosure of all assets and other important information.

I. What can be willed?

MARRIED: His/her one-half interest in community property

and in quasi-community property (see subject C).

BOTH: Each spouse's or mate's separate property.

J. Automatic protection for surviving spouse or mate:

MARRIED: Surviving spouse receives $12,000 homestead allowance if no homestead selected during life; exempt personal property of $3,500 and family allowance in reasonable amount.

UNMARRIED: No protection for surviving mate; minor dependent children of decedent receive allowances if they are entitled to inherit (see subject K).

K. If no will:

MARRIED: Surviving spouse receives decedent's half of community property and all separate property if there are no surviving children or parents of decedent; if children or parents survive, division is made between them and surviving spouse.

UNMARRIED: Surviving mate receives nothing. Illegitimate children inherit from mother; from father if parents marry or if paternity is established by adjudication.

L. Contracts:

BOTH: Each may contract with anyone, including each other.

M. Lawsuits:

MARRIED: Each may sue and be sued separately when separate property is involved; if community property is involved, both must participate.

UNMARRIED: Each may sue and be sued separately unless both involved.

N. Homestead law:

BOTH: $25,000 equity in family home over liens including mortgages for husband or wife, or for head of family.

UNMARRIED: $12,000 for mate who is not head of family.

O. Civil suits by spouses or mates against each other:

BOTH: Each may sue the other.

P. Legitimacy:

MARRIED: Children born during marriage are presumed legitimate.

UNMARRIED: Children born outside marriage are children of mother; also children of father if paternity established by adjudication.

BOTH: Children born before marriage are legitimized if parents marry each other.

Q. Adoption:

BOTH: Any adult may adopt any child if adult is fifteen years older than child, or at least twenty-five years old. Both spouses must consent.

R.   Division of property upon termination of relationship:
   MARRIED: Each spouse retains separate property; community and joint property divided as court deems fair; family home may be assigned to innocent spouse.
   UNMARRIED: Implied or express contracts, value of services, or unfair economic gain may create rights to property.

VI. RECENT EVENTS, TRENDS, AND CONCLUSIONS

A.   The estate of a deceased father is not liable for future child support payments.

B.   The courts' general disapproval of illicit sexual relationships and the fact that cohabitation, fornication, and adultery are illegal, seem to indicate that the *Marvin* case would not be followed. However, common-law marriages are recognized, and the courts have been willing to apply principles of fairness to settle property rights acquired during an illicit relationship when the relationship later developed into a common-law marriage.

ILLINOIS

I. MARRIAGE

A.   Legality:
   1.   Age: 18; between 16 and 18, need consent of parent or guardian.
   2.   License: Required.
   3.   Medical examination: Physician's certificate required, not more than 15 days before application for license, showing freedom from venereal disease. Sickle-cell anemia test may be required.
   4.   Waiting period: 3 days.

B.   Common-law marriages: Invalid.

C.   Out-of-state marriages: Void if prohibited in Illinois; otherwise valid if valid where entered into.

D.   Adultery: Illegal (misdemeanor) only if open and notorious.

E.   Property: Separate.

F. Partnerships: A partnership agreement between spouses is probably enforceable as long as there is a valid business purpose.

II. COHABITATION

A. Legality:
   1. Cohabitation: Illegal (misdemeanor) only if open and notorious.
   2. Fornication: Illegal (misdemeanor) only if open and notorious.
   3. All private, nonviolent sexual acts between consenting adults are legal.

B. Common-law marriage: Even though not recognized, if a marriage is invalid because of an undissolved prior marriage, and the parties continue to cohabit after the reason for invalidity is removed, they are lawfully married.

C. Putative marriage: Recognized to the extent of adjusting property rights.

D. Property:
   1. Divorcee may cohabit with a mate without losing alimony from ex-husband.
   2. Ex-husband's misconduct is not grounds for increasing alimony to ex-wife.

E. Partnerships: A partnership agreement between mates is probably enforceable as long as there is a valid business purpose and the agreement is not primarily based on sex.

III. DIVORCE (DISSOLUTION) AND LEGAL SEPARATION

A. Divorce or dissolution (grounds):
   1. Impotency.
   2. Bigamy.
   3. Adultery.
   4. Desertion for one year.
   5. Habitual drunkenness for two years.
   6. Attempt on life of spouse.
   7. Extreme and repeated mental or physical cruelty.
   8. Conviction of felony or infamous crime.
   9. Infection of spouse with venereal disease.
   10. Excessive use of addictive drugs for two years.

B. Legal separation (grounds): Same as for divorce.

C. Residency requirements: Either spouse must be domiciled or stationed in state at time legal action is filed. Domicile or military presence must be maintained for 90 days preceding final decree of divorce.

D.   Remarriage: Possible immediately after divorce is final.

E.   Court orders after filing for divorce and before divorce is final:
1. Orders to either spouse concerning custody, support, and visitation of minor children.
2. Temporary alimony, court costs, and attorneys' fees to either spouse.
3. Temporary court orders preventing sale or removal of property, removal of children from jurisdiction of court, molestation of one spouse or of child by other spouse, or any other restraint needed.

F.   Alimony: Court may order to either spouse if:
1. Lacks resources to provide for needs.
2. Cannot support self through appropriate employment or because child custody makes employment difficult.
3. Is otherwise without sufficient income.

G.   Child support and custody:
1. Court may order either spouse to pay support.
2. Court may order custody to either spouse, taking all circumstances into consideration.

H.   Property division by court in absence of written or oral agreement:
1. Court may dispose of family home as it deems fair.
2. Court assigns each spouse's nonmarital separate property to respective owning spouse. Nonmarital property includes:
   a. Property acquired before the marriage.
   b. Property acquired by gift or inheritance.
   c. Property acquired in exchange for that described in (a) or (b).
   d. Property acquired after a legal separation.
   e. Property excluded by agreement.
   f. The increase in value of property acquired before marriage.
3. Court divides marital property (all other property including jointly owned property) without regard to marital misconduct in fair proportions.

IV. TERMINATION OF COHABITATION

A.   Court jurisdiction: No judicial control; voluntary parting.

B.   Court orders: A court may make orders for child support and custody similar to those made in a divorce, once paternity is established.

C.   Property division (Recent court decisions have refused to recognize the property rights of mates).

1. Courts would probably honor express bone fide partnership agreements with a valid business purpose as a means of dividing property and money, but would probably not infer them.
2. Courts in almost all instances would not honor an oral contract. A written agreement might be enforceable, but it appears doubtful.
3. Courts might order return of property to rightful owner or grant an interest in property or an award of money to a mate to the extent of his/her contribution.

D. Putative marriage: Courts will adjust the property rights in a putative marriage.

E. Palimony: Court decisions seem to indicate that a mate would not be entitled to receive rehabilitative alimony or temporary or permanent alimony.

V. SPECIFIC SUBJECTS (No written agreements, except for A,E,I.)
Reference to "BOTH" means married and unmarried couples.

A. Prenuptial or precohabitation agreements:
MARRIED: Valid.
UNMARRIED: Written agreements may be recognized, but it appears doubtful. Oral or implied contracts would probably not be valid.
BOTH: Agreement must be made without duress and with full disclosure of assets and other important information.

B. Property:
BOTH: All property is separate property of acquiring mate or spouse.

C. Liability of separate property for other spouse's or mate's debts:
MARRIED: No liability except that both spouses are liable for family expenses and education of children.
UNMARRIED: No liability.

D. Management and control of separate property of each:
BOTH: Each controls own separate property.
MARRIED: Both spouses must sign for sale of family home.

E. Contracts made during marriage or cohabitation settling property rights:
MARRIED: Separation agreements are valid. Agreement must be made without duress and with full disclosure of assets and other important information.
UNMARRIED: An agreement settling property rights may not be recognized.

F.   What can be willed?
     BOTH: Each spouse's or mate's separate property.

G.   Automatic protection for surviving spouse or mate:
     MARRIED: Surviving spouse receives exemption in family
          home of $10,000 over and above mortgage liens; rea-
          sonable sum for support of spouse and dependent chil-
          dren for nine months.
     UNMARRIED: No protection for surviving mate. Dependent
          children receive allowance and homestead exemption
          until youngest is twenty-one; dependent illegitimate
          children would probably receive allowances and home-
          stead exemption if entitled to inherit (see subject H).

H.   If no will:
     MARRIED: Surviving spouse receives one-third of deceased
          spouse's estate if descendants of decedent survive; all
          if there are no descendants.
     UNMARRIED: Surviving mate receives nothing. Illegitimate
          children inherit from mother; from father if parents
          marry and children are acknowledged by father, or if
          paternity is adjudicated.

I.   Contracts:
     BOTH: May contract with anyone, including each other.

J.   Lawsuits:
     BOTH: Each may sue and be sued separately unless both
          involved.

K.   Homestead law:
     BOTH: $10,000 in family home over and above liens, in-
          cluding mortgages for every householder having a fam-
          ily. Includes proceeds of sale for one year after sale. No
          necessity to file for this protection.

L.   Civil suits by spouses or mates against each other:
     MARRIED: May sue each other for contracts, but not for per-
          sonal wrongs.
     UNMARRIED: Permitted.

M.   Legitimacy:
     MARRIED: Children born during marriage are presumed le-
          gitimate.
     UNMARRIED: Illegitimate children are heirs of mother. Le-
          gitimized if paternity is adjudicated.
     BOTH: Legitimate if parents marry and father acknowledges
          children.

N.   Adoption:
     BOTH: Any person of legal age may adopt any minor child.

Adult may be adopted in certain circumstances. Requires investigation of character, reputation, general standing in community, and whether petitioners are proper persons to adopt.

MARRIED: Both spouses must sign for adoption.

O. Division of property upon termination of relationship:

MARRIED: Court divides marital and joint property as it deems fair.

UNMARRIED: Court would probably not divide joint property. In the event of unfair economic gain, court might order return of property.

BOTH: Each spouse or mate retains his/her separate property.

VI. RECENT EVENTS, TRENDS, AND CONCLUSIONS

A. Although a court must consider the economic value of a homemaker when making a fair property division upon divorce, the court need not place a specific monetary value on these services.

B. Military retirement pensions are marital property subject to division upon divorce.

C. The state supreme court recently reversed the court of appeals and condemned a relationship in which an unmarried couple and their three children had lived as a family for 15 years. When the relationship ended, the court refused to order division of property as if the couple were married. The *Marvin* case was expressly rejected. The court states that the 1977 Marriage and Divorce Act lists as one of its purposes to "preserve the integrity of marriage." In addition, says the court, the act reaffirms the abolition of common-law marriages, rejects no-fault divorces, and extends legal recognition to nonmarital relationships only when there is a good-faith belief in a valid marriage.

D. In another recent Supreme Court case which reversed the lower court's ruling, a father acquired custody of his three daughters because his ex-wife was openly living with another man. The court pointed out that her relationship violated the state law against fornication as well as the moral policies expressed in the Marriage and Divorce Act.

INDIANA

I. MARRIAGE

A.   Legality:
1. Age: 18; under 18, need consent of parent or guardian.
2. License: Required; marriage must be within 60 days of issuance.
3. Medical examination: Report stating whether person has syphilis. Sickle-cell anemia test may be required.
4. Waiting period: 3 days.

B.   Common-law marriages: Not recognized.

C.   Out-of-state marriages: Valid if valid where entered into unless done with intention of avoiding laws of Indiana.

D.   Adultery: Not a crime.

E.   Property: Separate.

F.   Partnerships: A partnership agreement between spouses is probably enforceable as long as there is a valid business purpose.

II. COHABITATION

A.   Legality:
1. Cohabitation: Not a crime
2. Fornication: Not a crime.
3. All private, nonviolent sexual acts between consenting adults are legal.

B.   Common-law marriage: Continued cohabitation after the reason for an invalid marriage is removed will result in a valid marriage, even though common-law marriage is not recognized. However, if the relationship was illicit from the beginning, no marriage would result.

C.   Putative marriage: Recognized to the extent of compensating a putative spouse for household services.

D.   Property: A spouse who is living in adultery at time of death of other spouse receives no share of the deceased spouse's estate.

E.   Partnerships: A partnership agreement between mates is probably enforceable as long as there is a valid business purpose and the agreement is not primarily based on sex.

III. DIVORCE (DISSOLUTION) AND LEGAL SEPARATION

A.   Divorce or dissolution (grounds):
  1. Irretrievable breakdown of marriage (no fault).
  2. Conviction of infamous crime during marriage.
  3. Impotency existing at time of marriage.
  4. Incurable insanity for 2 years.

B.   Legal separation (grounds): Not available.

C.   Residency requirements: 6 months for either spouse before legal action is filed.

D.   Remarriage: Possible immediately after divorce is final.

E.   Court orders after filing for divorce and before divorce is final:
  1. Temporary orders for support and custody of children, court costs, attorneys' fees, and possession of property.
  2. Restraining orders:
    a. restraining either spouse from transferring, concealing or selling of property, or using it as collateral on a debt;
    b. preventing one spouse from disturbing peace of other;
    c. excluding either spouse from family dwelling.

F.   Alimony:
  1. May be granted by court to either spouse.
  2. May be arranged by agreement of spouses and merged into divorce decree.

G.   Child support and custody:
  1. Court may order either parent or both to pay support.
  2. Court determines custody in best interests of child. No presumptions favor either parent.

H.   Property division by court in absence of written or oral agreement:
  1. Courts have power to distribute all separate property including joint property, as it deems fair.
  2. Considerations: Contributions of each, extent of acquisition prior to marriage, economic circumstances of each, conduct of parties during marriage, earnings or earning ability of each.

IV. TERMINATION OF COHABITATION

    A.   Court jurisdiction: No judicial control; voluntary parting.

    B.   Court orders: A court may make orders for child support and custody similar to those made in a divorce, once paternity is established.

    C.   Property division (decisions in other states suggest the following possibilities):

        1. Courts could infer partnership agreements as a means of dividing property and money.

        2. Courts could order return or division of property and money if there had been an implied or express agreement.

        3. Courts could order return of property to rightful owner or grant an interest in property or an award of money to a mate to the extent of his/her contribution toward purchase of property.

        4. Since cohabitation is not illegal, recovery could be had for performing household duties as well as for financial contributions, so long as the implied or express agreement was not primarily based upon sex.

    D.   Putative marriage: The household services of a putative wife who believes in the validity of an invalid marriage will be compensated.

    E.   Palimony: There have been no court decisions to indicate that rehabilitative alimony or temporary or permanent alimony would be awarded to a mate, but such an award is a possibility.

V. SPECIFIC SUBJECTS (No written agreements, except for A,E,I.) Reference to "BOTH" means married and unmarried couples.

    A.   Prenuptial or precohabitation agreements:

        MARRIED: Valid.

        UNMARRIED: May be valid if sex is not the basis of the agreement and if meant for protection of property interests.

        BOTH: Agreements must be made without duress and with full disclosure of assets and other important information.

    B.   Property:

        BOTH: All property is separate property of acquiring spouse or mate.

    C.   Liability of separate property for other spouse's or mate's debts:

        MARRIED: Husband is liable for wife's premarital debts to the extent of personal property or rents received from

her before or during marriage. Otherwise, no liability.
UNMARRIED: No liability.

D. Management and control of separate property of each:
BOTH: Each controls own separate property.

E. Contracts made during marriage or cohabitation settling property rights:
MARRIED: Valid.
UNMARRIED: May be enforceable if based on earnings, property, etc., rather than on sex.
BOTH: Agreement must be made without duress and with full disclosure of assets and other important information.

F. What can be willed?
BOTH: Each spouse's or mate's separate property.
MARRIED: Surviving spouse may elect not to receive according to provisions of will and to take instead one-third of deceased spouse's property.

G. Automatic protection for surviving spouse or mate:
MARRIED: Surviving spouse receives $8,500 personal-property allowance and may stay in home for one year rent-free. Widow receives up to one-third interest in deceased husband's real estate free of creditors.
UNMARRIED: No protection for surviving mate. Minor children receive $8,500 allowance; minor illegitimate children, if they are entitled to inherit, receive same (see subject H).

H. If no will:
MARRIED: Surviving spouse receives everything of deceased spouse if there are no surviving children or parents; otherwise, division made between them.
UNMARRIED: Surviving mate receives nothing. Illegitimate children inherit from mother; from father if parents marry and father acknowledges children, or if paternity established in court before death of father.

I. Contracts:
BOTH: Each may contract with anyone, including each other.

J. Lawsuits:
BOTH: Each may sue or be sued separately unless both involved.

K. Homestead law:
BOTH: Every debtor domiciled in state has exemptions up to $5,000 over liens, including mortgages for personal residence, $2,000 for other real estate or tangible personal property, $100 for intangible personal property;

total not to exceed $6,000. Debtor must file with officer a sworn schedule of his property, credits, and effects, and specifically claim exempt property.

L.   Civil suits by spouses or mates against each other:

MARRIED: May sue each other for contract breach and for injuries to separate property, but not for negligent personal injuries.

UNMARRIED: Each may sue the other.

M.   Legitimacy:

MARRIED: Children born during marriage are presumed legitimate. Children born before marriage are legitimized if parents later marry and father acknowledges paternity.

UNMARRIED: Illegitimate children inherit from mother; from father if parents marry and father acknowledges children, or if paternity established in court before father's death. Establishment of paternity does not legitimize children for any purpose except inheritance.

N.   Adoption:

BOTH: Any resident may adopt. Both children and adults may be adopted. Financial strength is significant consideration.

MARRIED: Both husband and wife must sign for adoption.

O.   Division of property upon termination of relationship:

MARRIED: Court divides separate property, including joint property, acquired before or during marriage in a fair and reasonable manner.

UNMARRIED: Implied or express contracts, value of services, or unfair economic gain may create rights to property.

VI. RECENT EVENTS, TRENDS, AND CONCLUSIONS

A.   The Indiana Civil Liberties Union is testing the constitutionality of a law that requires an illegitimate child to take its mother's last name.

B.   It is permissible to deny a wife a portion of her husband's military retirement pay. However, a retirement plan may be considered a factor in dividing property, although payments are not being received when the property division is made.

C.   In compliance with a recent U.S. Supreme Court decision, a statute was declared unconstitutional which denied permission to a person with dependent children to remarry unless there was a showing of ability to support the children and compliance with earlier court orders.

    D.   Since cohabitation and fornication have been decriminalized, it is possible that a liberalization in attitude could occur and that some or all of the remedies suggested in the *Marvin* case would be followed.

IOWA

I. MARRIAGE

    A.   Legality:

         1. Age: 18; under 18, need consent of parents or guardian.

         2. License: Required; marriage must be performed within 30 days of issuance.

         3. Medical examination: Physician's certificate of freedom from syphilis within 20 days prior to license application.

         4. Waiting period: 3 days between application for license and issuance.

    B.   Common-law marriages: Recognized.

    C.   Out-of-state marriages: Valid if valid in state where entered into.

    D.   Adultery: Not a crime.

    E.   Property: Separate.

    F.   Partnerships: A partnership agreement between spouses is probably enforceable as long as there is a valid business purpose.

II. COHABITATION

    A.   Legality:

         1. Cohabitation: Not a crime.

      2. Fornication: Not a crime.

      3. All private, nonviolent sexual acts between consenting adults are legal.

B.   Common-law marriage: Recognized.

C.   Putative Marriage: Recognized for the purpose of adjusting property rights.

D.   Property: Courts will not imply the promise of either mate to pay for services rendered.

E.   Partnerships: A partnership agreement between mates is probably enforceable as long as there is a valid business purpose and the agreement is not primarily based on sex.

III. DIVORCE (DISSOLUTION) AND LEGAL SEPARATION

A.   Divorce or dissolution (grounds):

      1. Breakdown of marriage (no fault).

      2. Mental illness.

B.   Legal separation (grounds): Same as for divorce.

C.   Residency requirements: The spouse not filing for divorce must be a resident when divorce is filed. Otherwise, the spouse filing must be a resident for one year prior to time of filing.

D.   Remarriage: Possible immediately after divorce is final, but divorce is not final until 90 days after service of notice.

E.   Court orders after filing for divorce and before divorce is final:

      1. Support of spouse and children and temporary child custody.

      2. Court costs and attorneys' fees.

F.   Alimony: To either spouse as court deems fair.

G.   Child support and custody:

      1. Court orders support and custody to either parent as it deems fair.

      2. May also order joint custody.

H.   Property division by court in absence of written or oral agreement:

      1. Court has power to order division of all separate property, including joint property, as it deems fair.

      2. Fault is not considered.

IV. TERMINATION OF COHABITATION

A.   Court jurisdiction: No judicial control; voluntary parting.

B.   Court orders:
1. Court may make orders for child support and custody similar to those made in a divorce, once paternity is established.
2. Alimony for a putative spouse.

C.   Property division (decisions in other states suggest the following possibilities):
1. Courts would probably order return or division of property and money if there had been an express agreement. It is uncertain whether they would be willing to infer an agreement.
2. Courts could order return of property to rightful owner or grant an interest in property or an award of money to a mate to the extent of his/her contribution toward purchase of property.
3. Since living together is not illegal, recovery could be had for performing household duties as well as for direct financial contributions, so long as the agreement was express and was not primarily based upon sex.

D.   Putative marriage:
1. Courts will make adjustments for services rendered, even without an express agreement, if the person giving the services mistakenly believed marriage was valid.
2. A putative spouse may receive alimony.

E.   Palimony:
There have been no court decisions to indicate that rehabilitative alimony or temporary or permanent alimony would be awarded to a mate, but such an award is a possibility.

V. SPECIFIC SUBJECTS (No written agreements, except for A,E,I.)
Reference to "BOTH" means married and unmarried couples.

A.   Prenuptial or precohabitation agreements:
MARRIED: May not contract with each other for performance of traditional obligations of marriage, or to change interest one spouse has in other's property arising out of marriage; otherwise valid.
UNMARRIED: Probably valid if sex is not the basis of the agreement and if meant for protection of property interests.
BOTH: Agreements must be made without duress and with full disclosure of assets and other important information.

B.   Property:
BOTH: All property is separate property of acquiring spouse or mate.
MARRIED: Parties have limited rights to contract otherwise.

C. Liability of separate property for other spouse's or mate's debts:

MARRIED: No liability, except both liable for family expenses and education of children.

UNMARRIED: No liability.

D. Management and control of separate property of each:

MARRIED: Both spouses must sign to sell or encumber family home.

BOTH: Each controls own separate property.

E. Contracts made during marriage or cohabitation settling property rights:

MARRIED: Separation agreements recognized and enforced.

UNMARRIED: Probably enforceable if based on earnings, property, etc., rather than on sex.

BOTH: Agreements must be made without duress and with full disclosure of assets and other important information.

F. What can be willed?

BOTH: Each spouse's or mate's separate property.

MARRIED: Surviving spouse may elect to take either statutory share (see subject H) or family home for life instead of according to will provisions.

G. Automatic protection for surviving spouse or mate:

MARRIED: Surviving spouse, or decedent's minor children not living with surviving spouse, receive reasonable support for one year.

UNMARRIED: No protection for surviving mate. Children receive reasonable support for one year if entitled to inherit (see subject H).

H. If no will:

MARRIED: If issue of deceased spouse survive, surviving spouse receives one-third in value of all real estate owned by decedent at any time during marriage, provided no forced judicial sale nor a relinquishment of rights has been made by the surviving spouse, plus all exempt personal property that was owned by decedent and one-third of all other personal property possessed by decedent. If the foregoing does not amount to $50,000, surviving spouse receives that portion of remaining homestead and nonexempt real and personal property, after the payment of debts, to make up the difference. If there are no surviving issue, surviving spouse receives one-half in value of all real and personal property as stated above, up to $50,000. If foregoing does not amount to $50,000, surviving spouse receives other property to make up the difference.

UNMARRIED: Surviving mate receives nothing. Illegitimate children inherit from mother; from father if paternity proven during father's lifetime, or if father declares children to be his own.

I.   Contracts:
BOTH: Each may contract with anyone, including each other.
MARRIED: With exceptions noted in subject A.

J.   Lawsuits:
BOTH: Each may sue and be sued separately unless both involved.

K.   Homestead law:
MARRIED: Family home, owned by husband or wife, receives an exemption up to $500 over liens, including mortgages. Owner may select homestead and record it. If not done by owner, levying officer must do so before a forced sale.
UNMARRIED: Probably same if mate has family living in home with him/her.

L.   Civil suits by spouses or mates against each other:
MARRIED: May not sue each other for negligent injuries.
UNMARRIED: Permitted.

M.   Legitimacy:
MARRIED: Children born during marriage are presumed legitimate.
UNMARRIED: Illegitimate children inherit from mother; from father if paternity proven during father's lifetime, or if father declares children to be his own.
BOTH: Children are legitimized if parents marry.

N.   Adoption:
MARRIED: Husband and wife must consent to adoption.
UNMARRIED: An unmarried adult may adopt.
BOTH: Investigation required to determine whether home and adopting adult or adults are suitable.

O.   Division of property upon termination of relationship:
MARRIED: Court divides all separate property, including joint property, as it deems fair.
UNMARRIED: Implied or express contracts, value of services, or unfair economic gain may create rights to property.

VI. RECENT EVENTS, TRENDS, AND CONCLUSIONS

Since common-law marriages are recognized, and neither cohabitation, adultery, nor fornication is illegal, courts would probably follow some or all of the theories of the *Marvin* case.

KANSAS

I. MARRIAGE

    A.   Legality:
1. Age: 18; under 18, need consent of parents or guardian and judge of district court.
2. License: Required.
3. Medical examination: Blood test required within 30 days prior to issuance of license.
4. Waiting period: 3 days between application for license and issuance.

    B.   Common-law marriages: Recognized.

    C.   Out-of-state marriages: Valid if valid in state where entered into.

    D.   Adultery: Illegal (misdemeanor); fine and/or sentence; applies both to spouse and a mate who knows other party is married.

    E.   Property: Separate.

    F.   Partnerships: A partnership agreement between spouses is probably enforceable as long as there is a valid business purpose.

II. COHABITATION

    A.   Legality:
1. Cohabitation: Not a crime.
2. Fornication: Not a crime.

    B.   Common-law marriage: Recognized, can result from continued cohabitation with former spouse after divorce becomes final.

    C.   Putative marriage: Recognized for purposes of adjusting property rights.

    D.   Property: Cohabitation after divorce does not terminate alimony unless it becomes a common-law marriage.

    E.   Partnerships: A partnership agreement between mates is probably enforceable as long as there is a valid business purpose and the agreement is not primarily based on sex.

III. DIVORCE (DISSOLUTION) AND LEGAL SEPARATION

A.   Divorce or dissolution (grounds):
   1. Abandonment for one year.
   2. Adultery.
   3. Extreme cruelty.
   4. Habitual drunkenness.
   5. Gross neglect of duty.
   6. Conviction of felony and imprisonment therefor.
   7. Confinement for 3 years because of mental illness.
   8. Incompatibility (no fault).

B.   Legal separation (grounds): Same as for divorce.

C.   Residency requirements: Plaintiff must be resident for 60 days before divorce action filed.

D.   Remarriage: Possible 30 days after divorce is final.

E.   Court orders after filing for divorce and before divorce is final:
   1. Temporary alimony for either party.
   2. Court costs, including attorneys' fees, to either.
   3. Support and custody of minor children.

F.   Alimony: May be awarded to either spouse.

G.   Child support and custody:
   1. Court orders support and allowance for education.
   2. Each parent is equally considered in assigning custody.
   3. Joint custody may be awarded and parents will have equal rights and responsibilities.

H.   Property division by court in absence of written or oral agreement: Court may divide real estate and personal property including joint property, as it deems fair whether owned by either prior to marriage, acquired by either in his/her own right after marriage, or acquired by joint efforts.

IV. TERMINATION OF COHABITATION

A.   Court jurisdiction: No judicial control; voluntary parting.

B.   Court orders: Court may make orders similar to those made in a divorce, once paternity is established.

C.   Property division (decisions in other states suggest the following possibilities):
   1. Courts could infer partnership agreements as a means of dividing property and money.
   2. Courts could order return or division of property and money if there had been an implied or express agreement.

3. Courts could order return of property to rightful owner or grant an interest in property or an award of money to a mate to the extent of his/her contribution toward purchase of property.

4. Since living together is not illegal, it is possible that recovery could be had for performing household duties as well as for direct financial contributions, so long as the implied or express agreement was not based primarily upon sex.

D. Putative marriage: Courts will adjust the rights of a mate who had a good-faith belief in a valid marriage.

E. Palimony: There have been no court decisions to indicate that rehabilitative alimony or temporary or permanent alimony would be awarded to a mate and such an award seems unlikely.

V. SPECIFIC SUBJECTS (No written agreements, except for A,E,I.) Reference to "BOTH" means married and unmarried couples.

A. Prenuptial or precohabitation agreements:
MARRIED: Valid; homestead rights cannot be waived by agreement.
UNMARRIED: Probably valid if sex is not the basis of the agreement and if meant for protection of property interests.
BOTH: Agreements must be made without duress and with full disclosure of assets and other important information.

B. Separate property:
MARRIED: Property acquired before marriage or after marriage by gift or inheritance, plus earnings and profits from separate property. Other property acquired during marriage is marital property unless excluded by written agreement.
UNMARRIED: All property is separate property of acquiring mate.

C. Liability of separate property for other spouse's or mate's debts:
BOTH: No liability.

D. Management and control of separate property of each:
BOTH: Each controls own property.
MARRIED: Both spouses must sign for sale of family home or property in which he/she has dower rights.

E. Contracts made during marriage or cohabitation settling property rights:
MARRIED: Valid. Separation agreements are incorporated

into divorce decree and are nonmodifiable except for provisions for child support and custody.

UNMARRIED: Probably enforceable if based on earnings, property, etc., rather than on sex.

BOTH: Agreements must be made without duress and with full disclosure of assets and other important information.

F. What can be willed?
BOTH: Each spouse's or mate's separate property.

MARRIED: Subject to dower rights. Surviving spouse may elect to disregard (see subject H) instead of accepting the provisions of the will.

G. Automatic protection for surviving spouse or mate:
MARRIED: Surviving spouse has homestead exemption and dower rights. Surviving spouse and minor children receive support allowance consisting of clothing, household furnishings, and cash in amount of not less than $750 nor more than $7,500.

UNMARRIED: No protection for surviving mate. Minor children would probably receive homestead exemption and support allowance if entitled to inherit (see subject H).

H. If no will:
MARRIED: One-half to surviving spouse and one-half to surviving children of deceased spouse, or their descendants. Surviving spouse receives everything if there are no surviving children or their descendants.

UNMARRIED: Surviving mate receives nothing. Illegitimate children inherit from mother; from father if father openly or in writing declares children to be his own, or if paternity is judicially established during father's lifetime.

I. Contracts:
BOTH: Each may contract with anyone, including each other.

J. Lawsuits:
BOTH: Each may sue or be sued separately, unless both involved.

K. Homestead law:
MARRIED: Total value over liens, including mortgages, in family home occupied as residence by family of owner exempt from forced sale. Proceeds of sale also exempt until new home acquired. If homestead has not been selected and set apart, owner or spouse may notify levying officer in writing at time of levy or before a forced sale.

UNMARRIED: Could probably be claimed by a mate who owned home and occupied it with family.

L. Dower and/or curtesy:
MARRIED: Surviving spouse has undivided one-half interest in all real estate of deceased spouse held at any time during marriage, unless waived.

M. Civil suits by spouses or mates against each other:
MARRIED: Probably permitted.
UNMARRIED: Permitted.

N. Legitimacy:
MARRIED: Children born during marriage presumed legitimate. Children born before marriage are legitimized if parents later marry.
UNMARRIED: Illegitimate children inherit from mother; inherit from father if father openly or in writing declares children to be his own, or if paternity is judicially established during father's lifetime.

O. Adoption:
BOTH: Any adult may adopt minor or adult.
MARRIED: Both spouses must consent to adoption.

P. Division of property upon termination of relationship:
MARRIED: Court divides separate property, including joint property, as it deems fair.
UNMARRIED: Implied or express contracts, value of services, and unfair economic gain may create rights to property.

VI. RECENT EVENTS, TRENDS, AND CONCLUSIONS

A. A husband ordered to pay alimony until the wife remarried was not relieved of obligations when her later marriage was invalidated because she lacked mental capacity.

B. A former wife's cohabitation after divorce was not a sufficient reason to terminate alimony because it did not amount to common-law marriage.

C. Since cohabitation has recently been decriminalized, it is possible that some or all of the theories of the *Marvin* case would be followed.

KENTUCKY

I. MARRIAGE

A. Legality:
1. Age: 18; under 18, need consent of parent or guardian.
2. License: Required; good for 30 days.
3. Medical examination: Examination and tests by physician or laboratory for syphilis within 15 days prior to application for license.
4. Waiting period: 3 days between application for license and issuance.

B. Common-law marriages: Not valid; recognized if valid where entered into, even if Kentucky couple go to another state for this purpose.

C. Out-of-state marriages: Valid if valid in state where entered into.

D. Adultery: Not a crime.

E. Property: Separate.

F. Partnerships: A partnership agreement between spouses is probably enforceable as long as there is a valid business purpose.

II. COHABITATION

A. Legality:
1. Cohabitation: Not a crime.
2. Fornication: Not a crime.

B. Common-law marriage: Not recognized unless entered into in another state where it is valid. If a Kentucky couple goes to another state for the purpose of entering into a common-law marriage, the marriage will be recognized.

C. Putative marriage: Recognized for purpose of adjusting property rights.

D. Property: Property rights have been recognized, particularly when there was some agreement between mates.

E. Partnerships: A partnership agreement between mates is

probably enforceable as long as there is a valid business purpose and the agreement is not primarily based on sex.

III. DIVORCE (DISSOLUTION) AND LEGAL SEPARATION

A.   Divorce or dissolution (grounds): Irretrievable breakdown of marriage (no fault); must include living apart or without sexual cohabitation for 60 days.

B.   Legal separation (grounds): Any cause court finds sufficient. May be converted to decree of divorce after one year upon motion of either party.

C.   Residency requirements: 180 days by at least one party before divorce action filed.

D.   Remarriage: Possible immediately after divorce is final.

E.   Court orders after filing for divorce and before divorce is final:
1. Temporary alimony for either.
2. Court costs and attorney's fees.
3. Temporary child support and custody.
4. Any necessary restraining orders or other temporary orders.

F.   Alimony:
1. Granted by court to either spouse as it deems fair.
2. Grounds:
   a. Insufficient property available to provide for reasonable needs.
   b. Inability of spouse to support self.
   c. Condition or circumstances of child subject to custody.
3. Fault may be considered in determining amount.
4. Terminates upon death of either spouse or remarriage of recipient.

G.   Child support and custody:
1. Support is ordered to one or both, considering all relevant circumstances.
2. Custody ordered in best interests of child; both parents equally considered.

H.   Property division by court in absence of written or oral agreement:
1. Each spouse retains his/her separate property. Marital property is divided by court as it deems fair. (Marital property is all property acquired during the marriage whether title is held jointly or separately, except by gift or inheritance, or acquired after decree of sepa-

ration or as an increase in value of separate property, or as a result of the exchange of marital property for separate property.)

2. Fault may still be a factor, even though statute provides that marital misconduct is not to be considered.

3. Separation agreements are encouraged.

IV. TERMINATION OF COHABITATION

A. Court jurisdiction: No judicial control; voluntary parting.

B. Court orders:
   1. A court may make orders for child support and custody similar to those made in a divorce, once paternity has been established.
   2. Mother is favored for custody, but best interests of child are primary concern.

C. Property division (decisions in Kentucky and in other states suggest the following possibilities):
   1. Courts could infer partnership agreements as a means of dividing property and money.
   2. Courts could order return or division of property and money if there had been an implied or express agreement.
   3. Courts could order return of property to rightful owner or grant an interest in property or an award of money to a mate to the extent of his/her contribution toward purchase of property.
   4. Since living together is not illegal, recovery could be had for performing household duties as well as for direct financial contribution so long as the implied or express agreement was not primarily based upon sex.

D. Putative marriage: A putative spouse can have returned his/her interest in property.

E. Palimony: There have been no court decisions to indicate that rehabilitative alimony or temporary or permanent alimony would be awarded to a mate, but such an award is a possibility.

V. SPECIFIC SUBJECTS (No written agreements, except for A,E,I.)
Reference to "BOTH" means married and unmarried couples.

A. Prenuptial or precohabitation agreements:
   MARRIED: Valid.
   UNMARRIED: Probably valid if sex is not the basis of the agreement and if meant for protection of property interests.

BOTH: Agreements must be made without duress and with full disclosure of assets and other important information.

B. Property:
BOTH: All property is separate property of acquiring spouse or mate.

C. Liability of separate property for other spouse's or mate's debts:
MARRIED: No liability, except husband is liable for necessities furnished to wife.
UNMARRIED: No liability.

D. Management and control of separate property of each:
BOTH: Each controls own separate property.
MARRIED: Both spouses must sign to sell property affecting dower right (see subject L).

E. Contracts made during marriage or cohabitation settling property rights:
MARRIED: Separation agreements are encouraged; enforced if found fair and reasonable.
UNMARRIED: Probably enforceable if based on earnings, property, etc., rather than on sex.
BOTH: Agreements must be made without duress and with full disclosure of assets and other important information.

F. What can be willed?
BOTH: Each spouse's separate property.
MARRIED: Subject to dower rights (see subject L).

G. Automatic protection for surviving spouse or mate:
MARRIED: Homestead exemption, dower, or curtesy. If deceased spouse left no will, surviving spouse and minor children receive $3,500 in exempt personal property. Surviving spouse may remain in house until dower or curtesy assigned.
UNMARRIED: No protection for surviving mate. Children would probably get homestead exemption and exempt personal property if entitled to inherit (see subject H).

H. If no will:
MARRIED: Surviving spouse receives everything if deceased spouse leaves no surviving descendants, parents, or brothers and sisters. If any survive, surviving spouse receives dower rights and one-half personal property.
UNMARRIED: Surviving mate receives nothing. Illegitimate children inherit from mother only.

I. Contracts:
BOTH: Each may contract with anyone, including each other.

J.   Lawsuits:
      BOTH: Each may sue and be sued separately unless both involved.

K.   Homestead law:
      BOTH: $1,000 exemption allowed to householder with family using property as home. May be sold or used as collateral only by both spouses together. No filing required; levying officer sets homestead aside before any forced sale.

L.   Dower and/or curtesy:
      MARRIED: Surviving spouse receives one-half real estate owned at spouse's death and one-third real estate owned during marriage (but not at death), plus one-third surplus personal property (personal property remaining after payment of expenses, debts, and any family allowances).

M.   Civil suits by spouses or mates against each other:
      BOTH: Permitted.

N.   Legitimacy:
      MARRIED: Children born during marriage presumed legitimate. Children born before marriage are legitimized if father later marries mother and recognizes children.
      UNMARRIED: Illegitimate children inherit only from mother. Children of incestuous marriage are illegitimate; children of any other invalid marriage are legitimate.

O.   Adoption:
      BOTH: Any person over eighteen may adopt any person of any age. Adoption cannot be denied on religious, ethnic, or racial grounds. Investigation of home and background of prospective parent(s) required.

P.   Division of property upon termination of relationship:
      MARRIED: Court has power to divide all marital and joint property acquired during marriage except by gift or inheritance. Separate property acquired before marriage is retained by owner.
      UNMARRIED: Implied or express contracts, value of services, or unfair economic gain may create rights to property.

VI. RECENT EVENTS, TRENDS, AND CONCLUSIONS

A.   A 1973 court decision ruled that a marriage between two women is void.

B.   A dentist's license may be considered marital property to determine other spouse's monetary contribution to earning capacity to achieve fair result on divorce.

C. Cohabitation after a separation is not a reconciliation and does not void a separation agreement.

D. A husband's common stock in the family business owned before marriage is not marital property to be divided upon divorce.

E. Recent court decisions recognize property rights of mates, especially when an agreement is found. It seems likely that some or all of the theories of *Marvin* would be followed.

LOUISIANA

I. MARRIAGE

A. Legality:
1. Age: 18, male; 16, female; under 18, need consent of parents or tutor (guardian).
2. License: Available but not required; marriage without license is valid and not subject to annulment; only penalty is assessed against official performing marriage ceremony.
3. Medical examination: Required within 10 days of license application, with physician's certificate that applicant is free of venereal disease.
4. Waiting period: 72 hours between issuance of license and ceremony.

B. Common-law marriages: Not recognized; not recognized if entered into outside state by Louisiana residents.

C. Out-of-state marriages: Valid if valid in state where entered into.

D. Adultery: Not a crime.

E. Property: Community.

F. Partnerships: A partnership agreement between spouses is

probably enforceable as long as there is a valid business purpose.

II. COHABITATION

A. Legality:
  1. Cohabitation: Not a crime.
  2. Fornication: Not a crime.

B. Putative marriage: Recognized; a party in good faith and children receive civil effect of valid marriage.

C. Property:
  1. Concubinage is a recognized status. An unmarried female mate is a concubine. Concubinage is a relationship resembling marriage, in which the mates have not undergone a marriage ceremony but make no effort to conceal the illicit character of their relationship.
  2. A concubine assumes the legal responsibilities of a wife without receiving the privileges of a legal wife. Her services are presumed to be a gift.
  3. If the primary motive of the relationship is concubinage, the concubine has no claim to her lover's assets.
  4. If the initial motive for their coming together was not concubinage but rather some business interest, division of property will not be disallowed simply because the relationship is also illicit. Thus a concubine can claim rights arising out of a business relationship which is independent of the sexual relationship.

D. Partnerships: A partnership agreement between mates is probably enforceable as long as there is a valid business purpose and the agreement is not primarily based on sex.

III. DIVORCE (DISSOLUTION) AND LEGAL SEPARATION

A. Divorce or dissolution (grounds):
  1. No fault: Living apart for 2 years.
  2. No period of separation required:
     a. Adultery.
     b. Conviction of felony and sentenced to death or imprisonment at hard labor.
  3. After living apart for one year from date of legal separation:
     a. Habitual intemperance, excesses, cruel treatment, or outrages.
     b. Public defamation.
     c. Abandonment.
     d. Attempt on life of other.

      e. One charged with felony and has fled from justice and other spouse produces proof he actually is guilty of felony.

      f. Intentional nonsupport.

      g. Voluntarily living apart for one year.

      h. Voluntarily living apart for 6 months and affidavit showing irreconcilable differences.

B.   Legal separation (grounds): Same as for divorce except the no-fault ground. All are immediately available for legal separation.

C.   Residency requirements: None.

D.   Remarriage: Possible immediately after divorce; but if ground is adultery, guilty party cannot marry his or her accomplice.

E.   Court orders after filing for divorce and before divorce is final:

    1. Temporary alimony.

    2. If both parents seek custody during divorce, custody will be given to wife unless there are strong reasons for not doing so.

F.   Alimony:

    1. Granted to either spouse lacking sufficient means for support.

    2. Fault is a consideration and may preclude the award of alimony.

    3. Will be revoked if it becomes unnecessary, and terminates if recipient remarries.

G.   Child support and custody:

    1. Both parents are responsible for support.

    2. Custody is given according to the best interests of the child.

H.   Property division by court in absence of written or oral agreement:

    1. Each spouse receives his/her separate property.

    2. Community property divided by the court as it deems fair.

    3. Fault is a consideration.

IV. TERMINATION OF COHABITATION

A.   Court jurisdiction: No judicial control; voluntary parting.

B.   Court orders: A court may make orders for child support and custody similar to those made in a divorce, once paternity is established.

C. Property division (decisions in other states suggest the following possibilities):

1. Courts could infer partnership agreements as a means of dividing property and money.
2. Courts could order return or division of property and money if there had been an implied or express agreement.
3. Courts could order return of property to rightful owner or grant an interest in property or an award of money to a mate to the extent of his/her contribution toward purchase of property.
4. Since cohabitation is not illegal, it is possible that recovery could be had for performing household duties as well as for direct financial contributions, so long as the implied or express agreement was not primarily based on sex.

D. Putative marriage:

1. A mate with a good-faith belief in the validity of an invalid marriage may have valid claims to property accumulated during the relationship.
2. A putative spouse may receive all the privileges of a legal spouse, especially if the putative marriage is not bigamous.
3. If the putative marriage is bigamous, the legal spouse and the putative spouse may divide that part of the bigamist's estate that was acquired after the beginning of the putative marriage.

E. Palimony: There have been no court decisions to indicate that rehabilitative alimony or temporary or permanent alimony would be awarded to a mate, but such an award is a possibility.

V. **SPECIFIC SUBJECTS** (No written agreements, except for A,H,L.) Reference to "BOTH" means married and unmarried couples.

A. Prenuptial or precohabitation agreements:
   MARRIED: Valid. Law regulates property of married couples if there is a breach of the agreements. No agreements allowed that would alter established order of succession.
   UNMARRIED: Probably valid if sex is not the basis of the agreement and if meant for protection of property rights.
   BOTH: Agreements must be made without duress and with full disclosure of assets and other important information.

B. Separate property:
   MARRIED: All property acquired before marriage, acquired

during marriage with separate funds, or acquired during marriage by gift or inheritance.

UNMARRIED: All property is separate property of acquiring mate.

C. Community property:

MARRIED: All property acquired during marriage (unless purchased with separate funds), all profits of separate property, all earnings of both spouses. Community property belongs half to each.

D. Liability of separate property for other spouse's or mate's debts:

MARRIED: No liability if debts concern only spouse's separate property.

UNMARRIED: No liability.

E. Liability of community property for debts contracted by one spouse:

MARRIED: Debts contracted during marriage are community debts and community property is liable.

F. Management and control of separate property of each:

BOTH: Each controls own property.

G. Management and control of community property:

MARRIED: Each spouse may manage and control community property. One may not dispose of community—personal or real—property without the other's signature or consent. Each must sign for sale, mortgage, or lease of family home and furnishings.

H. Contracts made during marriage or cohabitation settling property rights:

MARRIED: Separation agreements in advance of divorce are illegal unless properly ratified after divorce or incorporated into divorce decree.

UNMARRIED: Probably enforceable if based on earnings, property, etc., rather than on sex.

BOTH: Agreements must be made without duress and with full disclosure of assets and other important information.

I. What can be willed?

BOTH: Each spouse's or mate's separate property.

MARRIED: Each spouse's half of community property.

J. Automatic protection for surviving spouse or mate:

MARRIED: Surviving spouse or minor children receive homestead exemption and a sum from the estate to total $1,000 in certain circumstances. Surviving spouse receives one-fourth of a rich deceased spouse's property, or life interest if there are children.

UNMARRIED: No protection for surviving mate. Minor children get homestead exemption and up to $1,000 allowance if entitled to inherit (see subject K).

K. If no will:
MARRIED: Surviving spouse receives deceased spouse's half of community property if there are no surviving parents or descendants of deceased spouse; one-half if there are parents but no descendants; none if there are descendants. If descendants are also children of surviving spouse, surviving spouse holds child's property for his/her use for life. Surviving spouse inherits deceased spouse's separate property only if there are no descendants or other relatives.
UNMARRIED: Surviving mate receives nothing. An acknowledged illegitimate child inherits from mother only if there are no legitimate children; from father only if there are no other heirs at all.

L. Contracts:
MARRIED: Each may contract with others; can contract with each other only in very limited circumstances.
UNMARRIED: Each may contract with anyone, including each other.

M. Lawsuits:
BOTH: Each can sue and be sued separately unless both involved.

N. Homestead law:
BOTH: Homestead owned and occupied by debtor exempt up to $15,000 over liens. Sworn declaration of homestead must be recorded.

O. Civil suits by spouses or mates against each other:
BOTH: Permitted.

P. Legitimacy:
MARRIED: Children born during marriage are presumed legitimate. Children born before marriage are legitimized if parents later marry and acknowledge them.
UNMARRIED: An illegitimate child must be acknowledged by mother as well as father. Acknowledgment made by registering birth or baptism, by declaration before notary and two witnesses, or by raising child as legitimate member of family. Natural mother or father may legitimize child by notarial act unless at time of conception or birth there was an invalid marriage, or unless parent has legitimate descendants at time of attempted legitimation. Acknowledged illegitimate children inherit from mother only if there are no legitimate descendants, in

which case child gets moderate alimony (support); inherit from father only if no other heirs. Unacknowledged or incestuous children do not inherit from father or mother, but get child support only. Acknowledged illegitimate children have no rights to estate of legitimate relatives of father or mother.

Q.   Adoption:
BOTH: Any person, married or single, 18 years of age or older, may adopt any child. Must be of same race. Investigation of health, character, financial fitness.
MARRIED: Both spouses must sign for adoption.

R.   Division of property upon termination of relationship:
MARRIED: Each spouse retains his/her separate property; community property divided by court as it deems fair.
UNMARRIED: Implied or express contracts, value of services, or unfair economic gain may create rights to property.

VI. RECENT EVENTS, TRENDS, AND CONCLUSIONS

A.   A recent case held that isolated sex acts between the spouses while legally separated do not necessarily annul the separation and husband's duty to pay alimony.

B.   A statute saying that the only domicile of the wife is that of her husband has been declared unconstitutional.

C.   A statute that designates the husband as "head and master" of the community estate and gives him power to sell or mortgage community property without the wife's consent is unconstitutional.

D.   A wife's share in her husband's retirement pension includes one-half of the husband's contributions made during the marriage to the fund and also one-half of the funds contributed by the employer during the marriage.

E.   Although cohabitation is not illegal, the theories of the *Marvin* case would probably not be followed unless there was a business venture on which to base recovery. As long as there is some kind of commercial agreement, a division of property between mates would probably be made even if sex formed a part of the agreement.

MAINE

I. MARRIAGE

A. Legality:
   1. Age: 18; under 18, need written consent of parents or guardians; under 16, need written consent of judge of probate.
   2. License: Required; must be issued within 5 days of application and must be used within 60 days of issuance. A divorced person must file certificate containing information on divorce.
   3. Medical examination: Need statement of physician that both applicants were examined and given blood test showing neither infected with communicable syphilis.
   4. Waiting period: 5 days.

B. Common-law marriages: Probably not recognized; probably valid if entered into in another state where they are recognized.

C. Out-of-state marriages: Valid unless entered into to evade law of Maine.

D. Adultery: Not a crime.

E. Property: Separate.

F. Partnerships: A partnership agreement between spouses may not be enforceable because a husband and wife cannot be business partners.

II. COHABITATION

A. Legality:
   1. Cohabitation: Not a crime so long as conducted in private.
   2. Fornication: Not a crime so long as conducted in private.
   3. All private, nonviolent sexual acts between consenting adults are legal.

B. Common-law marriage: Probably not recognized.

C. Putative marriage: Recognized to the extent that an innocent participant in bigamous marriage is not punished.

D.   Property: An interest in property acquired during cohabitation by a couple who later marry is not marital property subject to division on divorce.

E.   Partnerships: A partnership agreement between mates is probably enforceable as long as there is a valid business purpose and the agreement is not primarily based on sex.

III. DIVORCE (DISSOLUTION) AND LEGAL SEPARATION

A.   Divorce or dissolution (grounds):
1. Adultery.
2. Impotence.
3. Extreme cruelty.
4. Complete desertion for 3 years.
5. Gross and confirmed habits of intoxication from alcohol or drugs.
6. Nonsupport.
7. Cruel and abusive treatment.
8. Irreconcilable differences (no fault).

B.   Legal separation (grounds):
1. Desertion for one year.
2. Living apart for good cause for one year.

C.   Residency requirements:
1. Parties must have married in state or lived in state after marriage; or
2. Plaintiff must have resided in state when grounds for divorce arose; or
3. Plaintiff must be bona fide resident for 6 months; or
4. Defendant must be resident of state.

D.   Remarriage: Possible immediately after divorce is final.

E.   Court orders after filing for divorce and before divorce is final:
1. Attorney's fees and court costs to either.
2. Temporary alimony and child support to either.

F.   Alimony:
1. Court may order alimony to either spouse.
2. Court may assign real estate or rents and profits from real estate to one spouse for life or for a shorter period.
3. Court may order a specific sum of money instead of alimony.

G.   Child support and custody:
1. Court has power to make all orders for care, custody, and support.

        2. Financial support of minor children is equal responsibility of both parents.

H.   Property division in absence of written or oral agreement:
1. Court does not interfere with separate property of either spouse.
2. Court divides marital property acquired during marriage, including joint property, as it deems fair.
3. Considerations: Contributions of each during marriage, including contribution as homemaker; value of each spouse's separate property; economic circumstances of each.

IV. TERMINATION OF COHABITATION

A.   Court jurisdiction: No judicial control; voluntary parting.

B.   Court orders: A court may make orders for child support and custody similar to those made in a divorce, once paternity is established.

C.   Property division (decisions in other states suggest the following possibilities):
1. Courts might infer partnership agreements as a means of dividing property and money.
2. Courts might order return or division of property and money if there had been an implied or express agreement.
3. Courts might order return of property to the rightful owner or grant an interest in property or an award of money to a mate to the extent of his/her contribution toward purchase of property.
4. Since living together is not illegal, recovery might be had for performing household duties as well as for making direct financial contributions, so long as the implied or express agreement was not primarily based upon sex.

D.   Putative marriage: Recognized to the extent that an innocent participant in a bigamous marriage is not punished.

E.   Palimony: Court decisions seem to indicate that a mate would not be entitled to receive rehabilitative alimony or temporary or permanent alimony.

V. SPECIFIC SUBJECTS (No written agreements, except for A,E,I.)
Reference to "BOTH" means married and unmarried couples.

A.   Prenuptial or precohabitation agreements:
MARRIED: Valid.

UNMARRIED: Probably valid if sex is not the basis of the agreement and if meant for protection of property interests.

BOTH: Agreements must be made without duress and with full disclosure of assets and other important information.

B. Property:

BOTH: All property is separate property of acquiring spouse or mate.

C. Liability of separate property for other spouse's or mate's debts:

BOTH: No liability.

D. Management and control of separate property of each:

BOTH: Each controls own property.

MARRIED: Wife must cosign transfer of title or placement of lien upon family home.

E. Contracts made during marriage or cohabitation settling property rights:

MARRIED: Valid

UNMARRIED: Probably enforceable if based on earnings, property, etc., rather than on sex.

BOTH: Agreement must be made without duress and with full disclosure of assets and other important information.

F. What can be willed?

BOTH: Each spouse's or mate's separate property.

MARRIED: Surviving spouse may elect to receive intestate share (see subject H) instead of according to will.

G. Automatic protection for surviving spouse or mate:

MARRIED: Surviving spouse receives at least one-third of real estate owned by decedent spouse at death, even if not provided for in will. In addition, court grants allowance necessary for surviving spouse and children, and wife may remain in house for ninety days rent-free.

UNMARRIED: No protection for surviving mate. Minor children under 14 and children between 14 and 18, if unable to work, receive an allowance; illegitimate children receive allowance if entitled to inherit (see subject H).

H. If no will:

MARRIED: Surviving spouse receives one-third of deceased spouse's estate if there are surviving children; one-half if there are no children of deceased but other heirs; everything if there is not more than $10,000 in the estate, or if there are no children or other heirs of deceased.

UNMARRIED: Surviving mate receives nothing. Illegitimate

children inherit from mother; from father if adopted, or if acknowledged in writing before notary or justice of peace, or if legitimized by subsequent marriage of parents.

I. Contracts:

BOTH: Each may contract with anyone, including each other.

J. Lawsuits:

BOTH: Each may sue and be sued separately unless both involved.

K. Homestead law:

BOTH: Dwelling house in actual possession of householder exempt up to $6,500 in value over liens, including mortgages. Householder must claim the amount of the exemption at the time a forced sale should occur.

L. Dower:

MARRIED: Abolished and replaced by distributive share (see subject H).

M. Civil suits by spouses or mates against each other:

MARRIED: May sue to recover property withheld by the other; most other suits prohibited.

UNMARRIED: Permitted.

N. Legitimacy:

MARRIED: Children born during marriage are presumed legitimate.

UNMARRIED: Illegitimate children inherit from mother; from father if adopted, or if acknowledged in writing before notary or justice of peace.

BOTH: Children born before marriage are legitimized if parents subsequently marry.

O. Adoption:

BOTH: Any person may be adopted. Parents should be of same religion of true parents, if possible. Investigation must show suitability of home.

P. Division of property upon termination of relationship:

MARRIED: Each party retains separate property acquired before marriage and property acquired during marriage by gift or inheritance. Marital property acquired during marriage, including joint property, is divided as court deems fair.

UNMARRIED: Implied or express contract, value of services, or unfair economic gain may create rights to property.

VI. RECENT EVENTS, TRENDS, AND CONCLUSIONS

A.　The Uniform Marriage and Divorce Act gives the court the power to sell marital property and divide the proceeds or to divide the property itself.

B.　A divorced wife is not entitled to continued alimony when she and her mate share a home, commingle financial resources, and enjoy a relationship which has "all the practical attributes" of a marriage. Thus, living together after divorce may terminate alimony the same as remarriage.

C.　A recent court decision held that a one-half interest in real estate acquired by the spouses while living together before marriage is not marital property subject to division upon divorce.

D.　Since cohabitation is not illegal, perhaps some of the theories of the *Marvin* case would be followed. However, the court has cited an Illinois case that denied relief to a mate after a long period of cohabitation on the basis of public policy. Therefore, enforcement of rights between mates is doubtful.

MARYLAND

I. MARRIAGE

A.　Legality:
  1. Age: 16; under 16, need consent of parent or guardian, a certificate of physician that female is pregnant or has given birth, and approval of juvenile judge; between 16 and 18, need consent of parent or guardian unless female is pregnant.
  2. License: Required; 48 hours between application and issuance; license good for 6 months.
  3. Medical examination: None required.
  4. Waiting period: 48 hours.

B.   Common-law marriages: Not permitted; valid if valid where entered into.

C.   Out-of-state marriages: Valid if valid where entered into.

D.   Adultery: Illegal; nominal fine.

E.   Property: Separate.

F.   Partnerships: A partnership agreement between spouses is probably enforceable as long as there is a valid business purpose.

II. COHABITATION

A.   Legality:
   1. Cohabitation: Not a crime.
   2. Fornication: Not a crime.

B.   Common-law marriage: Not recognized.

C.   Putative marriage: Continued cohabitation after the removal of the reason for an invalid marriage does not result in a valid marriage.

D.   Property:
   1. Early court decisions indicate that a contract is void between mates which is based entirely on a sexual relationship.
   2. A contract is valid between mates if a sexual relationship is only incidental to the subject of the agreement.
   3. Performing household services for a mate would be considered an adequate and independent basis for an express agreement.

E.   Partnerships: A partnership agreement between mates is probably enforceable as long as there is a valid business purpose and the agreement is not primarily based on sex.

III. DIVORCE (DISSOLUTION) AND LEGAL SEPARATION

A.   Divorce or dissolution (grounds):
   1. Impotency at time of marriage.
   2. Any cause making marriage void from the beginning.
   3. Adultery.
   4. Abandonment for one year.
   5. Voluntary separation without cohabitation for one year (no fault).
   6. Conviction of felony or misdemeanor and three-year sentence.

        7. Involuntary separation without cohabitation for three years (no fault).

        8. Permanent and incurable insanity with three-year confinement.

B.   Legal separation (grounds):

        1. Cruelty.

        2. Excessively vicious conduct.

        3. Abandonment and desertion.

        4. Voluntary separation without reasonable expectation of reconciliation.

C.   Residency requirements: None if grounds arose within state; one year before filing for either spouse if grounds arose outside state; two years if ground is insanity.

D.   Remarriage: Possible immediately after divorce is final.

E.   Court orders after filing for divorce and before divorce is final:

        1. Temporary alimony to either spouse.

        2. Court costs and attorneys' fees to either.

        3. Child support to either.

F.   Alimony:

        1. Granted to either spouse.

        2. Ends on death of payor or remarriage of recipient.

        3. May be terminated because of flagrant sexual misconduct by recipient.

G.   Child support and custody:

        1. Court decides according to best interests of child.

        2. Both parents have equal rights and responsibilities.

H.   Property division by court in absence of written or oral agreement:

        1. Separate property acquired before marriage or by gift or inheritance during marriage retained by owner.

        2. Court may order division and/or sale of jointly owned property as it deems fair.

        3. Court may not divide, but it may determine value of marital property (obtained during marriage except by gift or inheritance) and award money to non-owning spouse to make a fair adjustment.

        4. Family home and property used by family may be granted to either spouse regardless of who holds title.

IV. TERMINATION OF COHABITATION

A.   Court jurisdiction: No judicial control; voluntary parting.

B. Court orders:
   1. A court may make orders for child support and custody similar to those made in a divorce, once paternity is established.
   2. Alimony may be awarded to a putative spouse. Unclear whether a court would award it to a mate.

C. Property division (decisions in other states suggest the following possibilities):
   1. Courts could infer partnership agreements as a means of dividing property and money.
   2. Courts could order return or division of property and money if there had been an implied or express agreement.
   3. Courts could order return of property to the rightful owner or grant an interest in property or an award of money to a mate to the extent of his/her contribution toward purchase of property.
   4. Since living together is not illegal, recovery might be had for performing household duties as well as for direct financial contributions so long as the implied or express agreement was not primarily based upon sex.

D. Putative marriage:
   1. Alimony can be granted to a mate who mistakenly believes in a valid marriage.
   2. A mate with such a belief can also receive compensation for benefits conferred.

E. Palimony: There have been no court decisions to indicate that rehabilitative alimony or temporary or permanent alimony would be awarded to a mate, but such an award is a possibility.

V. SPECIFIC SUBJECTS (No written agreements, except for A,E,I.) Reference to "BOTH" means married and unmarried couples.

A. Prenuptial or precohabitation agreements:
   MARRIED: Valid.
   UNMARRIED: Probably valid if sex is not the basis of the agreement and if meant for protection of property interests.
   BOTH: Agreements must be made without duress and with full disclosure of assets and other important information.

B. Property:
   BOTH: All property is separate property of acquiring spouse or mate.

C.   Liability of separate property for other spouse's or mate's debts:
      BOTH: No liability unless both involved.

D.   Management and control of separate property of each:
      BOTH: Each controls own property.

E.   Contracts made during marriage or cohabitation settling property rights.
      MARRIED: Binding and enforceable.
      UNMARRIED: Probably enforceable if based on earnings, property, etc., rather than on sex.
      BOTH: Agreements must be made without duress and with full disclosure of assets and other important information.

F.   What can be willed?
      BOTH: Each spouse's separate property.

G.   Automatic protection for surviving spouse or mate:
      MARRIED: $1,000 to surviving spouse and $500 to each unmarried minor dependent child are exempt from creditors. Surviving spouse may elect to receive one-third of net estate if children survive, or one-half if no children survive, instead of taking his/her share under the will.
      UNMARRIED: No protection for surviving mate. Unmarried minor dependent children receive $500 exemption if entitled to inherit (see subject H).

H.   If no will:
      MARRIED: Surviving spouse receives one-half of estate if children or parents of deceased spouse survive; otherwise surviving spouse receives everything.
      UNMARRIED: Surviving mate receives nothing. Illegitimate children inherit from mother; inherit from father if legitimized by adjudication or by written acknowledgment, or by open and notorious recognition, or by marrying mother and orally acknowledging child, or by adoption.

I.   Contracts:
      BOTH: Each may contract with anyone, including each other.

J.   Lawsuits:
      BOTH: Each may sue and be sued separately unless both involved.

K.   Homestead law:
      BOTH: No homestead law.

L.   Civil suits by spouses or mates against each other:
      MARRIED: May sue each other for contract breach. Wife may

not sue husband for personal wrongs such as assault.

UNMARRIED: Permitted.

M. Legitimacy:

MARRIED: Children born during marriage are presumed legitimate.

UNMARRIED: Illegitimate children inherit from mother; children are legitimized for all purposes including inheritance, if paternity is adjudicated, or if acknowledged by father in writing, or if openly and notoriously recognized, or if children are adopted by father.

BOTH: Legitimized if parents marry and father orally acknowledges children.

N. Adoption:

BOTH: Any person over eighteen may adopt any minor or adult.

MARRIED: Both spouses must consent to adoption.

O. Division of property upon termination of relationship:

MARRIED: Separate property distributed to each owner. Marital property (property acquired during marriage except by gift or inheritance) is valued and court awards money to one spouse to provide fair adjustment. Joint property may be sold by court order and proceeds divided equally. Family home and property used by family may be granted to either.

UNMARRIED: Implied or express contract, value of services, or unfair economic gain may create rights to property.

VI. RECENT EVENTS, TRENDS, AND CONCLUSIONS

A. Although a court may not modify permanent alimony without a finding of changed circumstances after divorce, it may award permanent alimony in a greater amount than that awarded for temporary alimony without such a finding.

B. A wife's conduct after divorce cannot be the sole reason for terminating or reducing alimony, but her conduct is relevant to determine changed financial conditions (for example, the court may consider if she is living with someone who provides her with support).

C. Early court decisions enforced contracts between mates unless the sole basis of the contract was sex. These decisions and the fact that neither cohabitation nor fornication is illegal suggest that some or all of the theories in the *Marvin* case would be followed.

MASSACHUSETTS

I. MARRIAGE

A.   Legality:
1. Age: 18; under 18, need consent of parent(s) or guardian.
2. License: Required; 3 days between application and issuance. Divorced person must file certificate evidencing divorce. License good for 60 days.
3. Medical examination: Physician's certificate showing blood test for syphilis was negative not more than 30 days before application for license.
4. Waiting period: 3 days.

B.   Common-law marriages: Not recognized.

C.   Out-of-state marriages: Void if resident of Massachusetts goes to another state to enter into a marriage that would be void in Massachusetts; otherwise valid if valid in state where entered into.

D.   Adultery: Illegal; fine or sentence.

E.   Property: Separate.

F.   Partnerships: A partnership agreement between spouses is probably enforceable as long as there is a valid business purpose.

II. COHABITATION

A.   Legality:
1. Cohabitation: Illegal; fine or sentence.
2. Fornication: Illegal; fine or sentence.
3. Persons divorced from each other and cohabiting as husband and wife or living together in the same house are guilty of adultery.

B.   Common-law marriage: Not recognized.

C.   Putative marriage: If one has a good-faith belief in a valid marriage when the marriage is in fact bigamous, continued cohabitation after the reason for the invalidity is removed will result in a valid marriage.

D.   Property: If a couple is not legally married, sale of real estate to them as tenants by the entirety will be considered tenancy in common.

E.   Partnerships: A partnership agreement between mates is probably enforceable as long as there is a valid business purpose and the agreement is not primarily based on sex.

III. DIVORCE (DISSOLUTION) AND LEGAL SEPARATION

A.   Divorce or dissolution (grounds): Can be sought only if couple has lived apart at least 30 days.
   1.   Adultery.
   2.   Impotency.
   3.   Desertion for one year.
   4.   Gross and confirmed habits of intoxication from alcohol or drugs.
   5.   Cruel and abusive treatment.
   6.   Gross and cruel failure to support.
   7.   Sentence to prison for 5 years or more.
   8.   Irretrievable breakdown of marriage (no fault). If both spouses file joint separation agreement, divorce becomes final 6 months after court approves agreement. If only one spouse files for divorce, divorce becomes final 12 months after filing.

B.   Legal separation (grounds):
   1.   Failure to support or desertion.
   2.   Justifiable cause for living apart.

C.   Residency requirements:
   1.   Spouses lived together in state as husband and wife and one is living in state at time of filing.
   2.   Plaintiff has lived in state for one year before filing if cause for divorce occurred outside state.
   3.   Plaintiff is living in state at time of filing if cause occurred in state.

D.   Remarriage: Possible immediately after divorce is final.

E.   Court orders after filing for divorce and before divorce is final:
   1.   Temporary alimony to either.
   2.   Court costs and attorneys' fees to either.

F.   Alimony:
   1.   Granted to either spouse.
   2.   Considerations: length of marriage; conduct of parties during marriage; age; health; station; employability; opportunity for future acquisition of assets and income; occupations; incomes; vocational skills; liabilities and needs; contributions of each to acquisition, preserva-

tion, and appreciation of estate; contributions as home-maker.
3. Remarriage of recipient results in reduction to nominal sum.

G. Child support and custody: Court orders custody and support at divorce or any time after divorce. Neither parent given preference for custody.

H. Property division by court in absence of written or oral agreement:
1. May be ordered in addition to or instead of alimony, applying same considerations during granting of alimony.
2. Separate or joint property is subject to division irrespective of how title is held or when it was acquired.

IV. TERMINATION OF COHABITATION

A. Court jurisdiction: No judicial control; voluntary parting.

B. Court orders: A court may make orders for child support and custody similar to those made in a divorce, once paternity is established.

C. Property division (decisions in Massachusetts and in other states suggest the following possibilities):
1. Courts could infer partnership agreements as a means of dividing property and money.
2. Courts could order return or division of property and money if there had been an implied or express agreement.
3. Courts could order return of property to the rightful owner or grant an interest in property or an award of money to a mate to the extent of his/her contribution toward purchase of property.
4. Since cohabitation is illegal, courts would probably not honor an agreement if the relationship was primarily sexual; thus it might be difficult to collect for performing household duties when no direct financial contribution can be shown.

D. Putative marriage:
1. Early cases do not give recovery for domestic services in a putative marriage.
2. Courts will order return of or reimbursement for property to which a putative spouse has contributed.

E. Palimony: Court decisions seem to indicate that a mate would not be entitled to receive rehabilitative alimony or temporary or permanent alimony.

V. SPECIFIC SUBJECTS (No written agreements, except for A,E,I.)
Reference to "BOTH" means married and unmarried couples.

    A.   Prenuptial or precohabitation agreements:
        MARRIED: Valid, but if property is designated between the parties, the contract must be recorded within ninety days after marriage or it will be void.
        UNMARRIED: Probably valid if sex is not the basis of the agreement and if meant for protection of property interests.
        BOTH: Agreements must be made without duress and with full disclosure of assets and other important information.

    B.   Property:
        BOTH: All property is separate property of acquiring mate or spouse.

    C.   Liability of separate property for other spouse's or mate's debts:
        MARRIED: No liability except for necessities.
        UNMARRIED: No liability.

    D.   Management and control of separate property of each:
        BOTH: Each controls own property.

    E.   Contracts made during marriage or cohabitation settling property rights:
        MARRIED: Enforceable.
        UNMARRIED: Probably enforceable if based on earnings, property, etc., rather than on sex.
        BOTH: Agreements must be made without duress and with full disclosure of assets and other important information.

    F.   What can be willed?
        BOTH: Each spouse's or mate's separate property.

    G.   Automatic protection for surviving spouse or mate:
        MARRIED: Allowances for immediate needs of surviving spouse and minor children; surviving spouse may remain in family home for six months. Surviving spouse may elect dower (real estate belonging to deceased spouse at death). Surviving spouse and minor children receive homestead exemption of $40,000 over liens, including mortgage liens.
        UNMARRIED: No protection for surviving mate. Minor children receive allowance for immediate needs, as well as homestead exemption, if entitled to inherit (see subject H).

    H.   If no will:
        MARRIED: Surviving spouse must sign election of dower within six months after death. If no election made, sur-

viving spouse divides estate with surviving children and
other heirs of deceased spouse; if there are no heirs,
surviving spouse receives everything.

UNMARRIED: Surviving mate receives nothing. Illegitimate
children inherit from mother; from father if he later
marries mother and either acknowledges children or
paternity is judicially established.

I.   Contracts:
     BOTH: Each may contract with anyone, including each
     other.

J.   Lawsuits:
     BOTH: Each may sue and be sued separately, unless both
     involved.

K.   Homestead law:
     BOTH: $40,000 exemption over liens, including mortgage
     liens, for owner of home or one who possesses by lease
     or otherwise, if owner has a family and occupies house
     as principal residence. Homestead created by declaration
     in deed at time of purchase or after acquisition, by writ-
     ing signed, sealed, acknowledged, and recorded in re-
     gistry of deeds in county where land is located.

L.   Dower and/or curtesy:
     MARRIED: Surviving spouse receives real estate owned by
     deceased spouse.

M.   Civil suits by spouses or mates against each other:
     BOTH: Permitted.

N.   Legitimacy:
     MARRIED: Children born during marriage are presumed le-
     gitimate. Children born before marriage are legitimized
     if parents later marry, and father acknowledges children.
     UNMARRIED: Illegitimate children are heirs of mother; inherit
     from father only if father later marries mother and either
     acknowledges children or is judicially established as
     father (a similar statute has been held to be uncons-
     titutional).

O.   Adoption:
     BOTH: Any single or married adult may adopt any person
     younger than self.
     MARRIED: Both spouses must consent to adoption.

P.   Division of property upon termination of relationship:
     MARRIED: Court has power to divide all separate and joint
     property.
     UNMARRIED: Implied or express contract, value of services,
     or unfair economic gain may create rights to property.

VI. RECENT EVENTS, TRENDS, AND CONCLUSIONS

A recent court case allowed a mate to recover for the fair value of services rendered in return for a promise to leave property by will. Although cohabitation is illegal, it seems likely that some or all of the theories of the *Marvin* case will be followed.

MICHIGAN

I. MARRIAGE

    A.   Legality:
        1. Age: Male, 18; female, 16; under 18, need written and notarized consent from one parent or guardian.
        2. License: Required; 3 days between application and issuance.
        3. Medical examination: Required, within 30 days preceding application for license, showing freedom from venereal disease.
        4. Waiting period: 3 days.

    B.   Common-law marriages: Not recognized.

    C.   Out-of-state marriages: Valid if valid where entered into, unless contrary to public policy.

    D.   Adultery: Illegal (felony); extends to those who live together after they have been divorced.

    E.   Property: Separate.

    F.   Partnerships: A partnership agreement between spouses is probably enforceable as long as there is a valid business purpose.

II. COHABITATION

- A.   Legality:
     1. Cohabitation: "Lewd and lascivious" cohabitation is illegal (misdemeanor); fine or sentence.
     2. Fornication: Illegal (misdemeanor); fine or sentence.

- B.   Common-law marriage: Not recognized.

- C.   Putative marriage:
     1. Continued cohabitation after one mate divorces will render a bigamous marriage valid, if the couple thought their marriage was valid. This would not be true if the marriage was known from the beginning to be invalid.
     2. A good-faith spouse would, upon the death of a mate, receive the property acquired during the putative marriage.

- D.   Property:
     1. A deed to husband and wife when they are not legally married establishes tenancy in common rather than tenancy by the entirety.
     2. Cohabitation alone will not give a mate rights in property of the other, but a written or oral agreement which was independent of the sexual relationship would be honored.

- E.   Partnerships: A partnership agreement between mates is probably enforceable as long as there is a valid business purpose and the agreement is not primarily based on sex.

III. DIVORCE (DISSOLUTION) AND LEGAL SEPARATION

- A.   Divorce or dissolution (grounds): Breakdown of marriage relationship (no fault).

- B.   Legal separation (grounds): Same as for divorce or dissolution.

- C.   Residency requirements:
     1. 180 days for a spouse before filing for divorce.
     2. If ground for divorce occurred outside Michigan, one year for either party.

- D.   Remarriage: Possible immediately after divorce is final, unless restriction is specified in divorce decree.

- E.   Court orders after filing for divorce and before divorce is final:
     1. Temporary alimony to either spouse.
     2. Court costs to either.

       3. Child custody and support to either.

F.   Alimony:
       1. Granted to either spouse.
       2. Remarriage of wife does not automatically terminate alimony, but may be a reason for its termination.
       3. Conduct of each spouse may be relevant in granting alimony.

G.   Child support and custody:
       1. Support ordered to either spouse, or either or both, if third party has custody.
       2. Custody awarded to one parent or to third party; neither parent gets preference.

H.   Property division by court in absence of written or oral agreement:
       1. Tenancy by the entireties or joint tenancy becomes tenancy in common.
       2. Court is given power to divide all separate property, including joint property, as it deems fair.
       3. Court must provide for wife to receive an award equal to her dower right.
       4. Court may give husband some or all of wife's separate property if he contributed to its acquisition or improvement.
       5. Conduct of each spouse may be considered in dividing property.

IV. TERMINATION OF COHABITATION

A.   Court jurisdiction: No judicial control; voluntary parting.

B.   Court orders: A court may make orders for child support and custody similar to those made in a divorce, once paternity is established.

C.   Property division (decisions in Michigan and in other states suggest the following possibilities):
       1. Courts could infer partnership agreements as a means of dividing property and money.
       2. Courts could order return or division of property and money if there had been an implied or express agreement.
       3. Courts could order return of property to the rightful owner or grant an interest in property or an award of money to a mate to the extent of his/her contribution toward purchase of property.
       4. Since living together (unless it is lewd and lascivious) is not illegal, recovery might be had for performing household duties as well as for direct financial con-

tributions, so long as the implied or express agreement was not primarily based upon sex.

D. Putative marriage: Courts will adjust the property rights to joint accumulations if there was a good-faith belief in a valid marriage.

E. Palimony: There have been no court decisions to indicate that rehabilitative alimony or temporary or permanent alimony would be awarded to a mate, but such an award is a possibility.

V. SPECIFIC SUBJECTS (No written agreements, except for A,E,I.)
Reference to "BOTH" means married and unmarried couples.

A. Prenuptial or precohabitation agreements:
MARRIED: Valid.
UNMARRIED: Probably valid if sex is not the basis of the agreement and if meant for protection of property interests.
BOTH: Agreements must be made without duress and with full disclosure of assets and other important information.

B. Property:
BOTH: All property is separate property of acquiring spouse or mate.

C. Liability of separate property for other spouse's or mate's debts:
BOTH: No liability.

D. Management and control of separate property of each:
BOTH: Each controls own separate property.
MARRIED: Both spouses must sign to sell jointly held property; wife waives dower if she joints in sale of husband's real estate. Wife must sign to transfer or encumber family home.

E. Contracts made during marriage or cohabitation settling property rights:
MARRIED: Valid.
UNMARRIED: Probably enforceable if based on earnings, property, etc., rather than on sex.
BOTH: Agreements must be made without duress and with full disclosure of assets and other important information.

F. What can be willed?
BOTH: Each spouse's or mate's separate property.
MARRIED: Rather than accepting the will provisions, surviving spouse may elect to take either entire dower (see subject L), or one-half intestate share (see subject H)

reduced by certain amounts received from other sources, if any.

G.   Automatic protection for surviving spouse or mate:

MARRIED: Surviving spouse and minor children of deceased receive allowance deemed necessary during administration of estate. Surviving spouse can remain in family home for one year. Surviving spouse and children receive homestead exemption of $3,500.

UNMARRIED: No protection for surviving mate. Minor children receive allowance and homestead exemption; illegitimate minor children probably would also, if entitled to inherit (see subject H).

H.   If no will:

MARRIED: Surviving spouse receives everything if no children or parents survive; if children of deceased spouse survive, all of whom are also children of surviving spouse, or if parents survive, surviving spouse receives $60,000 plus one-half of balance; if children survive who are not children of surviving spouse, surviving spouse receives one-half of estate. Widow may elect to receive dower and family home, instead of intestate share in real estate.

UNMARRIED: Surviving mate receives nothing. Illegitimate children inherit from mother as if legitimate; inherit from father only if legitimized by marriage to mother or by written acknowledgment.

I.   Contracts:

BOTH: Each may contract with anyone, including each other.

J.   Lawsuits:

BOTH: Each may sue and be sued separately unless both involved.

K.   Homestead law:

BOTH: Any resident who owns and occupies home has exemption up to $3,500 over and above liens, including mortgages. Occupancy of home is notice to all of homestead rights. No further notice or filing required.

L.   Dower:

MARRIED: Surviving spouse receives lifetime interest of one-third of estate owned by husband during marriage. Wife may release dower by contract or waive dower by joining husband in selling his property.

M.   Civil suits by spouses or mates against each other:

BOTH: Permitted.

N.   Legitimacy:
      MARRIED: Children born during marriage are presumed le-
          gitimate. Children born before marriage are legitimized
          if parents later marry.
      UNMARRIED: Illegitimate children inherit from mother as if
          legitimate; do not inherit from father unless legitimized
          (though such a distinction may be unconstitutional).
          Children are legitimized by marriage of parents or by
          written acknowledgment of father.

O.   Adoption:
      MARRIED: Both spouses must adopt together; may adopt
          child or adult.
      UNMARRIED: Single person may adopt child or adult.
      BOTH: Full investigation required.

P.   Division of property upon termination of relationship:
      MARRIED: Court is given power to divide all separate prop-
          erty, including joint property, as it deems fair. Joint
          tenancy and tenancy by the entireties become tenancy
          in common, which may be sold or divided.
      UNMARRIED: Implied or express contract, value of services,
          or unfair economic gain may create rights to property.

VI. RECENT EVENTS, TRENDS, AND CONCLUSIONS

A.   A husband's vested retirement pension must be considered
      marital property subject to division on divorce.

B.   An illegitimate child shares equally with a deceased parent's
      natural child in the proceeds of an insurance policy.

C.   To mandate termination of an unwed father's rights is not
      necessarily in the best interests of the child. Age and marital
      status are not proof of parental unfitness.

D.   A 1973 Michigan case established many property rights for
      mates that the *Marvin* case later established in California.
      In the Michigan case, although both mates were guilty of
      adultery, the court enforced an oral contract to convey prop-
      erty to the female mate, and found that she had contributed
      to their property accumulations pursuant to an agreement
      to pool assets and share them. The court also found an
      implied agreement and allowed recovery for household ser-
      vices rendered.

MINNESOTA

I. MARRIAGE

A. Legality:
1. Age: 18 for both male and female; between 16 and 18 for female, need parents' consent and approval of juvenile court judge.
2. License: Required; application at least 5 days before issuance.
3. Medical examination: None required.
4. Waiting period: 5 days.

B. Common-law marriages: Not recognized.

C. Out-of-state marriages: Valid if valid in state where entered into, unless the marriage violates strong public policy of Minnesota.

D. Adultery: Illegal; fine and/or sentence.

E. Property: Separate.

F. Partnerships: A partnership agreement between spouses is probably enforceable as long as there is a valid business purpose.

II. COHABITATION

A. Legality:
1. Cohabitation: Legal if it involves adults cohabiting in an ongoing voluntary relationship.
2. Fornication: Illegal (misdemeanor), unless part of ongoing relationship.

B. Common-law marriage: Not recognized.

C. Putative marriage: Continued cohabitation after the reason for the invalid marriage is removed will not result in a valid marriage.

D. Property: The state legislature recently enacted a law that only written contracts between mates are legally enforceable. Whether title is held separately or jointly should have a bearing on the rights of each party.

E. Partnerships: A partnership agreement between mates is

probably enforceable as long as there is a valid business purpose and the agreement is not primarily based on sex.

III. DIVORCE (DISSOLUTION) AND LEGAL SEPARATION

A.   Divorce or dissolution (grounds): Irretrievable breakdown of marriage (no fault).

B.   Legal separation (grounds): Granted upon showing of need.

C.   Residency requirements: 180 days for either spouse before legal action is filed.

D.   Remarriage: Possible immediately after divorce is final.

E.   Court orders after filing for divorce and before divorce is final:
      1.   Temporary alimony to either spouse.
      2.   Child support and custody.

F.   Alimony: Granted to a dependent spouse unable to support himself/herself through reasonable employment and lacking sufficient property.

G.   Child support and custody:
      1.   Court may order either spouse to pay support.
      2.   Custody determined according to children's best interest without favoring either parent.

H.   Property division by court in absence of written or oral agreement:
      1.   Court usually sets aside separate property to its owner and makes a fair division of marital property (acquired during marriage, including joint property) without regard to marital misconduct.
      2.   Division of property may be instead of or in addition to alimony.
      3.   Court may even divide separate property if needed.
      4.   Considerations: Length of marriage, age, health, occupation, amount of income, employability, needs, etc.

IV. TERMINATION OF COHABITATION

A.   Court jurisdiction: No judicial control; voluntary parting.

B.   Court orders: A court may make orders for child support and custody similar to those made in a divorce, once paternity is established.

C.   Property division (decisions in Minnesota and other states suggest the following possibilities):

1. Courts could infer partnership agreements as a means of dividing property and money.
2. Courts could order return or division of property and money if there is a written agreement.
3. Courts formerly could order return of property to the rightful owner or grant an interest in property or an award of money to a mate to the extent of his/her contribution toward purchase of property. This remedy may no longer be possible (see VI, F).
4. Since living together is not illegal, recovery might be had for performing household duties as well as for financial contributions, if there is a written agreement between the parties.

D. Putative marriage: Courts would probably make a fair property division between spouses if one or both of them thought they were validly married.

E. Palimony: Court decisions indicate that rehabilitative alimony or temporary or permanent alimony would be awarded to a mate if circumstances warranted.

V. SPECIFIC SUBJECTS (No written agreements, except for A,E,I.)
Reference to "BOTH" means married and unmarried couples.

A. Prenuptial or precohabitation agreements:
MARRIED: Valid.
UNMARRIED: Valid if in writing and sex is not the basis of the agreement, and if meant for protection of property interests.
BOTH: Agreement must be made without duress and with full disclosure of assets and other important information.

B. Property:
BOTH: All property is separate property of acquiring mate or spouse.

C. Liability of separate property for other spouse's or mate's debts:
MARRIED: No liability except husband's separate property liable for necessaries furnished to wife, and both spouses are liable for necessary household articles and supplies used by family.
UNMARRIED: No liability, except each might be held liable for necessary household articles used by "family."

D. Management and control of separate property of each:
BOTH: Each controls own separate property.
MARRIED: Selling of family home is subject to statutory right (see subject G).

E. Contracts made during marriage or cohabitation settling property rights:
   MARRIED: Valid.
   UNMARRIED: Enforceable if in writing and based on earnings, property, etc., rather than on sex.
   BOTH: Agreement must be made without duress and with full disclosure of assets and other important information.

F. What can be willed?
   BOTH: Each spouse's or mate's separate property.
   MARRIED: Family home cannot be willed.

G. Automatic protection for surviving spouse or mate:
   MARRIED: Family home descends automatically to surviving spouse if there are no surviving children, and to surviving spouse for life if children survive. Homestead exemption extends to surviving wife and minor children.
   UNMARRIED: No protection for surviving mate. Surviving minor children receive homestead exemption if they are entitled to inherit (see subject H).

H. If no will:
   MARRIED: Surviving spouse receives everything if there are no surviving descendants of deceased spouse; otherwise surviving spouse shares with surviving children or grandchildren, depending on number.
   UNMARRIED: Surviving mate receives nothing. Illegitimate children inherit from mother; from father if paternity is established in proceeding where written acknowledgment is produced.

I. Contracts:
   BOTH: Each may contract with anyone, including each other.
   MARRIED: May not contract with each other concerning real estate, except to create joint tenancy.

J. Lawsuits:
   BOTH: Each may sue and be sued separately unless both involved.

K. Homestead law:
   BOTH: No limitation of value over liens including mortgages for home owned and occupied by debtor. Proceeds of sale also exempt for one year. No filing necessary. Homestead created by occupation of home.
   MARRIED: Both spouses must sign to sell or mortgage.

L. Civil suits by spouses or mates against each other:
   BOTH: Permitted.

M. Legitimacy:

MARRIED: Children born during marriage presumed legitimate. Legitimized if parents later marry.

UNMARRIED: Illegitimate children inherit from mother as if legitimate; inherit from father if paternity is established in proceeding where written acknowledgment is produced.

N. Division of property upon termination of relationship:

MARRIED: Court makes fair and reasonable division of all property acquired during marriage, including joint property. Separate property acquired before marriage retained by owner with few exceptions.

UNMARRIED: Only written contracts are enforceable between mates. Oral agreements dividing property between mates will not be recognized by the court. If property is held jointly, then most likely the parties shall continue to hold title as is, and the courts will not allow oral testimony to show a different understanding between the parties.

VI. RECENT EVENTS, TRENDS, AND CONCLUSIONS

A. Pension benefits are property to be considered by the court upon division of property or alimony award.

B. Alimony to a lesbian ex-wife was terminated because the husband, when he agreed to pay alimony until wife died or remarried, did not know that remarriage would be a realistic impossibility. The prior assumptions within the agreement were no longer valid.

C. A three-week visit to Montana was not sufficient to establish a common-law marriage, though it might be valid in Montana.

D. A statute making the father alone responsible for the support of an illegitimate child has been declared unconstitutional.

E. A 1977 court case relying upon some of the theories of the *Marvin* case awarded an equal division of assets accumulated during 21 years of cohabitation; the female's share being granted for "wifely and motherly" services. The court found an implied contract because the couple held themselves out as husband and wife, raised a son, and held property as joint tenants. The principles used to divide property upon divorce were used to terminate cohabitation. The court expressly approved of the various theories suggested in the *Marvin* case.

F. The foregoing 1977 decision has been partially superseded by recent legislation providing that only written contracts between mates will be legally enforced.

MISSISSIPPI

I. MARRIAGE

A. Legality:
1. Age: Male, 17; female, 15; if under age, need consent of parents or guardian and written waiver by court.
2. License: Required; 3 days between application and issuance.
3. Medical examination: Certificate saying blood test shows freedom from syphilis within 30 days before application.
4. Waiting period: 3 days.

B. Common-law marriages: Not recognized.

C. Out-of-state marriages: Probably valid if valid where entered into.

D. Adultery: Illegal. Former spouses cohabiting after divorce are committing adultery.

E. Property: Separate.

F. Partnerships: A partnership agreement between spouses is probably enforceable as long as there is a valid business purpose.

II. COHABITATION

A. Legality:
1. Cohabitation: Illegal; fine and sentence.
2. Fornication: Illegal; fine and sentence.

B. Common-law marriage: Not recognized.

C. Putative marriage: Recognized to compensate party who believed marriage was valid.

D. Property: No recent court decisions, but see IV, C for possibilities as to division of property.

E. Partnerships: A partnership agreement between mates is probably enforceable as long as there is a valid business purpose and the agreement is not primarily based on sex.

III. DIVORCE (DISSOLUTION) AND LEGAL SEPARATION

A.   Divorce or dissolution (grounds):
1. Impotency.
2. Adultery.
3. Sentence in penitentiary.
4. Desertion for one year.
5. Habitual drunkenness.
6. Habitual excessive use of drugs.
7. Habitual cruel and inhuman treatment.
8. Insanity or idiocy at time of marriage.
9. Prior marriage undissolved (bigamy).
10. Pregnancy at time of marriage by person other than husband and unknown to husband.
11. Close blood relationship with spouse.
12. Incurable insanity with confinement for 3 years.
13. Irreconcilable differences, but only if not contested and parties make adequate provision for custody, maintenance of children, and settlement of property rights (no fault).

B.   Legal separation (grounds): Not obtainable by statute but court has power to provide for separate maintenance if separation is without fault of wife, and husband has abandoned her and refused to support her.

C.   Residency requirements: 6 months for either spouse before legal action is filed.

D.   Remarriage: Possible immediately after divorce is final; if grounds for divorce was adultery, court may prohibit remarriage of guilty party.

E.   Court orders after filing for divorce and before divorce is final:
1. Court costs and attorney's fees.
2. Temporary alimony to either spouse.

F.   Alimony:
1. May be granted to either spouse.
2. If both spouses are capable of supporting themselves adequately, no alimony should be granted.

G.   Child support and custody:
1. Court orders support and custody.
2. Each parent must contribute to support in proportion to ability.
3. Mother is given custody preference for young child so long as it is in the best interests of the child.

H. Property division by court in absence of written or oral agreement:
    1. Court has no power to divide separate property; title alone controls.
    2. Jointly owned property such as tenancy in common, joint tenancy, or tenancy of the entirety, is not affected by divorce, but it may be partitioned or sold and the proceeds distributed.

IV. TERMINATION OF COHABITATION

A. Court jurisdiction: No judicial control; voluntary parting.

B. Court orders: A court may make orders for child support and custody similar to those made in a divorce, once paternity is established.

C. Property division (decisions in other states suggest the following possibilities):
    1. Courts could recognize express partnership agreements as a means of dividing property and money, but they would be unlikely to infer them.
    2. Courts could order return or division of property and money if there had been an implied or express agreement, but this is doubtful.
    3. Courts could order return of property to the rightful owner or grant an interest in property or an award of money to a mate to the extent of his/her contribution toward purchase of property.
    4. Since cohabitation is illegal, courts would probably not honor an agreement if relationship was primarily sexual; thus it might be difficult to collect for performing household duties when no direct financial contribution can be shown.

D. Putative marriage: The property rights of one who believes in the validity of an invalid marriage will be adjusted.

E. Palimony: Court decisions seem to indicate that a mate would not be entitled to receive rehabilitative alimony or temporary or permanent alimony.

V. SPECIFIC SUBJECTS (No written agreements, except for A,E,I.)
Reference to "BOTH" means married and unmarried couples.

A. Prenuptial or precohabitation agreements:
    MARRIED: Valid.
    UNMARRIED: Doubtful. May be valid if sex is not the basis of the agreement and if meant for protection of property interests.

BOTH: Agreements must be made without duress and with full disclosure of assets and other important information.

B. Property:
    BOTH: All property is separate property of acquiring spouse or mate.
    MARRIED: Exception for homestead (see subject K).

C. Liability of separate property for other spouse's or mate's debts:
    MARRIED: No liability, except husband is liable for necessities.
    UNMARRIED: No liability.

D. Management and control of separate property of each:
    BOTH: Each controls own property.
    MARRIED: Both spouses must sign to sell home.

E. Contracts made during marriage or cohabitation settling property rights:
    BOTH: Agreements must be made without duress and with full disclosure of assets and other important information.
    MARRIED: Valid.
    UNMARRIED: May be enforceable if based on earnings, property, etc., rather than on sex, but there is less chance of enforceability than in most states.

F. What can be willed?
    MARRIED: Surviving spouse cannot be disinherited. If insufficiently provided for or disinherited in will, surviving spouse may receive intestate share not to exceed one-half of deceased's estate.
    UNMARRIED: Surviving mate can be disinherited entirely.
    BOTH: Each spouse's or mate's separate property.

G. Automatic protection for surviving spouse or mate:
    MARRIED: Certain exempt personal property to widow and children; one year's provision for widow and children. Widow may occupy family home rent-free during widowhood.
    UNMARRIED: No protection for surviving mate. Children would probably receive exempt property and year's provision, if entitled to inherit (see subject H).

H. If no will:
    MARRIED: Surviving spouse receives everything if there are no surviving children or descendants of children; otherwise, surviving spouse shares with children or their descendants.
    UNMARRIED: Surviving mate receives nothing. Illegitimate children inherit from mother; inherit from father if par-

ents marry and father acknowledges children.

I.   Contracts:
      BOTH: Each may contract with anyone, including each
            other.
      MARRIED: A spouse may not contract to pay the other for
            services.

J.   Lawsuits:
      BOTH: Each may sue and be sued separately unless both
            involved.

K.   Homestead law:
      BOTH: A householder has exemption up to $30,000 in value
            over liens including mortgages in family home. Married
            person or widow or widower over 60 years old receives
            exemption with or without family or home. Application
            must be made on or before April 1 of each year.

L.   Civil suits by spouses or mates against each other:
      MARRIED: Permitted, except for personal wrongs committed
            by one against the other.
      UNMARRIED: Permitted.

M.   Legitimacy:
      MARRIED: Children born during marriage are presumed le-
            gitimate.
      UNMARRIED: Illegitimate children inherit from mother; in-
            herit from father if parents marry and father acknowl-
            edges children.

N.   Adoption:
      BOTH: Any proper adult may adopt adult or child.
      MARRIED: Both spouses must consent to adopt either adult
            or child.

O.   Division of property upon termination of relationship:
      MARRIED: Court has no power to divide joint or separate
            property; title controls disposition.
      UNMARRIED: Implied or express contract, value of services,
            unfair economic gain may create rights to property, but
            this is doubtful.

VI. RECENT EVENTS, TRENDS, AND CONCLUSIONS

A.   Child-support payments for more than one child are not
      necessarily reduced when one child becomes an adult or
      gets married.

B.   The state's apparent determination to punish cohabitors,
      adulterers and fornicators indicate that the *Marvin* case the-
      ories would probably not be followed.

MISSOURI

I. MARRIAGE

A.   Legality:
1. Age: 18; under 18, need consent of one parent or guardian; under 15, not permitted.
2. License: Required; 3 days notice before issuance.
3. Medical examination: Negative laboratory blood test for syphilis and affidavit of applicant that he/she is not infected with syphilis, or certificate of physician that applicant is not infected, or that female applicant is not pregnant, or that one applicant is not on deathbed and unlikely to consummate marriage; must obtain within 15 days before issuance of license.
4. Waiting period: 3 days.

B.   Common-law marriages: Not recognized, but valid if valid in another state where entered into.

C.   Out-of-state marriages: Probably valid if valid in state where entered into.

D.   Adultery: Not a crime.

E.   Property: Separate.

F.   Partnerships: A partnership agreement between spouses is probably enforceable as long as there is a valid business purpose.

II. COHABITATION

A.   Legality:
1. Cohabitation: Not a crime.
2. Fornication: Not a crime.
3. All private, nonviolent sexual acts between consenting adults are legal.

B.   Common-law marriage: Not recognized.

C.   Putative marriage:
1. When one has a mistaken belief in the validity of an invalid marriage, courts will probably recognize the value of services rendered as a homemaker.
2. A sale of real estate to husband and wife when the

couple are not legally married establishes tenancy in common rather than joint tenancy.

D. Property: Courts will recognize and enforce agreements between mates.

E. Partnerships: A partnership agreement between mates is probably enforceable as long as there is a valid business purpose and the agreement is not primarily based on sex.

III. DIVORCE (DISSOLUTION) AND LEGAL SEPARATION

A. Divorce or dissolution (grounds): Marriage is irretrievably broken and court finds no likelihood that the marriage can be preserved (no fault).

B. Legal separation (grounds): Same as for divorce.

C. Residency requirements: 90 days for either spouse before filing of legal action.

D. Remarriage: Possible immediately after divorce is final.

E. Court orders after filing for divorce and before divorce is final:
1. Temporary alimony to either.
2. Temporary child support.
3. Temporary order protecting spouse or child from molestation, excluding one spouse from family home, protecting property interests.

F. Alimony:
1. Granted to either spouse.
2. Terminated on death of either or remarriage of recipient.
3. Modified only on showing after divorce of changed circumstances so substantial that original terms are unreasonable.

G. Child support and custody:
1. Court makes whatever orders seem reasonable.
2. Mother is generally given preference for custody of young child.

H. Property division by court in absence of written or oral agreement:
1. Each spouse retains own separate property.
2. Court divides marital property (acquired during marriage except by gift or inheritance, or acquired in exchange for income from property acquired before marriage).
3. Considerations: contributions, value of separate prop-

erty, economic circumstances of each, conduct of parties during marriage.

IV. TERMINATION OF COHABITATION

A. Court jurisdiction: No judicial control; voluntary parting.

B. Court orders: A court may make orders for child support and custody similar to those made in a divorce, once paternity is established.

C. Property division (decisions in other states suggest the following possibilities):
1. Courts could infer partnership agreements as a means of dividing property and money.
2. Courts could order return or division of property and money if there had been an implied or express agreement.
3. Courts could order return of property to the rightful owner or grant an interest in property or an award of money to a mate to the extent of his/her contribution toward purchase of property.
4. Since living together is not illegal, recovery might be had for performing household duties as well as for direct financial contributions, so long as the implied or express agreement was not primarily based upon sex.

D. Putative marriage: Courts would probably adjust the property rights of those invalidly married who believed in the existence of a valid marriage.

E. Palimony: There have been no court decisions to indicate that rehabilitative alimony or temporary or permanent alimony would be awarded to a mate, but such an award is a possibility.

V. SPECIFIC SUBJECTS (No written agreements, except for A, E, I.)
Reference to "BOTH" means married and unmarried couples.

A. Prenuptial or precohabitation agreements:
MARRIED: Valid; must be in writing and acknowledged by each party or proved by a witness.
UNMARRIED: Probably valid if sex is not the basis of the agreement and if meant for protection of property interests.
BOTH: Agreements must be made without duress and with full disclosure of assets and other important information.

B. Property:
MARRIED: Separate property is construed as property owned

before marriage; acquired by gift or inheritance; purchased with separate funds during marriage; or wages, income, and profits from separate property.

UNMARRIED: All property is separate property of acquiring mate.

C. Liability of separate property for other spouse's or mate's debts:
BOTH: No liability.

D. Management and control of separate property of each:
BOTH: Each controls own property.
MARRIED: Each must sign for sale of real estate of the other, or to sell or mortgage family home.

E. Contracts made during marriage or cohabitation settling property rights:
MARRIED: Valid.
UNMARRIED: Probably enforceable if based on earnings, property, etc., rather than on sex.
BOTH: Agreements must be made without duress and with full disclosure of assets and other important information.

F. What can be willed?
BOTH: Each spouse's or mate's separate property.
MARRIED: Surviving spouse may disregard will and receive one-half of the deceased's property if no surviving descendants; one-third otherwise.

G. Automatic protection for surviving spouse or mate:
MARRIED: Surviving spouse and unmarried minor children retain family Bible, books, clothing, household appliances and furniture, etc. Money allowance for one year's support. Homestead allowance up to $7,500 over liens, including mortgages.
UNMARRIED: No protection for surviving mate. Minor children receive household goods, year's support, and homestead allowance if entitled to inherit (see subject H).

H. If no will:
MARRIED: Surviving spouse receives everything if there are no surviving children or relatives of deceased spouse; one-half if any of them survive.
UNMARRIED: Surviving mate receives nothing. Illegitimate children inherit from mother; from father only if legitimized by subsequent marriage.

I. Contracts:
BOTH: Each may contract with anyone, including each other.

J. Lawsuits:
BOTH: Each may sue and be sued separately unless both involved.

K. Homestead law:
BOTH: Exemption for head of family up to $10,000 over liens, including mortgages. Proceeds of sale exempt for reasonable time for reinvestment. No filing necessary.

L. Civil suits by spouses or mates against each other:
MARRIED: Wife cannot sue husband for personal wrongs such as assault. Can sue each other for contract breach.
UNMARRIED: Permitted.

M. Legitimacy:
MARRIED: Children born during marriage are presumed legitimate. Children born before marriage are legitimized by later marriage of parents and recognition by father.
UNMARRIED: Illegitimate children inherit from mother. Inherit from father only if legitimized, which can be accomplished if parents later marry and father recognizes children, or if father adopts children.

N. Adoption:
MARRIED: Both husband and wife must consent to adoption. Child or adult may be adopted.
UNMARRIED: Any person may adopt any child or adult.
BOTH: Investigation of mental, physical, and hereditary background of all parties involved is made.

O. Division of property upon termination of relationship:
MARRIED: Each spouse retains separate property; court divides marital property as it deems fair.
UNMARRIED: Implied or express contract, value of services, or unfair economic gain may create rights to property.

VI. RECENT EVENTS, TRENDS, AND CONCLUSIONS

A. Unwed fathers are entitled to a hearing to terminate their parental rights. A natural father is afforded the same presumption of fitness as a married father.

B. Since neither cohabitation, fornication, nor adultery is illegal, and since the courts recognize and enforce agreements between mates, it would seem that some or all of the theories of the *Marvin* case would be followed.

MONTANA

I. MARRIAGE

A. Legality:
1. Age: 18; between 15 and 18, need consent of parents or guardian and authorization of district judge.
2. License: Required; expires 180 days after issuance.
3. Medical examination: Physician's certificate reporting test for rubella immunity and syphilis within 20 days prior to issuance of license.
4. Waiting period: 3 days.

B. Common-law marriages: Recognized.

C. Out-of-state marriages: Valid if entered into in another state where they are recognized.

D. Adultery: Illegal (misdemeanor) if open and notorious; fine or sentence.

E. Property: Separate.

F. Partnerships: A partnership agreement between spouses is probably enforceable as long as there is a valid business purpose.

II. COHABITATION

A. Legality
1. Cohabitation: Illegal (misdemeanor) if open and notorious and combined with adultery or fornication; fine or sentence.
2. Fornication: Illegal (misdemeanor) if open and notorious; fine or sentence.

B. Common-law marriage:
1. Recognized. If a marriage thought to be legal is in fact illegal and cohabitation continues after the illegality is discovered, a common-law marriage may result.
2. When mates are cohabiting, morality is presumed rather than immorality, and marriage is presumed rather than an illicit relationship.
3. Short-term or intermittent cohabitation will not be recognized as a common-law marriage.

C.   Putative marriage:
    1. Recognized by statute; putative spouse acquires rights of legal spouse.
    2. Knowledge of the illegality of the marriage terminates the status of a putative spouse.

D.   Property: No court decisions, but see IV, C.

E.   Partnerships: A partnership agreement between mates is probably enforceable as long as there is a valid business purpose and the agreement is not primarily based on sex.

III. DIVORCE (DISSOLUTION) AND LEGAL SEPARATION

A.   Divorce or dissolution (grounds): Marriage is irretrievably broken (no fault) together with a showing that the couple was not living together for 180 days or that serious marital discord existed.

B.   Legal separation (grounds): Same grounds as for divorce.

C.   Residency requirements: 90 days for either spouse before legal action is filed for divorce.

D.   Remarriage: Possible immediately after divorce is final.

E.   Court orders after filing for divorce and before divorce is final:
    1. Temporary child support.
    2. Court costs and attorneys' fees.
    3. Temporary alimony to either spouse.
    4. Temporary orders concerning disposal of property, removal of children from court's jurisdiction, and other needed relief.

F.   Alimony:
    1. Granted to either spouse without regard to marital misconduct, providing recipient lacks sufficient means and is unable to secure appropriate employment.
    2. Terminated upon remarriage of recipient or death of either.

G.   Child support and custody:
    1. Either or both spouses can be ordered to pay support, without regard to marital misconduct.
    2. Custody awarded according to best interests of child; other factors being equal, a mother will generally be given preference for custody of a young child.

H.   Property division by court in absence of written or oral agreement:
    1. Court has power to apportion all separate property, including joint property, as it deems fair, whether ac-

quired before or during the marriage,
2. Marital misconduct is not considered.

IV. TERMINATION OF COHABITATION

A. Court jurisdiction: No judicial control; voluntary parting.

B. Court orders:
1. Child support and custody available to either mate after review by court.
2. Alimony possible for putative spouse.

C. Property division (decisions in other states suggest the following possibilities):
1. Courts could infer partnership agreements as a means of dividing property and money.
2. Courts could order return or division of property and money if there had been an implied or express agreement.
3. Courts could order return of property to the rightful owner or grant an interest in property or an award of money to a mate to the extent of his/her contribution toward purchase of property.
4. Since living together is not illegal, except when it is open and notorious, recovery might be had for performing household duties as well as for direct financial contribution, so long as the implied or express agreement was not primarily based upon sex.

D. Putative marriage:
1. Putative spouse has rights of legal spouse, including right to alimony following termination.
2. If a legal spouse and a putative spouse both have rights, the court will apportion property and support rights.

E. Palimony: There have been no court decisions to indicate that rehabilitative alimony or temporary or permanent alimony would be awarded to a mate, but such an award is a possibility.

V. SPECIFIC SUBJECTS (No written agreements, except for A,E,I.)
Reference to "BOTH" means married and unmarried couples.

A. Prenuptial or precohabitation agreements:
MARRIED: Probably valid.
UNMARRIED: Probably valid if sex is not the basis of the agreement and if meant for protection of property interests.
BOTH: Agreements must be made without duress and with

full disclosure of assets and other important information.

B.   Property:
     BOTH: All property is separate property of acquiring spouse
     or mate.

C.   Liability of separate property for other spouse's or mate's
     debts:
     MARRIED: No liability, except for necessities, which are
     chargeable to both.
     BOTH: No liability.

D.   Management and control of separate property of each:
     BOTH: Each controls own separate property.
     MARRIED: Both must join in conveyance of family home.

E.   Contracts made during marriage or cohabitation settling
     property rights:
     MARRIED: Valid to settle child support, child custody, and
     spousal support; binding on court unless unconsciona-
     ble.
     UNMARRIED: Probably enforceable if based on earnings,
     property, etc., rather than on sex.
     BOTH: Agreements must be made without duress and with
     full disclosure of assets and other important information.

F.   What can be willed?
     BOTH: Each spouse's or mate's separate property.

G.   Automatic protection for surviving spouse or mate:
     MARRIED: Homestead allowance is $20,000; exempt prop-
     erty is $3,500; family allowance in a reasonable amount
     allowed.
     UNMARRIED: No protection for surviving mate. Minor or
     dependent children receive same allowances.

H.   If no will:
     MARRIED: Surviving spouse receives everything if there are
     no issue of deceased spouse, or if all issue of deceased
     spouse are also issue of surviving spouse. If there is
     issue of deceased spouse who is not issue of surviving
     spouse, a division is made between surviving spouse
     and issue of deceased spouse.
     UNMARRIED: Surviving mate receives nothing. Illegitimate
     children inherit from mother; from father if parents
     marry before or after birth, or if paternity is adjudicated
     before father's death, or established after death by clear
     and convincing evidence.

I.   Contracts:
     BOTH: Each may contract with anyone, including each
     other.

J.   Lawsuits:
      BOTH: Each may sue and be sued separately unless both
      involved.

K.   Homestead law:
      MARRIED: Husband or wife or both have exemption up to
      $20,000 over liens, including mortgages. Value means
      assessed valuation.
      UNMARRIED: Available to mate 60 years of age or older; to
      a mate under 60, if a child, grandchild, or other relation
      is residing with him/her and is supported by him/her.
      BOTH: Homestead must be selected and notice of selection
      recorded by head of family with county clerk and re-
      corder where land is located.

L.   Civil suits by spouses or mates against each other:
      MARRIED: Permitted except for personal wrongs, such as
      assault.
      UNMARRIED: Permitted.

M.   Legitimacy:
      MARRIED: Children born during marriage are presumed le-
      gitimate.
      UNMARRIED: Illegitimate children inherit from mother; from
      father if parents marry before or after birth, or if pa-
      ternity is established by adjudication before death of
      father, or by clear and convincing proof after death.

N.   Adoption:
      BOTH: Any individual may be adopted by any adult. Inves-
      tigation made to determine whether home is suitable and
      whether adoption is in best interests of child.
      MARRIED: Both spouses must consent to adoption.

O.   Division of property upon termination of relationship:
      MARRIED: Court divides all separate property, including
      joint property, acquired before or during marriage, as
      it deems fair, without regard to marital misconduct or
      recorded title.
      UNMARRIED: Implied or express contract, value of services,
      or unfair economic gain may create property rights.

VI. RECENT EVENTS, TRENDS, AND CONCLUSIONS

A.   A husband's support during a seven-year period of sepa-
      ration established a basis for determining the wife's needs
      upon divorce.

B.   It is error for the court to grant a divorce without a hearing
      to determine an irretrievable breakdown, although both
      spouses agree that the marriage is irretrievably broken.

C. A wife can have a divorce-settlement agreement revoked if the husband does not fully disclose all the property subject to division.

D. Cohabitation of a father after his divorce is not a reason to deny him custody of a child.

E. Custody was granted to a father, though both parents were found fit, overcoming the presumption that custody of a young child should go to the mother. The mother was about to enter medical school and the father was found to be more mature and more willing to provide a stable environment for the child.

F. Since common-law and putative marriages are recognized, and cohabitation, adultery, and fornication are legal providing they are not open and notorious, it seems likely that the courts would follow some or all of the theories of the *Marvin* case.

NEBRASKA

I. MARRIAGE

A. Legality:
    1. Age: 18; under 18, need consent of parent(s) or guardian.
    2. License: Required; application 2 days before issuance.
    3. Medical examination: Physician's certificate of examination and laboratory report of blood test showing applicants not infected with syphilis in communicable stage and that female immune to rubella; within 30 days previous to application.
    4. Waiting period: 2 days.

B. Common-law marriages: Not recognized. Valid if valid in another state where entered into.

C.   Out-of-state marriages: Valid if valid in state where entered into.

D.   Adultery: Illegal; sentence.

E.   Property: Separate.

F.   Partnerships: A partnership agreement between spouses is probably enforceable as long as there is a valid business purpose.

II. COHABITATION

A.   Legality:
1.   Cohabitation: Illegal; fine and sentence.
2.   Fornication: Not a crime.

B.   Common-law marriage: Not recognized.

C.   Putative marriage: Recognized to the extent of adjusting property rights.

D.   Property: A mate does not acquire property rights in the property of the other mate, but rights may be acquired under general principles of law.

E.   Partnerships: A partnership agreement between mates is probably enforceable as long as there is a valid business purpose and the agreement is not primarily based on sex.

III. DIVORCE (DISSOLUTION) AND LEGAL SEPARATION

A.   Divorce or dissolution (grounds): marriage irretrievably broken (no fault).

B.   Legal separation (grounds): No statutory grounds; within court's discretion.

C.   Residency requirements: One year for either spouse before filing for divorce.

D.   Remarriage: Possible immediately after divorce is final.

E.   Court orders after filing for divorce and before divorce is final:
1.   Temporary alimony.
2.   Allowance for court costs.
3.   Child support and custody.
4.   Orders protecting property and prohibiting one spouse from molesting the other.

F.   Alimony:
1.   Granted to either spouse as court finds reasonable.
2.   May be modified for good cause, but if no alimony is provided in divorce decree, it cannot be later modified to provide alimony.

3. Terminates on death of either or remarriage of recipient, but lump-sum alimony does not.
4. Later cohabitation is not a ground for modification.

G. Child support and custody: Court makes all suitable orders.

H. Property division by court in absence of written or oral agreement:
1. Court has power to divide all joint and separate property except that property acquired before marriage or by gift or inheritance during marriage is usually retained by owner.
2. Separation agreements are encouraged and enforced.

IV. TERMINATION OF COHABITATION

A. Court jurisdiction: No judicial control; voluntary parting.

B. Court orders: A court may make orders for child support and custody similar to those made in a divorce, once paternity is established.

C. Property division (decisions in other states suggest the following possibilities):
1. Courts could infer partnership agreements as a means of dividing property and money.
2. Courts could order return or division of property and money if there had been an implied or express agreement.
3. Courts could order return of property to the rightful owner or grant an interest in property or an award of money to a mate to the extent of his/her contribution toward purchase of property.
4. Since living together is illegal, courts would probably not honor an agreement if the relationship was primarily sexual; thus it might be difficult to collect for performing household duties when no direct financial contribution can be shown.

D. Putative marriage: Courts would probably make a fair division of property.

E. Palimony: There have been no court decisions to indicate whether rehabilitative alimony or temporary or permanent alimony would be awarded, but such an award is a possibility.

V. SPECIFIC SUBJECTS (No written agreements, except for A,E,I.)
Reference to "BOTH" means married and unmarried couples.

A. Prenuptial or precohabitation agreements:

MARRIED: Valid.

UNMARRIED: Probably valid if sex is not the basis of the agreement and if meant for the protection of property interests.

BOTH: Agreements must be made without duress and with full disclosure of assets and other important information.

B. Property:
BOTH: All property is separate property of acquiring spouse or mate.

C. Liability of separate property for other spouse's or mate's debts:
MARRIED: No liability, except separate property of both is liable for necessaries of family.
UNMARRIED: No liability.

D. Management and control of separate property of each:
BOTH: Each controls own property.
MARRIED: Both spouses must consent to sell real estate, including family home, and household goods.

E. Contracts made during marriage or cohabitation settling property rights:
MARRIED: Valid and binding on court except for provisions for minor children, or provisions found unfair. Agreement becomes part of divorce order.
UNMARRIED: Probably enforceable if based on earnings, property, etc., rather than on sex.
BOTH: Agreements must be made without duress and with full disclosure of assets and other important information.

F. What can be willed?
BOTH: Each spouse's or mate's separate property.

G. Automatic protection for surviving spouse or mate.
MARRIED: Homestead exemption of $4,000 over mortgage liens to surviving spouse. Homestead allowance is $5,000; exempt personal property, $3,500; reasonable family allowance for one year.
UNMARRIED: No protection for surviving mate. Homestead allowance, exempt property allowance, and family allowance available to minor children if they are entitled to inherit (see subject H).

H. If no will:
MARRIED: Surviving spouse receives everything if there are no surviving issue or parents of deceased; if issue or parents survive, surviving spouse divides with them.
UNMARRIED: Surviving mate receives nothing. Illegitimate

children inherit from mother; from father if parents later marry, or if paternity is established by adjudication before death of father, or after his death by clear and convincing proof.

I. Contracts:
BOTH: Each may contract with anyone, including each other.

J. Lawsuits:
BOTH: Each may sue and be sued separately unless both involved.

K. Homestead law:
BOTH: Exemption up to $4,000 over liens on dwelling house in which head of family resides. Head of family is defined as any person who has under his/her care and maintenance a minor child, minor brother or sister, or parent, grandparent, or any other relative who is dependent. No filing or recording required. If property is levied upon, debtor must notify levying officer as to property claimed as homestead.

L. Dower:
MARRIED: Abolished. Surviving spouse is allowed one-third of deceased spouse's estate. This is in addition to will provisions unless surviving spouse renounces will.

M. Curtesy:
MARRIED: Abolished (see subject L).

N. Civil suits by spouses or mates against each other:
BOTH: Permitted.

O. Legitimacy:
MARRIED: Children born during marriage are presumed legitimate. Children born before marriage are legitimized if parents later marry.
UNMARRIED: Illegitimate children are children of mother; of father if he married mother before or after children's birth, or if paternity is established by adjudication before death of father, or after his death by clear and convincing proof.

P. Adoption:
BOTH: Any minor child may be adopted by any adult.
MARRIED: Husband and wife must both consent.

Q. Division of property upon termination of relationship:
MARRIED: If there is no separation agreement, court distributes all joint and separate property as it deems fair. Property acquired before marriage, or by gift or inher-

itance during marriage, is usually retained by owner.
UNMARRIED: Implied or express contracts, value of services,
or unfair economic gain may create rights to property.

VI. RECENT EVENTS, TRENDS, AND CONCLUSIONS

A.   Alternating custody is not in the best interest of small children.

B.   Spouses can now sue each other with no restrictions.

C.   Although cohabitation is illegal, there are indications that agreements between mates would be honored so long as sex was not the only basis of the agreement; some or all of the theories of the *Marvin* case would probably be followed.

NEVADA

I. MARRIAGE

A.   Legality:
   1. Age: 18; between 16 and 18, need consent of parent or guardian; under 16, need authorization of district court and consent of parent or guardian.
   2. License: Required.
   3. Medical examination: None.
   4. Waiting period: None.

B.   Common-law marriages: Not recognized; will probably recognize if entered into in another state.

C.   Out-of-state marriages: Will probably recognize if valid in another state where entered into.

D.   Adultery: Not a crime.

E.   Property: Community.

F.   Partnerships: A partnership agreement between spouses is probably enforceable as long as there is a valid business purpose.

II. COHABITATION

A.   Legality:
   1. Cohabitation: Not a crime.
   2. Fornication: Not a crime.

B.   Common-law marriage: Not recognized.

C.   Putative marriage: No case law, but courts would probably recognize property rights of a putative spouse.

D.   Property: A female mate who had been divorced from her husband but continued to live with him received upon his death property that had been acquired during the marriage and that would have been community property had they still been married.

E.   Partnerships: A partnership agreement between mates is probably enforceable as long as there is a valid business purpose and the agreement is not primarily based on sex.

III. DIVORCE (DISSOLUTION) AND LEGAL SEPARATION

A.   Divorce or dissolution (grounds):
   1. Insanity for two years.
   2. Living apart for one year (no fault).
   3. Incompatibility (no fault).

B.   Legal separation (grounds): Not available.

C.   Residency requirements: 6 weeks for either spouse before filing for divorce.

D.   Remarriage: Possible immediately after divorce is final.

E.   Court orders after filing for divorce and before divorce is final:
   1. Temporary alimony to either spouse.
   2. Court costs and attorneys' fees to either.
   3. Child support to either.
   4. Orders affecting property of either.

F.   Alimony:
   1. Awarded to either spouse.
   2. Ceases upon death of either or remarriage of recipient.
   3. May be later modified upon finding of changed circumstances after divorce decree.

G.   Child support and custody:

1. Court decides according to best interests of child.
2. Either parent may be ordered to pay support.
3. Mother is no longer preferred for custody of young child.
4. Agreements are favored and generally approved.

H. Property division by court in absence of written or oral agreement:
   1. Court divides community property including other joint property, as it deems fair.
   2. Separate property is generally retained by the owning spouse, but the court may set aside the husband's separate property for support of wife; or the wife's separate property for support of husband, if he is disabled and unable to provide for himself; or separate property of either for support of children.
   3. Property settlement agreements are favored.

IV. TERMINATION OF COHABITATION

A. Court jurisdiction: No judicial control; voluntary parting.

B. Court orders: A court may make orders for child support and custody similar to those made in a divorce, once paternity is established.

C. Property division (decisions in Nevada and in other states suggest the following possibilities):
   1. Courts could infer partnership agreements as a means of dividing property and money.
   2. Courts could order return or division of property and money if there had been an implied or express agreement.
   3. Courts could order return of property to the rightful owner, or grant an interest in property or an award of money to a mate to the extent of his/her contribution toward purchase of property.
   4. Since living together is not illegal, recovery could be had for performing household duties as well as for direct financial contributions, so long as the implied or express agreement was not primarily based on sex.

D. Putative marriage: Courts would probably adjust property rights of a putative spouse.

E. Palimony: There have been no court decisions to indicate that rehabilitative alimony or temporary or permanent alimony would be awarded to a mate, but such an award is a possibility.

V. SPECIFIC SUBJECTS (No written agreements, except for A,H,L.)
Reference to "BOTH" means married and unmarried couples.

    A.   Prenuptial or precohabitation agreements:
        MARRIED: Valid. Couple cannot alter legal conjugal rela-
        tionship by agreement except to agree to legal separa-
        tion.
        UNMARRIED: Probably valid if sex is not the basis of the
        agreement and if meant for protection of property in-
        terests.
        BOTH: Agreements must be made without duress and with
        full disclosure of assets and other important information.

    B.   Separate property:
        MARRIED: Property of each owned before marriage, and all
        property acquired after marriage by gift or inheritance,
        or any award for personal injury; rents, issues, and prof-
        its of separate property.
        UNMARRIED: All property is separate property of acquiring
        mate.

    C.   Community property:
        MARRIED: All property acquired after marriage except that
        listed in subject B. Real estate may be held as joint
        tenancy, tenancy in common, or community property.

    D.   Liability of separate property for other spouse's or mate's
        debts:
        MARRIED: No liability, except that husband's separate prop-
        erty is liable for necessaries, if community property is
        insufficient.
        UNMARRIED: No liability.

    E.   Liability of community property for debts contracted by one
        spouse:
        MARRIED: Liable for debts contracted for the benefit of the
        community.

    F.   Management and control of separate property of each:
        BOTH: Each controls own property.

    G.   Management and control of community property:
        MARRIED: Either spouse acting alone may control all the
        community property, but neither may will more than
        his/her one-half share. Neither may give away com-
        munity property without consent of the other. Both
        spouses must sign for the sale or purchase of real estate,
        or the sale or collateralization of household goods and
        furnishings.

H. Contracts made during marriage or cohabitation settling property rights:

MARRIED: Valid. Usually approved.

UNMARRIED: Probably enforceable if based on earnings, property, etc., rather than on sex.

BOTH: Agreements must be made without duress and with full disclosure of assets and other important information.

I. What can be willed?

BOTH: Each spouse's or mate's separate property.

MARRIED: Same; also one-half share of the community property.

J. Automatic protection for surviving spouse or mate:

MARRIED: Homestead exemption of $50,000 over liens, including mortgages, to surviving spouse and legitimate children. Surviving spouse receives one-half of the community property. Widow receives same protections as minor children (see BOTH).

UNMARRIED: No protection for surviving mate. Homestead exemption does not go to illegitimate children.

BOTH: Minor children entitled to inherit may remain in family home, receive clothing, household furniture, and reasonable provision for support (see subject K).

K. If no will:

MARRIED: Surviving spouse receives all separate property of deceased spouse if there are no surviving children or other relatives of deceased spouse. Otherwise, surviving spouse divides with survivors. Surviving spouse always receives deceased spouse's one-half share of community property.

UNMARRIED: Surviving mate receives nothing. Illegitimate children inherit from mother; from father if acknowledged in writing before a witness, or if legitimized by marriage of parents.

L. Contracts:

BOTH: Each may contract with anyone, including each other.

M. Lawsuits:

BOTH: Each may sue and be sued separately unless both involved.

MARRIED: May also sue and be sued jointly even if both are not involved.

N. Homestead law:

BOTH: Exemption up to $50,000 over liens, including mortgages, upon dwelling house for head of family, both spouses, or a single person. Declaration of homestead must be recorded in county recorder's office in county where land is located.

O.   Civil suits by spouses or mates against each other:
MARRIED: May sue each other for injuries suffered in automobile accident. Other suits probably not permitted.
UNMARRIED: Permitted.

P.   Legitimacy:
MARRIED: Children born during marriage are presumed legitimate.
UNMARRIED: Illegitimate children inherit from mother; from father if acknowledged in writing before witness.
BOTH: Children born before marriage are legitimized if parents later marry.

Q.   Adoption:
BOTH: Any adult may adopt a minor if adoptive parent is ten years older than minor. Both spouses must join in adoption.

R.   Division of property upon termination of relationship:
MARRIED: Each spouse generally retains separate property. Court divides community property as it deems fair. Each spouse receives his/her share of other joint property.
UNMARRIED: Implied or express contracts, value of services, or unfair economic gain may create rights to property.

VI. RECENT EVENTS, TRENDS, AND CONCLUSIONS

A.   An ex-wife's cohabitation with another man is not necessarily a reason for terminating alimony.

B.   The "tender years" presumption that the mother is preferred for custody of young children has been abolished.

C.   In a recent case, a female mate tried to obtain property rights to accumulations acquired over a period of eight years on the basis of a partnership or joint venture, unfair economic gain, and value of services. The relief she asked for was denied because the court did not find evidence of an implied agreement. But the court discussed the *Marvin* case, and the implication is that, in the proper situation, some or all of the remedies of the *Marvin* case would be followed.

NEW HAMPSHIRE

I. MARRIAGE

A. Legality:
   1. Age: 18; between 14 and 18 for male or 13 and 18 for female need permission of judge of probate or superior court.
   2. License: Required; must be issued no less than 5 days after application; good for 90 days from issuance.
   3. Medical examination: Physician's certificate that each has had blood test for syphilis and is not infected; not more than 30 days before application for license.
   4. Waiting period: None.

B. Common-law marriages: Not recognized. But a statute provides that persons cohabiting and acknowledging each other as husband and wife and generally thought to be married for three years are thereafter deemed to have been legally married.

C. Out-of-state marriages: Valid if valid in state where entered into.

D. Adultery: Illegal (misdemeanor).

E. Property: Separate.

F. Partnerships: A partnership agreement between spouses is probably enforceable as long as there is a valid business purpose.

II. COHABITATION

A. Legality:
   1. Cohabitation: Not a crime.
   2. Fornication: Not a crime.

B. Common-law marriage: The statutory common-law marriage gives a woman all the rights of a wife (see I, B).

C. Putative marriage: If a marriage is void because it is bigamous, the courts will respect the rights of the mates to contributions made when acquiring property.

D. Property: Early cases held that a mate could not collect for household services, even if there was an agreement that she would be paid and sex was not the basis of the agreement.

E.   Partnerships: A partnership agreement between mates is probably enforceable as long as there is a valid business purpose and the agreement is not primarily based on sex.

III. DIVORCE (DISSOLUTION) AND LEGAL SEPARATION

A.   Divorce or dissolution (grounds):
   1. Impotency.
   2. Extreme cruelty.
   3. Conviction and imprisonment for felony.
   4. Adultery.
   5. Treatment to seriously injure mental or physical health.
   6. Absence for 2 years.
   7. Habitual drunkenness for 2 years.
   8. Joining any religious sect or society that believes relationship of husband and wife is unlawful, and refusal to cohabit for 6 months.
   9. Abandonment and refusal to cohabit for 2 years.
   10. Willing absence for 2 years without consent of other.
   11. Desertion and nonsupport for 2 years.
   12. Irreconcilable differences causing irremediable breakdown of marriage (no fault).

B.   Legal separation (grounds): Same as for divorce.

C.   Residency requirements:
   1. Both spouses domiciled in state where divorce action filed; or
   2. Plaintiff domiciled in state where action filed and defendant personally served in state; or
   3. Plaintiff domiciled in state for one year before action filed.

D.   Remarriage: Possible immediately after divorce is final.

E.   Court orders after filing for divorce and before divorce is final:
   1. Temporary alimony.
   2. Child support and custody.
   3. Restraining orders concerning property or children.

F.   Alimony:
   1. Granted to either spouse as court deems proper.
   2. If there are no minor children, award is for not more than three years, but may be renewed or modified not to exceed three years each time.
   3. May be modified for later changed circumstances after divorce.

G.   Child support and custody: Court orders support and custody according to best interests of child.

H.   Property division by court in absence of written or oral agreement: Court has power to divide all separate property, including joint property, as it deems fair. Usually each spouse receives his/her own separate property, but the court may award all or part of one spouse's property to the other, as justice requires.

IV. TERMINATION OF COHABITATION

A.   Court jurisdiction: No judicial control; voluntary parting.

B.   Court orders: A court may make orders for child support and custody similar to those made in a divorce, once paternity is established.

C.   Property division (decisions in New Hampshire and in other states suggest the following possibilities):
  1.   Courts could infer partnership agreements as a means of dividing property and money.
  2.   Courts could order return or division of property and money if there had been an implied or express agreement.
  3.   Courts could order return of property to the rightful owner or grant an interest in property or an award of money to a mate to the extent of his/her contribution toward purchase of property.
  4.   Since living together is not illegal, recovery might be had for performing household duties as well as for direct financial contribution, so long as the implied or express agreement was not primarily based on sex.

D.   Putative marriage: Property rights of a putative spouse would probably be recognized.

E.   Palimony: There have been no court decisions to indicate that rehabilitative alimony or temporary or permanent alimony would be awarded to a mate, but such an award is a possibility.

V. SPECIFIC SUBJECTS (No written agreements, except for A,E,I.)
Reference to "BOTH" means married and unmarried couples.

A.   Prenuptial or precohabitation agreements:
  MARRIED: Now allowed.
  UNMARRIED: Probably valid if sex is not the basis of the agreement and if meant for the protection of property interests. Agreements must be made without duress and

with full disclosure of assets and other important information.

B. Property:
    BOTH: All property is separate property of acquiring spouse or mate.

C. Liability of separate property for other spouse's or mate's debts:
    BOTH: No liability.

D. Management and control of separate property of each.
    BOTH: Each controls own property.
    MARRIED: Both spouses must sign to sell family home or use it as collateral for a loan.

E. Contracts made during marriage or cohabitation settling property rights:
    MARRIED: Invalid.
    UNMARRIED: Probably enforceable if based on earnings, property, etc., rather than on sex. Agreements must be made without duress and with full disclosure of assets and other important information.

F. What can be willed?
    BOTH: Each spouse's or mate's separate property.
    MARRIED: Surviving spouse may elect statutory share (specific share depending upon number of other surviving heirs) instead of will provisions and homestead rights (right to occupy home for life).

G. Automatic protection for surviving spouse or mate:
    MARRIED: Non-owning spouse may occupy family home for life after death of owner.
    UNMARRIED: No protection for surviving mate. No rights to minor children.

H. If no will:
    MARRIED: Surviving spouse receives everything if there are no surviving issue or parents of deceased spouse. Otherwise, surviving spouse divides with issue or parents.
    UNMARRIED: Surviving mate receives nothing. Illegitimate children inherit from mother; from father only if legitimized.

I. Contracts:
    MARRIED: Each may contract with anyone, probably including each other, except for antenuptial property settlement or separation agreement during marriage.
    UNMARRIED: Each may contract with anyone, including each other.

J. Lawsuits:

BOTH: Each may sue and be sued separately unless both involved.

K.   Homestead law:
BOTH: Any person is entitled to exemption to a limit of $2,500 over liens in family home. Superior court, on petition of owner, owner's spouse, or owner's creditor, may appoint appraisers to establish homestead right.

L.   Civil suits by spouses or mates against each other:
BOTH: Permitted.

M.   Legitimacy:
MARRIED: Children born during marriage are presumed legitimate.
UNMARRIED: Illegitimate children inherit from mother equally with legitimate children; from father if legitimized by father's petition that children be declared legitimate.
BOTH: Subsequent marriage of parents also legitimizes.

N.   Adoption:
BOTH: Any adult may adopt any other individual, except spouse. Investigation made of home conditions.
MARRIED: Both spouses must consent.

O.   Division of property upon termination of relationship:
MARRIED: Court has power to divide all separate property, including joint property, as it deems fair, but separate property of each is usually assigned to owner-spouse.
UNMARRIED: Implied or express contract, value of services, or unfair economic gain may create rights to property.

VI. RECENT EVENTS, TRENDS, AND CONCLUSIONS

A.   Proposed new legislation would allow spouses to make contracts before or during marriage, settling property, custody, duty, and separation.

B.   Female homemate who cohabited for five years with a man who passed away was awarded personal property which was given to her, one-half of the proceeds of a business in which they were joint venturers, and compensation for "intimate, confidential, and dedicated personal and business services" to the man. This decision is a good indication that some or all of the theories of the *Marvin* case would be followed.

NEW JERSEY

I. MARRIAGE

A. Legality:
1. Age: 18; under 18, need written consent (with 2 witnesses) of parents or guardian; under 16, consent must be approved by judge.
2. License: Required; issued 72 hours after application; good for 30 days after issuance.
3. Medical examination: Physician's certificate saying laboratory test shows applicant not infected with communicable syphilis.
4. Waiting period: 72 hours.

B. Common-law marriages: Not recognized; valid if valid in state where entered into.

C. Out-of-state marriages: Valid if valid where entered into.

D. Adultery: Not a crime.

E. Property: Separate.

F. Partnerships: A partnership agreement between spouses is probably enforceable as long as there is a valid business purpose.

II. COHABITATION

A. Legality:
1. Cohabitation: Not a crime.
2. Fornication: Not a crime.
3. All private, nonviolent sexual acts between consenting adults are legal.

B. Property: Both express and implied agreements between mates have been honored if sex is only incidental to the agreement.

C. Putative marriage:
1. A legal marriage does not automatically result from continuing to live together in a bigamous marriage after dissolution of the first marriage.
2. If a mate mistakenly believes he/she is married, and contributes to property acquired by the other mate,

reimbursement must be made upon termination of the relationship.

D.   Partnerships: A partnership agreement between mates is probably enforceable as long as there is a valid business purpose and the agreement is not primarily based on sex.

E.   Common-law marriage: not recognized.

III. DIVORCE (DISSOLUTION) AND LEGAL SEPARATION

A.   Divorce or dissolution (grounds):
   1.   Adultery.
   2.   Desertion for one year.
   3.   Extreme cruelty.
   4.   Living apart for 18 months (no fault).
   5.   Habitual addiction to drugs or habitual drunkenness for one year.
   6.   Commitment for mental illness for 2 years.
   7.   Imprisonment for 18 months.
   8.   Deviant sexual conduct.

B.   Legal separation (grounds): Same as for divorce.

C.   Residency requirements: One year for either spouse before filing for divorce.

D.   Remarriage: Possible immediately after divorce is final.

E.   Court orders after filing for divorce and before divorce is final:
   1.   Court costs and attorneys' fees to either spouse.
   2.   Temporary alimony to either.
   3.   Child support and custody.

F.   Alimony:
   1.   Granted to either spouse.
   2.   Considerations: need and ability to pay, duration of marriage.
   3.   Marital fault may be considered.
   4.   Terminates on remarriage of recipient.
   5.   Cohabitation of the recipient after divorce is not a sufficient reason for modification.

G.   Child support and custody: Court may order to either spouse as it deems fair.

H.   Property division by court in absence of written or oral agreement: Court divides all separate property, including joint property, acquired during marriage as it deems fair. Property acquired before marriage is retained by the owner-spouse.

IV. TERMINATION OF COHABITATION

A.   Court jurisdiction: No judicial control; voluntary parting.

B.   Court orders: A court may make orders for child support and custody similar to those made in a divorce, once paternity is established.

C.   Property division (decisions in New Jersey and in other states suggest the following possibilities):
1. Courts could infer partnership agreements as a means of dividing property and money.
2. Courts could order return or division of property and money if there had been an implied or express agreement.
3. Courts could order return of property to the rightful owner or grant an interest in property or an award of money to a mate to the extent of his/her contribution toward purchase of property.
4. Since living together is not illegal, recovery could be had for performing household duties as well as for direct financial contributions, so long as the implied or express agreement was not primarily based on sex.

D.   Putative marriage: Courts would probably adjust the property rights of a putative spouse.

E.   Palimony: Court decisions indicate that temporary or permanent alimony would be awarded to a mate if circumstances warranted.

V. SPECIFIC SUBJECTS (No written agreements, except for A,E,I.)
Reference to "BOTH" means married and unmarried couples.

A.   Prenuptial or precohabitation agreements:
MARRIED: Valid.
UNMARRIED: Probably valid if sex is not the basis of the agreement and if meant for protection of property interests.
BOTH: Agreements must be made without duress and with full disclosure of assets and other important information.

B.   Property:
BOTH: All property is separate property of acquiring spouse or mate.

C.   Liability of separate property for other spouse's or mate's debts:
MARRIED: No liability, except husband is probably liable for necessaries.
UNMARRIED: No liability.

D. Management and control of separate property of each:
    BOTH: Each controls own property.
    MARRIED: A sale cannot affect the rights of the other unless
    both sign.

E. Contracts made during marriage or cohabitation settling
    property rights:
    MARRIED: Valid.
    UNMARRIED: Probably enforceable if based on earnings,
    property, etc., rather than on sex.
    BOTH: Agreements must be made without duress and with
    full disclosure of assets and other important information.

F. What can be willed?
    BOTH: Each spouse's or mate's separate property.
    MARRIED: Surviving spouse can choose between real estate
    given according to the will, or dower or curtesy.

G. Automatic protection for surviving spouse or mate:
    MARRIED: Surviving spouse receives decedent's wearing
    apparel, up to $1,000 worth of decedent's personal prop-
    erty, and may remain in home rent-free until dower or
    curtesy is distributed.
    UNMARRIED: No protection for surviving mate. Minor chil-
    dren would probably receive wearing apparel and the
    $1,000 personal-property allowance if entitled to inherit
    (see subject H).

H. If no will:
    MARRIED: Surviving spouse receives everything if there are
    no surviving parents of deceased spouse; otherwise, es-
    tate is divided with parents.
    UNMARRIED: Surviving mate receives nothing. Illegitimate
    children inherit from mother; from father if legitimized
    by later marriage of parents, or if paternity is established
    by adjudication before death of father, or by clear and
    convincing proof after his death.

I. Contracts:
    BOTH: Each may contract with anyone, including each
    other.

J. Lawsuits:
    BOTH: Each may sue and be sued separately unless both
    involved.

K. Homestead law:
    BOTH: No homestead law.

L. Dower or curtesy:
    MARRIED: Surviving spouse receives one-half of real estate
    owned by decedent during marriage for life. May be

barred by spouse's will. Divorce terminates right.

M.   Civil suits by spouses or mates against each other:
      MARRIED: May sue each other for negligence in automobile
         accident. Otherwise, with few exceptions, spouses can-
         not sue each other.
      UNMARRIED: Permitted.

N.   Legitimacy:
      MARRIED: Children born during marriage are presumed le-
         gitimate. Children born before marriage are legitimized
         if parents later marry.
      UNMARRIED: Illegitimate children inherit from mother; from
         father if parents marry, or if paternity is established by
         adjudication during father's life, or by clear and con-
         vincing proof after his death.

O.   Adoption:
      BOTH: Any person ten years older than adoptee can adopt
         an adult or child.
      MARRIED: Husband and wife must both consent.

P.   Division of property upon termination of relationship:
      MARRIED: Court divides all separate property, including
         joint property, acquired during marriage as it deems fair.
         Property acquired before marriage is retained by owner-
         spouse.
      UNMARRIED: Implied or express contracts, value of services,
         or unfair economic gain may create rights to property.

VI. RECENT EVENTS, TRENDS, AND CONCLUSIONS

A.   An adoption was granted to a stepfather, but the natural
      father retained visitation rights with his two daughters.

B.   The father and mother of an illegitimate child cannot mu-
      tually waive the father's duty to pay child support.

C.   Trust property received by the husband during marriage is
      marital property divisible on divorce. A pension plan, the
      proceeds of which are presently unavailable, is not subject
      to distribution.

D.   Rehabilitative alimony after divorce is expressly rejected.

E.   A recent court decision provides that a joint venture, an
      implied and/or express (oral) contract, the value of services
      are all possibilities for relief after long-term cohabitation.
      Some or all of the theories of the *Marvin* case seem to be
      adopted in the state.

F.   A millionaire was ordered to pay $550 a month temporary

alimony to his mistress during a lawsuit in which she asked
for one-half of his $4,000,000 assets. She also was given
the right to live in his $100,000 house during the lawsuit.
The lawsuit is still pending final outcome.

NEW MEXICO

I. MARRIAGE

A.   Legality:
  1. Age: 18; under 18, need consent of parent or guardian;
     under 16, need order of children's court or family
     division of district court.
  2. License: Required.
  3. Medical examination: Required, not more than 30 days
     prior to application for license.
  4. Waiting period: None.

B.   Common-law marriages: Not recognized; valid if valid in
     another state where entered into.

C.   Out-of-state marriages: Valid if valid in state where entered
     into.

D.   Adultery: Not a crime.

E.   Property: Community.

F.   Partnerships: A partnership agreement between spouses is
     probably enforceable as long as there is a valid business
     purpose.

II. COHABITATION

A.   Legality:

1. Cohabitation: Illegal; warning by judge on first offense, conviction of misdemeanor after first offense.
2. Fornication: Not a crime.

B. Common-law marriage: Not recognized.

C. Putative marriage: Courts would probably recognize the property rights of an innocent putative spouse.

D. Property: No court decisions, but see IV, C for possibilities.

E. Partnerships: A partnership agreement between mates is probably enforceable as long as there is a valid business purpose and the agreement is not primarily based on sex.

III. DIVORCE (DISSOLUTION) AND LEGAL SEPARATION

A. Divorce or dissolution (grounds):
1. Adultery.
2. Cruel or inhuman treatment.
3. Abandonment.
4. Incompatibility (no fault).

B. Legal separation (grounds): Parties permanently separated and no longer live together.

C. Residency requirements: 6 months residence and domicile in state for either spouse before filing for divorce.

D. Remarriage: Possible immediately after divorce is final.

E. Court orders after filing for divorce and before divorce is final:
1. Temporary alimony to either spouse.
2. Court costs and attorneys' fees.
3. Orders for the protection of property.

F. Alimony: Granted to either spouse from other spouse's separate property in the form of property or money.

G. Child support and custody:
1. Either parent may be ordered to pay support.
2. Custody is granted according to best interests of child.

H. Property division by court in absence of written or oral agreement:
1. Court divides community property equally.
2. Court may allow either spouse a reasonable portion of other spouse's separate property.
3. Marital misconduct is not considered in division of community property.
4. Each spouse receives his/her share of other joint property.

IV. TERMINATION OF COHABITATION

A.   Court jurisdiction: No judicial control; voluntary parting.

B.   Court orders: A court may make orders for child support and custody similar to those made in a divorce, once paternity is established.

C.   Property division (decisions in other states suggest the following possibilities):
1. Courts could infer partnership agreements as a means of dividing property and money.
2. Courts could order return or division of property and money if there had been an implied or express agreement.
3. Courts could order return of property to the rightful owner or grant an interest in property or an award of money to a mate to the extent of his/her contribution toward purchase of property.
4. Since living together is illegal, courts would probably not honor an agreement if relationship was primarily sexual; thus it might be difficult to collect for performing household duties when no direct financial contribution can be shown.

D.   Putative marriage: Courts would probably adjust the rights of a putative spouse.

E.   Palimony: There have been no court decisions to indicate that rehabilitative alimony or temporary or permanent alimony would be awarded to a mate, but such an award is a possibility.

V. SPECIFIC SUBJECTS (No written agreements, except for A,H,L.)
Reference to "BOTH" means married and unmarried couples.

A.   Prenuptial or precohabitation agreements:
MARRIED: Valid; must be in writing.
UNMARRIED: Probably valid if sex is not the basis of the agreement and if meant for protection of property interests.
BOTH: Agreements must be made without duress and with full disclosure of assets and other important information.

B.   Separate property:
MARRIED: All property acquired before marriage; property acquired by gift or inheritance during marriage; property designated by written agreement; property held in joint tenancy or tenancy in common; rents, issues, and profits of separate property.

UNMARRIED: All property is separate property of acquiring mate.

C.   Community property:
MARRIED: All property acquired by either spouse during marriage, except separate property (see subject B).

D.   Liability of separate property for other spouse's or mate's debts:
BOTH: No liability.

E.   Liability of community property for debts contracted by one spouse:
MARRIED: All debts incurred during marriage are community debts unless they are specifically designated as separate debts; community property is liable for community debts. Debtor spouse's one-half of community property is liable for his/her separate debts after his/her separate property is depleted.

F.   Management and control of separate property of each:
BOTH: Each controls own property.
MARRIED: Both spouses must sign to sell family home.

G.   Management and control of community property:
MARRIED: Either spouse may manage or control community personal property. Both must sign for all sales of community real estate.

H.   Contracts made during marriage or cohabitation settling property rights:
MARRIED: Valid.
UNMARRIED: Probably enforceable if based on earnings, property, etc., rather than on sex.
BOTH: Agreements must be made without duress and with full disclosure of assets and other important information.

I.   What can be willed?
BOTH: Each spouse's or mate's separate property.
MARRIED: Same; also his/her half of community property.

J.   Automatic protection for surviving spouse or mate:
MARRIED: Surviving spouse receives family allowance of $10,000 and personal property allowance of $3,500; homestead exemption of $10,000 over liens, including mortgages; one-half of community property.
UNMARRIED: No protection for surviving mate. Minor or dependent children receive family and personal-property allowances if entitled to inherit (see subject K).

K.   If no will:
MARRIED: Surviving spouse receives all separate property

of deceased spouse if there are no surviving issue of deceased spouse; if issue survive, surviving spouse receives one-fourth. Surviving spouse always receives decedent's half of community property.

UNMARRIED: Surviving mate receives nothing. Illegitimate children inherit from mother; from father if parents later marry, or if father recognizes children in writing, or if paternity established by adjudication.

L.   Contracts:
BOTH: Each may contract with anyone, including each other.

M.   Lawsuits:
BOTH: Each may sue and be sued separately unless both involved.

N.   Homestead law:
BOTH: Exemption not to exceed $10,000 over liens, including mortgages, for married persons, widow, widower, or person supporting another. No requirements for filing or recording.

O.   Civil suits by spouses or mates against each other:
BOTH: Permitted.

P.   Legitimacy:
MARRIED: Children born during marriage are presumed legitimate.
UNMARRIED: Illegitimate children are children of mother; also of father if parents later marry, if father recognizes offspring in writing, or if paternity established by adjudication.

Q.   Adoption:
MARRIED: Both spouses must consent to adoption; may adopt adult or child.
UNMARRIED: Unmarried adult may adopt adult or child.
BOTH: Investigation as to suitability of home.

R.   Division of property upon termination of relationship:
MARRIED: Court divides community property equally and may grant either spouse a portion of other spouse's separate property. Each spouse receives his/her share of other joint property.
UNMARRIED: Implied or express contracts, value of services, or unfair economic gain may create rights to property.

VI. RECENT EVENTS, TRENDS, AND CONCLUSIONS

A.   A de facto marriage (cohabiting as if married) does not automatically cause termination of a prior alimony award, but income supplied by the third-party mate is considered in modifying or reducing payments.

B.   A husband's vested but unmatured pension and a disabled husband's pension earned during the marriage are community property in which the wife has a half-interest.

C.   A proposed law requiring contracts between mates to be in writing did not pass the legislature.

D.   Although cohabitation is illegal, it is punishable by reprimand. Since neither adultery nor fornication is illegal, it is likely that some or all of the theories of the *Marvin* case would be followed.

NEW YORK

I. MARRIAGE

A.   Legality:
1. Age: 18; under 18, need consent of parent or guardian; under 16, not permitted.
2. License: Required.
3. Medical examination: Physician's certificate required stating that blood tests show freedom from syphilis and gonorrhea, not more than 30 days prior to application. Sickle-cell anemia test may be required.
4. Waiting period: 24 hours after license issued; 10 days after medical examination.

B.   Common-law marriages: Not recognized.

C.   Out-of-state marriages: Valid if valid in state where entered into.

D.   Adultery: Illegal (misdemeanor); fine and/or sentence.

E.   Property: Separate.

F. Partnerships: A partnership agreement between spouses is probably enforceable as long as there is a valid business purpose.

II. COHABITATION

A. Legality:
1. Cohabitation: Not a crime.
2. Fornication: Not a crime.

B. Common-law marriage: Not recognized.

C. Putative marriage: A spouse who believes in the validity of an invalid marriage may retain his/her portion in tenancy by the entireties.

D. Property:
1. Property agreements between mates based on joint economic reasons rather than on sex would probably be enforced.
2. If a deed describes a couple who are not legally married as husband and wife, they take the property as joint tenants rather than as tenants in common, unless they are expressly described as tenants in common.

E. Partnerships: A partnership agreement between mates is probably enforceable as long as there is a valid business purpose and the agreement is not primarily based on sex.

III. DIVORCE (DISSOLUTION) AND LEGAL SEPARATION

A. Divorce or dissolution (grounds):
1. Cruel and inhuman treatment.
2. Abandonment for one year.
3. Imprisonment for 3 years.
4. Adultery.
5. Continuously living apart for at least one year after a decree of legal separation or written separation agreement (no fault).

B. Legal separation (grounds): Any of above grounds except number 5; in addition, husband's failure to support wife.

C. Residency requirements:
1. Both spouses residents before filing of legal action and reason for divorce arises in state.
2. One spouse a resident for at least one year and marriage occurred in state, or spouses have lived in state as husband and wife, or reason for divorce occurred in state.
3. Otherwise, one spouse must be a resident for 2 years before divorce is filed.

D.   Remarriage: Possible immediately after divorce is final.

E.   Court orders after filing for divorce and before divorce is final: Court may order either spouse to pay necessary expenses of the other spouse in a divorce or legal separation action, or in proceedings to enforce payment of alimony or support.

F.   Alimony: Court may require either spouse to support the other. Considerations:
   1. Duration of marriage.
   2. Wife's ability to be self-supporting.
   3. Circumstances of the situation and the respective parties.
   4. Marital misconduct is an absolute bar to alimony if divorce is granted under any fault ground.

G.   Child support and custody:
   1. Court may award custody to either parent.
   2. Each parent is responsible for child support.
   3. Neither parent is given preference for custody.

H.   Property division by court in absence of written or oral agreement:
   1. Each spouse retains his or her separate property, including marital property acquired during marriage.
   2. When wife secures divorce, husband loses all rights in wife's real estate or personal property in her possession or under her control.
   3. Wife's dower rights in husband's real property are not affected.
   4. Joint property divided equally.
   5. Recent legislation was enacted, providing for an equitable division of all separate property, including joint property. This new law applies to all divorce actions filed after the law became effective, and substantially changes division of property between spouses.

IV. TERMINATION OF COHABITATION

A.   Court jurisdiction: No judicial control; voluntary parting.

B.   Court orders: A court may make orders for child support and custody similar to those made in a divorce, once paternity is established.

C.   Property division (decisions in New York and in other states suggest the following possibilities):
   1. Courts could infer partnership agreements as a means of dividing property and money.

2. Courts could order return or division of property and money if there had been an implied or express agreement.

3. Courts could order return of property to the rightful owner or grant an interest in property or an award of money to a mate to the extent of his/her contribution toward purchase of property.

4. Since living together is not illegal, recovery could be had for performing household duties as well as for direct financial contributions, so long as the implied or express agreement was not primarily based on sex.

D. Putative marriage: If one mate is persuaded by the other's fraud into believing a valid marriage exists, property involved may be awarded to the defrauded mate or divided as if a valid marriage existed.

E. Palimony: Court decisions indicate that rehabilitative alimony or temporary or permanent alimony would be awarded to a mate if circumstances warranted.

V. SPECIFIC SUBJECTS (No written agreements, except for A,E,I.)
Reference to "BOTH" means married and unmarried couples.

A. Prenuptial or precohabitation agreements:
   MARRIED: Valid.
   UNMARRIED: Probably valid if sex is not the basis of the agreement and if meant for protection of property interests.
   BOTH: Agreements must be made without duress and with full disclosure of assets and other important information.

B. Property:
   BOTH: All property is separate property of acquiring spouse or mate.

C. Liability of separate property for other spouse's or mate's debts:
   MARRIED: No liability, except that husband may be liable for necessaries furnished to wife.
   UNMARRIED: No liability.

D. Management and control of separate property of each:
   BOTH: Each controls own property.

E. Contracts made during marriage or cohabitation settling property rights:
   MARRIED: Recognized and enforced.
   UNMARRIED: Probably enforceable if based on earnings, property, etc., rather than on sex.
   BOTH: Agreements must be made without duress and with

full disclosure of assets and other important information.

F. What can be willed?
    BOTH: Each spouse's or mate's separate property.

G. Automatic protection for surviving spouse or mate:
    MARRIED: Surviving spouse and children under 21 years of age receive household items, clothing, machinery, and money which is not subject to claims of creditors up to $5,000 in value, books up to $150, farm animals and machinery up to $5,000, money and other personal property up to $1,000. Widow may remain in home for 40 days rent-free.
    UNMARRIED: No protection for surviving mate. Children receive same protection as spouse if entitled to inherit (see subject H).

H. If no will:
    MARRIED: If there are no surviving children or descendants of deceased parent, surviving spouse receives everything; if children or descendants of deceased parent survive, division is made between them and surviving spouse.
    UNMARRIED: Surviving mate receives nothing. Illegitimate children inherit from mother; from father if paternity has been adjudicated or if father acknowledges paternity in writing and files it with state, or if parents later marry each other.

I. Contracts:
    BOTH: Each may contract with anyone, including each other.

J. Lawsuits:
    BOTH: Each may sue or be sued separately, unless both involved.

K. Homestead law:
    BOTH: Exemption for any person for land and buildings owned and used as principal residence, up to value of $10,000 above liens, including mortgages. Exemption continues, after death of owner, for surviving spouse and minor children. No filing necessary; occupancy is evidence of the claim of homestead.

L. Civil suits by spouses or mates against each other:
    BOTH: Each may sue the other.

M. Legitimacy:
    MARRIED: Children born during marriage are presumed legitimate.
    UNMARRIED: Paternity of an illegitimate child may be ad-

judicated within ten years of birth of particular child, or established by written acknowledgment of father.

BOTH: Children born before marriage are legitimized if parents later marry.

N.   Adoption:

BOTH: Both spouses together or single adults may adopt, subject to examination before a judge.

O.   Division of property upon termination of relationship:

MARRIED: See VI, J.

UNMARRIED: Implied or express contracts, value of services, or unfair economic gain may create rights to property.

VI. RECENT EVENTS, TRENDS, AND CONCLUSIONS

A.   A recent case brought by the mate of a rock star, alleging an oral contract and seeking (1) an equal division of his earnings since 1973, (2) a change of title of real estate to show joint ownership, and (3) an award of future earnings was dismissed by the court because the mates were adulterers, which was contrary to public policy.

B.   One court refused to allow recovery for domestic services to a woman who had lived with a man for over 25 years, borne him 2 children, and rendered services at his request, because no evidence was presented that he expressly agreed to pay her. The court also found no oral partnership agreement concerning domestic services.

C.   Another court awarded alimony, child support, and quasi-marital property to a homemate who had performed the duties of homemaker for 28 years.

D.   Permanent alimony was not awarded to a wife whose misconduct constituted grounds for separation or divorce.

E.   A court ruled that since a separation agreement stated that a husband's alimony payments ended if the wife cohabited, the obligations were not revived when the cohabitation ended.

F.   A husband has the right to seek attorney's fees and temporary or permanent alimony from his wife upon divorce.

G.   A statute that allows illegitimate children to inherit from their intestate father only if, before the father's death, there has been a judicial declaration of paternity, does not violate the rights of illegitimates.

H.   A father who has maintained a relationship with his illegitimate children and provided child support must give his consent before the children can be adopted by the mother's new husband.

I. New York courts have been inconsistent in property division awards upon the termination of nonmarital relationships. An express oral agreement may not be enforced unless a mate has relied on it. An express business agreement may not be enforced if there is also a sexual relationship which the court considers to be against public policy. On the other hand, implied contracts have been found, and property divisions and alimony granted, especially after a long marital-like period of cohabitation. Some aspects of the *Marvin* case might be followed, depending on the court and the particular circumstances of the case.

J. Recent legislation was enacted providing for an equitable division of all separate property, including joint property, assuming there is no contract between the spouses getting divorced. This new law applies to all divorce actions filed after the law became effective, and substantially changes former laws regarding division of property between spouses.

NORTH CAROLINA

I. MARRIAGE

A. Legality:
1. Age: 18; under 18, need written consent of parent or guardian; under 16, not permitted.
2. License: Required.
3. Medical examination: Physician's certificate showing freedom from venereal disease, tuberculosis, and mental incompetency, and that female has rubella immunity.
4. Waiting period: None.

B. Common-law marriages: Not recognized; valid if valid in another state where entered into.

C.   Out-of-state marriages: Valid if valid in state where entered into.

D.   Adultery: Illegal (misdemeanor); fine and/or sentence.

E.   Property: Separate.

F.   Partnerships: A partnership agreement between spouses is probably enforceable as long as there is a valid business purpose.

II. COHABITATION

A.   Legality:
1. Cohabitation: Illegal (misdemeanor); fine and/or sentence.
2. Fornication: Illegal (misdemeanor); fine and/or sentence.

B.   Common-law marriage: Not recognized.

C.   Putative marriage: A woman who mistakenly believes in a valid marriage can be repaid for her services less the value of support her mate has provided.

D.   Property:
1. Land granted to husband and wife before their marriage would establish tenancy in common; upon divorce, each would receive one-half.
2. An agreement between mates settling property rights would probably be enforced if it is not based specifically on sex.

E.   Partnerships: A partnership agreement between mates is probably enforceable as long as there is a valid business purpose and the agreement is not primarily based on sex.

III. DIVORCE (DISSOLUTION) AND LEGAL SEPARATION

A.   Divorce or dissolution (grounds): Grounds must have existed for at least 6 months prior to filing for divorce.
1. Adultery.
2. Impotency at time of marriage.
3. Pregnancy of wife at time of marriage by another man and without husband's knowledge.
4. Continuous separation for one year (no fault).
5. Separation for 3 years because of incurable insanity.
6. Crime against nature.
7. Bestiality.

B.   Legal separation (grounds):
1. Abandonment by either.

    2. Maliciously turning other out.
    3. Cruel and barbarous treatment endangering life.
    4. Indignities to person rendering life burdensome and conditions intolerable.
    5. Habitual drunkenness rendering life unbearable by excessive use of alcohol or drugs.

C.   Residency requirements: 6 months for plaintiff before filing for divorce.

D.   Remarriage: Possible immediately after divorce is final.

E.   Court orders after filing for divorce and before divorce is final: Temporary alimony and court costs to dependent spouse.

F.   Alimony:
    1. To either spouse who is dependent on the other, unless dependent spouse's adultery is grounds for divorce, or unless the dependent spouse filed the divorce suit on grounds of separation for one year.
    2. Fault of the supporting spouse is a consideration.

G.   Child support and custody:
    1. Custody is granted according to best interests of child; joint custody is allowed.
    2. No presumption as to which parent is better suited for custody.

H.   Property division by court in absence of written or oral agreement:
    1. An alimony settlement includes property settlement. Court has no power to divide property beyond alimony; title alone controls. Each spouse receives his/her share of joint property.
    2. Separation agreements are valid.

IV. TERMINATION OF COHABITATION

A.   Court jurisdiction: No judicial control; voluntary parting.

B.   Court orders: A court may make orders for child support and custody similar to those made in a divorce, once paternity is established.

C.   Property division (decisions in other states suggest the following possibilities):
    1. Courts could infer partnership agreements as a means of dividing property and money.
    2. Courts could order return or division of property and money if there had been an implied or express agreement.

3. Courts could order return of property to the rightful owner or grant an interest in property or an award of money to a mate to the extent of his/her contribution toward purchase of property.

4. Since living together is illegal, courts would probably not honor an agreement if relationship was primarily sexual; thus it might be difficult to collect for performing household duties when no direct financial contribution can be shown.

D. Putative marriage: A putative spouse would be compensated for household services.

E. Palimony: There have been no court decisions to indicate that rehabilitative alimony or temporary or permanent alimony would be awarded to a mate, and such an award seems unlikely.

V. SPECIFIC SUBJECTS (No written agreements, except for A,E,I.)
Reference to "BOTH" means married and unmarried couples.

A. Prenuptial or precohabitation agreements:
MARRIED: Valid.
UNMARRIED: Probably valid if sex is not the basis of the agreement and if meant for protection of property interests.
BOTH: Agreements must be made without duress and with full disclosure of assets and other important information.

B. Property:
BOTH: All property is separate property of acquiring spouse or mate.

C. Liability of separate property for other spouse's or mate's debts:
BOTH: No liability.

D. Management and control of separate property of each:
BOTH: Each controls own property.
MARRIED: Both husband and wife must sign to sell family home and property subject to elective life estate (see subject L).

E. Contracts made during marriage or cohabitation settling property rights:
MARRIED: Valid.
UNMARRIED: Probably enforceable if based on earnings, property, etc., rather than on sex.
BOTH: Agreements must be made without duress and with full disclosure of assets and other important information.

F.   What can be willed?

BOTH: Each spouse's or mate's separate property.

MARRIED: Surviving spouse may elect to take life interest in property of deceased spouse or intestate share instead of share provided by will.

G.   Automatic protection for surviving spouse or mate:

MARRIED: Surviving spouse receives one year's support of $2,000 (may be more if estate is large enough); minor children receive one year's support of $600 each. Homestead exemption of $1,000 over liens, including mortgages, to widow and minor children.

UNMARRIED: No protection for surviving mate. Minor children receive support and homestead exemption if entitled to inherit (see subject K).

H.   If no will:

MARRIED: Surviving spouse receives everything if there are no surviving children or parents of deceased. Otherwise, surviving spouse divides estate with descendants or parents.

UNMARRIED: Surviving mate receives nothing. Illegitimate children inherit from mother as if legitimate; from father if paternity judicially established, or if father acknowledges children in writing and files acknowledgment, or if children are legitimized. (See subject M).

I.   Contracts:

BOTH: Each may contract with anyone, including each other.

J.   Lawsuits:

BOTH: Each may sue and be sued separately unless both involved.

K.   Homestead law:

BOTH: Exemptions not exceeding $1,000 over liens, including mortgages, to any resident of state for any homestead or any real estate instead of homestead. Allotment of homestead must be filed within judgment roll in office of clerk of court in county where homestead located.

L.   Dower or curtesy:

MARRIED: Abolished, but surviving spouse may elect to receive life interest similar to dower in property of deceased spouse, instead of intestate share or as provided in the will.

M.   Civil suits by spouses or mates against each other: Permitted.

N.   Legitimacy:

MARRIED: Children born during marriage are presumed legitimate.

UNMARRIED: Illegitimate children inherit from mother as if legitimate; from father if father files written acknowledgment of paternity, or if paternity is judicially determined, or if children legitimized. Children may be legitimized upon petition by father to court.

BOTH: Children born before marriage are legitimized if parents later marry.

O. Adoption:

BOTH: Any proper adult may adopt child or adult. Investigation of suitability of home.

MARRIED: Both spouses must consent to adoption.

P. Division of property upon termination of relationship:

MARRIED: Separation agreements valid. Court has power to divide separate property for alimony, but not specifically for property settlement. Any property settlement will be included in alimony. Each spouse receives his/her share of joint property.

UNMARRIED: Implied or express contracts, value of services, or unfair economic gain may create rights to property.

VI. RECENT EVENTS, TRENDS, AND CONCLUSIONS

A. An illegitimate child may inherit from his/her father.

B. $30,000, which a female mate took from a joint account, was ordered returned when the court found that the money actually belonged to her male mate.

C. It is presumed, when evidence is given concerning alimony, that the wife is a dependent spouse, and the husband must present evidence to the contrary if he is to be relieved of payment.

D. Since cohabitation, fornication, and adultery are all illegal, it would appear that the courts would be unlikely to follow many of the theories of the *Marvin* case. However, early court decisions suggest that agreements of mates settling property rights probably would be enforced so long as the agreements were not exclusively based on sex.

NORTH DAKOTA

I. MARRIAGE

A.   Legality:
1.   Age: 18; 16 to 18, need consent of parents; under 16, not permitted.
2.   License: Required; good for 60 days. Other requirements: sworn testimony of credible person showing applicants' ages or consent of parents; sworn testimony of credible person showing that applicants are not habitual criminals; certified copy of divorce decree, if applicable.
3.   Medical examination: Affidavit of physician showing applicant is not feebleminded, imbecile, insane, a drunkard, or afflicted with contagious venereal disease; certificate of physician that blood test was given not more than 30 days before application for license.
4.   Waiting period: None.

B.   Common-law marriages: Not recognized.

C.   Out-of-state marriages: Valid if valid in state where entered into unless a North Dakota resident enters into a marriage in another state when the same marriage would be prohibited in North Dakota.

D.   Adultery: Illegal (misdemeanor).

E.   Property: Separate.

F.   Partnerships: A partnership agreement between spouses is probably enforceable as long as there is a valid business purpose.

II. COHABITATION

A.   Legality:
1.   Cohabitation: Illegal if open and notorious (misdemeanor).
2.   Fornication: Illegal if in a public place (misdemeanor).

B.   Common-law marriage: Not recognized.

C.   Putative marriage: No case law; a putative spouse might be given a share of accumulations to which he/she contributed.

D.   Property: No case law, but see IV, C.

E.   Partnerships: A partnership agreement between mates is probably enforceable as long as there is a valid business purpose and the agreement is not primarily based on sex.

III. DIVORCE (DISSOLUTION) AND LEGAL SEPARATION

A.   Divorce or dissolution (grounds):
1. Adultery.
2. Extreme cruelty.
3. Wilful desertion for one year.
4. Wilful neglect for one year.
5. Habitual intemperance for one year.
6. Conviction of felony.
7. Incurable insanity and confinement for 5 years.
8. Irreconcilable differences (no fault).
9. Separation decree in effect for one year and no reconciliation (no fault).

B.   Legal separation (grounds): Same as for divorce.

C.   Residency requirements: One year for plaintiff before filing for divorce. Must be citizen of United States or declare intention to become citizen.

D.   Remarriage: Neither may remarry except as permitted by divorce decree. Court must specify whether either or both may remarry, and when.

E.   Court orders after filing for divorce and before divorce is final:
1. Temporary alimony to either spouse.
2. Child support by either.
3. Court costs and attorneys' fees to either.

F.   Alimony:
1. Granted to either spouse as court deems fair.
2. Improper to terminate alimony on remarriage when alimony is part of a property settlement.

G.   Child support and custody:
1. Either parent may be ordered to pay support.
2. Custody granted as is necessary and proper; parents have equal rights.

H.   Property division by court in absence of written or oral agreement:
1. Court divides separate property, including joint prop-

erty, as it deems fair, no matter when property was acquired, or who has title.
2. Family home may be assigned to innocent spouse.

IV. TERMINATION OF COHABITATION

A. Court jurisdiction: No judicial control; voluntary parting.

B. Court orders: A court may make orders for child support and custody similar to those made in a divorce, once paternity is established.

C. Property division (decisions in other states suggest the following possibilities):
1. Courts could infer partnership agreements as a means of dividing property and money.
2. Courts could order return or division of property and money if there had been an implied or express agreement.
3. Courts could order return of property to the rightful owner or grant an interest in property or an award of money to a mate to the extent of his/her contribution toward purchase of property.
4. Since living together is illegal, courts would probably not honor an agreement if the relationship was primarily sexual; thus it might be difficult to collect for performing household duties when no direct financial contribution can be shown.

D. Putative marriage: It is possible that a putative spouse would be given a share in accumulations acquired during the invalid marriage.

E. Palimony: There have been no court decisions to indicate that rehabilitative alimony or temporary or permanent alimony would be awarded to a mate, but such an award is a possibility.

V. SPECIFIC SUBJECTS (No written agreements, except for A,E,I.)
Reference to "BOTH" means married and unmarried couples.

A. Prenuptial or precohabitation agreements:
MARRIED: Probably valid.
UNMARRIED: Probably valid if sex is not the basis of the agreement and if meant for protection of property interests.
BOTH: Agreements must be made without duress and with full disclosure of assets and other important information.

B.   Property:

BOTH: All property is separate property of acquiring spouse or mate.

C.   Liability of separate property for other spouse's or mate's debts:

MARRIED: No liability, except husband and wife are both liable for debts for necessary household supplies of food, clothing, fuel, shelter, and education of children.

UNMARRIED: No liability.

D.   Management and control of separate property of each:

BOTH: Each controls own property.

MARRIED: Both must sign to sell family home or use it as collateral for a debt.

E.   Contracts made during marriage or cohabitation settling property rights:

MARRIED: Valid.

UNMARRIED: Probably enforceable if based on earnings, property, etc., rather than on sex.

BOTH: Agreements must be made without duress and with full disclosure of assets and other important information.

F.   What can be willed?

BOTH: Each spouse's or mate's separate property.

MARRIED: Family home can pass by will, but is subject to homestead estate (see subject G). Surviving spouse may elect to receive one-third of estate and disregard provision of the will.

G.   Automatic protection for surviving spouse or mate:

MARRIED: Family home passes to surviving spouse for life or until remarriage. Surviving spouse receives exempt personal-property allowance of $5,000 and reasonable family allowance for one year.

UNMARRIED: No protection for surviving mate. Family home (until youngest child reaches 18), exempt property and family allowances received by decedent's minor children if they are entitled to inherit (see subject H).

H.   If no will:

MARRIED: Surviving spouse receives everything if there are no surviving children or parents of deceased spouse. Otherwise, estate is divided between surviving spouse and surviving descendants or parents.

UNMARRIED: Surviving mate receives nothing. Children inherit from parents regardless of marital status of parents; parent-child relationship may be established under Uniform Parentage Act.

I.   Contracts:
      BOTH: Each may contract with anyone, including each
      other.

J.   Lawsuits:
      BOTH: Each may sue and be sued separately unless both
      involved.

K.   Homestead law:
      BOTH: Exemption not exceeding $80,000 in value over
      liens, including mortgages, may be claimed by head of
      family. Head of family is regarded as any person who
      has various relatives residing with him/her and under
      his/her care and maintenance; head of family may be
      husband or wife, if married. Declaration of homestead
      should be recorded in office of registrar of deeds, but
      failure to record does not impair homestead rights.

L.   Civil suits by spouses or mates against each other:
      BOTH: Permitted.

M.   Legitimacy:
      MARRIED: Children born during marriage are presumed le-
      gitimate.
      UNMARRIED: Children are considered children of parents,
      regardless of marital status of parents. Parent-child re-
      lationship may be established under Uniform Parentage
      Act. Children are legitimized by subsequent marriage
      of parents, by adjudication of paternity, or by adoption
      (openly treating children as his/her own and having them
      in home).

N.   Adoption:
      BOTH: Any adult may adopt any person.
      MARRIED: Both spouses must consent to adoption.

O.   Division of property upon termination of relationship:
      MARRIED: Court divides all separate property, including
      joint property, as it deems fair.
      UNMARRIED: Implied or express contracts, value of services,
      or unfair economic gain may create rights to property.

VI. RECENT EVENTS, TRENDS, AND CONCLUSIONS

A.   Property division on divorce does not have to be equal to
      be fair.

B.   A law has been repealed that makes the husband the head
      of the family and the wife subject to his decisions as to their
      manner and way of family life.

C.   A profit-sharing fund is subject to division between the spouses upon divorce.

D.   Since cohabitation, adultery, and fornication are illegal, the court would be less likely to follow some or all of the theories of the *Marvin* case.

OHIO

I. MARRIAGE

A.   Legality:
1.   Age: Males, 18; females, 16; male or female under 18 needs consent of parents or guardian.
2.   License: Required; good for 60 days.
3.   Medical examination: Physician's statement that neither applicant is infected with syphilis; laboratory statement.
4.   Waiting period: Not less than 5 days nor more than 30 days between application for license and issuance.

B.   Common-law marriages: Recognized; validity determined by law of state where consummated. Marriage invalid in state where entered into may become valid if continued in Ohio.

C.   Out-of-state marriages: Valid if valid in state where entered into and not expressly forbidden by Ohio law.

D.   Adultery: Not a crime.

E.   Property: Separate.

F.   Partnerships: A partnership agreement between spouses is probably enforceable as long as there is a valid business purpose.

II. COHABITATION

A. Legality:
1. Cohabitation: Not a crime.
2. Fornication: Not a crime.
3. All private, nonviolent sexual acts between consenting adults are legal.

B. Property:
1. A contract based on sex is illegal.
2. Adultery is not a reason for denial of alimony upon divorce, but cohabitation after divorce may be a reason for the termination of alimony.

C. Common-law marriage:
1. Common-law marriage, though recognized, is disfavored by the courts as being against public policy.
2. Continued cohabitation after the reason for an invalid marriage is removed can result in a common-law marriage.

D. Putative marriage:
1. A person who knew marriage was invalid will be denied return of property he transferred to his mate who believed the marriage to be valid.
2. The rights of a putative spouse are recognized for the purpose of dividing property, but not if spouse seeking the property knew the marriage was bigamous.

E. Partnerships: A partnership agreement between mates is probably enforceable as long as there is a valid business purpose and the agreement is not primarily based on sex.

III. DIVORCE (DISSOLUTION) AND LEGAL SEPARATION

A. Divorce or dissolution (grounds):
1. Mutual consent; petition by both spouses, execution of separation agreement (providing for division of property and custody of minor children) and confirmation of agreement by court (no fault).
2. Bigamy.
3. Absence for one year.
4. Adultery.
5. Impotency.
6. Extreme cruelty.
7. Fraudulent contract.
8. Gross neglect of duty.
9. Habitual drunkenness.

          10. Imprisonment in penitentiary.

          11. Procurement of out-of-state divorce by other spouse.

          12. Living apart for 2 years (no fault).

          13. Living apart for 4 years because of confinement to mental institution.

B.   Legal separation (grounds): Not available. Husband and wife may make separation agreement.

C.   Residency requirements: 6 months for both spouses for mutual-consent divorce; 6 months for plaintiff before legal action is filed for divorce on other grounds.

D.   Remarriage: Possible immediately after divorce is final.

E.   Court orders after filing for divorce and before divorce is final:

      1. Child support and custody.

      2. Temporary alimony to either.

      3. Court costs and attorneys' fees.

F.   Alimony:

      1. Granted to either spouse.

      2. Court has discretion to divide property to provide for alimony.

      3. May be lump sum or periodic payments in real estate or personal property.

G.   Child support and custody:

      1. Court makes such orders as it deems fair.

      2. Each parent has equal consideration in custody decision.

      3. If custody of parents is not in best interests of children, children are assigned to juvenile court for further proceedings.

H.   Property division by court in absence of written or oral agreement:

      1. Alimony is a substitute for property settlement. Court has power to divide separate property to award alimony.

      2. Alimony award is not modifiable after divorce if it is a division of property.

IV. TERMINATION OF COHABITATION

A.   Court jurisdiction: No judicial control; voluntary parting.

B.   Court orders: A court may make orders for child support and custody similar to those made in a divorce, once paternity is established.

C. Property division (decisions in other states suggest the following possibilities):
1. Courts could infer partnership agreements as a means of dividing property and money.
2. Courts could order return or division of property and money if there had been an implied or express agreement.
3. Courts could order return of property to the rightful owner or grant an interest in property or an award of money to a mate to the extent of his/her contribution toward purchase of property.
4. Since living together is not illegal, recovery could be had for performing household duties as well as for direct financial contributions so long as the implied or express agreement was not primarily based on sex.

D. Putative marriage: The property rights of one who believes in the validity of an invalid marriage will be adjusted.

E. Palimony: There have been no court decisions to indicate that rehabilitative alimony or temporary or permanent alimony would be awarded to a mate, but such an award is a possibility.

V. SPECIFIC SUBJECTS (No written agreements, except for A,E,I.)
Reference to "BOTH" means married and unmarried couples.

A. Prenuptial or precohabitation agreements:
MARRIED: Valid.
UNMARRIED: Probably valid if sex is not the basis of the agreement and if meant for protection of property interests.
BOTH: Agreement must be made without duress and with full disclosure of assets and other important information.

B. Property:
MARRIED: A spouse has no interest in property of the other except right of support, dower, and right to remain in home after death of the other.
BOTH: All property is separate property of acquiring spouse or mate.

C. Liability of separate property for other spouse's or mate's debts:
BOTH: No liability.

D. Management and control of separate property of each:
BOTH: Each controls own separate property.
MARRIED: Agreement of both spouses is necessary to remove dower rights in real estate.

E.   Contracts made during marriage or cohabitation settling property rights:

MARRIED: Valid for separation and for support of either spouse or children, but the separation agreement cannot serve as a legal separation or divorce.

UNMARRIED: Probably enforceable if based on earnings, property, etc., rather than on sex.

BOTH: Agreements must be made without duress and with full disclosure of assets and other important information.

F.   What can be willed?

BOTH: Each spouse's or mate's separate property.

MARRIED: Surviving spouse may elect to take by intestacy statute (see subject H) rather than according to will.

G.   Automatic protection for surviving spouse or mate:

MARRIED: Surviving spouse has dower rights; $5,000 for support of surviving spouse and minor children, up to $2,500 in exempt personal property, right to stay in home free for one year, and homestead exemption of $1,000.

UNMARRIED: No protection for surviving mate. Surviving minor children receive homestead exemption, support allowance, and $1,000 each in exempt personal property; illegitimate minor children receive same if entitled to inherit (see subject H).

H.   If no will:

MARRIED: Surviving spouse receives everything if no children of deceased spouse survive. Otherwise, surviving spouse divides with children. Surviving spouse may elect family home and furnishings as part of his/her share of estate.

UNMARRIED: Surviving mate receives nothing. Illegitimate children inherit from mother; from father only if father marries mother and acknowledges children in probate proceedings and designates children as his heirs, or if he adopts children.

I.   Contracts:

BOTH: Each may contract with anyone, including each other.

J.   Lawsuits:

BOTH: Each may sue and be sued separately, unless both involved.

K.   Homestead law:

BOTH: Exemption of up to $1,000 over liens, including mortgages in family home for spouses or for surviving spouse or unmarried female living with unmarried minor

children; $500 personal-property exemption available
instead of homestead exemption. Debtor claiming exemption must apply before forced sale to officer in
charge of forced sale.

L.   Dower or curtesy:
MARRIED: Surviving spouse receives life interest of one-
third in all real estate owned by deceased spouse during
marriage; terminates on divorce. Released when both
agree to sell that property.

M.   Civil suits by spouses or mates against each other:
MARRIED: May sue each other in contract, but not for neg-
ligent personal injuries.
UNMARRIED: Permitted.

N.   Legitimacy:
MARRIED: Children born during marriage are presumed legitimate.
UNMARRIED: Illegitimate children inherit from mother; from
father if parents marry and father acknowledges children
in probate proceedings and designates children his heirs,
or if he adopts children or provides for children in his
will. Children can be legitimized by adjudication by
father with mother's consent, or by children filing application for their own legitimization.

O.   Adoption:
BOTH: Spouses together or an unmarried adult may adopt
any minor (or an adult in special circumstances.)
MARRIED: One spouse must be an adult.

P.   Division of property upon termination of relationship:
MARRIED: Court cannot divide separate property acquired
before or during marriage. The court has power to divide
separate property in order to grant alimony to either
spouse.
UNMARRIED: Implied or express contracts, value of services,
or unfair economic gain may create rights to property.

VI. RECENT EVENTS, TRENDS, AND CONCLUSIONS

A.   The State supreme court has refused to abolish interspousal
immunity; one spouse cannot sue the other for negligent
personal injuries.

B.   A mother's living with a male mate after divorce did not
warrant a custody change, since the court found no detri-
mental impact on the children.

C.   The intestacy statutes, which prevent an illegitimate child from inheriting from his father unless the father marries the mother, acknowledges the child in a formal proceeding, and names him as his heir, were found not to be unconstitutional.

D. Since common-law marriages are recognized and consensual sexual relations between adults are not criminal, it seems likely that some or all of the theories of the *Marvin* case might be followed.

OKLAHOMA

I. MARRIAGE

A. Legality:
   1. Age: 18; under 18, need consent of parent or guardian; under 16, not permitted.
   2. License: Required; good for 30 days.
   3. Medical examination: Examination for syphilis by physician within 30 days of issuance of license. Physician's certificate and statement of lab tests must be filed with clerk of the court.
   4. Waiting period: 72 hours between filing for license and issuance if either applicant is under 18.

B. Common-law marriages: Recognized; validity determined by laws of state where couple entered into marriage.

C. Out-of-state marriages: Probably valid if valid in state where entered into.

D. Adultery: Illegal; fine or sentence.

E. Property: Separate.

F. Partnerships: A partnership agreement between spouses is probably enforceable as long as there is a valid business purpose.

II. COHABITATION

A.   Legality:
1. Cohabitation: Not a crime.
2. Fornication: Not a crime.

B.   Common-law marriage:
1. Cohabitation, though illegal within 6 months after a divorce, may become a common-law marriage if the cohabitation continues longer than 6 months.
2. A cohabiting divorced couple could be remarried if common-law-marriage requirements are met.

C.   Putative marriage: A person who contributes to the accumulations of what he/she thinks to be a valid marriage will be compensated; the division will probably be equal unless different contributions can be shown.

D.   Property: A contract between mates to pay for domestic services will be enforced so long as the agreement is not based on sex.

E.   Partnerships: A partnership agreement between mates is probably enforceable as long as there is a valid business purpose and the agreement is not primarily based on sex.

III. DIVORCE (DISSOLUTION) AND LEGAL SEPARATION

A.   Divorce or dissolution (grounds):
1. Abandonment for one year.
2. Adultery.
3. Impotency.
4. Pregnancy of wife at time of marriage by someone other than husband.
5. Extreme cruelty.
6. Fraudulent contract.
7. Incompatibility (no fault).
8. Habitual drunkenness.
9. Gross neglect of duty.
10. Imprisonment for felony.
11. Procurement of divorce in another state by other spouse.
12. Insanity and confinement for 5 years.

B.   Legal separation (grounds): Same as for divorce.

C.   Residency requirements: 6 months in state for either spouse and 30 days in a county before legal action is filed.

D.   Remarriage: Must wait 6 months after divorce is final, or 30 days after appeal is decided. Marrying within this time period is bigamy; cohabiting within this period is adultery.

E. Court orders after filing for divorce and before divorce is final:
1. Temporary alimony.
2. Court costs and attorneys' fees.
3. Temporary orders protecting property.

F. Alimony:
1. Granted to either spouse.
2. Divorce order must state which part is for alimony and which part is for property settlement.
3. Property settlement is irrevocable; alimony portion terminates upon death or remarriage of recipient.

G. Child support and custody: Court orders to either spouse as it deems fair.

H. Property division by court in absence of written or oral agreement:
1. Court has power to distribute all jointly owned property as it deems fair.
2. Each spouse retains separate property acquired before or during marriage.

IV. TERMINATION OF COHABITATION

A. Court jurisdiction: No judicial control; voluntary parting.

B. Court orders: A court may make orders for child support and custody similar to those made in a divorce, once paternity is established.

C. Property division (decisions in other states suggest the following possibilities):
1. Courts could infer partnership agreements as a means of dividing property and money.
2. Courts could order return or division of property and money if there had been an implied or express agreement.
3. Courts could order return of property to the rightful owner or grant an interest in property or an award of money to a mate to the extent of his/her contribution toward purchase of property.
4. Since living together is not illegal, recovery could be had for performing household duties as well as for direct financial contributions, so long as the implied or express agreement was not primarily based upon sex.

D. Putative marriage: Courts would probably award property to the innocent party as if the marriage had been legal.

E.   Palimony: There have been no court decisions to indicate that rehabilitative alimony or temporary or permanent alimony would be awarded to a mate, but such an award is a possibility.

V. SPECIFIC SUBJECTS   (No written agreements, except for A,E,I.)
Reference to "BOTH" means married and unmarried couples.

A.   Prenuptial or precohabitation agreements:
MARRIED: Probably valid.
UNMARRIED: Probably valid if sex is not basis of agreement and if meant for protection of property interests.
BOTH: Agreements must be made without duress and with full disclosure of assets and other important information.

B.   Property:
BOTH: All property is separate property of acquiring spouse or mate.

C.   Liability of separate property for other spouse's or mate's debts:
MARRIED: No liability, except that husband's separate property is liable for necessaries furnished to wife and for debts of wife contracted during marriage.
UNMARRIED: No liability.

D.   Management and control of separate property of each:
BOTH: Each controls own property.
MARRIED: Both spouses must sign to sell family home or use it as collateral for a debt.

E.   Contracts made during marriage or cohabitation settling property rights:
MARRIED: Permitted, but not binding on court and will be closely scrutinized to see if reasonable and fair.
UNMARRIED: Probably enforceable if based on earnings, property, etc., rather than on sex.
BOTH: Agreements must be made without duress and with full disclosure of assets and other important information.

F.   What can be willed?
BOTH: Each spouse's or mate's separate property.
MARRIED: Surviving spouse may not receive less than he/she would receive if there were no will. If this happens, surviving spouse may disregard will.

G.   Automatic protection for surviving spouse or mate:
MARRIED: Surviving spouse may continue to occupy family home, and receive various personal and household items and provisions and fuel for one year; reasonable allowance for maintenance of family if needed.

UNMARRIED: No protection for surviving mate. Surviving minor children receive all benefits if entitled to inherit (see subject H).

H. If no will:

MARRIED: Surviving spouse receives everything if there are no surviving parents, brothers, or sisters of deceased spouse; otherwise, surviving spouse divides with them.

UNMARRIED: Surviving mate receives nothing. Illegitimate children inherit from mother; from father if father adopts children, acknowledges children in writing, receives children into home, or if paternity is judicially established.

I. Contracts:

BOTH: Each may contract with anyone, including each other.

J. Lawsuits:

BOTH: Each may sue and be sued separately unless both involved.

K. Homestead law:

BOTH: Resident homeowner or head of family receives exemption of up to $5,000 over liens, including mortgages, for family home. Claimed by informing levying officer before a forced sale by a creditor.

L. Civil suits by spouses or mates against each other:
BOTH: Permitted.

M. Legitimacy:

MARRIED: Children born during marriage are presumed legitimate.

UNMARRIED: All children are legitimate. Those born out of wedlock are mother's children; father's children if he acknowledges them in writing, or if parents later marry and father acknowledges or adopts children into family, or if father publicly acknowledges children, or if paternity is judicially established.

N. Adoption:

MARRIED: Both spouses together may adopt a child.
UNMARRIED: Any person 21 or older may adopt a child.
BOTH: Investigation must determine whether adoption is in child's best interest.

O. Division of property upon termination of relationship:

MARRIED: Court has power to distribute joint property as it deems fair. Separate property of each spouse is retained by the owner.

UNMARRIED: Implied or express contracts, value of services, or unfair economic gain may create rights to property.

VI. RECENT EVENTS, TRENDS, AND CONCLUSIONS

A. The court has ordered a jointly owned home sold and the proceeds divided upon divorce, when neither spouse was capable of buying the other's share.

B. Since remarrying within 6 months after divorce is prohibited and is a crime, prohibiting remarriage in a divorce order is not necessary. The remedy for breach is criminal prosecution, not contempt of court.

C. Jewelry and furs acquired during marriage are joint property.

D. Since common-law marriages are recognized, and neither cohabitation nor fornication is illegal, it seems likely that the courts would follow some or all of the principles of the *Marvin* case.

OREGON

I. MARRIAGE

A. Legality:
1. Age: 17; under 17, need consent of parent or guardian.
2. License: Required; good for 30 days.
3. Medical examination: Physician's certificate and laboratory test; certificate must state that applicant has no venereal disease.
4. Waiting period: 3 days.

B. Common-law marriages: Not recognized. Valid if valid in state where entered into.

C. Out-of-state marriages: Valid if valid in state where entered into.

D. Adultery: Not a crime.

E. Property: Separate.

F. Partnerships: A partnership agreement between spouses is probably enforceable as long as there is a valid business purpose.

II. COHABITATION

A. Legality:
1. Cohabitation: Not a crime.
2. Fornication: Not a crime.
3. All private, nonviolent sexual acts between consenting adults are legal.

B. Common-law marriage:
1. An Oregon couple who hold themselves out as husband and wife in a state that recognizes common-law marriages will not be validly married in Oregon.
2. When a couple cohabit as husband and wife, the law presumes marriage.

C. Putative marriage: When a couple mistakenly believes in a valid marriage, the court will presume a gift from the contributing mate and give the noncontributing mate a one-half interest in property held as tenants in common.

D. Property:
1. Property acquired when there is no valid marriage will be held as tenancy in common.
2. If the relationship is knowingly illicit, the court may adjust the division of real estate according to the amount of contribution of each, rather than making an equal division.
3. Courts will honor an oral agreement between mates as to division or disposition of property if cohabitation itself was not a basis for the agreement.

E. Partnerships: A partnership agreement between mates is probably enforceable as long as there is a valid business purpose and the agreement is not primarily based on sex.

III. DIVORCE (DISSOLUTION) AND LEGAL SEPARATION

A. Divorce or dissolution (grounds): Irreconcilable differences causing irremediable breakdown of marriage (no fault).

B. Legal separation (grounds): Same as for divorce.

C. Residency requirements: If couple was married in state and the suit for divorce is based upon a ground specified by Oregon divorce laws, residence or domicile of either in state before the lawsuit begins is sufficient. Otherwise, either spouse must be resident for 6 months before action is filed.

D. Remarriage: May not remarry for 60 days after divorce is final or until appeal is decided.

E. Court orders after filing for divorce and before divorce is final:
   1. Temporary alimony.
   2. Court costs.
   3. Child support and custody.
   4. Restraining orders not to molest minor children, or orders regulating disposal of property, occupancy of family home, and other appropriate orders.

F. Alimony:
   1. May be granted to either spouse in lump sum or in payments.
   2. Considerations: length of marriage, ages, health, work experience, financial resources, child-custody provisions, need for education or retraining, and other pertinent matters.
   3. A divorce decree should not provide for the automatic termination of alimony upon remarriage of the recipient, nor upon the later cohabitation of the recipient with a mate.

G. Child support and custody:
   1. Court orders support payments by parent without custody, or by both if there is joint custody.
   2. Best interest and welfare of child are primary, but not sole, concerns. Cohabitation of an ex-wife is not necessarily a reason for terminating custody.
   3. No special preference given to mother for custody.

H. Property division by court in absence of written or oral agreement:
   1. Court orders division of all separate property, including joint property, as it deems fair.
   2. A spouse's contribution as homemaker is considered a marital asset.
   3. Court will presume equal contribution to marital assets unless there is contrary evidence.
   4. Fault may not be considered when dividing property.
   5. Court may approve voluntary property settlement.

IV. TERMINATION OF COHABITATION

A.   Court jurisdiction: No judicial control; voluntary parting.

B.   Court orders: A court may make orders for child support and custody similar to those made in a divorce, once paternity is established.

C.   Property division (decisions in Oregon and in other states suggest the following possibilities):
1.   Courts could infer partnership agreements as a means of dividing property and money.
2.   Courts could order return or division of property and money if there had been an implied or express agreement.
3.   Courts could order return of property to the rightful owner or grant an interest in property or an award of money to a mate to the extent of his/her contribution toward purchase of property.
4.   Since living together is not illegal, recovery could be had for performing household duties as well as for direct financial contributions, so long as the implied or express agreement was not primarily based on sex.

D.   Putative marriage: Recognized for the purpose of dividing property. Marriage would be treated as if it had been valid.

E.   Palimony: There have been no court decisions awarding rehabilitative alimony or temporary or permanent alimony to a mate, but such an award would be likely in the proper circumstances.

V. SPECIFIC SUBJECTS (No written agreements, except for A,E,I.)
Reference to "BOTH" means married and unmarried couples.

A.   Prenuptial or precohabitation agreements:
MARRIED: Valid and binding.
UNMARRIED: Probably valid if sex is not the basis of the agreement and if meant for protection of property interests.
BOTH: Agreements must be made without duress and with full disclosure of assets and other important information.

B.   Property:
BOTH: All property is separate property of acquiring spouse or mate.

C.   Liability of separate property for other spouse's or mate's debts:

MARRIED: No liability, except for expenses of family and education of children.

UNMARRIED: No liability.

D. Management and control of separate property of each:
MARRIED: Each controls own property.

E. Contracts made during marriage or cohabitation settling property rights:
MARRIED: Valid.
UNMARRIED: Probably enforceable if based on earnings, property, etc., rather than on sex.
BOTH: Agreements must be made without duress and with full disclosure of assets and other important information.

F. What can be willed?
BOTH: Each spouse's or mate's separate property.
MARRIED: Surviving spouse may elect to take a one-fourth share of deceased spouse's estate instead of accepting the provisions of the will.

G. Automatic protection for surviving spouse or mate:
MARRIED: Surviving spouse and children receive reasonable amount for support from estate and may continue to live in home for up to one year.
UNMARRIED: No protection for surviving mate. Children get same protection as above if they are entitled to inherit (see subject H).

H. If no will:
MARRIED: Surviving spouse receives everything if there are no surviving issue of deceased spouse. If there are surviving issue, surviving spouse receives one-half and issue divide the rest.
UNMARRIED: Surviving mate receives nothing. Illegitimate children treated as legitimate except that, to inherit from father, paternity must be judicially established during children's lifetime, or father must acknowledge children in writing.

I. Contracts:
BOTH: Each may contract with anyone, including each other.

J. Lawsuits:
BOTH: Each may sue and be sued separately unless both involved.

K. Homestead law:
BOTH: Exemption from creditors limited to $12,000 over liens, including mortgages, for home occupied by owner

and spouse, parent(s), or child. Proceeds of sale also exempt for one year. Designation of homestead may be filed with deed records after judgment is entered, or owner, spouse, parent, child, or agent may claim exemption by notice to levying officer at time of levy or prior to sale.

L.   Civil suits by spouses or mates against each other:
MARRIED: May sue each other in contract, for damages to separate property, or for wilful wrong committed against other spouse; may not sue for wrongs caused by negligence.
UNMARRIED: Permitted.

M.   Legitimacy:
MARRIED: Children born during marriage are presumed legitimate. Children born before marriage are legitimized if parents later marry.
UNMARRIED: Illegitimate children are treated as legitimate except that, to inherit from father, paternity must be judicially established during children's lifetime, or father must acknowledge children in writing. Legitimacy can be established for all purposes by order of Administration of Support Enforcement Division, upon agreement of parties.

N.   Adoption:
BOTH: Any person may adopt a child or an adult. Investigation is made to decide whether parents are able to bring up child.
MARRIED: Both husband and wife must consent to adoption.

O.   Division of property upon termination of relationship:
MARRIED: Court orders division of separate property, including joint property, as it deems fair.
UNMARRIED: Implied or express contracts, value of services, or unfair economic gain may create rights to property.

VI. RECENT EVENTS, TRENDS, AND CONCLUSIONS

A.   The rights of mates to property and alimony is being considered by the legislature. Legislation, if passed, would provide that when mates have lived together for more than a year, one of the parties may, if the relationship breaks down, seek a court order for child custody, support, and/or property division.

B.   Before the *Marvin* case was decided, the court provided a property division for mates who had agreed to divide their joint accumulations. The woman was given a fair share for "living with defendant, caring for and keeping after him, and furnishing and providing him with all amenities of married life."

C. A recent decision held that property should be divided between mates according to their implied or expressed intention; if an agreement existed to share assets, distribution should be made according to the agreement.

D. Some or all of the theories of the *Marvin* case are presently followed.

PENNSYLVANIA

I. MARRIAGE

A. Legality:
   1. Age: Male, 14; female, 12; under 18, need written consent of parents or guardian; under 16, need approval of court.
   2. License: Required; good for 60 days; issued 3 days after application.
   3. Medical examination: Physician's statement that applicant has been examined for syphilis and found free of it, within 30 days of application for license.
   4. Waiting period: 3 days.

B. Common-law marriages: Recognized.

C. Out-of-state marriages: Probably valid if valid in state where entered into.

D. Adultery: Not a crime.

E. Property: Separate.

F. Partnerships: A partnership agreement between spouses is probably enforceable as long as there is a valid business purpose.

II. COHABITATION

A.   Legality:
1.   Cohabitation: Not a crime.
2.   Fornication: Not a crime.
3.   All private, nonviolent sexual acts between consenting adults are legal.

B.   Common-law marriage:
1.   Common-law marriage requires the so-called "words in the present tense" (words that demonstrate the intent of both that they are married), which should be witnessed.
2.   Common-law marriages are not encouraged by the courts.

C.   Putative marriage:
1.   If cohabitation begins while one mate is married to someone else, a common-law marriage between the mates will not automatically be grounds for a divorce of the original marriage.
2.   The putative wife of a man who is validly married to another woman cannot claim support from him.

D.   Property:
1.   When property is sold to an unmarried couple as husband and wife, and tenancy by the entireties was intended, joint tenancy will result; otherwise, a tenancy in common will result.
2.   A contract based entirely on sex is void.
3.   A mate would probably get an interest in property acquired during cohabitation, even though title was in the other mate's name.
4.   Courts could utilize the concept of common-law marriage to divide the property of mates living together.

E.   Partnerships: A partnership agreement between mates is probably enforceable as long as there is a valid business purpose and the agreement is not primarily based on sex.

III. DIVORCE (DISSOLUTION) AND LEGAL SEPARATION

A.   Divorce or dissolution (grounds):
1.   Bigamy.
2.   Adultery.
3.   One-year desertion.
4.   Cruel and barbarous treatment endangering life.
5.   Indignities rendering conditions intolerable and life burdensome.

      6. Conviction of certain crimes resulting in sentence of 2 years or more.
      7. Insanity or serious mental disorder with confinement for three years.
      8. Marriage irretrievably broken (no fault); both spouses must file affidavit of agreement.
      9. Living separately for three years (no fault).

B. Legal separation (grounds): Not available.

C. Residency requirements: One year for either spouse before legal action is filed.

D. Remarriage: An adulterous spouse may not marry the other party to the adultery during the lifetime of his/her former spouse; otherwise, remarriage is possible immediately after divorce is final

E. Court orders after filing for divorce and before divorce is final:
      1. Reasonable temporary alimony to either.
      2. Court costs and attorneys' fees to either.

F. Alimony:
      1. Prior to July 1, 1980, alimony was only awarded to an insane defendant who was divorced while sane; otherwise, no court-ordered alimony. A property settlement providing for periodic payments would be acceptable providing that it was not a guise for alimony.
      2. Since July 1, 1980, legislation now allows alimony awards.

G. Child support and custody:
      1. Court makes appropriate orders for support and custody.
      2. No preference for mother is allowed in custody award.

H. Property division by court in absence of written or oral agreement:
      1. Prior to July 1, 1980, the following applied:
        a. Court had no power to divide separate property; title alone controlled.
        b. Either party could force sale of jointly owned property (tenancy by the entireties) and the proceeds would be equally divided.
        c. If title was acquired after 1949, jointly held property (tenancy by the entireties) automatically became tenancy in common upon divorce, each spouse having an equal one-half share.
      2. Since July 1, 1980, new legislation provides for an equitable division of all separate property, including

joint property, except separate property acquired prior
to marriage, or separate property acquired before or
after marriage through gift or inheritance. This new
law substantially changes divisions of property between spouses.

IV. TERMINATION OF COHABITATION

A.   Court jurisdiction: No judicial control; voluntary parting.

B.   Court orders: A court may make orders for child support
and custody similar to those made in a divorce, once paternity is established.

C.   Property division (decisions in other states suggest the following possibilities):
1.   Courts could infer partnership agreements as a means
of dividing property and money.
2.   Courts could order return or division of property and
money if there had been an implied or express agreement.
3.   Courts could order return of property to the rightful
owner or grant an interest in property or an award of
money to a mate to the extent of his/her contribution
toward purchase of property.
4.   Since living together is not illegal, recovery could be
had for performing household duties as well as for
direct financial contribution so long as the implied or
express agreement was not primarily based upon sex.

D.   Putative marriage: Courts would probably adjust the property rights of a putative spouse.

E.   Palimony: There have been no court decisions to indicate
that rehabilitative alimony, temporary, or permanent alimony would be awarded to a mate, but such an award is
a possibility.

V. SPECIFIC SUBJECTS (No written agreements, except for A,E,I.)
Reference to "BOTH" means married and unmarried couples.

A.   Prenuptial or precohabitation agreements:
MARRIED: Valid.
UNMARRIED: Probably valid if sex is not the basis of the
agreement and if meant for the protection of property
interests.
BOTH: Agreements must be made without duress and with
full disclosure of assets and other important information.

B.   Property:

BOTH: All property is separate property of acquiring spouse or mate.

C. Liability of separate property for other spouse's or mate's debts:

MARRIED: No liability, except that both husband and wife are liable for necessaries furnished to wife.

UNMARRIED: No liability.

D. Management and control of separate property of each:

BOTH: Each controls own property.

MARRIED: Neither husband nor wife required to sign when separate property is sold, but buyer usually requires joinder to prevent husband's claiming curtesy rights to the property.

E. Contracts made during marriage or cohabitation settling property rights:

MARRIED: Valid and will be enforced.

UNMARRIED: Probably enforceable if based on earnings, property, etc., rather than on sex.

BOTH: Agreements must be made without duress and with full disclosure of assets and other important information.

F. What can be willed?

BOTH: Each spouse's or mate's separate property.

MARRIED: Surviving spouse may elect to disregard will of deceased spouse and take a one-third share of the estate.

G. Automatic protection for surviving spouse or mate:

MARRIED: Surviving spouse receives $2,000 exemption in personal or real property of decedent's estate.

UNMARRIED: No protection for surviving mate. Children receive the $2,000 exemption if entitled to inherit (see subject H).

H. If no will:

MARRIED: Surviving spouse receives everything if there are no surviving issue or parents of deceased spouse; otherwise, spouse divides with issue or parents.

UNMARRIED: Surviving mate receives nothing. Children born out of wedlock inherit from mother; from father if parents later marry, or if father openly holds children out as his during children's lifetime, or upon clear and convincing evidence of paternity.

I. Contracts:

BOTH: Each may contract with anyone, including each other.

J. Lawsuits:

BOTH: Each may sue or be sued separately unless both involved.

K. Homestead law:
BOTH: No homestead law.

L. Dower or curtesy:
MARRIED: Abolished. Intestate share or share of surviving wife or husband electing to disregard will replaces dower or curtesy rights (see subjects F and H).

M. Civil suits by spouses or mates against each other:
MARRIED: Not permitted except for divorce or annulment, or to protect or recover separate property.
UNMARRIED: Permitted.

N. Legitimacy:
MARRIED: Children born during marriage are presumed legitimate.
UNMARRIED: All children are legitimate. Those born out of wedlock are children of mother; of father if parents later marry, or if father openly holds children out as his during children's lifetime, or upon clear and convincing evidence that may include prior judicial determination of paternity.

O. Adoption:
BOTH: Any individual may adopt any other individual. No restrictions on age or marital status.

P. Division of property upon termination of relationship:
MARRIED: Prior to July 1, 1980, the court held no power to divide separate property; title controlled. Jointly held property became tenancy in common, with each spouse holding one-half interest, or property could be sold and proceeds divided evenly. Since July 1, 1980, new legislation provides for an equitable division of all separate property, including joint property, except separate property acquired before marriage, or separate property acquired before or during marriage by gift or inheritance.
UNMARRIED: Implied or express contracts, value of services, or unfair economic gains may create rights to property.

VI. RECENT EVENTS, TRENDS, AND CONCLUSIONS

A. A wife whose husband left her to live with another woman was denied support because, two years later, the wife also had an adulterous relationship.

B. The Pennsylvania Equal Rights Amendment, a state law,

requires both parents to share equally in the responsibility of child support.

C.   A Pennsylvania statute provides that a person who commits adultery may not marry the person with whom the adultery was committed while that person's spouse is alive. A federal court of appeals, however, decided that a Pennsylvania court could, because of federal and state interests in providing for the aged, disregard this statute and award widow's Social Security benefits to a woman who had committed adultery and then married her lover after he divorced his previous wife, who was still alive.

D.   Because common-law marriages are recognized and neither cohabitation, adultery, nor fornication is illegal, there is reason to believe that some or all of the theories of the *Marvin* case would be followed.

E.   Recent legislation provides that since July 1, 1980, strict separate-property laws shall no longer prevail upon divorce. At divorce, all separate property, including joint property, shall be equitably divided, assuming the parties cannot arrive at a private settlement agreement between themselves, except that separate property acquired prior to marriage, or separate property acquired before or during marriage by gift or inheritance, cannot be so divided.

RHODE ISLAND

I. MARRIAGE

A.   Legality:
   1. Age: 18; under 18, need written consent of parent or guardian.
   2. License: Required; copy of divorce required, if applicable.

        3. Medical examination: Statement of physician that each
          had examination and blood test, that female under 55
          had rubella test, and that applicant is not infected with
          gonorrhea or syphilis.
        4. Waiting period: None.

B.   Common-law marriages: Recognized.

C.   Out-of-state marriages: Valid if valid in state where entered
        into.

D.   Adultery: Illegal; fine or sentence.

E.   Property: Separate.

F.   Partnerships: A partnership agreement between spouses is
        probably enforceable as long as there is a valid business
        purpose.

II. COHABITATION

A.   Legality:
        1. Cohabitation: Not a crime.
        2. Fornication: Illegal; maximum fine $10.

B.   Common-law marriage: Recognized.

C.   Putative marriage: Courts would probably recognize the
        property rights of a putative spouse.

D.   Property: A tenancy by the entireties cannot be created in
        a void marriage; it will be declared a tenancy in common.

E.   Partnerships: A partnership agreement between mates is
        probably enforceable as long as there is a valid business
        purpose and the agreement is not primarily based on sex.

III. DIVORCE (DISSOLUTION) AND LEGAL SEPARATION

A.   Divorce or dissolution (grounds):
        1. Marriage originally void or voidable by law.
        2. Either party, because of crime, deemed to be civilly
          dead.
        3. Impotency.
        4. Adultery.
        5. Extreme cruelty.
        6. Wilful desertion for 5 years.
        7. Continual drunkenness.
        8. Habitual, excessive, or intemperate use of opium,
          morphine, or chloral.
        9. Neglect and refusal for one year for husband to provide
          necessaries.

10. Any other gross misbehavior and wickedness repugnant to and in violation of marriage covenant.

11. Living apart for 3 years (no fault). 20-day waiting period before final decree.

12. Irreconcilable differences causing irremediable breakdown of marriage (no fault).

B. Legal separation (grounds): Same as for divorce.

C. Residency requirements: One year for either spouse before filing for divorce.

D. Remarriage: Possible immediately after divorce is final.

E. Court orders after filing for divorce and before divorce is final:
1. Attorneys' fees and court costs to either spouse.
2. Temporary child support and custody to either spouse.

F. Alimony:
1. Granted to either spouse.
2. Terminated by remarriage of recipient.

G. Child support and custody:
1. Court makes all orders concerning support and custody.
2. Mother has preference for custody of young child, but best interests of child control.

H. Property division by court in absence of written or oral agreement:
1. Court may assign to husband or wife a portion of the separate property of the other acquired during the marriage.
2. Separate property acquired before marriage cannot be divided, but income from such property can.
3. Jointly held property may be divided as court deems fair.
4. Property division may be in addition to or instead of alimony.

IV. TERMINATION OF COHABITATION

A. Court jurisdiction: No judicial control; voluntary parting.

B. Court orders: A court may make orders for child support and custody similar to those made in a divorce, once paternity is established.

C. Property division (decisions in other states suggest the following possibilities):

1. Courts could infer partnership agreements as a means of dividing property and money.
2. Courts could order return or division of property and money if there had been an implied or express agreement.
3. Courts could order return of property to the rightful owner or grant an interest in property or an award of money to a mate to the extent of his/her contribution toward purchase of property.
4. Since living together is not illegal, recovery could be had for performing household duties as well as for direct financial contribution, so long as the implied or express agreement was not primarily based upon sex.

D. Putative marriage: Courts would probably adjust the property rights of a putative spouse.

E. Palimony: There have been no court decisions to indicate that rehabilitative alimony or temporary or permanent alimony would be awarded to a mate, but such an award is a possibility.

V. SPECIFIC SUBJECTS (No written agreements, except for A,E,I.) Reference to "BOTH" means married and unmarried couples.

A Prenuptial or precohabitation agreements:
MARRIED: Probably valid.
UNMARRIED: Probably valid if sex is not the basis of the agreement and if meant for protection of property interests.
BOTH: Agreements must be made without duress and with full disclosure of assets and other important information.

B. Property:
BOTH: All property is separate property of acquiring spouse or mate.

C. Liability of separate property for other spouse's or mate's debts:
BOTH: No liability.

D. Management and control of separate property of each:
BOTH: Each controls own property.
MARRIED: Husband and wife should sign to sell real estate in order to release dower or curtesy rights that may have accrued before curtesy laws were abolished (see subject L).

E. Contracts made during marriage or cohabitation settling property rights:

MARRIED: Valid.

UNMARRIED: Probably enforceable if based on earnings, property, etc., rather than on sex.

BOTH: Agreements must be made without duress and with full disclosure of assets and other important information.

F.   What can be willed?

BOTH: Each spouse's or mate's separate property.

MARRIED: If will does not state that its provision for surviving spouse is instead of statutory life estate (see subject L), then it is in addition to it. If will provision is instead of statutory life estate, surviving spouse must elect either the life estate or the will provision.

G.   Automatic protection for surviving spouse or mate:

MARRIED: Widow, for family, receives household effects and supplies, personal property of husband, and reasonable allowance for one year. If no issue of decedent survive, widow receives a reasonable portion of real estate for her support in addition to statutory share (see subject L).

UNMARRIED: No protection for surviving mate. Minor children receive household supplies and personal property of deceased if they are entitled to inherit (see subject N).

H.   If no will:

MARRIED: Surviving spouse receives ownership for life of all real estate; receives one-half or more of all personal property, amount depending on whether issue of deceased spouse survive; receives everything only if there are no surviving relatives.

UNMARRIED: Surviving mate receives nothing.

I.   Contracts:

BOTH: Each may contract with anyone, including each other.

J.   Lawsuits:

BOTH: Each may sue and be sued separately unless both involved.

K.   Homestead law:

BOTH: No homestead law.

L.   Dower or curtesy:

MARRIED: Abolished. Surviving spouse or mate receives lifetime ownership in real estate owned by deceased spouse at time of death. This takes precedence over will. Surviving spouse or mate must elect between life ownership or will provision.

M.   Civil suits by spouses or mates against each other:
     BOTH: Permitted.

N.   Legitimacy:
     MARRIED: Children born during marriage are presumed le-
          gitimate. Children born before marriage are legitimized
          if parents later marry and children are acknowledged by
          father (though it is possible that acknowledgment is not
          necessary).
     UNMARRIED: Illegitimate children inherit from mother only;
          from father if legitimized by later marriage of parents
          and acknowledged by father.

O.   Adoption:
     BOTH: Any person may adopt anyone younger than him/
          herself.
     MARRIED: Both spouses must sign for adoption.

P.   Division of property upon termination of relationship:
     MARRIED: Court may assign separate marital property of
          either spouse to the other. Separate property acquired
          before marriage is not assignable, but income of such
          property is. Jointly held property may be divided by
          court as it deems fair.
     UNMARRIED: Implied or express contracts, value of services,
          or unfair economic gain may create rights to property.

VI. RECENT EVENTS, TRENDS, AND CONCLUSIONS

Since common-law marriages are recognized and cohabitation is not
illegal, it seems likely that some or all of the theories of the *Marvin*
case would be followed.

SOUTH CAROLINA

I. MARRIAGE

A. Legality:
1. Age: 18; under 18, need consent of parent or guardian; males under 16 not permitted; females under 14 not permitted.
2. License: Not required. Application must be filed 24 hours before issuance; must furnish evidence of age unless older than 25.
3. Medical examination: Not required.
4. Waiting period: 24 hours.

B. Common-law marriages: Valid.

C. Out-of-state marriages: Probably valid if valid in state where entered into.

D. Adultery: Illegal; fine and/or sentence.

E. Property: Separate.

F. Partnerships: A partnership agreement between spouses is probably enforceable as long as there is a valid business purpose.

II. COHABITATION

A. Legality:
1. Cohabitation: Illegal; fine and/or sentence.
2. Fornication: Illegal; fine and/or sentence.

B. Property:
1. A promise made in return for future illicit cohabitation will not be enforced because it is against public policy.
2. An express agreement will not be enforced if the primary basis is illicit cohabitation, and household services are only incidental.

C. Common-law marriage:
1. There is a strong presumption in favor of a common-law marriage when a couple cohabits.
2. A bigamous marriage will not be validated as a com-

mon-law marriage even if the former spouse of the
bigamous partner is divorced or dies.

D.   Putative marriage: If one party enters a bigamous marriage
in good faith, the children of the marriage are legitimate.

E.   Partnerships: A partnership agreement between mates is
probably enforceable as long as there is a valid business
purpose and the agreement is not primarily based on sex.

III. DIVORCE (DISSOLUTION) AND LEGAL SEPARATION

A.   Divorce or dissolution (grounds):
1.   Adultery.
2.   Desertion for one year.
3.   Physical cruelty.
4.   Continuous separation for one year (no fault).
5.   Habitual drunkenness or drug addiction.

B.   Legal separation (grounds): Not available.

C.   Residency requirements: One year for either spouse or 3
months for both spouses prior to filing for divorce.

D.   Remarriage: Possible immediately after divorce is final.

E.   Court orders after filing for divorce and before divorce is
final:
1.   Temporary alimony to either spouse.
2.   Allowance for court costs and legal fees to either.

F.   Alimony:
1.   Granted to either spouse in lump sum or installments.
2.   Adultery bars alimony.
3.   If custody of children is involved, alimony award
should be allocated between spouse and children.

G.   Child support and custody:
1.   Court has power to order support and custody.
2.   Support award should be separate from alimony.
3.   Mother is given preference for custody of young children unless it is not in the child's best interests.

H.   Property division by court in absence of written or oral
agreement: Courts may not divide separate property acquired before marriage; title alone controls. Courts may
recognize a "special equity" of one spouse in the separate
property of the other as a result of his/her homemaker contributions to the marriage. Thus, the court can, in effect,
divide any property acquired during the marriage as it deems
fair.

IV. TERMINATION OF COHABITATION

    A.   Court jurisdiction: No judicial control; voluntary parting.

    B.   Court orders: A court may make orders for child support and custody similar to those made in a divorce, once paternity is established.

    C.   Property division (decisions in South Carolina and in other states suggest the following possibilities):
        1.   Courts could infer partnership agreements as a means of dividing property and money.
        2.   Courts could order return or division of property and money if there had been an implied or express agreement.
        3.   Courts could order return of property to the rightful owner or grant an interest in property or an award of money to a mate to the extent of his/her contribution toward purchase of property.
        4.   Since living together is illegal, courts would probably not honor an agreement if the relationship was primarily sexual; thus it might be difficult to collect for performing household duties when no direct financial contribution can be shown.

    D.   Putative marriage: Courts would probably adjust the rights of a putative spouse.

    E.   Palimony: There have been no court decisions to indicate that rehabilitative alimony or temporary or permanent alimony would be awarded to a mate, and such an award seems unlikely.

V. SPECIFIC SUBJECTS (No written agreements, except for A,E,I.)
Reference to "BOTH" means married and unmarried couples.

    A.   Prenuptial or precohabitation agreements:
        MARRIED: Valid.
        UNMARRIED: Probably valid if sex is not the basis of the agreement and if meant for protection of property interests.
        BOTH: Agreements must be made without duress and with full disclosure of assets and other important information.

    B.   Property:
        BOTH: All property is separate property of acquiring mate or spouse.

    C.   Liability of separate property for other spouse's or mate's debts:

MARRIED: No liability, except that husband is liable for necessaries for wife and children.

UNMARRIED: No liability.

D. Management and control of separate property of each:

BOTH: Each controls own property.

MARRIED: Both spouses must sign to sell family home.

UNMARRIED: Amount that can be given to illegitimate children or a mate, if there is a legal wife or legitimate children, is restricted.

E. Contracts made during marriage or cohabitation settling property rights:

MARRIED: Valid.

UNMARRIED: Probably enforceable if based on earnings, property, etc., rather than on sex.

BOTH: Agreements must be made without duress and with full disclosure of assets and other important information.

F. What can be willed?

BOTH: Each spouse's or mate's separate property.

MARRIED: Widow can disregard will of husband and elect to receive dower instead.

UNMARRIED: Amount that can be willed to illegitimate children or a mate, if there is a surviving legal wife or legitimate children, is restricted.

G. Automatic protection for surviving spouse or mate:

MARRIED: Widow has dower and homestead exemption. No allowances or right to stay in home.

UNMARRIED: No protection for surviving mate. Homestead exemption given to minor children if entitled to inherit (see subject H).

H. If no will:

MARRIED: Surviving spouse receives everything if there are no issue, parents, or other relatives of deceased spouse; receives one-third if there are surviving issue; one-half if there are no surviving issue but other surviving relatives. If widow accepts this share, she does not receive dower.

I. Contracts:

BOTH: Each may contract with anyone, including each other.

J. Lawsuits:

BOTH: Each may sue and be sued separately unless both involved.

K. Homestead law:

BOTH: Exemption of $1,000 over liens to head of family or

husband and wife. No filing necessary. Sheriff, before a forced sale, appoints three appraisers who designate the homestead.

L.   Dower:

MARRIED: Wife receives lifetime ownership of one-third of all real estate owned by husband at any time during marriage, or complete ownership of one-sixth of all real estate, including land of which she is joint owner. Wife may accept intestate share (subject H) instead of dower. Divorce ends dower right, as do various marital wrongs.

M.   Civil suits by spouses or mates against each other:

BOTH: Permitted.

N.   Legitimacy:

MARRIED: Children born during marriage are presumed legitimate.

UNMARRIED: Illegitimate children inherit from mother; from father if parents later marry. Children born before marriage are legitimized if parents later marry.

O.   Adoption:

MARRIED: Both spouses must sign for adoption.

UNMARRIED: An unmarried father or mother of any age may adopt.

BOTH: An adult or a child may be adopted. Investigation to determine suitability of home.

P.   Division of property upon termination of relationship:

MARRIED: Separate property acquired prior to marriage cannot be divided by court. Marital property acquired during the marriage may be divided by court as it deems fair, primarily as a result of services rendered to the marriage.

UNMARRIED: Implied or express contract, value of services, or unfair economic gain may create rights to property.

VI. RECENT EVENTS, TRENDS, AND CONCLUSIONS

A.   Giving birth after a divorce to an illegitimate child who lives with the children of a former marriage does not make the mother an unfit parent or necessitate a change of custody to the father.

B.   A revision of the divorce code provides that support and alimony apply equally to husband and wife.

C.   The legislature has ratified a constitutional amendment allowing divorce on the ground of separation for one year rather than three.

D.   After cohabitating for 20 years, a female mate asked a half-interest in the family home, which the court denied her because she had not actually contributed to the purchase price at the time of purchase (though she had contributed money at other times).

E. A male mate asked for an interest in the property owned by his mate, to which he had made large contributions. The court denied his request because the couple had been married at common law and a gift was thus presumed.

F. Though the law in South Carolina is unclear, perhaps some of the theories of the *Marvin* case would be followed.

SOUTH DAKOTA

I. MARRIAGE

A. Legality:
    1. Age: 18; under 18, need consent of parent or guardian.
    2. License: Required; good for 20 days.
    3. Medical examination: Physician's certificate that applicant is free from syphilis or that the disease is not in communicable stage; within 20 days of application for license.
    4. Waiting period: None.

B. Common-law marriages: Not recognized.

C. Out-of-state marriages: Valid if valid in state where entered into.

D. Adultery: Not a crime.

E. Property: Separate.

F. Partnerships: A partnership agreement between spouses is probably enforceable as long as there is a valid business purpose.

II. COHABITATION

A. Legality:
   1. Cohabitation: Not a crime.
   2. Fornication: Not a crime.
   3. All private, nonviolent sexual acts between consenting adults are legal.

B. Common-law marriage: Not recognized.

C. Putative marriage: No case law, but courts would probably recognize the property rights of a putative spouse.

D. Property: Cohabiting mates who purchase property with joint contributions will be declared joint owners, no matter who has title to the property. If there is no express contract, the court will divide the property according to the contributions of each.

E. Partnerships: A partnership agreement between mates is probably enforceable as long as there is a valid business purpose and the agreement is not primarily based on sex.

III. DIVORCE (DISSOLUTION) AND LEGAL SEPARATION

A. Divorce or dissolution (grounds):
   1. Adultery.
   2. Extreme cruelty.
   3. Wilful desertion for one year.
   4. Habitual intemperance for one year.
   5. Wilful neglect for one year.
   6. Conviction of felony.
   7. Incurable, chronic insanity (mania or dementia) for 5 years with confinement.

B. Legal separation (grounds): Same as for divorce.

C. Residency requirements: Plaintiff must be resident when divorce is filed and until it is final.

D. Remarriage: Possible immediately after divorce is final.

E. Court orders after filing for divorce and before divorce is final:
   1. Care and custody of children by either.
   2. Temporary alimony to either.
   3. Court costs and attorneys' fees.

F. Alimony: Granted to either spouse after divorce for life or for any shorter period.

G. Child support and custody:
   1. Court orders custody, care, and education as seems necessary and proper.

       2. Fault cannot be considered in custody award except as it is relevant to fitness of parent.

H.   Property division by court in absence of written or oral agreement:
       1. Court can divide separate property, including joint property, as it deems fair.
       2. Fault cannot be considered except for unique circumstances.
       3. Joint property is usually divided or sold and the proceeds divided equally.

IV. TERMINATION OF COHABITATION

A.   Court jurisdiction: No judicial control; voluntary parting.

B.   Court orders: A court may make orders for child support and custody similar to those made in a divorce, once paternity is established.

C.   Property division (decisions in other states suggest the following possibilities):
       1. Courts could infer partnership agreements as a means of dividing property and money.
       2. Courts could order return or division of property and money if there had been an implied or express agreement.
       3. Courts could order return of property to the rightful owner or grant an interest in property or an award of money to a mate to the extent of his/her contribution toward purchase of property.
       4. Since living together is not illegal, recovery could be had for performing household duties as well as for direct financial contributions, so long as the implied or express agreement was not primarily based upon sex.

D.   Putative marriage: Courts would probably adjust the property rights of a putative spouse.

E.   Palimony: There have been no court decisions to indicate that rehabilitative alimony or temporary or permanent alimony would be awarded to a mate, but such an award is a possibility.

V. SPECIFIC SUBJECTS (No written agreements, except for A,E,I.)
Reference to "BOTH" means married and unmarried couples.

A.   Prenuptial or precohabitation agreements:

MARRIED: Valid, but will not necessarily be honored by court.

UNMARRIED: Probably valid if sex is not the basis of the agreement and if meant for protection of property interests.

BOTH: Agreements must be made without duress and with full disclosure of assets and other important information.

B. Property:
BOTH: All property is separate property of acquiring spouse or mate.

C. Liability of separate property for other spouse's or mate's debts:
MARRIED: No liability, except that husband and wife are both liable for food, clothing, and fuel purchased by either.
UNMARRIED: No liability.

D. Management and control of separate property of each:
BOTH: Each controls own property.
MARRIED: Both spouses must sign to sell family home or use it as collateral for a loan.

E. Contracts made during marriage or cohabitation settling property rights:
MARRIED: Valid.
UNMARRIED: Probably enforceable if based on earnings, property, etc., rather than on sex.
BOTH: Agreements must be made without duress and with full disclosure of assets and other important information.

F. What can be willed?
BOTH: Each spouse's or mate's separate property.
MARRIED: Surviving spouse receives will provisions and homestead rights (see subject K) unless will clearly states that a choice must be made.

G. Automatic protection for surviving spouse or mate:
MARRIED: Surviving spouse and minor children receive possession of family home, up to $2,500 in money and property, and an additional reasonable allowance for one year if needed; certain personal property and household furnishings.
UNMARRIED: No protection for surviving mate. Minor children receive possession of family home and allowances if entitled to inherit (see subject H).

H. If no will:
MARRIED: Surviving spouse receives everything if there are no surviving issue or other relatives of deceased spouse;

otherwise, surviving spouse divides with surviving issue
or other relatives.

UNMARRIED: Surviving mate receives nothing. Illegitimate
children inherit from mother as if legitimate; from father
only if acknowledged in writing before witness, or if
legitimized by marriage of parents and acknowledgment
and acceptance into family by father.

I.   Contracts:

BOTH: Each may contract with anyone, including each
other.

MARRIED: May not alter legal relationship by contract with
each other.

J.   Lawsuits:

BOTH: Each may sue and be sued separately unless both
involved.

K.   Homestead law:

BOTH: Any person may claim exemption up to $30,000 over
liens, including mortgages, in family home. No designation or recording required and no claim of exemption
necessary.

L.   Civil suits by spouses or mates against each other:
BOTH: Permitted.

M.   Legitimacy:

MARRIED: Children born during marriage are presumed legitimate. Children born before marriage are legitimized
if parents later marry and father acknowledges child and
adopts him into family.

UNMARRIED: Illegitimate children inherit from mother as if
legitimate; from father only if acknowledged in writing
before witness.

N.   Adoption:

BOTH: Any minor may be adopted by any adult at least ten
years older. An adult may adopt another adult. Investigation made of financial ability and moral fitness.

O.   Division of property upon termination of relationship:

MARRIED: Court divides separate property, including joint
property, as it deems fair. Joint property, however, is
usually sold and the proceeds divided equally.

UNMARRIED: Implied or express contracts, value of services,
or unfair economic gain may create rights to property.

VI. RECENT EVENTS, TRENDS, AND CONCLUSIONS

A.   An agreement limiting a wife's right to alimony is not enforceable.

B. Equal rights of spouses to alimony, divorce costs, and financial support have become law.

C. The presumption that a mother is preferred for custody of a young child has been discarded in custody cases.

D. A spouse, by previous agreement, can waive the right to his/her share of a jointly owned home.

E. A mother, separated but not divorced from her husband, lost custody of the children to the father because she lived with another man during the separation.

F. Although marital misconduct (adultery) of a mother would not necessarily result in a loss of child custody after divorce, her unsuitable lifestyle (several evenings a week drinking in bars) does warrant granting custody to the father.

G. Since neither cohabitation, fornication, nor adultery is illegal, it seems likely that some or all of the theories in the *Marvin* case would be followed.

TENNESSEE

I. MARRIAGE

A. Legality:
   1. Age: 18, between 16 and 18, parents must join in application; under 16, not permitted.
   2. License: Required; good for 30 days.
   3. Medical examination: Physician's certificate showing freedom from venereal disease, accompanied by statement of laboratory tests.
   4. Waiting period: 3 days.

B. Common-law marriages: Not recognized; valid if valid where entered into.

    C.   Out-of-state marriages: No provision; probably valid if valid in state where entered into.

    D.   Adultery: Not a crime.

    E.   Property: Separate.

    F.   Partnerships: A partnership agreement between spouses is probably enforceable as long as there is a valid business purpose.

II. COHABITATION

    A.   Legality:
            1. Cohabitation: Legal unless openly and notoriously lewd.
            2. Fornication: Legal unless openly and notoriously lewd.

    B.   Common-law marriage: Courts will presume a valid marriage if there has been a long period of cohabitation.

    C.   Putative marriage: Not recognized.

    D.   Property:
            1. Oral partnership agreements have been found to exist when cohabiting mates are involved in business together.
            2. A contract based on immoral sexual relationship is not enforceable unless the basis was past rather than future cohabitation.

    E.   Partnerships: A partnership agreement between mates is probably enforceable as long as there is a valid business purpose and the agreement is not primarily based on sex.

III. DIVORCE (DISSOLUTION) AND LEGAL SEPARATION

    A.   Divorce or dissolution (grounds):
            1. Irreconcilable differences (no fault):
                a. If no contest or denial by defendant
                b. If parties have executed notarized property settlement referring to divorce action, no service of complaint on defendant is necessary.
                c. Court must find that parties have made adequate provision in written agreement for child custody, child support, and fair settlement of property rights.
            2. Impotency.
            3. Bigamy.
             4. Adultery.

5. Desertion or absence for one year.
6. Conviction of infamous crime.
7. Conviction of felony and sentence to penitentiary.
8. Attempt to murder other.
9. Refusal of wife to move with husband and absence from him for 2 years.
10. Wife pregnant by another at time of marriage without husband's knowledge.
11. Habitual drunkenness or abuse of narcotic drugs by either.
12. Granted by petition to either party when there has been no reconciliation after two years of legal separation.

B.   Legal separation (grounds):
1. Irreconcilable differences (see above).
2. Cruel and inhuman treatment.
3. Husband renders wife's life intolerable so that she is forced to leave.
4. Abandonment of wife by husband and his refusal to provide for her.

C.   Residency requirements: Plaintiff a bona fide resident, or, if not, 6 months residence for one spouse before divorce suit is filed.

D.   Remarriage: Possible immediately after divorce is final.

E.   Court orders after filing for divorce and before divorce is final:
1. Temporary alimony to spouse filing for divorce (plaintiff).
2. Child support.
3. Attorneys' fees for plaintiff spouse.

F.   Alimony:
1. Granted to spouse filing for divorce at discretion of court.
2. Marital misconduct by spouse filing for divorce is an automatic bar to alimony payments.
3. May be later modified when circumstances change after divorce is final.

G.   Child support and custody:
1. Court orders support and awards custody to either parent or to third party according to best interests of the child.
2. Custody of mother preferred for young child unless it is not in best interests of child.

H.   Property division by court in absence of written or oral agreement:

1. Court has power to distribute all jointly owned property as it deems fair.
2. In certain cases, court may grant one spouse's real estate to the other, but generally each spouse retains his/her separate property.
3. Court may grant homestead to spouse in whose favor divorce is granted.

IV. TERMINATION OF COHABITATION

A. Court jurisdiction: No judicial control; voluntary parting.

B. Court orders: A court may make order for child support and custody similar to those made in a divorce, once paternity is established.

C. Property division (decisions in other states suggest the following possibilities):
1. Courts could infer partnership agreements as a means of dividing property and money.
2. Courts could order return or division of property and money if there had been an implied or express agreement.
3. Courts could order return of property to the rightful owner or grant an interest in property or an award of money to a mate to the extent of his/her contribution toward purchase of property.
4. Since living together is not illegal, recovery could be had for performing household duties as well as for direct financial contributions, so long as the implied or express agreement was not primarily based upon sex.

D. Putative marriage: Not recognized, but courts might make adjustments to allow for fair division of property.

E. Palimony: There have been no court decisions to indicate that rehabilitative alimony or temporary or permanent alimony would be awarded to a mate, but such an award is a possibility.

V. SPECIFIC SUBJECTS (No written agreements, except for A,E,I.)
Reference to "BOTH" means married and unmarried couples.

A. Prenuptial or precohabitation agreements:
MARRIED: Valid; must be in writing.
UNMARRIED: Probably valid if sex is not the basis of the agreement and if meant for the protection of property interests.
BOTH: Agreements must be made without duress and with

full disclosure of assets and other important information.

B.   Property:
     BOTH: All property is separate property of acquiring spouse or mate.

C.   Liability of separate property for other spouse's or mate's debts:
     BOTH: No liability.

D.   Management and control of separate property of each:
     BOTH: Each controls own separate property.
     MARRIED: Both spouses must sign to sell family home or use it as collateral for a debt.

E.   Contracts made during marriage or cohabitation settling property rights:
     MARRIED: Valid.
     UNMARRIED: Probably enforceable if based on earnings, property, etc., rather than on sex.
     BOTH: Agreements must be made without duress and with full disclosure of assets and other important information.

F.   What can be willed?
     BOTH: Each mate's separate property.
     MARRIED: Surviving spouse may elect to disregard will and take one-third of estate plus automatic protection (see subject H).

G.   Automatic protection for surviving spouse or mate:
     MARRIED: Surviving spouse receives homestead exemption of $5,000 over liens, including mortgages, plus one year's support allowance and certain exempt property.
     UNMARRIED: No protection for surviving mate. Unmarried minor children of deceased receive same protection surviving spouse would get if they are entitled to inherit (see subject H).

H.   If no will:
     MARRIED: Surviving spouse receives everything if none of decedent's issue survive; surviving spouse receives children's share (but not less than one-third of estate) if children survive.
     UNMARRIED: Surviving mate receives nothing. Children born out of wedlock inherit from mother; from father if parents marry, if paternity is judicially established before death of father or afterward by clear and convincing proof, or if children have lived with father who has openly acknowledged and supported them.

I.   Contracts:

BOTH: Each may contract with anyone, including each other.

J. Lawsuits:
BOTH: Each may sue and be sued separately unless both involved.

K. Homestead law:
BOTH: Any individual receives exemption from creditors up to $5,000 over liens, including mortgages, on family home. Levying officer designates disinterested three people to select the exempt property of $5,000 from the homestead.

L. Civil suits by spouses or mates against each other:
MARRIED: Permitted, except may not sue each other for personal wrongs.
UNMARRIED: Permitted.

M. Legitimacy:
MARRIED: Children born during marriage are presumed legitimate.
UNMARRIED: Illegitimate children inherit from mother; inherit from father if parents marry, if paternity is judicially established before death of father or afterward, by clear and convincing proof, or if children have lived with father who has openly acknowledged and supported them. Children are legitimized by adjudication of paternity signed by either father or mother.
BOTH: Children born before marriage are legitimized if parents later marry.

N. Adoption:
BOTH: Any person over 18 may adopt a minor.

O. Division of property upon termination of relationship:
MARRIED: Court has power to distribute all jointly owned property as it deems fair. Court may grant part of one spouse's separate real estate to the other, and family home may be granted to spouse in whose favor divorce is granted. Separate property is usually retained by owner.
UNMARRIED: Implied or express contracts, value of services, or unfair economic gain may create rights to property.

VI. RECENT EVENTS, TRENDS, AND CONCLUSIONS

A. A new law requires any reference to "wife" to read "spouse" in relation to divorce, alimony, or child support.

B. A willingness by the courts to make adjustments, and the fact that neither cohabitation nor fornication is illegal, seem to indicate that the court would follow some or all of the theories suggested in the *Marvin* case.

TEXAS

I. MARRIAGE

A. Legality:
1. Age: 18; under 18, need consent of parent or guardian; under 14, court order necessary.
2. License: Required: good for 21 days.
3. Medical examination: Physician's certificate showing examination made and applicant free of venereal disease, not more than 21 days before issuance of license.
4. Waiting period: None.

B. Common-law marriages: Recognized.

C. Out-of-state marriages: Valid if valid in state where entered into, unless contrary to state policy.

D. Adultery: Not a crime.

E. Property: Community.

F. Partnerships: A partnership agreement between spouses is probably enforceable as long as there is a valid business purpose.

II. COHABITATION

A. Legality:
1. Cohabitation: Not a crime.
2. Fornication: Not a crime.

B. Common-law marriage:
   1. Continued cohabitation after reason for an illegal marriage is removed will result in a common-law marriage.
   2. Private vows between out-of-state residents will not form a common-law marriage.
   3. Living together without the intention of being married will not result in a common-law marriage.

C. Putative marriage:
   1. A putative wife has legal status and can share equally in community property acquired prior to learning the marriage is invalid.
   2. The putative marriage ends when the putative spouse learns the marriage is invalid.

D. Property:
   1. A mate may have property rights if a business relationship exists between them, but no community property can be established.
   2. Value of homemaker's services may be recognized if sexual favors are not the primary reason for the express or implied agreement.
   3. If the basis for an agreement is future sexual favors, the agreement is not enforceable.
   4. If a mate can prove a contribution toward the purchase of property, he/she can receive compensation to that extent.

E. Partnerships: A partnership agreement between mates is probably enforceable as long as there is a valid business purpose and the agreement is not primarily based on sex.

III. DIVORCE (DISSOLUTION) AND LEGAL SEPARATION

A. Divorce or dissolution (grounds):
   1. Cruel treatment or treatment rendering living together intolerable.
   2. Abandonment for one year.
   3. Adultery.
   4. Living apart for 3 years (no fault).
   5. Conviction of a felony and imprisonment.
   6. Incurable mental illness and confinement for 3 years.
   7. Marriage has become insupportable because of discord or personality conflicts (no fault).

B. Legal separation (grounds): Not available.

C. Residency requirements: 6 months in state and 90 days in county for either spouse before legal action is filed.

D.   Remarriage: Neither may remarry for 30 days after divorce is final.

E.   Court orders after filing for divorce and before divorce is final:
     1. Temporary alimony.
     2. Temporary orders concerning property.
     3. Court costs.

F.   Alimony:
     1. Court cannot award alimony.
     2. Parties can agree on periodic payments as part of property settlement agreement.

G.   Child support and custody:
     1. Court orders support as necessary.
     2. Court grants custody to either parent according to best interests of child.

H.   Property division by court in absence of written or oral agreement:
     1. Community property is divided as the court deems fair.
     2. Marital misconduct may be considered in dividing community property.
     3. Separate-property real estate may not be awarded to the non-owning spouse.
     4. Jointly held property is divided as the court deems fair.
     5. Separate personal property may be divided by the court if it deems it fair to do so.

IV. TERMINATION OF COHABITATION

A.   Court jurisdiction: No judicial control; voluntary parting.

B.   Court orders: A court may make orders for child support and custody similar to those made in a divorce, once paternity is established.

C.   Property division (decisions in Texas and other states suggest the following possibilities):
     1. Courts could infer partnership agreements as a means of dividing property and money.
     2. Courts could order return or division of property and money if there had been an implied or express agreement.
     3. Courts could order return of property to the rightful owner or grant an interest in property or an award of money to a mate to the extent of his/her contribution toward purchase of property.

4.   Since living together is not illegal, recovery could be had for performing household duties as well as for financial contributions, so long as the implied or express agreement was not primarily based upon sex.

D.   Putative marriage: Courts will recognize property rights of a putative spouse who mistakenly believes a valid marriage exists.

E.   Palimony: There have been no court decisions to indicate that rehabilitative alimony or temporary or permanent alimony would be awarded to a mate, but such an award is a possibility.

V. **SPECIFIC SUBJECTS** (No written agreements, except for A,H,L.) Reference to "BOTH" means married and unmarried couples.

A.   Prenuptial or precohabitation agreements:
MARRIED: Valid. However, contract to end deceased spouse's interest in community property when he/she dies is invalid.
UNMARRIED: Probably valid if sex is not the basis of the agreement and if meant for protection of property interests.
BOTH: Agreement must be made without duress and with full disclosure of assets and other important information.

B.   Separate property:
MARRIED: Property owned before marriage or acquired during marriage by gift or inheritance; personal injury awards.
UNMARRIED: All property is separate property of acquiring mate.

C.   Community property:
MARRIED: Rents and profits of separate property; all property acquired by either spouse during marriage except by gift or inheritance.

D.   Liability of separate property for other spouse's or mate's debts:
BOTH: No liability unless both involved.

E.   Liability of community property for debts contracted by one spouse:
MARRIED: Either or both spouses liable for personal wrongs committed during marriage; spouse who does not manage is not liable for wrongs committed before or after marriage. Not liable for contracts during marriage signed by spouse who does not manage.

F.   Management and control of separate property of each:
     BOTH: Each controls own separate property.
     MARRIED: Spouses must both sign to sell homestead or use
        it as collateral for a debt.

G.   Management and control of community property:
     MARRIED: Controlled by spouse who would have owned
        property had they been single, or by spouse whose name
        is on title. Both spouses manage family home.

H.   Contracts made during marriage or cohabitation settling
     property rights:
     MARRIED: Valid.
     UNMARRIED: Probably enforceable if based on earnings,
        property, etc., rather than on sex.
     BOTH: Agreement must be made without duress and with
        full disclosure of assets and other important information.

I.   What can be willed?
     MARRIED: Each spouse's separate property. If will attempts
        to dispose of community property, surviving spouse may
        elect to accept the terms of the will or to take his/her
        one-half share of the community property.
     UNMARRIED: Each mate's separate property.

J.   Automatic protection for surviving spouse or mate:
     MARRIED: Reasonable allowance for one year; homestead
        and property exemptions (or, if none, $5,000 instead
        of homestead, and $1,000 instead of other exempt prop-
        erty); right to occupy homestead.
     UNMARRIED: No protection for surviving mate. Allowances
        for minor children who are entitled to inherit (see subject
        K).

K.   If no will:
     MARRIED: Surviving spouse receives all separate property
        if no children or other close family of deceased spouse
        survive; otherwise, divided between surviving spouse
        and children or other heirs. Surviving spouse receives
        all community property if no children survive; one-half
        if there are children surviving.
     UNMARRIED: Surviving mate receives nothing. Illegitimate
        children inherit from mother as if legitimate; from father
        if parents marry, or if legitimized by court decree, or
        if father makes written statement of paternity.

L.   Contracts:
     BOTH: Each may contract with anyone, including each
        other.

M.   Lawsuits:

BOTH: Each may sue and be sued separately unless both involved.

N. Homestead law:
BOTH: Every head of family and single adult receives exemption up to $10,000 over liens, including mortgages. Limited to 200 acres for family and 100 acres for single adult.

O. Civil suits by spouses or mates against each other:
MARRIED: Permitted only when necessary for protection of property rights.
UNMARRIED: Permitted.

P. Legitimacy:
MARRIED: Children born during marriage are presumed legitimate; children born before marriage are legitimized if parents later marry.
UNMARRIED: Voluntary legitimization occurs by obtaining court decree if father makes statement of paternity. Illegitimate children inherit from mother; from father if parents marry, or if legitimized by court decree, or if father makes a statement of paternity.

Q. Adoption:
BOTH: Any adult may adopt a child. Study of home may be ordered.

R. Division of property upon termination of relationship:
MARRIED: Community and joint property divided by court as it deems fair. Separate real estate may not be divided, but separate personal property may be divided if the court deems it fair to do so.
UNMARRIED: Implied or express contracts, value of services, or unfair economic gain may create rights to property.

VI. RECENT EVENTS, TRENDS, AND CONCLUSIONS

A. A jury awarded $20,000 to a female mate who had lived with a male for two years. Although the basis of her request was for a division of property from a common-law marriage, the jury did not recognize their relationship as a marriage.

B. Based upon the above decision, since cohabitation and fornication are not illegal, the court would probably follow some or all of the theories of the *Marvin* case.

UTAH

I. MARRIAGE

A. Legality:
   1. Age: 16; under 18, need consent of parent or guardian; under 14, not allowed.
   2. License: Required; good for 30 days.
   3. Medical examination: Certificate showing freedom from venereal disease.
   4. Waiting period: None.

B. Common-law marriages: Not recognized; out-of-state common-law marriage not recognized if entered into by Utah resident who went to another state for that purpose.

C. Out-of-state marriages: Valid if valid where entered into.

D. Adultery: Illegal (misdemeanor); fine or sentence.

E. Property: Separate.

F. Partnerships: A partnership agreement between spouses is probably enforceable as long as there is a valid business purpose.

II. COHABITATION

A. Legality:
   1. Cohabitation: Not a crime.
   2. Fornication: Not a crime.

B. Common-law marriage: Not recognized.

C. Putative marriage: Courts will recognize rights of partners acting in good faith in an invalid marriage and distribute assets fairly.

D. Property: Courts will make a fair distribution of assets acquired during cohabitation.

E. Partnerships: A partnership agreement between mates is probably enforceable as long as there is a valid business purpose and the agreement is not primarily based on sex.

III. DIVORCE (DISSOLUTION) AND LEGAL SEPARATION

A.   Divorce or dissolution (grounds):
  1. Impotency at time of marriage.
  2. Adultery.
  3. Desertion for more than one year.
  4. Neglect to provide necessaries of life.
  5. Habitual drunkenness.
  6. Conviction of felony.
  7. Cruelty causing bodily injury or great mental distress.
  8. Permanent insanity.
  9. Separation for 3 years under decree of separate maintenance (no fault).

B.   Legal separation (grounds): Allowed to wife when husband deserts or fails to support, or when wife, without her fault, must live separately (separate maintenance).

C.   Residency requirements: 3 months for either spouse before legal action is filed.

D.   Remarriage: Prohibited during appeal period; otherwise, no restriction.

E.   Court orders after filing for divorce and before divorce is final:
  1. Allowance for court costs and attorneys' fees.
  2. Child support.
  3. Temporary alimony.

F.   Alimony:
  1. Awarded to either spouse at court's discretion.
  2. Terminated on remarriage or cohabitation of recipient.

G.   Child support and custody:
  1. Court awards money for support of minor children.
  2. Court determines custody considering best interests of child and past conduct and moral standards of each parent.
  3. No particular preference given either parent.

H.   Property division by court in absence of written or oral agreement: Court divides all separate property, including joint property, as it deems fair.

IV. TERMINATION OF COHABITATION

A.   Court jurisdiction: No judicial control; voluntary parting.

B.   Court orders: A court may make orders for child support and custody similar to those made in a divorce, once paternity is established. Mother has primary right to custody of young illegitimate child.

C. Property division (decisions in Utah and other states suggest the following possibilities):
1. Courts could infer partnership agreements as a means of dividing property and money.
2. Courts could order return or division of property and money if there had been an implied or express agreement.
3. Courts could order return of property to the rightful owner or grant an interest in property or an award of money to a mate to the extent of his/her contribution toward purchase of property.
4. Since cohabitation is not illegal, recovery could be had for performing household duties as well as for direct financial contributions, so long as the implied or express agreement was not primarily based upon sex.

D. Putative marriage: Courts will recognize rights of putative spouse to property accumulated during relationship.

E. Palimony: There have been no court decisions to indicate that rehabilitative alimony or temporary or permanent alimony would be awarded to a mate, but such an award is a possibility.

V. **SPECIFIC SUBJECTS** (No written agreements, except for A,E,I.) Reference to "BOTH" means married and unmarried couples.

A. Prenuptial or precohabitation agreements:
MARRIED: Probably valid.
UNMARRIED: Probably valid, if sex is not the basis of the agreement and if meant for protection of property interests.
BOTH: Agreement must be made without duress and with full disclosure of assets and other important information.

B. Property:
BOTH: All property is separate property of acquiring spouse or mate.

C. Liability of separate property for other spouse's or mate's debts:
MARRIED: No liability, except that husband and wife are both liable for family expenses.
UNMARRIED: No liability.

D. Management and control of separate property of each:
BOTH: Each controls own separate property.

MARRIED: Both spouses must sign to sell or mortgage home, and wife must sign to waive statutory right (see subject L).

E. Contracts made during marriage or cohabitation settling property rights:

MARRIED: Valid, but not binding on court.

UNMARRIED: Probably enforceable if based on earnings, property, etc., rather than on sex.

BOTH: Agreement must be made without duress and with full disclosure of assets and other important information.

F. What can be willed?

MARRIED: Each spouse's separate property, except wife's statutory share (see subject L). Surviving spouse may elect to disregard the will and inherit as if there were no will (see subject H).

UNMARRIED: Each mate's separate property.

G. Automatic protection for surviving spouse or mate:

MARRIED: Possession of family home exempt from foreclosure as long as court directs; certain exempt property; reasonable allowance up to one year.

UNMARRIED: No protection for surviving mate; minor children receive certain allowances and may remain in family home; minor illegitimate children receive same, if entitled to inherit (see subject H).

H. If no will:

MARRIED: Surviving spouse receives everything if there are no children or other relatives of deceased spouse surviving; surviving spouse's share is not in addition to statutory share (see subject L). Surviving spouse divides estate with children of deceased spouse or with other relatives of deceased spouse, the amount depending on the number of children or their issue.

UNMARRIED: Surviving mate receives nothing. Illegitimate children are heirs of mother and of person acknowledging himself to be father.

I. Contracts:

BOTH: Each may contract with anyone, including each other.

J. Lawsuits:

BOTH: Each may sue and be sued separately unless both involved.

K. Homestead law:

MARRIED: Husband or wife may select homestead from separate property of either. Exemption of $6,000 in home over liens, including mortgages, plus $2,000 for wife and $800 for each additional family member. Declaration of homestead must be filed in office of county recorder in which property is located, and must contain statement showing person is head of family, plus description and value of property.

UNMARRIED: Same as for spouse, if owner can show he/she is head of family.

L.   Dower:

MARRIED: None, but there is a statutory share upon death of husband providing that one-third in value of all real estate owned by husband during marriage passes to wife.

M.   Civil suits by spouses or mates against each other:

MARRIED: May enforce property rights against each other; other suits not allowed.

UNMARRIED: Permitted.

N.   Legitimacy:

MARRIED: Child born during marriage is presumed legitimate unless the result of adulterous intercourse.

UNMARRIED: Illegitimate children are children of mother; of father if paternity is judicially established before his death, or afterward by clear and convincing proof; or if father adopts by acknowledging children and with mother's consent.

BOTH: Children born before marriage are legitimized if parents later marry.

O.   Adoption:

BOTH: An adult may adopt anyone at least ten years younger. Consent of spouse required if adult is married.

P.   Division of property upon termination of relationship:

MARRIED: Court has power to divide separate property, including joint property, as it deems fair.

UNMARRIED: Implied or express contracts, value of services, or unfair economic gain may create rights to property.

VI. RECENT EVENTS, TRENDS, AND CONCLUSIONS

A.   An award to the wife of 90 percent of the couple's assets accumulated during a 25-year marriage was not allowed, since property division in a divorce is not meant as punishment to the "guilty" spouse.

B.   New legislation provides for termination of alimony upon remarriage of recipient, or proof that recipient is cohabitating with someone of the opposite sex.

C.   In a recent case, the court ordered a property distribution to a female mate, even though the man she was living with was married to another woman at the beginning of the cohabitation.

D.   Court decisions, together with the fact that cohabitation is not illegal, seem to indicate that some or all of the theories of the *Marvin* case would be followed.

VERMONT

I. MARRIAGE

A.   Legality:
   1. Age: 18; under 18, need consent of parents or guardian; under 16, need consent of parent or guardian and court; under 14, not permitted.
   2. License: Required; void after 60 days.
   3. Medical examination: Required within 30 days of application for license.
   4. Waiting period: 5 days.

B.   Common-law marriages: Not recognized.

C.   Out-of-state marriages: Valid if valid where entered into, unless entered into with intention of avoiding laws of Vermont.

D.   Adultery: Illegal; fine and/or sentence.

E.   Property: Separate.

F.   Partnerships: A partnership agreement between spouses is probably enforceable as long as there is a valid business purpose.

II. COHABITATION

A. Legality:
1. Cohabitation: Not a crime.
2. Fornication: Not a crime.

B. Common-law marriage: Not recognized.

C. Putative marriage: In an invalid marriage that is thought to be valid, the transfer of property between mates will be recognized and rights restored.

D. Property: If sex is not the basis of an agreement, an express contract will be recognized, but an old court decision refused to infer a contract to compensate for household services.

E. Partnerships: A partnership agreement between mates is probably enforceable as long as there is a valid business purpose and the agreement is not primarily based on sex.

III. DIVORCE (DISSOLUTION) AND LEGAL SEPARATION

A. Divorce or dissolution (grounds):
1. Adultery.
2. Confinement at hard labor in state prison for 3 years.
3. Intolerable severity.
4. Disappearance for 7 years.
5. Neglect and refusal to provide maintenance when able to do so.
6. Incurable insanity and confinement for 5 years.
7. Living apart for 6 months (no fault).

B. Legal separation (grounds): Same.

C. Residency requirements: 6 months for a spouse before filing for divorce and one year before final hearing; 2 years if ground is insanity.

D. Remarriage: Possible immediately after divorce is final.

E. Court orders after filing for divorce and before divorce is final:
1. Temporary alimony.
2. Restraining orders concerning personal and property rights.

F. Alimony:
1. Granted to either spouse according to the circumstances.
2. Living together with a mate after divorce will not necessarily cause a reduction of alimony to recipient.

G. Child support and custody: Court may order to either party.

H.   Property division by court in absence of written or oral agreement: Court may divide all separate property, including joint property, as it deems fair.

IV. TERMINATION OF COHABITATION

A.   Court jurisdiction: No judicial control; voluntary parting.

B.   Court orders: A court may make orders for child support and custody similar to those made in a divorce, once paternity is established.

C.   Property division (decisions in other states suggest the following possibility):
  1.   Courts could infer partnership agreements as a means of dividing property and money.
  2.   Courts could order return or division of property and money if there had been an implied or express agreement.
  3.   Courts could order return of property to the rightful owner or grant an interest in property or an award of money to a mate to the extent of his contribution toward purchase of property.
  4.   Since living together is not illegal, recovery could be had for performing household duties as well as for direct financial contribution, so long as the implied or express agreement was not primarily based upon sex.

D.   Putative marriage: If a marriage thought to be valid is actually void, courts will nevertheless divide any property accumulated during the relationship as it deems fair.

E.   Palimony: There have been no court decisions to indicate that rehabilitative alimony or temporary or permanent alimony would be awarded to a mate, but such an award is a possibility.

V. SPECIFIC SUBJECTS (No written agreements, except for A,E,I.)
Reference to "BOTH" means married and unmarried couples.

A.   Prenuptial or precohabitation agreements:
  MARRIED: Valid.
  UNMARRIED: Probably valid if sex is not the basis of the agreement and if meant for protection of property interests.
  BOTH: Agreements must be made without duress and with full disclosure of assets and other important information.

B.   Property:

BOTH: All property is separate property of acquiring spouse or mate.

C. Liability of separate property for other spouse's or mate's debts:
MARRIED: No liability, except for necessaries.
UNMARRIED: No liability.

D. Management and control of separate property of each:
BOTH: Each controls own separate property.
MARRIED: Spouses must both sign to sell family home or use it as collateral for a loan.

E. Contracts made during marriage or cohabitation settling property rights:
MARRIED: Valid.
UNMARRIED: Probably enforceable if based on earnings, property, etc., rather than on sex.
BOTH: Agreements must be made without duress and with full disclosure of assets and other important information.

F. What can be willed?
BOTH: Each mate's separate property.
MARRIED: Surviving spouse may disregard will and receive dower or curtesy instead (see subject L).

G. Automatic protection for surviving spouse or mate:
MARRIED: Widow and children receive reasonable support, not to exceed eight months; homestead exemption rights pass to surviving spouse.
UNMARRIED: No protection for surviving mate. Minor children receive support allowance; illegitimate minor children would probably receive allowance if entitled to inherit (see subject H).

H. If no will:
MARRIED: Surviving spouse receives at least one-third of personal property and one-half or one-third of real estate (see subject L); if there are no surviving issue of decedent, surviving spouse receives up to $25,000 of real and/or personal property and one-half of everything over $25,000.
UNMARRIED: Surviving mate receives nothing. Illegitimate children inherit from mother; from father if paternity is judicially established, or if father has openly and notoriously claimed children as his.

I. Contracts:
MARRIED: Each may contract with anyone. Contracts between husband and wife are enforceable if fair. Spouses

may make partnership agreements with each other.
UNMARRIED: Each may contract with anyone, including each other.

J. Lawsuits:
BOTH: Each may sue and be sued separately unless both involved.

K. Homestead law:
BOTH: Exemption of value up to $30,000 over liens, including mortgages, on dwelling house used by housekeeper or head of family. Designation of homestead is made at time of levy.

L. Dower or curtesy:
MARRIED: One-third of all real estate owned by spouse at death, or one-half if spouse left only one heir who is also child of spouse. Dower may be waived by either in written contract, or by a will provision, or by electing to receive under conditions outlined in subject H.

M. Civil suits by spouses or mates against each other:
MARRIED: Wife may sue husband for injuries received while riding in automobile driven by husband. Other suits not allowed.
UNMARRIED: Permitted.

N. Legitimacy:
MARRIED: Children born during marriage are presumed legitimate.
UNMARRIED: Illegitimate children inherit from mother; from father if paternity is judicially established, or if father has openly and notoriously claimed children as his.
BOTH: Children born before marriage are legitimized if parents later marry and father acknowledges children.

O. Adoption:
BOTH: Any proper adult may adopt any other person.
MARRIED: Husband and wife must consent.

P. Division of property upon termination of relationship:
MARRIED: Court has power to divide separate property, including joint property, as it deems fair.
UNMARRIED: Implied or express contracts, value of services, or unfair economic gain may create rights to property.

VI. RECENT EVENTS, TRENDS, AND CONCLUSIONS

A. Granting of joint custody is presumed contrary to the child's best interests and would be ordered only in extraordinary circumstances.

B.   Early court cases recognize express agreements, but not implied agreements between mates. Since neither cohabitation nor fornication is illegal, some or all of the theories of the *Marvin* case may be followed.

VIRGINIA

I. MARRIAGE

A.   Legality:
   1.   Age: 18; under 18, need consent of parent or guardian.
   2.   License: Required; good for 60 days.
   3.   Medical examination: Statement of physician that blood test was made to determine infection from syphilis. If syphilis found, parties must take treatment if they marry.
   4.   Waiting period: None.

B.   Common-law marriages: Not recognized. Valid if valid in another state where entered into.

C.   Out-of-state marriages; Valid if valid in state where entered into. If resident leaves Virginia to avoid its marriage laws, the validity of the marriage will be determined according to laws of Virginia.

D.   Adultery: Illegal (misdemeanor).

E.   Property: Separate.

F.   Partnerships: A partnership agreement between spouses is probably enforceable as long as there is a valid business purpose.

II. COHABITATION

A.   Legality:

        1. Cohabitation: Illegal (misdemeanor) if lewd and lascivious; fine and/or sentence.
        2. Fornication: Illegal (misdemeanor); fine.

B.   Common-law marriage: Not recognized.

C.   Putative marriage: In a recent case, when both parties mistakenly believed in the validity of an invalid marriage, a female mate's claim on the basis of implied partnership was denied because she was unable to prove an agreement existed.

D.   Property: An express agreement would probably be honored; an implied agreement will not be recognized without strong proof.

E.   Partnerships: A partnership agreement between mates is probably enforceable as long as there is a valid business purpose and the agreement is not primarily based on sex.

III. DIVORCE (DISSOLUTION) AND LEGAL SEPARATION

A.   Divorce or dissolution (grounds):
    1. Sodomy or buggery outside marriage.
    2. Adultery.
    3. Conviction of felony and confinement for more than one year.
    4. Cruelty after one year of separation for such.
    5. Desertion for one year.
    6. Separation without cohabitation for one year (no fault).
    7. Legal separation with no reconciliation after one year or upon application to court by either party.

B.   Legal separation (grounds): If decree is for perpetual separation, it is the same as a divorce, except that neither may remarry.
    1. Cruelty.
    2. Reasonable apprehension of bodily harm.
    3. Abandonment or desertion.

C.   Residency requirements: 6 months for one spouse before filing for divorce.

D.   Remarriage: Court may order that neither spouse may remarry while case is appealed; otherwise, possible immediately after divorce is final.

E.   Court orders after filing for divorce and before divorce is final:
    1. Temporary alimony.
    2. Child support and custody.
    3. Court costs.

    4. Orders to preserve property.

F.   Alimony:
    1. May be granted to either spouse.
    2. May be payments or lump sum.
    3. Ceases upon remarriage or death of recipient.
    4. No permanent alimony granted to dependent spouse if the payor was granted the divorce based upon any fault ground. If the dependent spouse obtains the divorce based upon a fault ground, or if a no-fault divorce is granted, alimony may be awarded.

G.   Child support and custody:
    1. Court makes all orders concerning support and custody, taking into consideration all relevant factors.
    2. Each parent is equally considered for custody.

H.   Property division by court in absence of written or oral agreement:
    1. Courts have no power to distribute property; title alone controls.
    2. Rights of either spouse in property of other are extinguished on divorce.
    3. Tenancy with right of survivorship becomes tenancy in common. Each spouse receives his/her share.

IV. TERMINATION OF COHABITATION

A.   Court jurisdiction: No judicial control; voluntary parting.

B.   Court orders: A court may make orders for child support and custody similar to those made in a divorce, once paternity is established.

C.   Property division (decisions in Virginia and in other states suggest the following possibilities):
    1. Courts could infer partnership agreements as a means of dividing property and money.
    2. Courts could order return or division of property and money if there had been an implied or express agreement.
    3. Courts might order return of property to the rightful owner or grant an interest in property or an award of money to a mate to the extent of his/her contribution toward purchase of property.
    4. Since living together is illegal, courts would probably not honor an agreement if the relationship was primarily sexual; thus it might be difficult to collect for performing household duties when no direct financial contribution can be shown.

D.   Putative marriage: Court would probably adjust the property rights of a putative spouse, but any implied agreement would require proof.

E.   Palimony: There have been no court decisions to indicate that rehabilitative alimony or temporary or permanent alimony would be awarded to mate, and such an award seems unlikely.

V. SPECIFIC SUBJECTS (No written agreements, except for A,E,I.) Reference to "BOTH" means married and unmarried couples.

A.   Prenuptial or precohabitation agreements:
MARRIED: Probably valid.
UNMARRIED: Probably valid if sex is not the basis of the agreement and if meant for protection of property interests.
BOTH: Agreement must be made without duress and with full disclosure of assets and other important information.

B.   Property:
BOTH: All property is separate property of acquiring spouse.

C.   Liability of separate property for other spouse's or mate's debts:
BOTH: No liability.

D.   Management and control of separate property of each:
BOTH: Each controls own property.
MARRIED: Subject to dower and curtesy rights (see subjects L and M).

E.   Contracts made during marriage or cohabitation settling property rights:
MARRIED: Valid.
UNMARRIED: Probably enforceable if based on earnings, property, etc., rather than on sex.
BOTH: Agreements must be made without duress and with full disclosure of assets and other important information.

F.   What can be willed?
BOTH: Each spouse's or mate's separate property.
MARRIED: Whether or not surviving spouse is included in will, he/she may disregard will and receive dower or curtesy and distributive rights, i.e., one-third if children of deceased spouse or their descendants survive, or one-half if no children of descendants survive.

G.   Automatic protection for surviving spouse or mate:
MARRIED: Either may receive homestead exemption or personal-property exemption until remarriage or death (but

not if surviving spouse accepts dower or curtesy). Another personal property exemption may be available.
Right to stay in house until assignment of dower or
curtesy.

UNMARRIED: No protection for surviving mate. Unmarried
minor children receive homestead exemption and exempt personal property if entitled to inherit (see subject
H).

H.   If no will:
MARRIED: Children of deceased spouse receive all real estate
over and above dower or curtesy. If there are no surviving children, surviving spouse receives everything.
Personal property: Surviving spouse receives one-third
if there are surviving children of deceased spouse; all
if there are no children.

UNMARRIED: Surviving mate receives nothing. Illegitimate
children inherit from mother; from father if parents later
marry or if paternity is judicially established.

I.   Contracts:
BOTH: Each may contract with anyone, including each
other.

J.   Lawsuits:
BOTH: Each may sue and be sued separately unless both
involved.

K.   Homestead law:
BOTH: Householder or head of family receives exemption
of value up to $5,000 over liens, including mortgages,
in real estate or personal property.

L.   Dower:
MARRIED: One-third real estate owned by husband during
marriage. Wife may relinquish by joining in sale, by
willful desertion, by waiver in will, by court order if
wife is insane, or by court-ordered division.

M.   Curtesy:
MARRIED: Same as dower (see subject L) as would be applied to husband.

N.   Civil suits by spouses or mates against each other.
MARRIED: Suits to settle property rights permitted. Suits for
personal injuries, except auto accidents, not permitted.
UNMARRIED: Permitted.

O.   Legitimacy:
MARRIED: Children born during marriage are presumed legitimate. Children born before marriage are legitimized

if parents later marry and both parents acknowledge.

UNMARRIED: Illegitimate children inherit from mother; from father if parents later marry or if paternity judicially established.

P.   Adoption:

BOTH: Any resident may adopt a child. Both spouses must consent to adoption. Investigation of suitability of parents.

Q.   Division of property upon termination of relationship:

MARRIED: Courts may not divide separate property; title alone controls. Tenancy with right of survivorship becomes tenancy in common; each spouse receives his/her share.

UNMARRIED: Implied or express contracts, value of services, or unfair economic gain may create rights to property.

VI. RECENT EVENTS, TRENDS, AND CONCLUSIONS

A.   The court held that a woman could not be barred from admission to the state bar because she lived with someone of the opposite sex. Unmarried cohabitation does not bear a rational relationship to fitness and capacity to practice law.

B.   Courts may consider both earnings and earning capacity in awarding alimony, but they cannot consider possible future inheritance rights.

C.   In a recent case, a couple lived together as husband and wife for 23 years, thinking that they were validly married. They had three children and ran a business together. When they separated, the woman sued for part of the business partnership. The court found no express partnership agreement and put the burden on her to prove an implied agreement. She was unable to do so and was granted no share.

D.   Since cohabitation, adultery, and fornication are all illegal, and since common-law marriage is not recognized, it appears that the *Marvin* case would not be followed, except that an express agreement would probably be recognized; implied agreements might be recognized if they could be proved.

WASHINGTON

I. MARRIAGE

A. Legality:
1. Age: 18; under 18, need consent of parent or guardian: under 17, not permitted.
2. License: Required; good for 60 days. Must also file affidavit of disinterested person certifying qualifications of parties.
3. Medical examination: Not required. Must file affidavit showing applicant not infected with venereal disease.
4. Waiting period: 3 days.

B. Common-law marriages: Not recognized; valid if valid in another state where entered into, unless spouses are Washington residents.

C. Out-of-state marriages: Valid if valid in state where entered into, unless one spouse is trying to avoid restrictions imposed by Washington law.

D. Adultery: Not a crime.

E. Property: Community.

F. Partnerships: A partnership agreement between spouses is probably enforceable as long as there is a valid business purpose.

II. COHABITATION

A. Legality:
1. Cohabitation: Not a crime.
2. Fornication: Not a crime.
3. All private, nonviolent sexual acts between consenting adults are legal.

B. Putative marriage: If either mate believes that an invalid marriage is valid, the court will divide the property as it deems fair.

C. Partnerships: A partnership agreement between mates is probably enforceable as long as there is a valid business purpose and the agreement is not primarily based on sex.

D.   Property:
    1. Property acquired by mates living together is not community property.
    2. A contract which would be enforceable under ordinary circumstances does not become invalid because of a sexual relationship between the parties.
    3. If neither mate has any belief that there is a valid marriage, and title to property is in the names of both, each would probably be given a half-interest.
    4. Earlier decisions held that if property was in only one name, no adjustment would be made and title would control. This theory was followed in a 1978 case.
    5. In other recent decisions, the theories of partnership, contract, unfair economic gain, or return of contribution have been used to divide property.

E.   Common-law marriages: Not recognized; valid if valid in another state where entered into, unless spouses are Washington residents.

III. DIVORCE (DISSOLUTION) AND LEGAL SEPARATION

A.   Divorce or dissolution (grounds): Marriage is irretrievably broken (no fault).

B.   Legal separation (grounds): Same as for divorce.

C.   Residency requirements: Spouse filing for divorce must be a resident of the state before legal action is filed (no specific duration required).

D.   Remarriage: Possible immediately after divorce is final.

E.   Court orders after filing for divorce and before divorce is final: Court may make temporary orders regarding property and children.

F.   Alimony:
    1. Granted to either spouse without regard to marital misconduct.
    2. Considerations: Financial resources of each; time necessary to gain training for eimployment; standard of living during marriage; duration of marriage; age and physical and emotional condition of spouse seeking maintenance.

G.   Child support and custody:
    1. Court may order either parent or both to pay support, without regard to marital misconduct.
    2. Court determines custody according to children's best interests.

H. Property division by court in absence of written or oral agreement:
1. Court divides community and separate property, including joint property, as it deems fair, without regard to marital misconduct.
2. Considerations: Nature and extent of separate and community property, duration of marriage, and economic circumstances of each.

IV. TERMINATION OF COHABITATION

A. Court jurisdiction: No judicial control; voluntary parting.

B. Court orders: A court may make orders for child support and custody similar to those made in a divorce, once paternity is established.

C. Property division (decisions in Washington and other states suggest the following possibilities):
1. Courts could infer partnership agreements as a means of dividing property and money.
2. Courts could order return or division of property and money if there had been an implied or express agreement.
3. Courts could order return of property to the rightful owner or grant an interest in property or an award of money to a mate to the extent of his/her contribution toward purchase of property.
4. Since living together is not illegal, recovery could be had for performing household duties as well as for direct financial contributions, so long as the implied or express agreement was not primarily based upon sex.

D. Putative marriage: If either mate believes that an invalid marriage is valid, the court will divide property as it deems fair.

E. Palimony: There have been no court decisions to indicate that rehabilitative alimony or temporary or permanent alimony would be awarded to a mate, but such an award is a possibility.

V. SPECIFIC SUBJECTS (No written agreements, except for A,H,L.)
Reference to "BOTH" means married and unmarried couples.

A. Prenuptial or precohabitation agreements:
MARRIED: Valid.
UNMARRIED: Probably valid if sex is not the basis of the

agreement and if meant for protection of property interests.

BOTH: Agreement must be made without duress and with full disclosure of assets and other important information.

B. Separate property:

MARRIED: All property owned by either spouse before marriage, or acquired after marriage by gift or inheritance.

UNMARRIED: All property is separate property of acquiring mate.

C. Community property:

MARRIED: Property acquired by either spouse during marriage, except that acquired by gift or inheritance, or from sale, rents, issues, or profits of separate property.

D. Liability of separate property for other spouse's or mate's debts:

BOTH: No liability.

E. Liability of community property for debts contracted by one spouse:

MARRIED: Liable for debts entered into for the benefit of the community.

F. Management and control of separate property of each:

BOTH: Each controls own separate property.

MARRIED: Husband and wife must each sign to sell family home.

G. Management and control of community property:

MARRIED: Each spouse, acting alone, may manage or control community property except:

1. Neither may will more than one-half community property.

2. Neither may give, sell, encumber, or purchase community property without consent of the other.

3. Neither may deal with business assets where both participate without consent of other.

H. Contracts made during marriage or cohabitation settling property rights:

MARRIED: Valid. Binding on court except for custody, support, and visitation, unless unfair.

UNMARRIED: Probably enforceable if based on earnings, property, etc., rather than on sex.

BOTH: Agreement must be made without duress and with full disclosure of assets and other important information.

I. What can be willed?

MARRIED: All separate property and one-half of community property. If deceased spouse tries to will surviving spouse's share of community property, surviving spouse must elect either to receive according to the will or to take his/her share of community property.

UNMARRIED: Each mate's separate property.

J.   Automatic protection for surviving spouse or mate:

MARRIED: One-half of community property; reasonable cash allowance for family expenses during administration of estate. $20,000 homestead exemption in home over mortgage liens; other property up to $20,000 instead of homestead. If homestead is less than $20,000, difference awarded in other property.

UNMARRIED: No protection for surviving mate. Homestead exemption or award instead of homestead to minor children.

K.   If no will:

MARRIED: Surviving spouse receives deceased spouse's share of community property; one-half of separate property if children of deceased survive; three-fourths if no children survive but other relatives survive; everything to surviving spouse if sole survivor.

UNMARRIED: Surviving mate receives nothing. Illegitimate children inherit from both father and mother.

L.   Contracts:

BOTH: Each may contract with anyone, including each other.

M.   Lawsuits:

MARRIED: When wife is a party to a lawsuit, husband must be joined except:

1.   When action is between herself and husband.
2.   When she is living separate and apart from husband.

Apparently these procedures do not apply to the husband, and he alone can be a party to a lawsuit.

UNMARRIED: Each can sue or be sued separately unless both involved.

N.   Homestead law:

MARRIED: Exemptions for married person of $20,000 over liens, including mortgages, for family home or land on which dwelling house will be built. May be selected from community or separate property of one spouse. To obtain the exemption, an acknowledged declaration of homestead must be recorded in office of auditor of county where property is located.

UNMARRIED: An unmarried head of family receives the same exception.

O.   Civil suits by spouses or mates against each other:
     BOTH: Permitted.

P.   Legitimacy:
     MARRIED: Children born during marriage are presumed le-
        gitimate.
     UNMARRIED: Inheritance does not depend on whether parents
        have been married; children inherit from both parents.

Q.   Adoption:
     MARRIED: Any husband and wife may adopt together.
     UNMARRIED: Any unmarried person may adopt.

R.   Division of property upon termination of relationship:
     MARRIED: Court divides all community and separate prop-
        erty, including joint property, as it deems fair, without
        regard to marital misconduct.
     UNMARRIED: Implied or express contracts, value of services,
        or unfair economic gain may create rights to property.

VI. RECENT EVENTS, TRENDS, AND CONCLUSIONS

A.   Good will in a professional practice is a community-property
     asset subject to division upon divorce, though its value may
     be difficult to determine.

B.   Upon divorce, the wife is entitled to one-half of the con-
     tribution to the husband's state pension fund during their
     marriage. An omission in an earlier property settlement later
     merged into a divorce decree does not preclude her from
     later claiming this pension interest.

C.   A wife may be awarded a percentage of her husband's
     military disability pay upon divorce.

D.   Social Security benefits are community property and are
     divisible upon divorce.

E.   Most of the theories in the *Marvin* case have been followed.

WEST VIRGINIA

I. MARRIAGE

    A.   Legality:
        1. Age: Males, 18; females, 16; under 18, need consent of parents or guardian.
        2. License: Required; must be filed 3 days prior to issuance.
        3. Medical examination. Physician's certificate that applicant is not infected with syphilis.
        4. Waiting period: 3 days.

    B.   Common-law marriages: Not recognized; valid if valid in another state where entered into.

    C.   Out-of-state marriages: Valid if valid in state where entered into, and if not against public policy of West Virginia.

    D.   Adultery: Illegal (misdemeanor); fine.

    E.   Property: Separate.

    F.   Partnerships: A partnership agreement between spouses is probably enforceable as long as there is a valid business purpose.

II. COHABITATION

    A.   Legality:
        1. Cohabitation: Illegal if lewd and lascivious; fine and/or sentence.
        2. Fornication: Illegal (misdemeanor); fine.

    B.   Common-law marriage: Not recognized.

    C.   Putative marriage: Might be recognized to the extent of adjusting property rights.

    D.   Property: No case law, but see IV, C.

    E.   Partnerships: A partnership agreement between mates is probably enforceable as long as there is a valid business purpose and the agreement is not primarily based on sex.

III. DIVORCE (DISSOLUTION) AND LEGAL SEPARATION

A. Divorce or dissolution (grounds):
   1. Adultery.
   2. Conviction of felony.
   3. Abandonment or desertion for 6 months.
   4. Cruel or inhuman treatment.
   5. Habitual drunkenness during marriage.
   6. Addiction to narcotic drugs.
   7. Living apart for one year (no fault).
   8. Permanent and incurable insanity.
   9. Abuse or neglect of child.
   10. Irreconcilable differences if one party files sworn complaint and other files sworn answer (no fault); 60-day waiting period required.

B. Legal separation (grounds): Not available, but financial support may be ordered for failure to provide, upon any grounds for divorce.

C. Residency requirements: Either spouse must be a bona fide resident for one year before legal action is filed.

D. Remarriage: Possible immediately after divorce is final.

E. Court orders after filing for divorce and before divorce is final:
   1. Temporary alimony.
   2. Court costs.
   3. Custody and support of children.
   4. Orders concerning property.

F. Alimony:
   1. Granted to either spouse.
   2. No alimony granted in no-fault divorce unless some fault (inequitable conduct) can be shown.
   3. Cohabitation after divorce with someone of opposite sex may be grounds for changing the amount of alimony.

G. Child support and custody:
   1. Court decides as necessary to promote welfare of child.
   2. Custody of young child given to mother unless contrary to best interests of child.

H. Property division by court in absence of written or oral agreement:
   1. Courts have no power to divide separate property; title alone controls. Each spouse receives his/her share of joint property.

2. Rights to dower are barred by divorce, but court may order guilty party to compensate innocent party for loss of dower rights.
3. Court may restore to one spouse his/her separate property that is being controlled by the other.

IV. TERMINATION OF COHABITATION

A. Court jurisdiction: No judicial control; voluntary parting.

B. Court orders: A court may make orders for child support and custody similar to those made in a divorce, once paternity is established.

C. Property division (decisions in other states suggest the following possibilities):
1. Courts could infer partnership agreements as a means of dividing property and money, but this is doubtful.
2. Courts could order return or division of property and money if there had been an implied or express agreement.
3. Courts could order return of property to the rightful owner or grant an interest in property or an award of money to a mate to the extent of his/her contribution toward purchase of property.
4. Since living together is illegal, courts would probably not honor an agreement if the relationship was primarily sexual; thus it might be difficult to collect for performing household duties when no direct financial contribution can be shown.

D. Putative marriage: Might be recognized to the extent of adjusting property rights.

E. Palimony: There have been no court decisions to indicate that rehabilitative alimony or temporary or permanent alimony would be awarded to a mate, and such an award seems unlikely.

V. SPECIFIC SUBJECTS (No written agreements, except for A,E,I.)
Reference to "BOTH" means married and unmarried couples.

A. Prenuptial or precohabitation agreements:
MARRIED: Probably valid if in writing and signed.
UNMARRIED: Doubtful, but may be valid if sex is not the basis of the agreement and if meant for the protection of property interests.
BOTH: Agreements must be made without duress and with full disclosure of assets and other important information.

B. Property:

BOTH: All property is separate property of acquiring spouse or mate.

C. Liability of separate property for other spouse's or mate's debts.

MARRIED: No liability except for reasonable and necessary services of physician, rent of residence, or necessaries of family.

UNMARRIED: No liability.

D. Management and control of separate property of each:

BOTH: Each controls own separate property.

MARRIED: Both spouses must sign to sell dower property (see subject L).

E. Contracts made during marriage or cohabitation settling property rights:

MARRIED: Permitted.

UNMARRIED: May be enforceable if based on earnings, property, etc., rather than on sex.

BOTH: Agreements must be made without duress and with full disclosure of assets and other important information.

F. What can be willed?

BOTH: Each spouse's or mate's separate property.

MARRIED: Provision in will providing for surviving spouse replaces dower, unless clearly stated otherwise. Surviving spouse may elect to disregard will and accept intestate share (see subject H).

G. Automatic protection for surviving spouse or mate:

MARRIED: Exempt personal property of $200; possession of home until dower distributed.

UNMARRIED: No protection for surviving mate. Possession of family home for minor children until youngest reaches age 21; exempt personal property to minor children who are entitled to inherit (see subject H).

H. If no will:

MARRIED: Surviving spouse receives everything if there are no surviving descendants of deceased spouse. If descendants survive, they receive everything except dower of surviving spouse.

UNMARRIED: Surviving mate receives nothing. Illegitimate children inherit from mother only (but this law is probably unconstitutional).

I. Contracts:

BOTH: Each may contract with anyone, including each other.

MARRIED: Between spouses, contract must be in writing.

J.   Lawsuits:
BOTH: Each may sue or be sued separately unless both involved.

K.   Homestead law:
BOTH: Husbands, parents, heads of household, or infant children of deceased or insane parents receive exemption of up to $5,000 over liens. No filing required.

L.   Dower:
MARRIED: Surviving husband or wife receives ownership for his/her life in one-third of all real estate owned by deceased spouse during marriage. Court may award cash instead of property. Dower is in addition to right of inheritance. Dower barred in real property sold if surviving spouse consented to sale, or if either spouse lives in adultery unless there is a subsequent reconciliation, or if one deserts the other.

M.   Curtesy:
MARRIED: Abolished. Husband has dower in wife's estate (see subject L).

N.   Civil suits by spouses or mates against each other:
BOTH: Permitted.

O.   Legitimacy:
MARRIED: Children born during marriage are presumed legitimate.

UNMARRIED: Illegitimate children inherit from mother only (but this law is probably unconstitutional).

BOTH: Children born before marriage are legitimized if parents later marry.

P.   Adoption:
BOTH: Any person may adopt a child or adult. Investigation is made to determine whether home life is suitable.

MARRIED: Spouses must consent.

Q.   Division of property upon termination of relationship:
MARRIED: Title alone controls separate-property distribution. Each spouse receives his/her share of joint property. Right to dower barred by divorce, but party at fault may be ordered to compensate innocent party for loss of dower rights.

UNMARRIED: Implied or express contracts, value of services, or unfair economic gain may create rights to property.

VI. RECENT EVENTS, TRENDS, AND CONCLUSIONS

A.   A child conceived a few weeks prior to marriage is presumed legitimate unless the husband is able to prove that he did not have sexual relations with his wife prior to the marriage.

B.   Although the general rule is that alimony ceases on the death of the payor, a separation agreement stating that it would end only on death or remarriage of wife (the recipient) is binding, and payments continue after the husband's death.

C.   Although no alimony may be granted without a finding of fault, it does not mean that the fault has to be great enough to merit the granting of a fault divorce; "fault," in this sense, means substantial unfair conduct.

D.   A proposed law that there be no presumption favoring one parent over another for child custody failed to pass the legislature. Thus, the "tender years" presumption, which favors a mother for custody of a young child, remains. This has been confirmed by a recent court decision.

E.   Since cohabitation, fornication, and adultery are illegal, and common-law marriages are not recognized, the courts would probably not follow the theories of the *Marvin* case.

WISCONSIN

I. MARRIAGE

A.   Legality:
1. Age: 18; between 16 and 18, need written, sworn, and verified consent of parent(s) or guardian.
2. License: Required; good for 30 days.
3. Medical examination: Examination for presence of venereal disease, blood test for syphilis, physician's

certificate of negative finding, within 20 days prior
to application for license.

4. Waiting period: 5 days between application for license
and issuance.

B. Common-law marriages: Not recognized.

C. Out-of-state marriages: Valid if valid in state where entered
into, unless a Wisconsin resident goes to another state to
enter into a marriage prohibited in Wisconsin.

D. Adultery: Illegal (felony).

E. Property: Separate.

F. Partnerships: A partnership agreement between spouses is
probably enforceable as long as there is a valid business
purpose.

II. COHABITATION

A. Legality:
1. Cohabitation: Illegal (misdemeanor); fine and/or sentence.
2. Fornication: Illegal (misdemeanor); fine and/or sentence.

B. Common-law marriage: Not recognized.

C. Putative marriage:
1. An invalid marriage becomes a valid marriage after
the removal of the reason for the invalidity, and if
cohabitation continues.
2. A mate who believes in the validity of an invalid
marriage will be compensated for the value of services
rendered less the value of the support received.

D. Property:
1. Joint tenancy between mates is recognized.
2. If both mates know that their marriage is invalid,
courts give property to the mate who has title; a partnership or other agreement might be recognized.

E. Partnerships: A partnership agreement between mates is
probably enforceable as long as there is a valid business
purpose and the agreement is not primarily based on sex.

III. DIVORCE (DISSOLUTION) AND LEGAL SEPARATION

A. Divorce or dissolution (grounds): Marriage is irretrievably
broken (no fault), when:
1. Both parties so state under oath.

      2. One party so states and parties have lived apart for one year.

      3. One party so states, and parties have not lived apart for one year, and court finds no prospect of reconciliation.

B.   Legal separation (grounds): Same as for divorce. Legal separation may be converted to divorce after one year upon stipulation of both spouses or upon motion of either.

C.   Residency requirements: 6 months in state and 30 days in county for either spouse before filing of legal action.

D.   Remarriage: Each must wait 6 months after divorce becomes final, whether obtained in Wisconsin or elsewhere.

E.   Court orders after filing for divorce and before divorce is final:

      1. Temporary alimony.

      2. Court costs and attorneys' fees.

      3. Support of minor children.

      4. Orders to protect persons and property.

F.   Alimony:

      1. Granted to either spouse after all relevant factors are considered.

      2. Cohabitation after divorce is a ground for termination.

      3. Terminated upon remarriage of recipient.

G.   Child support and custody:

      1. Court may order either parent or both parents to pay child support.

      2. Court grants custody according to best interests of child and without preference for one sex over other.

      3. Court may grant joint custody if it is in the best interests of child.

H.   Property division by court in absence of written or oral agreement:

      1. Court has the power to distribute all separate property, including joint property, except inherited property.

      2. The presumption is that all separate property, including joint property, will be divided equally, but the court may allow one spouse more than half if circumstances dictate.

      3. Court may not consider marital misconduct, but economic misconduct may be considered.

      4. Divorce bars dower or curtesy rights.

IV. TERMINATION OF COHABITATION

A.   Court jurisdiction: No judicial control; voluntary parting.

B.   Court orders: A court may make orders for child support and custody similar to those made in a divorce, once paternity is established.

C.   Property division (decisions in Wisconsin and in other states suggest the following possibilities):
   1. Courts could infer partnership agreements as a means of dividing property and money.
   2. Courts could order return or division of property and money if there had been an implied or express agreement.
   3. Courts could order return of property to the rightful owner or grant an interest in property or an award of money to a mate to the extent of his/her contribution toward purchase of property.
   4. Since living together is illegal, courts would probably not honor an agreement if the relationship was primarily sexual; thus it might be difficult to collect for performing household duties when no direct financial contribution can be shown.

D.   Putative marriage: Courts would probably recognize property rights of a mate who believed that the marriage was valid.

E.   Palimony: There have been no court decisions to indicate that rehabilitative alimony or temporary or permanent alimony would be awarded to a mate, but such an award is a possibility.

V. SPECIFIC SUBJECTS (No written agreements, except for A,E,I.)
Reference to "BOTH" means married and unmarried couples.

A.   Prenuptial or precohabitation agreements:
   MARRIED: Valid, as concerns property rights during marriage. Void, as contrary to public policy, if prepared as a condition of divorce; may assist court in arriving at fair property division.
   UNMARRIED: Probably valid if sex is not the basis of the agreement and if meant for the protection of property interests.
   BOTH: Agreements must be made without duress and with full disclosure of assets and other important information.

B. Property:
> BOTH: All property is separate property of acquiring spouse or mate.

C. Liability of separate property for other spouse's or mate's debts:
> BOTH: No liability.

D. Management and control of separate property of each:
> BOTH: Each controls own separate property.
> MARRIED: Both spouses must sign to sell family home or property owned by both.

E. Contracts made during marriage or cohabitation settling property rights:
> MARRIED: Valid and enforceable unless unfair.
> UNMARRIED: Probably enforceable if based on earnings, property, etc., rather than on sex.
> BOTH: Agreements must be made without duress and with full disclosure of assets and other important information.

F. What can be willed?
> BOTH: Each spouse's or mate's separate property.
> MARRIED: Surviving spouse may elect to receive one-third of value of the estate, reduced by value of any property provided for according to a will, instead of accepting the will provisions.

G. Automatic protection for surviving spouse or mate:
> MARRIED: Reasonable allowances for surviving spouse and minor children. Support and education of minor children until specified age. Exempt property up to $1,000. Surviving spouse may petition court to set aside property up to $10,000 for support (may include home).
> UNMARRIED: No protection for surviving mate. Minor children receive support allowance if entitled to inherit (see subject H).

H. If no will:
> MARRIED: Surviving spouse receives everything if there are no surviving children of deceased spouse. If children survive, divided according to number of children. Home passes to surviving spouse. Surviving spouse may elect to take one-third of the value of the estate instead of intestate share.
> UNMARRIED: Surviving mate receives nothing. Illegitimate children inherit from mother; from father if paternity is adjudicated, or if father admits paternity in open court or acknowledges paternity in writing.

I.   Contracts:
BOTH: Each may contract with anyone, including each other.

J.   Lawsuits:
BOTH: Each may sue and be sued separately unless both involved.

K.   Homestead law:
BOTH: Every resident receives exemption up to $25,000 over liens, including mortgages, for homestead owned. Proceeds of sale, up to $25,000, exempt for two years. No filing required. Claim is made at time of filing.

L.   Dower and curtesy:
MARRIED: Surviving spouse has right to one-third of estate, reduced by value of property given him/her in will. Right is only in property owned by deceased spouse at his/her death. Right is barred by divorce.

M.   Civil suits by spouses or mates against each other:
BOTH: Permitted.

N.   Legitimacy:
MARRIED: Children born during marriage are presumed legitimate. Children born before marriage are legitimized if parents later marry.
UNMARRIED: Illegitimate children inherit from mother; from father if paternity is adjudicated, or if father admits paternity in open court, or acknowledges paternity in writing.

O.   Adoption:
BOTH: Any person may adopt a child. An adult may adopt another adult. Adopter and adopted should be of same religious faith, if possible. Personal qualities of adoptive parent(s) are strong consideraton. Both spouses must consent.

P.   Division of property upon termination of relationship:
MARRIED: Court distributes all separate property, including joint property, except property acquired by inheritance.
UNMARRIED: Implied or express contract, value of services, or unfair economic gain may create rights to property.

VI. RECENT EVENTS, TRENDS, AND CONCLUSIONS

A.   A higher court decided that when a husband failed to disclose ownership of corporate stock at the time of divorce, it was proper for the trial court to value the stock and grant the wife a monetary award.

B.   In a case involving a 24-year marriage, a higher court decided that the trial court should not have granted a fifty-fifty property division instead of alimony; it should have retained the right to grant alimony later, if warranted.

C.   In a 1977 decision, the court refused to permit a male mate to retain all the benefits of cohabitation without compensating his mate for her services.

D.   Though cohabitation, fornication, and adultery are all illegal, it appears that courts may follow some of the theories in the *Marvin* case.

WYOMING

I. MARRIAGE

A.   Legality:
1.   Age: 16; under 18, need oral or written consent of parent or guardian (if written, must be witnessed); under 16, need consent of court.
2.   License: Required.
3.   Medical examination: Physician's certificate showing freedom from venereal disease, including report of blood test for syphilis, within 30 days of application.
4.   Waiting period: None.

B.   Common-law marriages: Not recognized; valid if valid in another state where entered into.

C.   Out-of-state marriages: Valid if valid in state where entered into.

D.   Adultery: Not a crime.

E.   Property: Separate.

F.   Partnerships: A partnership agreement between spouses is

probably enforceable as long as there is a valid business purpose.

II. COHABITATION

A.   Legality:
   1. Cohabitation: Not a crime.
   2. Fornication: Not a crime.
   3. All private, nonviolent sexual acts between consenting adults are legal.

B.   Common-law marriage: Not recognized.

C.   Putative marriage:
   1. Continued cohabitation after the removal of the reason for the invalidity of marriage will not result in a valid marriage.
   2. The property rights of one who mistakenly believes in a valid marriage will be recognized.

D.   Property: A claim for value of services in an illicit relationship was not recognized in early cases, since no implied promise was inferred.

E.   Partnerships: A partnership agreement between mates is probably enforceable as long as there is a valid business purpose and the agreement is not primarily based on sex.

III. DIVORCE (DISSOLUTION) AND LEGAL SEPARATION

A.   Divorce or dissolution (grounds):
   1. Irreconcilable differences in marital relationship (no fault).
   2. Incurable insanity and confinement for at least 2 years.

B.   Legal separation (grounds): Same as for divorce. Court may grant lifelong separation or impose a time limitation.

C.   Residency requirements: 60 days for plaintiff spouse before filing legal action for divorce.

D.   Remarriage: Possible immediately after divorce is final.

E.   Court orders after filing for divorce and before divorce is final:
   1. Temporary alimony.
   2. Temporary child support.
   3. Court costs and attorney's fees.
   4. Restraining orders concerning property and personal rights.

F. Alimony:
  1. Granted in reasonable amount to wife only. (A similar law in another state has recently been declared unconstitutional.)
  2. May be in form of rents and profits from husband's real estate or a specific sum to be paid.

G. Child support and custody:
  1. Child support is ordered by the court to either parent.
  2. Custody awarded according to the best interests of the child.
  3. No custody is awarded solely on the basis of the parent's sex.

H. Property division by court in absence of written or oral agreement:
  1. Court makes division of all separate property, including joint property, as it deems fair.
  2. Considerations:
    a. Respective merits of spouses.
    b. Condition in which each is left by divorce.
    c. Which spouse acquired the property.
    d. Extent to which property is used for the benefit of either spouse or children.

IV. TERMINATION OF COHABITATION

A. Court jurisdiction: No judicial control; voluntary parting.

B. Court orders: A court may make orders for child support and custody similar to those made in divorce, once paternity is established.

C. Property division (decisions in other states suggest the following possibilities):
  1. Courts could infer partnership agreements as a means of dividing property and money.
  2. Courts could order return or division of property and money if there had been an implied or express agreement.
  3. Courts could order return of property to the rightful owner or grant an interest in property or an award of money to a mate to the extent of his/her contribution toward purchase of property.
  4. Since living together is not illegal, recovery could be had for performing household duties as well as for direct financial contribution, so long as the implied or express agreement was not primarily based upon sex.

D.   Putative marriage: Property rights of a putative spouse would probably be recognized by the courts.

E.   Palimony: There have been no court decisions to indicate that rehabilitative alimony or temporary or permanent alimony would be awarded to a mate, but such an award is a possibility.

V. SPECIFIC SUBJECTS (No written agreements, except for A,E,I.)
Reference to "BOTH" means married and unmarried couples.

A.   Prenuptial or precohabitation agreements:
MARRIED: Probably valid.
UNMARRIED: Probably valid if sex is not the basis of the agreement and if meant for protection of property interests.
BOTH: Agreement must be made without duress and with full disclosure of assets and other important information.

B.   Property:
BOTH: All property is separate property of acquiring spouse or mate.

C.   Liability of separate property for other spouse's or mate's debts:
BOTH: No liability.
MARRIED: Both spouses are liable for necessary expenses of family and education of children.

D.   Management and control of separate property of each:
BOTH: Each controls own separate property.
MARRIED: Both spouses must sign to sell family home or use it as collateral for a loan.

E.   Contracts made during marriage or cohabitation settling property rights:
MARRIED: Recognized and enforced if part of final divorce decree. Probably valid as private agreement.
UNMARRIED: Probably enforceable if based on earnings, property, etc., rather than on sex.
BOTH: Agreements must be made without duress and with full disclosure of assets and other important information.

F.   What can be willed?
BOTH: Each spouse's or mate's separate property.
MARRIED: Surviving spouse can elect to disregard will and receive one-half of deceased spouse's property if there are no surviving children by previous or present marriage, or one-fourth if surviving spouse is not a parent of any surviving children of deceased spouse.

G.   Automatic protection for surviving spouse or mate:

MARRIED: Widow and children receive reasonable provision
for support. Homestead exemption up to $6,000 over
liens, including mortgages, continues. Surviving spouse
may remain in possession of family home, and use family wearing apparel and furniture of deceased spouse.

UNMARRIED: No protection for surviving mate. Minor children receive homestead exemption and may remain in
possession of family home and use family wearing apparel and furniture of deceased spouse. Illegitimate
minor children receive same if entitled to inherit (see
subject H).

H.   If no will:

MARRIED: Surviving spouse receives everything of deceased
spouse if no children or other relatives of deceased
spouse survive; otherwise, surviving spouse, children,
or relatives divide estate.

UNMARRIED: Surviving mate receives nothing. Illegitimate
children inherit from mother; from father if parents
marry and father recognizes children, or if parentage is
established according to Uniform Parentage Act.

I.   Contracts:

BOTH: Each may contract with anyone, including each
other.

J.   Lawsuits:

BOTH: Each may sue and be sued separately unless both
involved.

K.   Homestead law:

BOTH: Every householder who is head of family, or who is
60 years old or more, has exemption up to $6,000 in
value over liens, including mortgages. No requirement
for filing or recording of homestead.

L.   Civil suits by spouses or mates against each other:

MARRIED: Wife may not sue husband for injuries caused by
husband's gross negligence in automobile accident.
Otherwise, no law concerning interspousal suits.

UNMARRIED: Permitted.

M.   Legitimacy:

MARRIED: Children born during marriage are presumed legitimate. Children born before marriage are legitimized
if parents later marry.

UNMARRIED: Illegitimate children inherit from mother; from
father if parents marry and father recognizes children,
or if paternity is established according to Uniform Parentage Act.

N. Adoption:
BOTH: Any adult may adopt any other person. Investigation required.

O. Division of property upon termination of relationship:
MARRIED: Court has power to divide all separate property, including joint property, as it deems fair.
UNMARRIED: Implied or express contracts, value of services, unfair economic gain may create rights to property.

VI. RECENT EVENTS, TRENDS, AND CONCLUSIONS

A. Though the court has authority to modify alimony and child support after divorce, it has no authority to modify a property-settlement agreement.

B. Workmen's compensation laws denying death benefits to a surviving spouse in a common-law marriage, validly contracted out of state, are unconstitutional.

C. Since cohabitation is not illegal, the courts would probably follow some or all of the theories in the *Marvin* case.

GLOSSARY

(These definitions apply as generally used in this book; exceptions or variations in meaning occur in some jurisdictions).

acknowledged illegitimate child A child whose paternity has been legally established by the oral statement, written statement, or conduct of the father as determined by each state's laws.

acknowledgment Admission, confession, or assumption of the responsibility for one's acts; may be by oral statement, written agreement, conduct, or by other satisfactory evidence according to each state's laws.

action A lawsuit or judicial proceeding.

adjudication Formal decision by a court of law, deciding the legal rights of parties.

adoption Court process which provides that a person or persons become the legal parent for a minor child or adult who is the biological child of other parents.

adultery Voluntary sexual intercourse between a married person and a person of the opposite sex who is not his/her spouse.

affidavit A notarized written statement under oath.

alimony Court-ordered payments for one spouse to furnish financial support to another spouse in a legal action for divorce or separation.

annulment A court order, decree, or judgment terminating a marriage on grounds of invalidity.

antenuptial (prenuptial) Before marriage, as in a property settlement entered into before marriage.

bigamy The criminal offense of entering into another marriage while a former marriage is still valid.

blood relationship (See consanguinity)

bona fide Honest, in good faith, truthful, straightforward. A bona fide agreement is one that is valid and entered into in good faith.

breach A failure to carry out a legal duty or obligation, as a breach of contract.

casual mate A cohabitant (mate) who lives together with another in a relationship characterized by informality, lack of permanent commitment, and relatively short duration. There is little possibility of property rights arising between them. Rehabilitative or restorative alimony may be possible.

child custody The care, control, and financial support of a child(ren), which can be partial or total. A noncustodial parent is also almost always financially responsible for a child(ren).

child support Payments made by a noncustodial parent to a custodial or foster parent(s) for the support of a child(ren).

cohabitation Living together; generally living together without being married. (Spouses and children, of course, also cohabit.)

cohabitation agreement An oral or written agreement between two people who live together without being married, settling all or part of their property and/or legal rights.

common-law marriage A marriage that arises, expressly or impliedly, without a state-recognized ceremony, in one of the fourteen jurisdictions that recognize such marriages. It is usually required that the couple agree to be married, live together as husband and wife, and hold themselves out to the community as a married couple.

community property Property acquired after marriage, except by gift or inheritance, by a married couple who reside in a community-property state. (Property acquired after marriage from the proceeds of separate property is usually not community property.)

consanguinity The relationship among persons descended from a common ancestor, a blood relationship.

conservator A person appointed by the court to manage another person's property.

consideration The transfer of something of value, or the commission of an act, in return for a benefit; an exchange of one detriment (sacrifice) for another.

contract A bona fide oral or written agreement with enforceable legal rights.

creditor A person who has loaned something of value, usually money.

cruelty Unreasonable mental or physical infliction of pain upon one's spouse; usually a ground for divorce or legal separation.

curtesy Once referred to a life estate in the real property owned by a deceased wife during marriage, but has been abolished. In some states it has been replaced by statutory distributive shares, and is similar to the wife's dower right.

decedent A dead person.

decree A final order of the court adjudging the rights of the parties.

defendant The person(s) sued for divorce, sued in a lawsuit, or accused in a criminal action.

descendant Lineal offspring of another, including child, grandchild, great-grandchild, etc., to the remotest degree.

dissolution A court order, decree, or judgment terminating a marriage; divorce, but not annulment. It may include a division of property and/ or financial support and/or child custody.

divorce A court order, decree, or judgment terminating a marriage; dissolution, but not annulment. It may include a division of property and/or financial support and/or child custody.

domicile The place where a person intends to have his/her true, fixed, and permanent home.

dower Property right of a surviving wife in certain property (usually real estate) owned by her deceased husband. In most states it has been abolished, but it has been replaced by a statutory distributive share.

duress Unreasonable physical and/or mental force or pressure influencing another to do something he/she probably would not have done voluntarily.

encumbrance A lien upon property, such as a mortgage.

equity 1. The net value of an owner in property over and above liens and encumbrances.
2. In special circumstances, principles of fairness applied by the courts instead of technical rules of law to provide justice to a wronged party.

estate All the real and personal property owned by a person while alive or upon his/her death.

exempt property (exemption) That portion of real or personal property which is free from the claims of creditors according to state laws.

express contract (agreement) A valid oral or written agreement; that is, one which has been affirmatively stated orally or set forth in writing between two or more parties.

extreme cruelty Acts of extreme wretchedness toward a spouse, seriously endangering health and causing a breakdown in the marriage relation; usually a ground for divorce or legal separation.

family allowance Fixed or reasonable sums allotted by state law for a surviving spouse and/or children from the estate of a deceased spouse and/or parent. Usually it is allotted only during the administration of the estate until final distributions are made.

family home A home used by spouses or mates living together as their primary dwelling place, with or without children; may include one adult, often a parent, having a child(ren) living with him/her in some states.

fault The act of committing a legal wrong. In some states it is a ground or reason for terminating a marriage.

felony A serious crime, more serious than a misdemeanor, often punishable by a prison term in a state penitentiary.

fornication Heterosexual intercourse between unmarried people.

gift A voluntary irrevocable conveyance and delivery of all right, title, and interest in property to another, without anything in return.

good faith Honesty and truthfulness of intentions and actions.

ground The fundamental basis for a divorce lawsuit; for example habitual intemperance is a ground for divorce in some states.

guardian A person appointed by the court to take care of another person and/or that person's property.

habitual intemperance The habit of frequent drunkenness.

heir A natural successor to real- or personal-property ownership, upon the death of the owner, usually if there is no will. It may also refer to one who inherits by will.

homemate A cohabitant (mate) who lives with another in a serious personal relationship of a sustained duration with the probability of property and/or legal rights arising between them, either by express or implied contract, or by other legal theory.

homestead allowance A state law providing payments and/or equity for survivors, usually a spouse or children, from a deceased person's estate.

homestead exemption or law A state law providing that a certain amount of net value in the family home is exempt from creditors' claims. Usually it only protects spouses and/or children, but in some states it may also protect mates. Valid liens and encumbrances, such as mortgages upon the family home, remain enforceable.

illegitimate A child born out of wedlock, who has not been legitimized according to the laws of a particular state.

impediment A legal hindrance that negates the validity of a marriage; a flawed divorce, for example, makes a later marriage invalid.

implied contract A contract that is inferred from oral statements and/or conduct of the parties.

incompatibility Inability to live together because of personality conflicts, misconduct, or conflicting lifestyles.

inheritance (inherit) The right to successive property ownership upon the death of the owner.

intangible personal property Property that has no intrinsic value, but is representative of something of value, such as stock certificates.

intestacy (intestate) The state of dying without having made a valid will (or failing to dispose of all property by will).

intestate succession The disposition of a deceased person's property by state law, rather than according to the terms of a valid will, joint tenancy, or other dispositive instrument. It is invoked when someone dies without having made a will, and occasionally when a will exists but is held invalid.

irretrievable breakdown The establishment, usually by the testimony of a spouse, that the marriage has deteriorated to the extent that the spouses can no longer live together; generally referred to as *no fault*.

issue Same as *descendant*.

joint property Undivided ownership in property by two or more persons, such as tenancy in common, joint tenancy, community property, tenancy by the entireties. Usually the term is not used to refer to community property.

joint tenancy Undivided joint ownership in property by two or more persons, usually with automatic passage of ownership upon the death of one joint tenant to the surviving tenant(s).

joint venture Usually a single business enterprise or investment undertaken for profit by two or more persons.

judicial Related to or connected with the courts, or a court proceeding.

jurisdiction Power of a court to preside over a specific legal matter.

legal separation A court decree lawfully terminating cohabitation between spouses, although they remain married.

legitimacy Lawful birth; generally the condition of being born in wedlock, but some states make all children the legitimate children of their biological parents, and others provide means for legitimizing children born out of wedlock.

lewd and lascivious Notorious, socially unacceptable; usually refers to acts of a sexual nature.

liability Responsibility for debts and/or other obligations.

license A written certificate by law granting permission, such as a marriage license.

lien A claim on personal or real property as security for the payment of a debt; usually it is a mortgage or other security instrument.

life estate An interest in property only during a person's lifetime.

life interest Same as *life estate*.

marital Having to do with or related to a valid marriage.

marital property Property acquired after a valid marriage, except by gift or inheritance, in a separate-property state.

mate An unmarried person who cohabits with another unmarried person.

meretricious In the legal sense, an intimate relationship outside of marriage that has little standing in the law because it provides for an exchange of money for sexual services, or is primarily based upon a sexual relationship, or both.

misdemeanor A minor crime, usually punishable by a fine and/or a short period of incarceration.

necessaries Basic purchases, usually food and clothing, to furnish minimum standards of sustenance and protection, according to the accustomed standard of living of the parties.

no fault Divorce (dissolution) granted by the court without a finding of misconduct or fault by either spouse.

notarization The placing of a designated public official's signature and official seal on a document to openly declare authenticity of a signature.

open and notorious Usually an act committed in a public manner.

palimony A recently coined expression for court-ordered financial support between ex-mates.

partnership An association of two or more people for a business purpose.

paternity The state or condition of being a father. A court adjudication or a father's admission that he is the parent of a child(ren) born out of wedlock.

personal property All property except real property.

personal wrong A negligent or intentional illegal act against another.

plaintiff The person(s) who initiates or files a lawsuit, including a divorce action.

polygamy Having more than one spouse at the same time.

precohabitation agreement A property and/or financial support agreement entered into between mates prior to living together.

prenuptial agreement (antenuptial agreement) A property and/or alimony agreement entered into prior to and in contemplation of marriage.

presumptive marriage A marriage which is presumed to exist because a couple has cohabited and has established the appearance and general reputation of being husband and wife.

probate A court procedure to determine the validity of a will and to provide for the payment of debts and the distribution of assets according to the will provisions; or, in the absence of a will, according to the laws of intestacy.

property All real and personal property, including intangibles such as stocks, bonds, notes, cash.

putative marriage A marriage entered into in good faith and in ignorance of impediments that render the marriage invalid.

putative spouse A partner in a putative marriage who mistakenly believes that the marriage is valid.

quasi-community property Separate property acquired in a separate-property state, which would have been community property if acquired in a community-property state. If the owner of such property moves to a community-property state, the property is treated as community property for purposes of divorce (Arizona), distribution at the death of one spouse (Idaho), or both (California).

real estate Land, improvements, and attached fixtures.

real property Same as *real estate*.

rehabilitative alimony Court-ordered payments by one former spouse or mate to furnish financial support to another for a relatively short period, to restore a person to a former earning position or to establish skills to achieve reasonable earning ability.

sentence The judgment of the court pronounced upon a defendant after conviction of a crime.

separate maintenance A court order for support of a spouse or mate while living apart without being divorced.

separate property Property acquired by a person before, during, or after marriage that is not owned by his/her spouse. In some states, at the time of divorce or death, a non-owning spouse will acquire property rights in the separate property of the owning spouse.

separation agreement An agreement between spouses or cohabitants dividing all or part of their legal and property rights.

sequestration   The separation or removal of property from the person in possession so that a court or other authority may deal with it.

service of process (to serve)   The delivery of judicial orders and summons to a person, as the notification that the recipient is being sued.

spouse   A wife or husband.

statute   A state or federal law passed by the legislature.

suit (lawsuit)   A legal action instituted by one party against another to obtain a monetary award, a determination of legal rights, or other remedies.

surviving spouse   A husband or wife who outlives his/her spouse.

temporary alimony   Court-ordered payments for one spouse to furnish financial support to the other spouse before a divorce or legal separation lawsuit is final.

tenancy by entirety (entireties)   Ownership between husband and wife, which can only be terminated by joint action; upon death, all ownership passes to the surviving spouse.

tenancy in common   Undivided ownership in property by two or more persons without automatic passage of ownership to the surviving owner(s) when one dies.

testacy   Reference to a person dying and leaving a valid will that disposes of all or part of his property.

unjust enrichment   Unfair economic gain to the disadvantage or loss of another.

verification   A written statement confirming the truth of a document, usually under oath.

vested   Accrued, settled, or absolute, as *vested property rights*, which are property rights that are presently owned.

will   Usually a valid written document, duly witnessed, providing for the disposition of a person's property after death.

Notes

PROLOGUE

¹Alvin Toffler, *Future Shock* (New York, Bantam Book published by arrangement with Random House, Inc., 1971), 251.

CHAPTER ONE

¹Nathaniel Lande, *Mindstyles/Lifestyles* (Los Angeles, Price/Stern/ Sloan, 1976).
²J. K. Footlick, "Legal Battle of the Sexes," *Newsweek*, April 30, 1979.
³*Anchorage* (Alaska) *News*, December 29, 1979.
⁴R. Pinner, "Heartbreak, Inc.," *TV Picture Life*, January 1980.
⁵D. Zimmerman, interview with Peter Frampton, *Hit Parade*, December 1979.
⁶*Washington Star*, 1978.

CHAPTER TWO

¹J. Otten, "Living in Syntax," *Newsweek*, December 30, 1974.
²B. DeMott, "After the Sexual Revolution," *The Atlantic*, Vol. 238, No. 5, November 1976.
³B. Hirsch, *Living Together: A Guide to the Law for Unmarried Couples* (Boston, Houghton, Mifflin, 1976).
⁴Blackstone, *Commentaries on the Laws of England*, 1765.
⁵*Baltimore Morning Sun*, May 30, 1980.
⁶W. Durant, *The Life of Greece* (New York, Simon and Schuster, 1939).

CHAPTER THREE

¹D. Walden, *Nelson, A Biography* (New York, Dial Press, 1978).
²*Richmond* (Virginia) *Afro-American*, June 16, 1979.
³H. C. Black, *Black's Law Dictionary*, 5th ed. (St. Paul, West Publishing Co., 1979).

[4]*Journal of the American Bar Association*, July 1979.
[5]*Boston Herald American*, January 17, 1980.
[6]*Framingham*, (Massachusetts) *News*, September 11, 1979.
[7]*Los Angeles Daily Journal*, January 25, 1980.

CHAPTER FOUR

[1]*Tucson Daily Citizen*, November 29, 1978.
[2]*People Weekly*, January 22, 1979.
[3]*Marvin vs. Marvin*, 134 California Reporter, 815 (1976).
[4]Ibid.
[5]Ibid.
[6]Ibid.
[7]Ibid.
[8]*Marvin vs. Marvin* trial, Superior Court of the State of California for the County of Los Angeles, Case No. C 23303, *Family Law Reporter*, Vol. 5, No. 24, April 24, 1979.
[9]Ibid.
[10]Ibid.
[11]"Tomorrow" (TV show), January 31, 1980.
[12]*Marvin vs. Marvin* trial, Superior Court of the State of California for the County of Los Angeles, Case No. C 23303, *Family Law Reporter*, Vol. 5, No. 24, April 24, 1979.
[13]Ibid.
[14]Ibid.
[15]Ibid.
[16]Ibid.
[17]*The New York Times*, July 20, 1979.
[18]Ibid.
[19]*The New York Times*, June 7, 1980.
[20]*Paterson* (New Jersey) *Morning News*, October 19, 1979.
[21]Ibid.
[22]"Tomorrow," January 31, 1980.
[23]*Marvin vs. Marvin*, 134 California Reporter, 815 (1976).
[24]Ibid.
[25]*Mansfield* (Ohio) *News-Journal*, October 6, 1979.
[26]*Hewitt vs. Hewitt*, Supreme Court of Illinois ruling, 394 Northeastern Reporter, 2d Series, 1204.
[27]Ibid.
[28]Ibid.
[29]Ibid.
[30]*Los Angeles Times*, November 24, 1977.

CHAPTER FIVE

[1]*New Kensington* (Pennsylvania) *Valley News Dispatch*, August 10, 1979.

[2]Judge Hyde, in *The Dictionary of Legal Quotations*, Norton-Kyshe, J. W., (London, Sweet and Maxwell, 1904).

[3]*Arizona Daily Star*, August 1, 1980.

[4]*Family Law Reporter*, 2962, October 16, 1979.

[5]*Baltimore News American*, April 10, 1980.

CHAPTER SIX

[1]*People Weekly*, May 7, 1979.

[2]*People Weekly*, November 5, 1979.

[3]*The Annapolis Capital*, November 10, 1979.

[4]*People Weekly*, November 5, 1979.

[5]"The law does not concern itself with trifles."

[6]R. L. Taylor, *W.C. Fields: His Follies and Fortunes* (New York, Doubleday, 1949).

[7]Ibid.

[8]*Los Angeles Times*, May 21, 1980.

[8a]*Los Angeles Herald-Examiner*, July 6, 1979.

[9]D. J. Freed and H. H. Foster, "Divorce in the Fifty States: An overview as of August 1, 1979," *Family Law Reporter*, Vol. 5, No. 43.

[10]*Wall Street Journal*, June 27, 1978.

[11]A. Pietropinto and J. Simenauer, *Husbands and Wives: A Nationwide Survey of Marriage* (New York Times Books, 1979).

[12]*New York Post*, April 11, 1980.

[13]*Hewitt vs. Hewitt*, Supreme Court of Illinois ruling, 394 North Eastern Reporter, 2d series, 1204.

[14]*Boulder* (Colorado) *Camera*, July 29, 1979.

Index